I0630723

Also by Kenneth E. Nelson:
Thoughts of a Boy Growing Up. Christopher Publishing House, Hanover, MA 1999

NEIGHBORS

A Summer-Winter Affair

KENNETH E. NELSON

iUniverse, Inc.
New York   Bloomington

Neighbors
A Summer-Winter Affair

Copyright © 2010 Kenneth E. Nelson

All rights reserved. No part of this book may be used or reproduced by any means, graphic, electronic, or mechanical, including photocopying, recording, taping or by any information storage retrieval system without the written permission of the publisher except in the case of brief quotations embodied in critical articles and reviews.

This is a work of fiction. All of the characters, names, incidents, organizations, and dialogue in this novel are either the products of the author's imagination or are used fictitiously.

iUniverse books may be ordered through booksellers or by contacting:

iUniverse
1663 Liberty Drive
Bloomington, IN 47403
www.iuniverse.com
1-800-Authors (1-800-288-4677)

Because of the dynamic nature of the Internet, any Web addresses or links contained in this book may have changed since publication and may no longer be valid. The views expressed in this work are solely those of the author and do not necessarily reflect the views of the publisher, and the publisher hereby disclaims any responsibility for them.

ISBN: 978-1-4502-3386-6 (pbk)
ISBN: 978-1-4502-3388-0 (cloth)
ISBN: 978-1-4502-3387-3 (ebook)

Printed in the United States of America

iUniverse rev. date: 6/30/10

Dedication

To Karen Micili, my teacher friend and enthusiastic fellow gardener, without whose entry into my life, her inspiration and encouragement, this story would likely never have been conceived or written.

Acknowledgments

(in alphabetical order)

Suzanna Anderson, Ross, CA; Bruce Black, Oakland, CA; Juliana Combs, Manteca, CA' Isabel Gallagher, Mercer Is. WA; Shirley Gallagher, Walnut Creek, CA; Dr. William Garman, Palm Desert, CA; Florence Holbrook, Fresno, CA; James Lindley, Fresno, CA; Stephanie Salzer, Los Gatos, CA; Gordon Sharafinski, San Francisco, CA; and Mary Webb, Berkeley, CA.

Editor: Robin Martin, Two Songbirds Press, Orangevale, CA

ONE

Getting Acquainted

It was almost eight-thirty when his golden-haired neighbor, Lauren, answered his knock. "Well, hello Ted. We've already drunk all of the margaritas." She stepped back and swept her arm ushering him inside.

Ted had hesitantly accepted the evening's invitation to toast her roommate Ellen's 60th birthday because he knew he might be delayed. However, earlier in the week he'd delivered half-dozen fresh tomatoes from his garden to his new neighbors as a way of saying "Welcome," and been invited for a drink. It seemed un-neighborly to turn it down.

Lauren Haas had been outside pulling weeds from around the neglected front walkway when he crossed the street with the tomatoes. At forty-something, she was the younger of the two women teachers who were moving into the rental unit directly across the street from Ted's home of forty years. She accepted the tomatoes with an open and friendly smile.

"I just love fresh tomatoes! I know it's too late now for a summer garden, but if I stay here I want one for myself next spring. There's some space out back."

Ted's interest picked up, and he immediately offered his help. "When the time comes, and if you can use a hand, I'm pretty good with a spade."

She glanced appreciatively up and down Ted's trim figure, which was surprisingly fit for a seventy-five year old grandfather, made a muscle with her right arm and gave him a quick "You're on!"

Lauren seemed in no hurry to get back to what she was doing. "Why don't you come in, and I'll show you what's going on?" She took off her gardening gloves, and brought him in the front door through the house.

"This will be my bedroom and also my office. I can look through this big window while using the computer." Then, with another smile, "I'm glad you keep your house and front yard looking so nice because I'll be forced to look at it while I'm working."

His wife of fifty years had died unexpectedly a year earlier, Ted explained to Lauren. "I'm trying to keep the place looking presentable. My wife insisted on having the shrubs and flowers at their best, and spent a lot of time at it. She was equally meticulous around the house and would have applauded what is being done to yours."

Lauren led the way to another room. "This will be my roommate, Ellen's bedroom. It has its own bathroom. Don't you just love those oak floors? They've been covered with old, dirty carpet for too many years. We plan to place rugs around that can be cleaned easily. There will be a lot less dust to breathe."

Their final stop was the living room. "Do you see that pad by the fireplace? I'm sleeping there during the renovation. We can't put up the beds until the rooms are painted." Her eyes softened and small lines appeared at their edges as she seemed to note Ted's pained expression. "It's not really comfy, but I can put up with it for a couple of weeks. Besides, it's sort of like camping out. Ellen wont move in until this house is completely ready. But, my lease ended a few days ago, so I decided to move on in. It's a little inconvenient, but there's no rent to pay until the work is finished. And you can't beat that deal."

He was aware that the home was owned by Ellen's mother. She had been in declining health for a number of years. Occasionally, if Ted was entering his driveway when Ellen was across the street, he would inquire about her mother's health. Ted thought back to the many times he and his wife had been awakened by ambulance sirens responding to her calls for help. Now, she was confined to a convalescent hospital.

Lauren explained that she had known Ellen for almost ten years, with their friendship starting when they attended college courses together. Ted had been surprised with her explanation of her role in Ellen's mother's life.

"I'm really no stranger to this home. For about a year, I worked as a paid companion for Ellen's mother. On several days each week, I'd come over and help with laundry, bathing and some housework. She still liked to get out a little, so I would drive her to lunch and to meetings with friends. Along towards the end of the year she became rather obnoxious to be around and her physical health was visibly declining, but the work fit in well with my college teaching, and I sure did need the money."

"Do you mean you were the young woman loading her wheelchair and walker into the car trunk and helping Ellen's mother into the car?" Ted asked. "I have to confess that I thought you were a pretty athletic chick being able to toss that heavy wheelchair around."

Ted found himself staring at Lauren while shaking his head. He reflected on the home's history. One guy's wife had mental problems and was institutionalized, prompting the family to move. A single woman with two teenaged daughters had committed suicide just inside the front door. Ellen's mother had owned the property for about fifteen years, but Ted's wife had been very specific about not getting involved with her when she moved into the house that had formerly been inhabited by such complicated stories.

"I remember you and your wife as an older couple who kept up a lovely home but didn't seem too involved with the neighbors. I thought your wife looked awfully thin and fragile."

Ted's eyes dropped. His wife, Joan, was then thin and fragile, and though they didn't know it, her heart was struggling. It hadn't always been that way. He'd married a vibrant and lovely young woman, slightly taller and more slender than Lauren. Joan had led the way, raising two healthy, well-adjusted children. And yes, she was reserved, not one to immediately want to meet new neighbors. Her cadre of women-friends, developed while they lived in an earlier rental home and mostly mothers of young families, had remained stable long after the children were grown. Their social life, other than family get-togethers, was built around several couples their age, and came through Ted's old business relationships. He and his wife had had little social contact with Ellen's mother during the period she owned the home across the street from them.

As he came through the doorway into the freshly painted hallway, Ellen joined Lauren and Ted stepped forward to greet her.

"The paint makes the place look better already."

"Thanks. I suppose Lauren told you, we are out of margaritas, but would you like a cold beer or some wine as a substitute?"

Ted accepted a beer while Ellen poured herself a glass of wine. She directed him to a spare chair, and sat down nearby.

3

"Thank you for the beer, and I understand this is your birthday, Ellen. Happy birthday!"

He noticed Lauren disappear and could hear her in the background busying herself around the house.

"Lauren showed me through the house several days ago. You're putting a lot of work and money into fixing up the place. I'm impressed."

"Thank you. I didn't realize how things had become so neglected since my mother became ill and began to lose her strength and even some of her memory. On top of not feeling up to doing housekeeping, she didn't throw anything away, and stuff was stacked everywhere. It's going to cost my mother a lot of money, but whether it's for Lauren and me or for another renter, the house has to be made attractive. A new roof and an outside paint job will also help sell this house when we have to face that some day."

Ted watched the salt and pepper haired woman while she motioned with her hands from one room to the next indicating the various work locations. He noticed that her hands were strong and her nails were short, very utilitarian, to match other aspects of her appearance. He couldn't avoid looking through the open door and into the almost empty dining room. Finally, he raised a question.

"What have you done with the furniture that was your mother's? Lauren doesn't seem to have a lot but I'm assuming you'll both want to use your own."

"My mother would be sick if she knew we have already put much of her furniture and other belongings into storage. You should also see the garage! It's loaded! There's no room for a car. But, we had to give the workmen space to do their jobs." Ellen grimaced, and added: "It was awful. I was here and could hardly breathe when they tore up all of the old carpeting. We're lucky, though. There were barely any stains on that beautiful original oak flooring that has been hidden all of these years."

Ted chuckled aloud. "I never gave it much thought but I've lived in that house across the way for forty years and don't believe I've seen a stitch of hardwood for thirty-five of those years. Maybe I got a glimpse if I happened to be home when my wife was having some carpeting replaced."

Ellen tilted her head to the side. She leaned slightly forward and looked at his blue eyes. "I'm sorry about your wife's death. It wasn't until almost a month later that a neighbor walked by as I was about to leave and asked if I knew that the old guy across the street had lost his wife."

"Well, thank you, Ellen. At the time it felt so unbelievable. Here were paramedics and an ambulance at my house instead of at your mother's. Some of the close-by neighbors were standing outside on their sidewalks at about ten that night when the ambulance slowly pulled away. I was numb."

Ted was silent for a minute. "I know you'll understand what I mean when I tell you that I'm now glad her death was so sudden, a heart attack, not like your mother's seems destined to be." Ellen nodded and waited for him to continue.

"In a way my situation was fortunate. I couldn't easily drop out of life, so I didn't. My grandchildren counted on us to visit them pretty regularly. How could I let that drop? Also, I had two summer school lectures to give on the day following my wife's funeral. It seemed best to not even tell the teacher what had happened. It helped me to have to concentrate on the program I was giving."

Ellen brightened. "I'm a high school teacher. What do you lecture about?"

He could picture Ellen in front of her class, tall and in charge, using her hands for vivid descriptions. "Well, my topics are pretty much limited to alcohol abuse and drunk-driving as these relate to teenagers. It's volunteer work that I've done for almost fifteen years. It's been a rewarding retirement career. When school starts again I'll be doing lots of speaking."

She put down her drink and turned completely towards him so that her denim-covered knees were almost touching his. "I teach English, but I'm sure what you say would have a positive impact. Would you consider being a guest speaker for my classes?"

"Yes, of course! You can be sure I don't turn down many invitations. I work at filling most of my spare hours because living alone in an empty house and not being busy can be pretty awful. Most of my classes are health or driver ed, but I'm sure you're correct in feeling that your English students would listen. I get a wonderful response from most teenagers."

Ted nodded at Ellen with his entire upper body as if he were just completing a business deal with a favorite customer. "Just let me know after the new semester begins if you have an appropriate date. But, enough of that! Right now I'm more interested in fishing and hiking at my place near Truckee. Are you a hiker, or like to trout fish by any chance? It's a spectacular wilderness place that a bunch of us own, and it's less than a three hour drive from Sacramento."

"I like to eat trout that someone else catches," Ellen laughed a hearty, throaty laugh. "But I haven't the slightest idea of how to go about it myself. I love to hike, though, and envy you." Ellen glanced at her watch and stood. "I really must go now. I'm glad you came over."

Ted stood to leave and shook Ellen's hand. "Me too. I've enjoyed the visit. Again, Happy birthday! Now, I'd like to say so long to your roommate as well."

Lauren showed up almost immediately, hugged Ellen and saw her to the door. Lauren closed the door and turned to Ted.

"Ellen is a nice woman," Lauren said, as she placed her hand on Ted's elbow and gently turned him back into the room.

"She certainly is," Ted replied.

"I hope you'll stay a bit longer."

"Well, I…"

She turned him towards her, looked directly into his eyes, and gave Ted a challenging grin. "I feel really horny tonight."

Dumbfounded and trying to gain composure, he blurted out,

"The hell you do!"

"I think I'm also kind of drunk."

"That isn't surprising if you drank my share of the margaritas. I did enjoy the beer and the visit with Ellen, however." He began walking slowly with her into the bare-walled living room. Music from a transistor radio in the kitchen wafted barely audibly into the room. "You don't look drunk, though, and I could hear you in the kitchen doing the dishes. Would you like me to make you some coffee?" Noticing her hesitation and her expression, he added, "You look mighty beautiful tonight."

"No thanks on the coffee, but aren't you sweet. Why don't you stretch out on my pad? I'm going to get into something comfortable."

She turned again as she entered the hall illuminated by a bare bulb. "I'll turn this off," she said, gesturing to the light, "And why don't you take off your pants and relax."

In the dark room, the windows framed the inky sky and the silhouette of the tree in the front yard. Ted's thoughts raced back to his early relationship with Joan. She was part of a large East Coast family. His brief meetings with her family prior to their marriage convinced him that her mother dominated the roost. Sex for a girl was not before marriage; love making from the start needed to be thoughtfully discussed and limited. Although seldom spontaneous, Ted had always considered his intimate times with Joan as being wonderful and fulfilling, but vastly different from what this free-wheeling young woman seemed to be offering.

Like a wide-eyed robot, Ted did what he was told. He was stretched out on the pad in his T-shirt and shorts when Lauren returned, her long blonde hair loose around her smooth, tanned shoulders, dressed in a short, see-through garment and bikini panties. There was no doubt now that this young, highly attractive woman thirty years his junior was serious. What an unexpected invitation!

At seventy-five and without sex for several years, Ted's excitement was tempered by alarm bells. What if he couldn't respond? That would be a terrible disaster! What if she was promiscuous, and he contracted some disease? Supposing she became pregnant and insisted on marriage? One glance provided the answer. What the heck! He'd take his chances. It had been a long while and might be long again. Damn, why hadn't he taken the time for a shower?

All of the house lights were out except for a muted glow coming from a corner table lamp. Lauren closed the horizontal Venetian blinds tightly. He had no concerns about their privacy as she stretched out beside him on the narrow pad. He momentarily wished he'd had a second drink.

Ted pulled her close to him and these two neighbors kissed for the first time. Their kissing increased in intensity and she pressed her body tightly to his. He began to feel a youth he had almost forgotten. This night was going to be all right after all.

She did things to him he had never known a woman would do, and he wanted it never to end. Afterwards, they remained stretched out on the uncomfortable pad and talked quietly. Ted's confidence level had been raised several notches, but for the first several minutes he did more listening than talking while his heartbeat subsided. He realized that he had layered some new sweat over what he had earned in the afternoon's basketball game with the grandchildren.

"You don't smell very good!" she suddenly blurted out. "Didn't you take a shower today?"

"Not since morning," he admitted. "I worked hard in my grandchildren's garden for an hour and then played basketball with them for thirty minutes before begging off. It was hot. Then, after dinner, I raced home and came directly over here so as not to be late for the birthday margaritas with you two ladies. I missed the drinks anyway, so, I'm sorry, I should have taken time for a shower."

She reached over and squeezed his hand. "You're forgiven. I'm sure you weren't expecting this kind of a reception. How old are these grandchildren? Do you have any others?"

"These two were my daughter Kathy's twin boys; they will be eleven soon. They are enthralled with basketball and had to show me how easily they could beat me. Their parents recently sent them to a three-day basketball camp. They just about wore me out."

Ted rolled over on his side and gently kissed her on her bare shoulder, then continued, "My son, Matthew, is three years younger than Kathy. They have a fourteen-year-old daughter and a son about the age of Kathy's twins. They live further away and I don't see them as often. The whole family seems to have always gotten along fine, and I feel fortunate about that."

How he had loved this unbelievable, intimate encounter with a woman Matthew's age. Several times, Lauren had exclaimed, "God, how I love sex!" Although he had no problem in building up excitement, he couldn't help but wonder if it was he who was turning this sensuous woman on. Could it be that she just had an insatiable desire for sex, something that maybe he would be hard-pressed to match? Right now, though, he had been her man, and it was a luxurious feeling.

He walked across the street to his house in a daze. Her parting words had been, "Why don't you come over in a few weeks and we can talk about my spring garden? And do you have a few more tomatoes for me?"

What a bizarre way for two neighbors to get acquainted. He pictured Lauren stretched out on the temporary bed in the living room. It was a little after ten. He knew he'd have a good night's sleep; he'd wondered how she was faring on that uncomfortable pad.

He smiled sheepishly as he turned the key in his front door lock. An old saying had suddenly come to mind: "There's no fool like an old fool." He didn't like the feeling. Maybe their tryst had been triggered by Lauren's drinking, an event she might later pass off as having been a nothing. But then, hadn't she suggested that he plan to come help with her garden? He'd be there when she called.

TWO   Mountain Love

Ted crossed the street when he saw Ellen and Lauren come out of the front door with a can of paint and a drop cloth.

"You look like you've got a project in mind."

"We're going to pretty up that old mailbox. How are you today, Ted?"

"Never felt better." He looked at Lauren, directly into her eyes to make sure she understood his hidden meaning. "I'm heading up to my wilderness cabin in the Sierra Nevada with my daughter and her kids tonight. My wife and I have owned the place jointly with other families for over twenty years. It's still pretty rustic. Joan was a great sport, and we camped out a dozen times in a tent before I built a trailer shelter about ten years after we bought in. There is still no electricity, and the group's idea is to strictly limit development. The kids love it: hiking, fishing, boating, starlight like you wouldn't believe. We sleep out on the deck when it's warm enough. Real special times up there. I bet you ladies would like it."

Both women expressed enthusiasm to see his place, although Lauren asked more questions about personal comfort.

"It sounds fine for hiking around, but I'm more concerned about having some conveniences: The idea of a smelly outhouse or taking a shovel into the woods turns me off. Count me out, there."

Ted tried to paint a reasonably attractive picture.

"You can be sure that would have turned Joan off too! Our rules are that trailers can't have individual septic tanks, so my trailer bathroom is a linen closet for my towels. I'm lucky that we chose a location close to a community bathroom where we have both hot water and showers."

Ted, Ellen, and Lauren set a date for an overnight a week out. He looked forward to this opportunity to include these women, although he inwardly wished he could have more alone time with the lovely Lauren. During his morning ritual, he began to notice her routine. He broke from his breakfast dishes to wave to her through his kitchen window when she walked out onto the porch to pick up the paper.

As the date for the trip neared, Ellen backed out, and his wish to be alone overnight with Lauren seemed to be coming true. Ellen's excuse was something about required summer teacher training interfering with the particular Saturday they had chosen.

"It might be even more exciting with just the two of us! I'll be ready at seven. We can take Ellen next time," Lauren said.

When the day came, Ted couldn't restrain his excitement. He got up at five, read the morning paper while occasionally glancing at the clock, and was packing his Explorer shortly after six. They were to stop at a little restaurant in Truckee for a late breakfast and then drive on into the valley where his year around trailer was located. Lunch goodies and drinks were packed in ice, and trout fishing gear and items for the rowboat filled the back of his vehicle.

Ted watched the clock pass seven with no sight of or word from Lauren. At 7:15 he hesitantly phoned and was jolted by the response to his question whether she was ready to go.

"I'm not going. I changed my mind."

"Is there something wrong? Why didn't you tell me before I got the truck all packed?"

"I don't know. I guess I just didn't get around to it. I'm sorry, but you love the place so much, why don't you just go."

Ted didn't appreciate her tone, but tried not to show his anger. He hung up the phone and slowly unpacked the truck. What kind of a woman was this who would back out of a planned trip without a word of explanation?

Despite her strange withdrawal from the trip, Lauren continued to be a constant admirer of his garden that was now producing an array of tomatoes, peppers, sweet corn, and cucumbers. Stopping by after checking the mail, and always greeting him with a smile and a compliment, Lauren often went home with as many vegetables as she could carry.

Ellen, too, was warm and open with her compliments.

"These veges are just great. We don't often eat together, Lauren and I, but I always include some in my dinner. Thank you so much, Ted."

After hearing that Lauren and Ellen didn't usually dine together, he decided to invite Lauren to have dinner with him. He knew the puzzling matter of the aborted mountain trip needed to be addressed, but wasn't sure how to approach the issue. So he didn't say anything. After a lovely dinner followed by lovemaking that rivaled that of their first encounter, he figured she had forgotten about it, so he would too.

A week later, he had an early Saturday morning call from Lauren.

"Will you come over and help me find a place in my back yard for next spring's garden? My father always had this huge garden, almost a farm, and he insisted we all help, so I know how to grow stuff."

Within a few minutes, Ted showed up with four three foot stakes, a hammer, and twine. He was greeted with a big smile and a warm hug.

"The first thing we need to do is to locate the area where the direct sun hits for the most number of hours each day. You have an awful lot of shade. That's why it is so pleasant back here. The people who designed this yard weren't thinking of vegetable gardens."

She nodded and he continued: "Do you have a spot in mind?"

She didn't hesitate, and together they pounded in corner stakes and wrapped the twine around them. As he was pounding in the last stake, Ted offered some additional help. He also wanted to get her reaction: was he to be involved beyond this step?

"Later in the year, before it really starts to rain, I'll bring over a shovel and spade up this plot. There will be many tree and bush roots to dig out. You can't see them, but they're under here."

"How about bringing over two shovels? I think I can probably handle a shovel as well as you can. Remember, I helped my dad." "Yes, I don't have any doubts about your gardening abilities, Lauren. You proved yourself by picking the exact spot that I would have chosen. Count on two shovels." Ted smiled to himself.

The job was finished too quickly, and Lauren handed him the partial ball of twine.

"Thanks for helping me. I'm glad we really work well together."

Ted was encouraged that she too seemed to want a more substantial relationship. The casual way she had cancelled the mountain trip, however, still rankled him. As much as he desperately wanted to share his special retreat with her, he shuddered at the thought of another refusal. He responded as he walked toward her back gate.

11

"You're welcome. There wasn't much to do. You already had everything figured out."

She followed him quietly to the gate. He turned, startled, as she touched his shoulder. She almost blurted it out:

"You haven't asked me to go to your mountain place again. Are you going to? I'd really like to see it."

He felt as if a huge burden had been lifted from his shoulders. Had she too been wanting to clear the air over the failed trip?

"Yes, I've been wanting to do it, but you'd have to promise that you won't back out. I can't handle another one of those."

She showed no hesitation. "I promise. That was terribly wrong of me, and I don't know why I did it. For some reason I got nervous about going. I did say I was sorry."

It was almost a question. Lauren smiled hesitantly and continued to look directly at him. Ted put down the hammer and twine and grabbed her hand.

"I'd like us to make this trip an overnight. Would you consider that? If it's a clear night, we can even sleep under the stars. There's a large, raised redwood deck and the elevation there is almost sixty-five hundred feet. You won't believe how spectacular the stars look."

She let go of his hand and threw her arms around him.

"Stop it! I said I wanted to go. Quit worrying."

He stepped back and picked up his tools.

"I hear you and I'm glad. If it fits, let's do it this weekend before it starts getting too chilly at night. I don't have any other commitments if you don't. Why don't we consider this to be a trial run for other overnight trips? If we can stand each other in the mountains for two days with all of the mosquitoes, bugs, dust and other inconveniences, who knows what might appeal to us. How about Carmel? It's right on the ocean and a real favorite of mine. I know you would love it."

Her response was a little wave and a bright "We'll see. Let's do this first."

Ted breathed a sigh of relief.

That Saturday morning, they left their houses at seven o'clock sharp without a hitch. But about halfway into the three-hour drive, Lauren lowered the radio volume and unexpectedly exclaimed: "I don't feel good about this! You should be making this trip with your wife and not with me. Even though she's gone, I feel like I'm intruding."

He pulled the truck off of the freeway at the first wide spot, his mind racing, thinking of how to respond. Ted felt that he needed to avoid any hint of irritation or impatience and touched her arm gently.

"Look, Lauren, we can turn around and go home right now if this is bothering you too much. It's important that you spend these special times with me because you want to and feel comfortable. I'm not going to push you. We sort of agreed that this would be a trial run to see if we can handle it. Maybe it isn't time yet."

Within a few minutes Ted sensed that Lauren was beginning to relax. She acknowledged that maybe she wasn't being realistic by feeling that she was doing something wrong.

"But I keep thinking about you and your wife."

Ted squeezed her hand as he pulled back onto the highway. "I do appreciate your feelings. You are very sensitive."

He watched her spirits lift immediately. She inserted a Harry Belafonte tape into the player and smiled at his approval.

Little more was said until they were over the Donner Summit and driving along a rancher's private dirt road, part of the final three miles of the trip. They caught a glimpse of Prosser Creek running through the meadow and sometimes parallel to the one lane road. He suggested she keep an eye out for deer.

"You might see one grazing among the trees. My guess, though, is that they have finished their morning feeding and are somewhere bedded down and resting in the shade."

Ted was beginning to feel an elevated level of excitement even though he had made the drive hundreds of times. He was watching Lauren's attentiveness and now was certain that he had been right in persuading her to continue the trip.

"This is my favorite part. Can you smell the freshness of the forest pine? There must have been a small thunderstorm yesterday because there isn't any dust at all on the road."

He stopped to unlock the padlocked gate into the club's property, and then climbed back into the truck. Lauren made no comment and Ted continued.

"The rancher brings cattle in each summer to eat up the grass in this big meadow along the creek. If I come through here quite early in the morning, some deer are often grazing with the cattle. They seem to get along well together. Once in a while, we've had a real treat and have seen tiny fauns or even a big buck." Ted pointed to their left. "As a matter of fact, there are a couple dozen Herefords way over there across the creek."

"It's such a beautiful place," she said as she jumped out of the Explorer now parked in a grassy area near the trailer shelter. "I never expected it to be like this!"

Ted pointed out the large bathroom less than fifty feet away.

"My family and guests definitely appreciate this. That big propane tank near the road heats the water for the four individual bathrooms in the building. Some of our club members have to walk several hundred yards to a bathroom, and that can be a little tough at night. Everyone says we made a great selection for a campsite."

Lauren didn't hesitate to check out one of the bathrooms, calling over her shoulder, "Then, I'm anxious to see the inside of your trailer. It looks almost new from the outside."

Ted carried the heavy car battery from the truck and connected it to the trailer terminals. When she returned, he was turning on the propane valve to the trailer's stove. Her voice was filled with excitement.

"I'd like to see the lake, and we can eat the lunch I made out there. What can I do to help get us ready?"

"Can you use a broom? These two decks need to be swept clean of pine needles so we can set up some tables and put down the foam rubber mats for sleeping."

He unlocked the trailer door and handed her a broom.

"I'll hook up the water and make sure the propane system is working."

Lauren finished sweeping and he now found her inside the trailer pulling out drawers and examining cupboards for supplies. She finally opened the refrigerator door.

"Why'd you bring all of that ice when you have a great fridge? Doesn't the thing work?"

"Oh, yes, it works, sometimes too well. We got it started easily a couple of times but couldn't regulate the temperature. One night all of a guest family's milk froze. They had small kids, and you can imagine how upsetting that was. Another time, all the veggies for the salad froze. The milk was the final straw. Now I simply bring lots of ice. The refrigerator serves as a great storage space for food that doesn't need to be chilled."

"You mean you gave up just because no one was smart enough to figure out how to adjust a gas refrigerator? How do we get this thing started? I'm going to put our stuff in it. Digging into ice for everything doesn't make sense."

In his view, bringing lots of ice had proven to be a fully acceptable solution to accommodate guests. If one or two overnights were involved, he brought along a separate chest filed with spare ice. Besides, Ted told himself, his guests felt more like they were camping out this way. But he wasn't willing to fight Lauren's persistence for long. She seemed to be headstrong, and he didn't want to start off on the wrong foot with her.

Ted instructed her to come outside and watch as he removed the cover panel and pointed to where the pilot orifice was located, then, he handed her the igniter.

"I'll go inside and get things adjusted. You light the flame when I tell you. Let me know when about a minute is up and if the pilot remains lighted when I release the button."

He lay down on the trailer floor, removed the cover over the refrigerator control panel and read the instructions with the help of a flashlight. He almost hoped the damned thing wouldn't work at all. He didn't need this!

Lauren continued to express her impatience.

"What's taking so long? I want to get our food stored so we can go to the lake. Besides, I'm hungry."

"I'm ready now. I have the button pushed in that opens the gas to the pilot light. See if you can get a flame."

"Of course there's a flame. This is easy. Why did you make such a production of it?"

Ted adjusted the needed settings, replaced the cover, got to his feet and faced a silent but "I told you so" Lauren.

"I have the dials set to where the temp should level out. We'll have to keep a watch on the inside temperature, though."

She seemed not to be listening, and in several quick trips, she stowed their drinks, milk, cheese, meat and vegetables. Lauren wasn't through yet.

"I can't believe anyone being so dumb as not to use this convenient refrigerator!"

Ted scowled and Lauren changed the subject: "Let's go see the lake now."

They quickly loaded oars, life jackets, anchor, a folding table and the small ice chest containing their lunch into the Explorer. Within ten minutes, the tranquil, sparkling surface of the lake brought exclamations of delight from her.

"How did you ever find a hidden place like this? I don't see anyone else. Are we the only ones here?"

He acknowledged that they probably were. "Most of the members live further away than I do and may come up only once or twice each year. They often stay a week or more, though. I like to drive up lots of times each summer but mainly only for a day at a time. I get too busy doing other things to spend a whole week."

They set the table and chairs up in a shaded, level area alongside the lake. Ted watched while she deftly laid out the sandwiches, napkins, and an apple to share. Lauren got a beer for him and a soda for herself.

While they were eating, he explained how the twenty-acre lake had originally been a marshy area in the cradle scraped out by a glacier.

"This isn't the way it used to be. The few owners of the club property before my wife and I bought in did a lot of dredging. They put up that big levee with the dirt from the marsh." Her eyes followed as Ted pointed to a several hundred-yard stretch of bare levee. He sipped his beer while she scanned the lake, the far shore, and the surrounding mountain ranges with his binoculars.

"There are thousands of little evergreens on the other side of the lake. They can't be very old. Why are they so dense?" Lauren handed the binoculars to him and he looked at the new growth area she had asked about. Then he focused on some water flowing down a mountain gorge about half mile away, far to their left.

"When we go out in the boat, we can look down and see a dozen or two stumps of huge trees that were well over one hundred years old. They were cut down and dragged out because they would have died anyway as the lake filled. Those new trees you see can't be over twenty or thirty years old. The growing conditions along the edge of the lake must have become perfect for them. They're so thick that none will ever grow into a large tree." He felt strength in his role as a teacher.

"I hear the sound of water running. Where's it coming from?"

"The lake is pretty full now, with more water coming in than is needed. What you hear is the overflow water going over our spillway into a big drainpipe that leads to the creek we saw coming in. The snowmelt keeps our lake full until midsummer. Then there's a spring high up on that mountain that keeps some fresh water coming in." Ted pointed to a barely visible waterfall located in a rocky gorge that he had verified through the binoculars.

"Once we depend entirely on that spring, the lake level drops quickly. That's not too good for fishing because the water warms up some and we get lots of bottom weeds." As he spoke, he noticed her attention drifting off. The lecture time must be over, he thought. With lunch finished, he installed the oarlocks, loaded the oars, ice chest, net, rod and tackle box into the boat and announced that they were ready to go fishing. Lauren climbed in, carrying her sunscreen, a tape deck and a container of tapes. He pushed the boat into the water and jumped in as it cleared the shore.

Ted soon discovered that trout fishing wasn't for her. Although she had claimed to be an experienced and enthusiastic angler, Lauren now turned her head and covered her eyes every time he pulled a fish towards the boat for netting. He was puzzled and disappointed. After several nice trout were landed, Ted asked her what was wrong.

"I used to go fishing with my dad a lot. At first I wanted to, but then I began to hate it. Part of my job was to put the worm on a hook and I just couldn't bear to see it squirm. I also could never come to grips with the fish losing their lives. They were so beautiful and seemed to be pleading with me not to kill them. After a while, every fishing trip with my dad was horrible, but I can't help my feelings. I'm sorry if it's spoiling your fishing."

Ted quietly stowed his fishing gear.

"No, that's okay. I think I understand. Besides, we already have several nice fish. I'm going to pull up the anchor now." He saw relief on Lauren's face and continued, "Why don't I row around the lake and show you some interesting spots? The water is so clear that you might see a stray rainbow swimming around. Most are in deep water and aren't actively feeding unless you catch them off guard and drop bait in front of them."

He had now taken up the oars and was maneuvering the small craft towards one shore.

"If we have a little luck, we might see a family of geese that I know is here. The five goslings are half grown and can't fly yet. They make a spectacular picture, with an adult in the lead, then the goslings, followed by the other parent. You'll love watching them if they're in the water."

Ted alternately rowed and drifted. There was a slight breeze that slowly pushed the boat to the north when he wasn't using oars. A few strokes kept them from being brushed by overhanging willows along the shoreline. They welcomed the shade, and drifted quietly for fifteen minutes. Lauren played a Linda Ronstadt tape and sang along, singing Ted a Mexican love song. Ted couldn't believe any sounds could be so beautiful, sung only for him. Only the goose family moving in line less than a hundred yards away shared this experience. Could he be falling in love with this lovely, unpredictable young woman? She reached across and squeezed Ted's hand. Could Lauren possibly be pondering the same question?

Back in camp, Lauren seemed relaxed and enthusiastic about their evening.

"I'm going to take a shower and then fix up the salad and beans. I also put in half a loaf of French bread to warm in the oven. Your big job is to get the charcoal going and take care of the steaks."

She turned after going several steps up the path to the community bathroom.

"I like my meat medium rare."

Ted grinned. "Yes, I hear those instructions. I'll also lay out the logs and stuff for the fire tonight. Save a little hot water for me."

At dinner, Lauren surprised him with her toast, "To our first night in your mountain place! I never expected it to be so gorgeous. I'm glad you insisted that I come." But in spite of this delightful start, dinner was less than a complete success. The charcoal had been difficult to light and then got too hot. He also misjudged the cooking time for the steaks that he had so carefully selected. She ate very little of the meat, but told him it was okay. Feeling relieved, Ted reached across the table and touched Lauren's arm. How little he knew about his unpredictable companion.

He had carefully laid out the makings for a fire in the pit. He knew from experience where to get dry pine needles even following brief thundershowers. Now, while Lauren was washing and putting dinner things away, he lit the fire and carried over two chairs. She soon joined him. Together they watched the burning needles ignite smaller sticks and finally the larger pieces of wood.

Sitting close to one another in the semi-darkness around the fire, Ted told Lauren about the fire pit's history.

"I first dug a hole six feet across and almost two feet deep. That was the easy part. It then took about ten trips to bring in these huge stones that I had selected from the side of the road on that steep, downhill grade coming in."

Lauren reached over and squeezed his hand, then left hers resting on his lap. He was thinking of the summer, fifteen years earlier when he had hauled in the heavy rocks.

"I didn't have the Explorer then, of course, and had to divide each load of stones in my sedan, some on the floor of the front seat, some in the back, and a few in the trunk. It was a lousy way to treat a nice new car!"

She was watching the fire intensely and put her feet up on the rock wall.

"How long did it take? Didn't you have anyone to help you?" Lauren seemed almost annoyed.

"It took most of a summer, and no, I chose to do it all myself. Once I had stockpiled several loads of rocks, I mixed mortar in a bucket. It was tiring, but I only worked a couple of hours at a time. I admit that it tore up my hands, but I was thrilled each time over the progress. I always separated the rocks that had smooth, flat tops, and were fairly thin, and set them aside. You can see what a convenient sitting place the top layer made. It's great for coffee mugs too."

"Why did you build the walls so high? Most fire pits I've seen have ledges just above the ground level."

"Most of my grandchildren were very little then. I had nightmares about them chasing each other around and one stumbling into the fire. It took away that worry for my wife and myself."

Lauren didn't ask any more questions but squeezed his hand again. The fire was burning steadily, and Ted put on another log. Occasionally the smoke forced them to shift their chairs to the other side of the pit. But neither complained. The increasing chill prompted them to don hooded sweatshirts. They snuggled closer.

Night came quickly in the dense mountain forest. Ted had experienced this many times in his earlier years of camping in other mountain areas with his son, Matthew. As nine o'clock approached, the only light other than that from the fire came from a spectacular full moon slowly showing itself above the mountains to the east of them.

There seemed to be no need for talk. They pushed their chairs tightly together, and she rested her head on his shoulder. He put his arm snugly around Lauren and drew her even more closely to him. For half an hour they quietly watched the fire burn itself down, mesmerized by the flickering flames and crackling sounds.

She was the first to break the silence.

"I'm getting kind of cold. Will you put another log on the fire?"

Ted carefully disengaged himself and glanced at the outside thermometer nailed to the trailer shelter.

"Do you realize that it's under fifty degrees already? No wonder we're getting cold. It's time to drown the fire and go to bed. I'll get our sleeping bags and bed ready."

Ted was starting to lay out the foam pads on the deck when Lauren asked how cold it would get during the night. His response that it wouldn't drop below thirty brought an outburst from her:

"You can do this with the grandkids if you want. I'm no teenager! Or sleep on the deck yourself and watch your darned stars if you want to. I'm sleeping inside!"

A quick glance revealed her silhouette in the brightening moonlight, feet spread apart, hands on hips.

Ted realized that he wasn't on firm enough ground to pursue the outdoor sleeping suggestion. He knew too, that the interior of the trailer, even without heat, would be at least ten degrees warmer than outside. This was a night when he desperately wanted things to go well.

"You're likely right. If you'll help zip these two sleeping bags together, I can then make up the kitchen seating area into a good double bed in just a few minutes."

With the trailer door closed and locked, and only one dim, battery-powered light in the hallway on, the cozy double sleeping bag completed a perfect setting for their first night of mountain lovemaking. Neither suggested a break to admire the full moon or the unlimited twinkling stars.

Ted found himself tiring more quickly than he normally did. He felt the effects of the long drive, several hours on the lake, and the altitude. It was more difficult for him to become fully aroused. His anxiety didn't help, but Lauren's eagerness and encouragement led him, although not her, to complete fulfillment.

He felt guilty because he wanted so much to bring her to climax. "It's okay," she said softly. I get really excited when you come."

Ted knew that this assurance couldn't always be true for any woman. Coming from her though, as they held each other in a final goodnight embrace, it made a relaxed sleep possible.

The sun was already showing above the mountain range and the deck partly covered in sunshine when he awakened and opened the trailer door. Lauren briefly opened her eyes and returned his "good morning" with a smile. She then pulled his pillow over to her side and held it tightly. Although her eyes were closed now, he was sure she was awake.

"I'm going to put heat under the water for coffee and then walk to the bathroom to wash up. Will you keep an eye on the water? It won't take long."

She nodded her head without opening her eyes. When Ted returned, she was partly dressed sitting on the edge of the bed. The flame had been turned down and the steam from the heated water was visible in the cold air. He bent over and kissed her forehead.

"It's your turn now. Don't rush. I'm going to fix some coffee and roll up the sleeping bags so I can get the kitchen table ready. I may even have a sweet roll in the oven and be cutting up the melon when you get back."

Lauren picked up a towel, washcloth, and small overnight bag and stood in the open doorway.

"You're sweet. The sunshine feels wonderful on my back. It's warmer outside than in the trailer. I won't be long."

After a leisurely breakfast, he began talking about getting back to the lake for a few more trout.

"If you remember, I promised Ellen enough for a couple of dinners. On top of that, my daughter's family will be looking forward to getting a few nice fish."

Lauren, though, was having nothing to do with rushing to the lake. He noticed some irritation in her voice.

"What's wrong with staying around camp for a while? Don't you ever relax?"

Ted reluctantly acknowledged that he didn't often take time out for relaxing.

"Many of my guests are here to fish, hike, or do some boating. I get used to rushing around to try and fit in all these activities. Some only come up once a year and buy expensive fishing licenses for the chance to catch a few fish."

"Well, I'm not your ordinary guest, Ted, and I want to sit on the deck in this great morning sunshine and just talk." Then, half angrily, she added, "can't we just sit and visit for an hour or two? Then we can go out to your damned lake?"

Ted had no comeback. He put two captain's chairs on the deck overlooking the open meadow, stirred up another cup of coffee for each of them, and sat down. Even though he had no idea where their conversation might lead, he reasoned that it could be a pleasant hour or two. But, couldn't they do the same sitting in his boat? Fishing was usually better in the morning hours.

21

Then he remembered their wonderful lovemaking of the night before. What on earth was he complaining about? He smiled and greeted her brightly as she joined him on the deck.

"You look awfully nice this morning. The mountain air agrees with your complexion."

She wanted to talk about her past relationships. He'd heard bits and pieces but had never encouraged any detailed revelations. Now he was relaxed. Let it be Lauren's hour. He didn't feel threatened by men long out of her life.

"When I was a senior in high school, I fell in love with a college man. I would cut classes and walk over to the student union to be with him. We secretly began to have sex and it really screwed up my schoolwork. I could have graduated with honors, but I didn't. I got married right out of high school and it only lasted five years."

Lauren seemed to Ted to almost be dreaming about what might have been as she told him about the elegant wedding, a big, Catholic affair. His wedding to Joan was a typical wartime event, hastily arranged and attended by a handful of close relatives and two fellow officers and their wives. Ted smiled to himself as he reflected on the contrast.

"We then had to move to a base in Germany, because my husband was suddenly called up for active army duty. He was really upset, but I thought it would be exciting. It was my chance to get out of a little town and see the world."

Ted now listened to her intently. As a WWII naval officer himself, he was interested in her reaction to military life as the young wife of an officer.

"It was exciting for a while, but really I did very little that meant anything. Much of the time we wives talked about where the next party would be when the men were off duty. I did enjoy shopping and loved the short trips we took to other parts of Europe."

Shortly after those army years, she had become pregnant. Her voice quivered when she related to Ted that the baby had serious health problems and died within three weeks. The loss had devastated her.

"But my husband just didn't get it! He had finished college and had a good job by that time and was excited about his work. He kept insisting that we had to put this sad event behind us and move on with our lives. I also couldn't seem to fit in with the social life that went with his job. Most of my husband's co-workers had college degrees, and I felt inadequate having only a high school diploma."

She told Ted that she had finally asked her husband for a divorce because he didn't have the ability to really care about her feelings and their son's death. Now, sitting in the warm, tree-filtered sun, she told him about other relationships with men, some lasting only a few months and others several years. She had decided that a second marriage just wasn't for her.

Lauren related that she had lived in several western areas, including Arizona, San Diego, and South Lake Tahoe. Ted was fascinated by her story about a sixty-eight year old insurance company executive she had met while dealing blackjack at a South Lake Tahoe casino.

"I was twenty-eight at the time. For some reason I found that I could handle dealing blackjack well. It allowed me a lot of time with my friends. With the tips I got, I could pay my bills and have money for partying which I seemed to do in most of my free time."

She paused and took a sip of coffee, not seeming to notice or care that it had become cold.

"This older guy played at my table for three nights and kept teasing me and flirting with me. It didn't seem to bother him that he lost a lot of money. Most men were fun at my table as long as they were winning, but they became sarcastic and verbally obnoxious when they lost. This Texan, in his white linen suit and Stetson just smiled and kept on playing and losing."

Ted was astonished as Lauren continued to recall her experience with the Texan millionaire.

"He kept asking me what a beautiful, talented woman like me was doing dealing blackjack. He wanted me to be his personal secretary at a salary of three thousand dollars a month. On the third night he was there, he told me he had to leave to return to work and almost begged me to go with him to Texas."

She paused and looked at Ted as if asking him to understand her actions, shrugged her shoulders and continued.

"I know you'll find this hard to believe, but at the end of my shift, I climbed into his Lear jet, and off I went. I didn't even go back to my apartment for any clothes or other stuff. He said there was plenty to buy in Texas and it would all be on him. My roommate was shocked when I called her the next morning from Austin. I told her to do what she wanted with my clothes because I was starting a brand new life."

Ted couldn't help but feel a little jealous. Here was a tall, distinguished gentleman, appealing so much to Lauren that she flew away with him. She, no doubt, pictured herself living a life of luxury with this big spending, fun loving sixty eight year old man. He knew he couldn't provide Lauren with that many material goods, nor could he ever be that spontaneous.

He watched his lovely camping companion's expression of acceptance of what followed as she concluded her story.

"I bought only four hundred dollars worth of clothes, despite his insisting that I buy more. I just didn't feel right about it. My job was mostly lying by the pool and answering his phone when he was away. He was gone a lot of the time and I was bored. On two occasions I traveled to meetings with him. He introduced me as his lady, and I didn't feel comfortable with that. And to top it off, he was impotent! After three weeks I insisted that he put me on a plane back to California. He told me that if I would stay, everything he had might be mine some day. Even that wasn't worth it. I realized I had made a big mistake and wanted out."

She hadn't mentioned the man's name once. Maybe she had forgotten. Ted didn't ask. The casino gave Lauren her job back. She was a vibrant, attractive and quick-witted woman, all desirable attributes for a card dealer, so it really was no surprise to Ted. The male customers would have loved her quick smiles and flirtatious glances. She would have been tipped generously.

Ted interrupted her reminiscing only occasionally with brief questions. At one point, he asked her where she had developed her avid interest in the Mexican culture and language.

"It started after I met this young Mexican guy, Antonio, while I was living in Arizona. He imported Indian silver jewelry from Mexico. I quit a medical receptionist job and moved in with him. He had a jewelry retail store. We flew to Mexican cities several times a year on his buying trips. Antonio had a small plane and was a good pilot. We always stayed in very nice places. While he was dealing with suppliers, I would spend most of my time in the towns or cities, watching and listening to the native people. Sometimes I bought food to cook for us when we stayed in places with a kitchenette, but mostly we dined out. On each trip I learned more Spanish and just loved it."

Ted had to ask, "Everything seemed so right. The guy was your age. He sounds like he was successful and you were doing interesting things. Why aren't you with him today?"

"I lasted almost five years. He didn't want me to get a job, and I was often bored. I began jogging regularly around a park to keep in shape and simply for something to stimulate me. Sometimes I would stop briefly and chat with men standing near the running path. I got so I could run a mile in seven minutes. If men were nearby, they would cheer me as I ran past and call out, 'Nice going, Lauren!' Antonio got very jealous and he became quite possessive. I would spot him watching me from his truck. I became almost afraid of him. One day I left and never saw him again."

Ted began to think about what these stories had in common: exciting men with traveling lifestyles, extreme generosity, and more than a bit of possessiveness over Lauren. They wined and dined her and with both of them she was bored! Some day, in one of these stories, if he listened hard enough, he would find the key to her happiness and his satisfaction too. She was obviously a hard woman to please.

"Tell me, Lauren, you seem to have been the one to end your relationships. Is this always the way it happens?" He asked this seriously, but put a teasing look in his eye, which she didn't seem to notice.

"Most of the time, yes, but there was one guy I met after I decided I'd better face the fact that I was going nowhere and needed a college education if I wanted to get a steady job with a good salary and a retirement plan. I met him at a bar in San Diego, which, I'll admit, doesn't bode well. But he was a couple of years younger than I was and had a good job. His parents were wealthy and seemed to like and respect me a lot, especially for my determination to get my degree. They had a beautiful place on the coast near Fort Bragg. We stayed there on weekends several times. After two years, I thought things were going great, and I would have married him. He phoned me one day after I got home from classes and said he was going back to an old girlfriend but 'thanks for a great couple of years.' I called him dozens of times, but he was cold."

Ted's curiosity pushed him to another question: "Did he marry this woman?"

"Yes, and they're still married. Jim calls me every year, almost always on my birthday…" Her voice trailed away.

Ted thought he could see tears forming in her eyes and leaned closer to her. She stood up.

"It was close as I ever came to killing myself."

She walked several steps across the deck and faced Ted.

"What is wrong with me? Why do you have to be so old?"

A surge of jealousy overwhelmed Ted. Could Lauren still be yearning for this younger man? He was too stunned to answer. Lauren's demeanor then shifted as if she had just walked from darkness into sunlight. She smiled brightly and said, "Well, Ted, we've talked for over an hour. Thanks. We can go fishing now, but I won't fish. I'll sit and read and watch you from shore. Let me put a lunch together while you load the truck." She disappeared into the trailer but within a minute was back outside.

"What happened to the fridge? The thermometer reads forty-eight now and you said it was thirty eight when we went to be last night."

"Yes, I remember, but you also should remember it was dropping. I woke up three times and was so concerned that I got up to check the temperature. At three this morning it was twenty-eight degrees! We had the gas set as low as possible so I turned the whole thing off. Nothing had become frozen yet. We'll need to get some of it back on ice."

She turned again as she re-entered the trailer.

"It looks like I came down on you too hard yesterday about your not wanting to use the fridge. I'm sorry."

Ted had the two folding chairs in his hands. "That's alright. There has to be an answer somewhere. I just haven't found it yet. And it's too expensive to have experts come in."

He completed loading the truck with the boat oars, a life jacket and the anchor. She joined him with the packed ice chest. Within ten minutes the sight of the tranquil surface of the lake was again bringing exclamations of delight from Lauren. He was thinking about an added way to enhance their afternoon.

"Before we unload and you start reading, would you like to hike around the lake? I've done it only once."

She approved immediately. "With all of our sitting this morning, I'm really ready for some walking. It's a wonderful idea."

Ted wasn't sure what to expect. He knew the trail wasn't very distinct because few members chose the back, brushy area on the far side of their lake for hiking. Recently fallen trees could make for backtracking or fighting their way through the brush. Lauren insisted that she could manage in shorts and was soon applying insect repellent to the exposed skin. He, too, was getting excited. Here was a woman who might share the limited number of summers he would have left to enjoy in these mountains.

"Why don't you lead during the first quarter mile around the edge of the lake and up along the levee and into the forest beyond it. There used to be a fairly well-marked trail," he said.

After fifteen minutes of steady walking, they lost the trail, and Ted suggested that he lead. Several times he asked her to wait while he retraced their steps to locate the missed turn and then called for her to join him.

They climbed a large, recently fallen evergreen rather than detour around it, and then stood together atop the five-foot diameter log. She turned and embraced him.

"Do you suppose," she asked, "that we are the first people on earth to stand here since this old tree came down during a storm?"

"I'm almost sure of it. There were big storms last winter. There's little reason for people being here in this part of the forest."

He climbed down from the log and then steadied her descent. They held each other tightly, adding a deep kiss. He whispered in her ear, "thanks again for last night," and gently released her with a playful pat on her bottom. Ted quickly dismissed the temptation to suggest they make love on the nearby grassy area. Suppose he couldn't perform, or Lauren got a sudden painful insect bite on her exposed skin. Her quick smile and the sparkle in her eyes reassured him that he was on firm ground. Nothing more was needed. Ted continued:

"For the most part, we make sure the deer aren't disturbed. I'm not a hunter, but some of the owners are, and club rules do allow for deer hunting during the late fall season, but only up on the mountain slopes."

Twice a doe trotted away, disturbed by their voices or footsteps. The curious animals stopped after going fifty feet and stared at the intruders. They soon returned to grazing. Ted relished this situation. He knew how much Lauren loved the sight of wild animals living their lives naturally and peacefully.

"If we had been here a month earlier, one or likely two spotted fawns would be lying hidden close by. Even now, they can't be far away, but they're slowly gaining the needed independence."

They came to a narrow stream that fed the lake. Mud on either side of the water caused them to hesitate. They moved upstream to a point where jumping across was possible without getting their shoes muddy. He pointed to a mountainside of boulders dotted with scattered trees and shrubs.

"Do you think you might one day want to climb those rocks with me? If we followed that gorge up for a quarter mile or so, I believe we could locate the spring feeding this stream."

Her faint smile and shrug told him there was a limit to her wanting to experience his wilderness. Soon, they rounded the south end of the lake and came out of the thick brush and trees. They skirted a marshy area and climbed onto a more-traveled trail lined by knee-high grass. Lauren pointed to large patches of trodden-down grass.

"What caused this? I haven't seen any cattle around, and you said deer bedded down among the trees for safety."

Ted laughed.

"Yes, I used to ask myself the same question. It turns out that these are the mid-day resting places for itinerant geese! They seem to love to spend several hours each day just being quiet and enjoying the sunshine. From the boat you can sometimes spot them because one or both of the adult geese will poke their black heads above the grass. You have to assume they're watching out for danger. Geese that can't fly yet aren't very safe out of the water."

She now took the lead. The edge of the lake ahead had several boats pulled up on the shore, including his own. He had to increase his pace to barely keep up with her. Lauren ducked through a final cluster of lakeside evergreens and onto the open, gravelly beach.

Ted walked to the truck a few yards away and pulled out the two folding chairs, setting them up in the shade near the water's edge and settled into one. After a moment, he went back to the vehicle for yesterday's newspaper, the folding table, and the ice chest with their drinks and lunch. While she sipped a soda, he assembled his rod and cast to where he knew was a fairly deep part of the lake. She glanced up from her paper at the sound of the splash.

"I thought you were going out in the boat."

"I've decided to forget the boat and just be here with you. There are almost sure to be some hungry trout in this deeper water. Besides, I feel great and want to enjoy my lunch leisurely. I'll try not to disturb your reading."

"Well, okay, but I hope you don't catch any of those beautiful fish while I'm looking. Will you clean those you do catch somewhere where I can't see you doing it?'

"Of course."

She said, "Thanks for suggesting that wonderful hike," and turned back to her paper.

THREE   By The Sea

THREE

The summer was quickly passing. Lauren was busy fulfilling her contract to teach an adult education class four days a week. She frequently commented about her dissatisfaction with the lax teaching atmosphere. Ted was pleased that she, like him, demanded accountability from the class.

"There isn't much of a future in what I'm doing with these older people. There aren't any attendance requirements. I spend hours preparing lessons for twenty-five people and only ten show up. I often feel like a babysitter for those who do attend. Yesterday, the attendance sheet showed 22 students present but I counted only 10! The others had checked in and then left at the break. Good thing it helps pay the rent. "

Ted learned to listen carefully to these regular complaints, agreeing with most, cautioning her on others.

Ted's trips with guests to his mountain place filled one day of most weeks. Twice, he saved an overnight for Lauren and himself. They hiked, boated, fixed special dinners, and spent hours by the warm fire before their ritual of lovemaking.

Visits with his grandchildren were irregular as special activities filled many of their summer vacation days. His garden also required less attention. He fit in the necessary watering and regularly carried baskets of tomatoes, peppers and beans to neighbors. They would reciprocate with cookies, or fresh peaches or apricots if they had back yard orchards. The two neighbors shared dinners when their schedules allowed it. Ted and Ellen were both regularly invited when Lauren prepared a meal at her place. Ted really enjoyed the discussion between the two women, which mostly centered on education.

Several times during the summer, he suggested that Lauren accompany him to Carmel for a weekend or a single overnight. But each time, she had demurred.

"I'm not sure Ted. From what you told me, this has always been a very special place for you and your wife. It probably is nice, and I've always loved the coast, but let's not rush into going."

He was acutely aware that time was getting short. She would soon be adding her college teaching hours to her adult education schedule. Putting three days together for even a short vacation would be difficult.

Ted considered one last appeal. Maybe he could tease her into looking at Carmel as a challenge, an adventure.

"Now that you've been to my mountains three times and survived so well, will you gamble on two nights in Carmel? The summer is almost over!"

Lauren looked at him squarely, then almost laughed.

"Yes, I think I can handle it, but do we have to stay at the same place you always did?"

"Give it a try. It's the nicest place in town, Lauren, and I want it to become our ocean spot, just as you want my wilderness camp to be. Let me make reservations. You wont be disappointed."

Ted was fully aware that a time would come when his two children, Kathy and Matthew, would have to be told about his relationship with Lauren. His male friends were immediate recipients of the news of this dramatic change in his life. He loved watching their startled expressions when he told them about his romance with this "Polish bombshell."

The best he was going to get from his children, he figured, would be muted enthusiasm, and more likely expressed doubts and even criticism. Ted wasn't used to the latter, so he had delayed telling his children about Lauren. At first, he justified waiting because this might be just an exciting dream he was having, and she might just as quickly back out of his life. But, she gave no signs of planning to do so.

Taking Lauren to his mountain retreat hadn't led to any questioning from either Matthew or Kathy. If one had asked who he was taking there for a day or for an overnight, his response of "a friend" or "a teacher" or "a neighbor" had triggered no further questions. Both of his children liked the idea of his having someone along in the event of car trouble. And handling the twelve-foot rowboat alone wasn't something either felt was wise, regardless of Ted's assurance that it was a piece of cake.

Carmel, now, was different; they would be staying two nights. You just don't grab a friend or neighbor and take the long trip to this romantic seaside city. Ted knew he had run out of time. He stared at the phone for a long minute before making the first call, to his son, Matthew.

He was relieved when his son, and not his daughter-in-law, answered the phone. After the usual pleasantries, he got down to the purpose of his call.

"Listen, Matt, I just wanted you and Susan to know that I'll be away for three days next week in Carmel, in the event you call and get no answer. I don't want you to worry."

"Carmel?" Matt asked.

"Yes. I'm taking a neighbor woman who I've become acquainted with over the past couple of months. Her name is Lauren. She is a college instructor."

There was a brief pause, and then Matt replied. "That sounds nice, Dad. I'm glad you called because we would have been concerned. You said she's a neighbor? Which house?"

"Right across the street. I'm sure you remember your mother and my telling you about the old lady who was always being taken away in the ambulance. Her health has finally put her in a permanent-care facility. Her daughter moved in, and Lauren is renting with her."

"Nice. I remember hearing about that old woman. How old is her daughter? About sixty?"

"Yes, she just had her sixtieth birthday."

"And Lauren's about the same?"

"Actually, Matt, she's forty-five." Ted held his breath as he waited for the response.

"Seriously, Dad? Forty-five? Are you sure you can handle this? What do you two do together? I mean…"

Ted sighed and chuckled just a bit. "Lauren loves to garden. She loves the mountains and hiking and boating and stuff."

"Just keep your head on straight, Dad. And good luck."

Matthew was concerned, but not critical, and this reassured Ted. The tougher hurdle was still to come. He somehow knew his daughter, Kathy, would not be so understanding.

"Daddy!" She exclaimed, after Ted told her about his trip, his new neighbor, and his new relationship. "A new woman friend? What are the boys going to think?"

"They'll see that a man can continue to have relationships with women even late in life, Kathy. Even with someone younger."

"Younger? How old is this Lauren person?"

"She's forty five."

"Oh— what can you be thinking? She's younger than I am! What do you see in her? What can you possibly have in common?"

"Lauren really likes gardening, and she thinks what I'm doing talking with high school kids about alcohol and driving is great; and, she really likes the mountains and hiking." Ted trailed off and waited.

"Do you mean you've taken her to Truckee?"

"Yes, and…"

"Do you stay overnight?" Kathy interrupted.

"Yes. We do. Why?" He hoped his tone carried a challenge she wouldn't dare confront.

"It just seems to me that you're forgetting your family. What will your grandchildren think? They want to remember their grandmother, not another strange woman."

"Please don't worry about that part. Kids are resilient. Besides, Lauren is lots of fun with children. She comes from a big family."

"I don't want to offend you, Daddy, but you're not a young man. You're seventy-five. And she's forty?"

"Forty five."

"Does she know you have money? Who's paying for this Carmel trip? I bet it's not her!"

"We don't discuss my money, Kathy. I'm paying for it, of course. Lauren's just beginning to teach. She doesn't have a lot of spare cash. She does her share. Don't you worry about that."

"An unmarried woman her age is after money and little else. I hope you realize this before it's too late. We all love you so much. This is really upsetting."

Realizing he wouldn't be able to change his daughter's reaction, Ted tried a more conciliatory approach. "Who knows, Kathy, maybe you're right. But only time will tell. One of these days, perhaps you'll have a chance to meet her. She's really nice, I know you'd like her."

"Well, please don't bring her here, Daddy. I'm not sure I ever want to meet her."

Ted sat down with a magazine after their conversation ended with his assurance that he'd be calling soon about coming up to bring some of the last of his tomato crop and count on some basketball with his grandchildren.

Alternately, he read and leaned back in the rocker to review the conversations with his children. Conflict wasn't something he'd ever handled well. Avoiding it was always his first approach. But he wasn't going to give up Lauren. So what if she cost him a little money? She made him feel young again. Ted slept well; he doubted that Kathy did.

As the Carmel departure day approached, Ted found himself actually looking forward to the four-hour drive to the coast town. He hoped that Lauren would have many questions that he could answer concerning the crops growing on farms along the way. He had concluded that her interest in gardening was real, and farming was just the commercial extension of that. He wasn't disappointed as the first huge corn field, almost perfectly manicured, led into a long discussion about corn varieties and enabled him to show off his knowledge.

"I have a degree in agriculture and worked as an agronomist for thirty years. A lot of the growers in this area became good friends of mine." He glanced wistfully at Lauren. "I now see too many of their pictures on the obituary page. Maybe their kids or grandchildren are farming these same acres now."

Ted was again enjoying his role as a sort of teacher. He pointed to several fields of dark green sugar beets, looking almost like spinach, on Lauren's right.

"If you peeled and sliced one of those beets when it was ready, it would taste quite sweet. I would guess, though, that beets have only about half as much sugar as cane. It takes a lot of expensive machinery to separate the sugar out of the beets and a whole lot of pulp is left over. Some of the pulp can be dried and used as animal feed. If you mix it with molasses, cows like the stuff."

He hesitated while thinking back much further than his employment years. "We used quite a bit of what was called molasses-dried beet pulp as part of the feed mix when my parents had a dairy."

His further observation that beets wouldn't be grown for sugar without government subsidy seemed to spark no interest on his passenger's part, and though she had turned away from him, Ted felt it was important and that he needed to finish.

"It was because of the wars. The argument was that this country needed a safe supply of sugar if friendly nations producing cane sugar were overrun by an enemy. I'm sure it made good sense at the time, and maybe still does."

They were now driving due west and the highway took them over a range of low mountains. Hundreds of windmills were standing erect like sentinel soldiers. Lauren couldn't control her exclamations of surprise:

"They look so stately! Why are many turning and others stand completely still? Why do those," she said, pointing to one side and then to the other, "look different from those other ones on that hill?"

"I really don't have many answers, but am always fascinated by them, as you are. The wind has certainly been pushing the car around."

They drove in silence down the western slope of the pass. Lauren seemed engrossed in watching the scenery change from small farms with cattle or horse pastures to condominium developments.

"In another two miles we'll be getting onto the main highway going south. It's only another hour and a half to Carmel."

Lauren's response was a quick smile. "Are you ready for lunch? I'm hungry." She leaned over to the back seat and got out a block of Swiss cheese, an apple, and sweet hot mustard from the small ice chest along with a box of crackers and a bag of pretzels. Out of the paper bag she also pulled napkins, cups, and a small paring knife.

"Would you like orange juice or wine?"

"I'd prefer a beer, but under the circumstances, I'll go with the juice."

He glanced appreciatively as she prepared small pieces of cheese and apple slices. She put his cup into the holder on the dashboard and then chose a Garth Brooks tape to listen to.

"I bet you were never this prepared for a long drive. Look at the time we'll save by not stopping. And we can even have music with our lunch."

"Yes, I've always stopped somewhere along this trip." She popped an apple slice in his mouth but he continued to talk. "You're pretty wonderful; you'll spoil a guy."

They registered at the hotel, and while they were heading towards the room, Lauren nudged him. "Did you see the looks they gave me in the lobby?"

"No, I'm afraid I didn't. I was busy signing in. Were they wondering what a beauty like you was doing checking in with an old geezer? Hah. I'm sure it does happen. I guess we'll have to accept all of the unasked questions as being normal considering our obvious age difference."

She seemed to him to have accepted his response, and immediately fallen in love with their poolside room. Ted could see that he'd made no mistake in asking her to go along with his choice of a place to stay.

"How about a walk on the beach while the sun is still high?" He knew from experience that the fog would drift in before five. Lauren had other ideas.

"I'd rather spend some time right here. Just feel that wonderful air! Why don't you fix us a drink? We need to celebrate just being here. You'll find a container of dip in the ice chest. I know where I packed the bag of snacks, so I'll get the chips."

Ted readily agreed. Soon, they were sitting on comfortable patio chairs with a tray of snacks between them. Young swimmers from family groups were excitedly playing in the pool. He raised his glass and she followed.

"I can't think of any appropriate toast, Lauren. I'm so awfully glad you decided to come here with me."

She smiled in agreement, then stood up and kissed his forehead but offered no toast. Two hours later the fog came in on schedule. The pool was soon vacated and Lauren commented on how chilly it had become.

"I'm ready to go inside and watch a movie for a while. We can stretch out on the bed and prop ourselves up with pillows."

He felt euphoric simply being beside her. He could also feel the effects of the alcohol. Her enthusiasm for a movie was often greater than his, and this early evening was no exception. He watched as Lauren became totally engrossed in the plot. Ted wasn't hungry and saw no reason to interrupt and suggest a break for dinner. When the movie ended, it was almost eight o'clock.

"I didn't realize it was so late!" she said when she looked at the clock. "Where are we going to eat? I'd like some seafood if you can find a restaurant we can walk to. I'll take the first shower."

When she emerged he told her that he had called three places and that there was a waiting time of an hour or more at each. Her annoyance wasn't well veiled.

"Why didn't you call earlier? Didn't you remember how crowded Friday nights are here in these touristy places in the summer?"

Ted bit his tongue. "I didn't call because we nibbled so much I wasn't hungry and doubted you were either. I don't mind waiting the hour. We can have a glass of wine at their bar."

"If you think I'm going to wait a whole hour, then you're crazy. You know you should have called earlier. I don't want to eat at all. I'm not hungry any more."

"Like hell you're not hungry. Get your jacket on and we're going to walk downtown. We'll find some place open where we can at least get a bowl of clam chowder. I'll get my shower later." He'd quickly sensed that this was the only approach that might prevent a ruined evening.

They sat at the counter of a downtown joint and quickly ate a bowl of soup and shared a basket of hot sourdough bread. They didn't speak. Ted thought their dinner, except for the bread, was rather tasteless. Lauren said it was okay and thanked him for dinner. The chilly walk back to the inn was in silence.

He missed the lovemaking that he had anticipated all day, but accepted her casual assurance that things were okay.

"I'm really tired. Besides, I think we both had too much to drink and the late eating didn't help. You can watch TV with me for a while if you want. I don't mind if you fall asleep."

She reached over, grabbed Ted's hand and followed that with a long, passionate kiss. Their good nights were warm, and Ted was reassured.

The next day, they enjoyed a room service breakfast and a Monterey Bay newspaper on the room's patio before heading to the wharf and the aquarium they both wanted to visit for the day. Their plan was to be back at the room for a timely dinner.

As they stood together at the base of the aquarium centerpiece, a huge two story cylindrical tank containing millions of gallons of seawater and more fish than either of them had ever seen before, Ted felt elated by Lauren's reaction. For twenty minutes they edged around the tank, watching hundreds of fish swimming among twenty foot strands of growing, swaying seaweed. Ted found he could identify very few of the dozens of species. Lauren concentrated on matching each fish with the pictures and names that were on plaques at the base of the tank. He didn't see that detail as too important, but followed her, regardless. She touched his arm.

"Don't you love to watch these schools of tiny fish? They're constantly moving and changing direction, but they seem to stay in an exact formation. I've been watching, though, and they don't get too close to the really big fish."

Ted moved closer to hear her. The noise level had increased with the rapidly growing crowd. He touched her shoulder and guided the way to the octopus tank. They linked fingers to traverse the bustling groups of people. Lauren gasped and clutched his hand when the octopus head, the size of a pumpkin, came into view followed by eight-foot tentacles. She whispered in his ear. "I can see why there have been so many horror stories about being trapped by those long arms and suction cups."

They stood motionless, watching the tentacles whip lazily through the water. The animal's huge brown bladder inflated and shrunk as it drew in and expelled water.

For five minutes they watched in amazement, moving only enough to allow some small children to squeeze between their legs and the window for a close up look.

Ted knew she would fall in love with the pair of sea otters and led the way to their upstairs glass enclosure. He wasn't disappointed. He loved her excitement. The otters' antics entertained both of them. One minute the animals were suspended close to the viewing glass, and in a second they were simply a flash of brown fur, playfully romping and rolling through the maze that was their home.

In this way, moving from one exhibit to the next, they enjoyed their morning in the aquarium. Two hours had passed so quickly, and after leaving the building they walked along the wharf, marveling at the sea lions and mimicking their sounds, admiring the pelicans looking for a fishing boat's handout.

Soon it was time for lunch and they started to look around. Lauren noticed an unlocked gate leading down a flight of stairs to a long row of private docks. The gate was half open and a sign read, *Private. No entry.*

"I'd really like to see some of those yachts up close," Lauren said. "Do you think it would be okay?"

"Not really, but the worst that could happen is that someone will ask us to leave. But I thought we were going to get lunch." He was apprehensive, but tried to feign enthusiasm.

"Let's try it."

No one questioned their stroll down the floating dock. A few owners were cleaning the decks of their elegant crafts. They didn't even look up at the intruders. On several vessels, small groups were enjoying their drinks and lunch. Lauren gave a little wave and a quick smile to those who glanced up.

"Do you suppose we could ever live like that? Why don't you buy one of those? You can afford it!"

Ted took a minute to respond, then smiled and shrugged his shoulders. "Come on, let's don't go overboard! Even if I could afford it, why spend a hundred and fifty thousand for one of these beauties when you likely can rent one for five thousand a week? With your job and the stuff I do, we'd never use it for over two or three weeks a year. And you can't imagine what those dock fees are. I can hardly picture us up on the deck, like those guys back there, scrubbing and painting for hours at a time."

"Cheapskate!" A smiling Lauren grabbed his hand to lead them further along the floating dock.

Near the end of the dock the two were surprised by a huge sea lion that had pulled itself up on the dock for sunning. As the two of them walked closer to the animal, Lauren hesitated.

"Do you think he'll dive into the water?"

Ted walked toward the sea lion and clapped his hands sharply. Instead of plunging into the water, the apparently sleepy animal came right awake and ferociously charged towards Ted. Startled, he took a few quick steps back and nearly fell into the water. Embarrassed, he faced a laughing crowd watching from the wharf railing above, and Lauren's teasing remark:

"Chicken. I guess he showed you who's boss of this dock!"

Even with all the ruckus, the sea lion flopped down again and shut his eyes.

"I'm starving," said Lauren. "Let's go back to the wharf."

On the way back from the dock, she spotted a small sign directing people down a narrow stairway to a water level restaurant.

"Let's try this place. It looks romantic, and the smells coming up from it are great!"

They shared a hot crab and melted cheese sandwich on sourdough. Each had a small green salad and a glass of wine.

"To us, by the sea!"

After lunch, Lauren said she figured her feet were good for another hour of walking, so he suggested a walk down Cannery Row, keeping them fairly close to where they parked the car.

"You can get in some window shopping. Something may catch your eye that's worth buying. I'll promise to hang back and not rush you. I like to look at window displays too," he lied.

Ted thought that most of the shop windows were attractive and appropriately colorful for the tourist trade. He nodded or responded briefly to her outbursts of delight.

"I just love the color of this blouse! I'm going in to see if they have it in my size. Look at these great shell wind chimes. It has the name of the local designer right on it. They would look wonderful in your patio, don't you think?"

She entered a half dozen shops but made no purchases. He suggested that they cross the street and work their way back to the parking lot. Lauren agreed.

"My feet are getting a little tired and you must be awfully bored. It's been an hour and a half. We'll walk fast and I'll just barely look in each window."

When they were at the car, she threw her arms around him.

"Thanks for the wonderful time. We've had a perfect day. I couldn't ask for anything better than what we did."

She massaged the back of his neck with her left hand as they started the drive back to the inn. Ted was tired, but happy. That afternoon they repeated their before-dinner snacks and cocktail hour and enjoyed watching the young swimmers in the pool. He was watching the time very carefully. Their previous night had been a lesson to him. Was she prone to violent outbursts over minor things? He wondered if there could be a permanent relationship between them. Could he keep up? Could he handle her unpredictable volatility?

When it was time to start looking for a place for dinner, they decided to chance finding a good restaurant by walking towards the main part of town, but to try several new streets. Lauren soon found a second story Vietnamese restaurant and insisted on trying it. Though Ted was hesitant, he followed her up the stairs and was surprised when Lauren greeted the waiter in Vietnamese. The waiter grinned widely and answered most of her questions in broken English. Ted watched and listened as she navigated the menu selections in a hybrid of English and Vietnamese.

"We can order this one for you and this one for me and share them. Are you game?"

"If you and the waiter agree, count me in."

After the waiter departed, she explained that she studied Vietnamese in night classes for two years and had some Vietnamese students who helped her pick it up a bit.

"Thank you for agreeing to come here so I can use it!"

Before dinner was over, Ted's satisfaction equaled hers. "I'm glad you brought me here. Let's put this place at the top of our list for our next visit." Lauren walked over and said good night to the busy waiter while Ted paid the cashier.

Lauren had already readied herself for bed and pulled an extra pillow from the closet. He had taken a shower and was brushing his teeth when she called through the half opened door.

"I see there's a movie on that I'd like to watch, but there aren't any more pillows. You'll have to prop yourself up beside me."

He loved the way she was always so casual and comfortable as she led him into lovemaking. They watched in silence for a while. When he looked at her, her response was a little smile, but the mischievous look in her eyes was an unspoken greater promise. Ted was content to wait for her signals. It was difficult, though, to keep his mind on the film.

His hand searched for hers and couldn't avoid brushing the pajamas that covered her thighs. He held his hand there for a few seconds. Lauren raised her hips slightly and kissed him. Soon kisses became more frequent and lasted longer. Ted was no longer even pretending to watch the film, but she seemed to have the extraordinary ability to concentrate on the movie while still building his excitement with the subtle, yet so sensuous movements of her hips which followed his hand.

He turned on his side and put his hand under her pajama top and she finally gave her full attention to him while the movie played in the background.

He became totally lost in the magic of this woman, as he had been so many times during this brief, sometimes frantic romance. He held off for as long as he could, hoping that Lauren would experience climax. They both wanted and needed this to happen. They now lay close together with him completely relaxed. Lauren must have read his thoughts.

"It's okay, I really loved tonight and was so close to coming several times. I think I'll sleep as well as you will. Good night and thanks for a perfect day."

Finally, they got their walk on the long, white sand beach of Carmel. It was midmorning of the day of check out. They held hands for half minute stretches. Occasionally Lauren would dash towards the receding surf to grab a bright shell. Ted knew she couldn't completely ignore the curious glances from other beach walkers, but for now she pretended to be oblivious to them. He watched their eyes move from her shapely legs in shorts to her golden hair and then to his sparse white hair and the rolled up pant legs revealing extremely white skin. But he was feeling young today. He thought, to hell with them! Last night she was mine, by her choice! Even the sky was already rid of the morning fog, and no clouds hid any part of the sun.

On their way home, he pulled into a gas station adjacent to a huge artichoke field and was cleaning the windshield and putting gas in the car when Lauren stuck her head out the window.

"I want to go to Salinas. See the sign?"

"We are not going to Salinas. It will take us out of our way." He continued to wipe the window without looking up.

"Please? I've heard so much about the place. John Steinbeck has even written a short story and a novel connected with the area. I remember discussing them in one of my college English courses."

"It will take us at least a half hour. Can't we do it another time?"

"We're not in a hurry, are we?"

Ted suddenly realized how thoughtless and ridiculous he was being. She was right! Why should he be in such a hurry? It had been a fabulous three days with this charming young woman. Why not add a little reward for her?

"Okay," he relented, "you're right. Let's do it. Besides, I haven't been through Salinas in a long time myself."

She reached across and touched his forearm but said nothing. Her eyes told him that she was glad he understood. He knew that Lauren wasn't at all anxious to have their little trips end. For her, it signaled the start of another workweek. She had openly expressed her envy of his retired situation on several occasions and did so again.

"I wish I was retired like you and didn't have to work. You are so lucky; you have the money and good health to do whatever you feel like doing. I wish I were in your place."

Ted bit his lip and tried not to show his irritability. He was tempted to remind her that he had worked steadily since he was nine years old helping on the family dairy and since then had never been able to slow down until he retired at sixty. Instead, he pushed it from his mind and enjoyed their drive through the farming community of Salinas. They turned north again on Highway 101.

Conversations centered on what they had seen and done. After about an hour, Lauren tilted her seat back and closed her eyes. Ted admired her now serene and relaxed expression. What a beautiful woman! How lucky he was!

As they neared home, they listened to her tapes, and drove the final fifty miles with very little talking. An occasional squeezing of hands and shy smiles kept the magic alive. He wondered if she, too, was allowing herself dreams of a more permanent relationship.

He tuned into her driveway. Before turning off the engine, he reached over and grabbed her knee.

"Hey you—we managed another overnight trip together! Was it all that bad?" Ted could afford to tease. This time he knew the answer without waiting for one.

Monday morning came quickly and he was at his chosen spot to blow her a kiss as she sped away to teach her morning adult education class. Ted reluctantly returned to his paper, which covered the kitchen table. He felt no pressure to begin any project. There was little mail that had been picked up by a neighbor. As he looked at what he considered to be neat, organized stacks, he thought about Lauren's almost regular comment when she entered his kitchen:

"How can you possibly know where anything is?"

Watering the garden was his first task after unloading from their trip. He completed it well before dark. He fixed himself a bowl of soup and a salad but hadn't suggested dinner together. She told him she needed time to prepare for the next week's classes. Lauren's good night call included a warm thank you for the weekend.

Ted slept well and found the next morning's paper and coffee especially enjoyable. Yes, it had been a rewarding weekend. Thinking of the things they spent time talking about, he remembered her asking him what it was about her that he liked. What did he like? he mused. He had put her off with a promise to think about it and tell her later. Why not do it now? She might like it even better if he put it in writing. He enjoyed writing and never felt uneasy about putting his words into print.

Two hours later, he let himself into her house with the key Ellen had given him for emergencies, and placed a vase of a dozen mixed red and yellow roses on the kitchen counter with an envelope marked with Lauren's name. With a verbal greeting to her pet cockatiel, he let himself back out.

The note read like this:

Dear Lauren,

On a couple of occasions you have asked that I tell you why I like you so much. This is my attempt to do just that because it is a fair request.

How can I not like your youth and beauty? I'm not sure how to handle it, but I love you for sharing them so intimately with me.

I vividly remember our first night on your camping pad by the fireplace. I puzzled a lot about why you wanted to make love with me, an older guy, whom you had only known for a few weeks. It was wonderful, though, because I've always felt that when a woman so fully shares herself with a man, it means everything. There is not a greater expression of trust.

I learned a lot from the stories of your past relationships. This doesn't make me apprehensive because I see in you a woman who enters into a relationship with a 100% commitment. I'm no different there.

I like you for your sensitivity. Although I might tease you for not wanting to watch the trout being caught and cleaned, I understand and respect your desire not to want to see living things hurt. But doesn't someone always have to do the catching?

I like you for your insistence that things be clean and attractive whether it is in your home, yard, or yourself. I like you for your love and mastery of the outdoors, whether it be your yard and the gardens, or my mountain camp. You are a full partner, and I delight in watching the way you do these things well. But please don't get back on that refrigerator kick!

I like you for the effort you are putting into becoming a professional in your work. You show a great desire to benefit the students you teach as well as yourself. Somehow, during those several years when you worked as a blackjack dealer and pursued your degrees, you lived with those tough late Friday drives back to Tahoe and the dangerous trips home on Sunday nights down those two lane roads back to Sacramento. After fifteen years of knocking around, you had the ability to change. I like you for your level of perseverance. The student loans you took out and now worry so much about would have been much greater had you not made the effort to work those long weekend hours. I hope you'll allow me to help you with some of these loans along the way.

I like you for your sense of humor. I tend to look at most sides of life quite seriously. It's good to have someone like you poke holes in some of my overly serious expressions.

Finally, I like you for your ability to love and express love. For you, it seems the only way. You draw a real distinction between love and caring. Although I'm not certain where one ends and the other begins, it's nice to know someone who seems to be sure.

Ted

Shortly after Lauren pulled into her driveway after school, Ted's phone rang, and he picked it up after a half-ring.

"Thanks Ted, the roses are just beautiful. Is it all right if I tell you, though, that I like carnations better? Most roses don't last but a day or two, and I know they have to be more expensive. I haven't hurt your feelings, have I?"

Ted's laugh was genuine. "No, not at all. I'll remember your preference. I'm not too experienced in giving you flowers. Roses just seemed to fit this occasion." He paused. "Did you read my letter?"

"Yes, twice. Thanks for saying those nice things. I'll always treasure it. I know there are some things about me that you don't like."

"When would you like a letter telling you about those? We have to look at both sides of a valuable coin, don't we?"

"Don't you dare! I'd tear that thing up without reading it. I know I can be a bitch sometimes, but I don't want to have to see it in writing. Forget that whole idea!"

He knew that no response was expected and invited her to dinner.

FOUR
Seasons Change

Ted had been watching the weather change and badly wanted one final trip with Lauren to his mountain hideout. October snows in the high country would soon close out vehicle entry. The task of winterizing for the coming seven months of snow was not difficult and he hoped she might agree to be a part of it. To him, it was routine. Usually he had reserved the day for one of his regular guests, who jumped at the chance for some late season fishing even though he told them ahead of time about the work that would be involved.

"Of course I want to help you button things down at your place! You know I can use a hammer. And you do need someone to help you lift those boats up on end. It's a wonder you haven't killed yourself!"

Ted wanted to make sure he wasn't making a big mistake.

"I've been watching the night temperatures up in Truckee. Can you handle thirty degrees?" Then without waiting for an answer, added:

"It does look like there are a series of decent days ahead, though, so we have a good chance for some boating. A strong wind over the lake would be the only problem."

"We can always do the work first and leave early. It doesn't have to be an overnight. I do so want to be a part of this last day so I can remember it for next summer."

He smiled at her mention of being with him again next summer, for it meant she, like him, was picturing them in a long-term situation despite the things that made them different from one another.

When they got to the mountain, she was the first to comment on the mountainside changes: The yellows and the orange and reds that decorated the slopes and the slightly lower angle of the sun through the branches. They were met at the camp by the caretaker, who welcomed Ted, greeted Lauren, and advised them that they were the last ones to close up.

"We could get a real blanket down here any day now. If you plan to fish, I want to tell you that very few trout are being caught. The water may have turned cold already and the fish think it's time to go dormant."

Ted thanked the man, shook his hand and told them their plan to watch the sky, grab a last boat ride and then get to work.

After an hour's ride in the boat, with both of them tightly bundled up to offset the chilly air, he gladly took Lauren's suggestion that he do some fishing.

"While you fish," she said, "I'll sit in the warm truck with my book. I'm almost through with it. Good luck."

Ted caught a nice limit and was off the lake joining her in less than an hour, but it was past two o'clock. He quickly unloaded the boat and cleaned and iced the trout. Then, he asked Lauren for her help.

They found that roping the boat upright against evergreen trees took more time than he had expected. Twice he had to get the heavy pruning shears and remove several tree limbs. He admired Lauren's strength and the ease with which she handled her part of each task. Finally, they had snug fits for the boat and Ted tied them in place. It was time to stand by the water's edge and say good-bye for the winter. They held hands tightly. She spoke softly:

"It almost makes me cry to realize that it will be seven months before I get to come back here with you. I just love this place."

When they returned to the camp, he pulled a sack out of the truck.

"I brought these two sunflower heads from our garden. From the chattering and calls I hear, the blue jays, chipmunks and squirrels haven't finished their harvest season yet. We have time. Let's watch them."

He placed the heads filled with ripe seeds on a nearby tree stump while Lauren set up two chairs on the deck. Ted poured each of them a glass of wine. Soon three tiny chipmunks were opening the seeds and discarding the shells. A single mountain jay sent the little animals scurrying while it crowded several seeds into its beak and flew to a tree limb above their heads. The chipmunks promptly returned and resumed their feeding.

"It's only five and I'm getting cold already," Lauren said.

"So am I! There's really no point in starting an outside fire. Maybe we can play some Scrabble inside after dinner. I love for us to sit by the fire, but this just isn't the night."

Once inside, he set up the kitchen table and opened a can of baked beans. She took a small package of ground meat from the ice chest and handed Ted a container of salad ingredients. Together they cooked the meal. The warmth of the flames from the gas stove slowly reduced the chill in the trailer. Neither had removed their hooded sweatshirts. As he flipped the burgers and she placed a slice of cheese on each, she drew him close for a kiss.

"I'm awfully glad you asked me to come on this trip. Do you mind if I wear this sweatshirt to bed until I get warmed up? The way I'm feeling, our Scrabble game may not last long!" It was Ted's turn to bring her close and press his mouth to hers.

They awakened to a cloudy sky and an occasional distant clap of thunder.

"At least it's not raining yet," Ted said as he opened the trailer door to peer outside.

"Maybe we'd better give up on our plan to hike around the lake. I'll get coffee going and turn on the oven for the cinnamon rolls. It will help warm the place up a little too."

Lauren slid out of the double zipped bag and sat on the edge of the bed.

"I had a wonderful night sleep and wish it could have lasted another two hours." She reached out and snapped the elastic on his pajama bottoms. "Do you remember our first time up here? You tried to convince me to sleep outside on that hard deck. I told you to get lost. I think you've learned something since you met me!"

"Yes, it's a different world I live in now, and I do love most of it. Now, will you get up and get the cereal ready? I'll slice up an apple just as soon as I get our bed made back into a kitchen table." He began rolling up the sleeping bags.

Lauren pushed open the door and quickly pulled it shut again. "It's raining already. We're not going to be able to have a cup of coffee on the deck this morning." She ran out and dashed across to the bathrooms and Ted watched her through the window.

He insisted that they not rush their breakfast. He pulled the window curtains open to be able to watch the changing weather. "Nothing can happen in the hour and a half it will take us to enjoy a decent breakfast and close up this place."

47

She seemed to relax a little but finished eating well ahead of him. He continued with a second cup of coffee and a sweet roll while watching her quickly pack her overnight bag. Reluctantly he finished and carried his dishes to the small sink.

"There's more than enough hot water on the stove if you have a few minutes to wash the dishes. I'll grab a rain jacket and take care of the battery, the propane tanks, and drain the water system."

In fifteen minutes, Ted was back. Lauren had washed the dishes and was pouring scalding water on them. He noticed that the kitchen was completely in order and that she had packed his bag, too. The rain had increased enough to badly soak his shoes, but he'd brought an extra pair.

"We're looking fine. Here's another jacket for you when you're ready to help me with the plywood. I'll be outside, leaning the boards against the shelter."

She joined him in a few minutes. He handed Lauren the hammer and several twelve penny galvanized nails.

"I'll put the boards up and hold them steady while you do the nailing. The nails don't need to be pounded in all the way, just enough to hold the plywood in place."

He had positioned the third board making sure it was directly in front of two trailer windows. Lauren hesitated with the hammer in mid-air.

"Why do you put these up at all? Someone could jerk them right off!"

Ted laughed, "Yes you're right. It isn't people we worry about. If they feel they need in, they're welcome to come in; it's mostly a precaution. The snowdrifts here get twelve to fifteen feet deep and the pressure all pushes inward. I don't want to come up next summer and find the side of the trailer crushed or the windows broken and a lot of water inside. If a tree falls in a big storm and crushes the shelter and trailer, we can't help that."

Just as he had hoisted the last of the four by eight plywood sheets into place, Lauren interrupted her hammering.

"Look what's happening now! It's hailing! We've got to get out of here before we get stuck!"

Ten minutes later, Ted was standing by the loaded Explorer making a last minute survey. He had remembered to put four boxes of rodent bait near possible entry points in the trailer. A light snow was falling. Lauren was watching him while managing to keep warm inside the heated Explorer. His feelings of sadness were divided. Yes, he would miss his wonderful mountain retreat. But, worse, would its loss affect Lauren? Diminish her closeness to him? He knew that their time spent here had developed into something very special as he had originally hoped it would. Was there a way he could replace it during the long winter months ahead?

He climbed into the vehicle and glanced at her. Were her thoughts the same as his? There were signs of a tear in her eye. She put a tape in the player as the truck slowly rolled over the thin layer of hail now being covered with snow. She returned his glance and smiled.

"I love you, Ted."

FIVE   Fireplace Magic

Early November came, and with it, cool nights. Ted shared Lauren's spoken enthusiasm for a bright fireplace and the prospect of dinners together in that atmosphere. He carried in two dozen oak logs and a large bundle of kindling wood and stacked these neatly in one corner of the covered patio. Assuring himself of a starting supply of dry wood wasn't a new routine, but one he had followed for forty years. Use of the fireplace had become less and less frequent after his two children had begun their college years, followed by marriages, but he continued to bring in a good supply of logs each year. Perhaps they might have company who enjoyed an evening fire. Much of the use in recent years centered on the year-end holiday season when the grandchildren were visiting. When April arrived Ted found himself often restacking the oak outside. He saw this as a small job to do for the possible enjoyment it could provide.

They fitted in two casual dinners a week apart, set up close to the open fire. Pleasant conversations centered around memories of their recent visits to his mountain retreat and the pressures of her increased teaching load. Dinner dishes had been washed and put away and Lauren heading home by eight. Ted had been settling into his leather chair and reading while the flames died down.

But this time was different. He felt an added level of excitement. Just the prospect of setting up a card table and sharing dinner with Lauren while watching the flames raised his expectations. He watched her coming up his driveway with a big candle in one hand and her dinner contribution in the other.

"Let's turn out all of the lights tonight and just go with the fireplace and this candle. Won't it be romantic?" She situated the candle on the corner of their dinner table. He ignited a long match in the fireplace and lit the candle. They stood side by side with their arms around each other. Ted was pleased with the effect but a little embarrassed.

He belatedly remembered that he had candles stored in a high service porch cabinet and wondered why candlelight had never occurred to him. He was trying his best to portray himself as romantic and winced at the occasional nudging that bordered on deserved criticism from her. Shortly after dinner, after bringing in the dinner dishes and folding up the card table, he began filling the dishpan. Lauren walked over and gave him a gentle poke in the ribs.

"Why don't you forget the dishes? And get your pajamas. Do you have a pair I can wear?"

He quickly brushed his teeth, slipped into his pajamas then rummaged through the drawer, returning with a colorful pair he hoped would please her.

With nothing but the living room carpet to cushion them, and the pillows pulled from the bed for their heads, they stretched out by the warm fire. Up on one elbow, Ted marveled at the added loveliness in his partner's face, brought on by the glow of the coals.

The night had started differently from any others they had shared intimately. Ted wasn't exactly sure why he felt this new level of excitement, but he relished it. Other times when Lauren had chosen to stay over, or he at her place, she had never held back and seemed to welcome any romantic overtures he might initiate. But this first night by the glowing fireplace seemed to be enveloped in even more magic. Soon forgetting the fact that there was no comfortable mattress to cushion their moves, she responded to every touch, sometimes with a demand he had not before experienced. Something new seemed about to happen. Then he remembered her comment during their very first tryst on the pad in her unfurnished rental house, "You will know when I come!"

Did he ever! He knew it was happening. After what seemed like a multitude of explosions, Lauren relaxed, and he realized that a barrier had been crossed in their fairly brief relationship. They had fulfilled her sex needs together. She confided to him that this was one of the very few times she had reached a climax during intercourse, and she loved him for that. He felt an increased sense of appreciation for this young woman. Could it be, too, that her need for him would lead to a more solid partnership? This was tempered with doubts about the longevity of his own virility.

As winter enveloped them, romance by the fireplace became a ritual. It seemed to Ted that it enhanced the lovers' confidence in each other. Ted knew his feeling of elation. Her assurance that he was fulfilling a need for her that other men had not met was an invigorating tonic. The first question he would ask when it was agreed they dine at his house was, "May I start the fireplace?"

Only if she had after-dinner work that was pressing, such as correcting student papers or designing tests, was Lauren's answer other than what he had hoped for. Then, he accepted her response reluctantly.

Their evening lovemaking would sometimes begin even before dinner was served and eaten. Each would touch the other in passing as they set the table. They spoke few words. At times they would stop for a brief kiss with plates or pots in their hands. It was an atmosphere of anticipation and confidence. If there was a question about the evening ending in fulfillment, neither voiced it.

Some practical steps were taken. Ted's down-filled sleeping bag now became a favorite cushion. Lauren would arrive with her own pajamas tucked under her arm. She would move the candle from the card table to a lower, more intimate level and would be watching the flames when he joined her after putting away the table and brushing his teeth. Ted loved the way she kissed and seldom rushed this part. They stopped briefly to lie back on the pillows to listen to the subtle popping of the flames while hands continued to explore exciting bare skin.

He had found it a little difficult at first not to rush right in. Here was this delightful, sensuous woman showing him in every way that she was his alone and happy to move at his pace. Now he knew he could take his time. She wasn't going to run away.

She would open her pajama top, and he would watch the flickering firelight accentuate the beauty of her firm, pink breasts. His touches and kisses always brought responses. Now and then she nearly smothered him by lifting her body and holding her breasts against his face. Then he would hear a delighted laugh as he freed himself enough to catch a breath. Ted's hands would trace a path up and down her inner thigh, always he marveled aloud about how any skin could be so delicate and smooth. She teasingly stroked and caressed him while his hips unconsciously followed every move. Neither could stand the anticipation and suspense forever.

Little then became off limits. Hands and mouths played together. Lauren never once said, "Please I've had enough!"

He was completely taken by this dynamo who seemed to want to go on forever. Mostly it was he who could stand no more foreplay and asked the question:

"Are you ready for me now?"

At times he felt he absolutely could have held back no longer had she answered in the negative. Once she had reached a climax with him it had almost become a regular occurrence. Ted knew that all of the patience and holding back had been worth the effort. He couldn't believe how one woman could express her fulfillment so beautifully.

The flames died down as they continued to hold each other tightly. He asked himself silently, how could any seventy five year old man be so lucky? Life was good, from his point of view.

They shared intimate moments over meals, where they discussed monogamy and marriage, and he came to feel he understood her better as a person.

SIX   Hot And Cold

In the morning paper, Ted saw a travel agency's advertisement for an early winter cruise down the Mexican Coast, and he thought he might have found a way to brighten up the winter and fill some of the gap left by closing up the mountain home. He'd have to mention it to Lauren. But this time of year always got busy, as he received the expected phone calls from schools asking him to speak to their classes. He had accepted three days of lecturing during late October, and more were coming, but he was confident that the volunteer work wouldn't interfere with available time with Lauren or his family obligations. Though Lauren had called several times during the week, she hadn't suggested staying over. Ted was beginning to feel anxious. It had been well over a week.

He picked up the phone after seeing her arrive home on Wednesday.

"How about dinner on Friday night? I froze two trout from our last trip. Can you steal away from your work?"

"That sounds wonderful! I'm finished working at noon and will have time to make some coleslaw. Do you have a head of cauliflower? We could steam it."

He assured her that he'd have his part ready. "There doesn't have to be any hurry or set time. We can start preparing the food after you arrive. Take time to do any work that you need to get done."

"I'll be there on the early side and I want to stay over. Ellen has a man coming over for dinner tonight. She seems to like him, but I can't stand the guy."

Ted noticed a car pulling in front of Lauren's house and saw Ellen welcoming the man at the door. Not long after, he watched Lauren walk determinedly across the street, carrying her bowl of coleslaw. She slammed the door as she entered, passing him without a kiss.

"I absolutely cannot stand that man. He makes me feel uncomfortable. I don't know what Ellen sees in him."

Ted wasn't sure where to begin. "Whoa! Tell me what this is all about. You've always encouraged Ellen to get out and meet men. What's wrong with this one? I would think you'd be pleased."

Lauren set the bowl of slaw on the kitchen counter and faced him.

"I'll tell you what's wrong with him! His name is Bill and he's been over three nights this week. He's almost bald and has a silly looking potbelly. When I get home from work, I like to change into something comfortable. Many times I don't wear a bra, and this guy Bill leers at me! I feel like I almost have to stay in my room. He stares at my boobs. He hovers over me. If Ellen's noticed it, she hasn't said anything."

Ted nodded. "That's not good at all. I don't know if there's anything you can do, though."

"I've got to get out of there. I want to move in with you. You've got the room and we love each other."

He couldn't meet her blazing dark eyes and stared instead at the floor.

"I can definitely understand the uneasiness you're feeling right now, Lauren, but it's a big step to take just because you don't like your roommate's boyfriend. He won't last long if he's a big jerk like you say. Ellen will kick him out on his ass soon enough."

"I don't see how you can claim to want to be near me all the time and then tell me I can't move in."

He had thought several times about inviting the move, but had always edged away.

"It's not that I wouldn't want to have you beside me each morning. I can't imagine anything nicer. I think, though, that it would be a mistake to try to live together, at least for now. Our interests and temperaments are so different." He forced a smile and added:

"I love to see you coming across the street for a visit or to stay overnight. Don't you feel that it keeps our relationship more exciting?"

He sensed she wasn't going to be easily placated.

"It's pretty convenient for you to have me across the street. What sort of a man are you? You don't really mean what you say when you tell me you care for me a lot."

"I'd like for us to keep our independence." He wanted to add that at his age he liked to go to bed early most nights, and that he didn't want the TV to be on every evening, even while they were trying to visit, and that his favorite morning routine began at five with the early reading of the newspaper and coffee. He said nothing more and awaited the next salvo.

"Sometimes I feel that all you want me for is sex. I want us to do a lot of things together."

"I love our intimate times together, yes. You tell me you do too. We've done a lot of wonderful things together—the mountains, the ocean, the garden, movies, dinner. It hasn't been one sided. How can you possibly say my interest in you has only been sex? It's simply that I'm not ready for us to live together. The door isn't closed forever."

Visible signs of her agitation were lessening and her stare was no longer piercing. He drew her close, but was aware of her unresponsiveness.

"I suggest that you be frank with Ellen and tell her what's happening. She'll likely dump the guy if he doesn't change his act."

Lauren pulled away.

"That's easy for you to say! I'm the one who has to put up with that kind of crap. I'm not going to leave because that would make you mad. We can eat and then watch some TV for a while, but at ten I'm going home to sleep. That guy makes me sick, but I can't stand the thought of staying here and sleeping with a man who doesn't want to live with me!"

Ted heard the TV go on in the living room. It wasn't going to be a good evening for him. How could she turn her anger over this man's crudeness into an attack on him? As he got ready to prepare the dinner, he thought more about it and got increasingly angry. He walked into the living room planning to tell her to take her coleslaw and leave, but saw her on the couch with her long legs up on the coffee table and offered her a glass of wine instead.

"Yes, thank you," Lauren said, without glancing up.

Dinner was eaten in silence. The TV was tuned to a film they had both recently seen and the commercial breaks were long and frequent. Before ten, Lauren stood, thanked Ted for dinner and left without offering him a goodnight kiss.

Ted had forgotten to mention the cruise ad.

SEVEN   Four Balmy Days

The next day, Ted finished his morning coffee and paper and noticed the travel section again had the reasonably priced cruise. It was the second time in a matter of a week that his eyes had caught this same thing. It wasn't extravagant; offering it to Lauren as a show of contrition could only help get their relationship back on track. Indeed, he felt very bad about the way their Friday evening had gone and wanted to make it up to her. He looked out the window and spotted Lauren beginning to rake the leaves from under the huge liquid amber tree. He walked across the street to meet her.

He handed her the folded page. "You've mentioned to me a couple of times that you might like to go on a cruise. This was in the morning paper. It's only a week, and there are several different departure dates. What do you think?"

She looked up at him and he looked back with eyes that showed his apologies for the night before. She nodded and touched his hand as she moved the paper to look at it.

"It looks great, but I'd have to take off several days of work for any of those dates listed. I'm sorry, Ted, but I can't afford to lose the pay." She went back to raking the leaves and added, "I'd much rather fly to Mexico for a shorter trip that fits my Christmas break. I've never done it, but getting all dressed up on those cruises isn't exactly my idea of a good time. Besides, a shorter trip would cost you less."

"Where would you like to go?"

She didn't hesitate to suggest Puerto Vallarta or Cabo San Lucas. She'd never been to Cabo, and told him she'd really love to go there.

Ted thought back to their first summer morning at his mountain place when Lauren had told him about Antonio, the young Mexican importer of Indian Jewelry. She had enjoyed her many flights across the border. He thought, too, about her present classes where so many of her adult students were of Mexican heritage. Maybe this would be a good opportunity to indulge her desire to immerse herself in the culture for a few days.

But, he thought, it is such a long flight. Supposing we eat contaminated food and it ruins the entire trip? He wouldn't even understand what people were saying. He looked at Lauren's eyes, which were focused on him as if she was trying to penetrate his thoughts. On the other hand, Lauren would be his exclusively for those four days. He fantasized about afternoon cavorting, and petting in the gentle warm Cabo surf, ignoring envious glances. He'd go for it.

"I'll set it up," he said. And she threw her arms around his neck, all signs of the anger from the night before gone.

Ted visited several travel agents to find the perfect flight: A four-day three night stay in Cabo with the return flight just before Christmas. It coincided with her holiday break from classes. He decided not to tell Lauren that the near-year end dates had made the price of the four days almost equal to the seven day cruise that he had first offered her. He told her the plan, and had not seen her so excited in a long time. They checked out maps and the descriptions of the available hotels on or near the beach. Lauren was ecstatic.

"I can just see us being a part of the life in that warm, tropical place for those four days. Let's stay there!" She pointed to a hotel on the map. "It says that it's located on a small hill with a veranda overlooking the beach, and the map shows that it's close to town so I can shop."

Ted left his deposit check with the travel agency the next morning while Lauren was at work. He chose not to take out trip cancellation insurance.

As the trip neared, Ted watched the daily reports of weather in Cabo San Lucas and relayed them to Lauren. His enthusiasm was also building. Since he had made the plans, their visits had been free of dissention. He couldn't wait to experience an expansion of intimacy in the exotic location of Mexico. The tickets came two weeks before their departure date and Lauren surprised him by announcing that she was almost already all packed.

"Let me know if they're talking about bad weather. I've saved some room for a warmer jacket. I bet you haven't even started packing yet!"

He knew it would take him less than an hour to pack, once he pulled his big bag down from the loft in the garage.

"My big concern is you, Lauren. You'll be working right up until noon, and I'd like to be on the way to San Francisco around two so we'll be at the motel before dark. That's not too much time for last minute stuff. Let me know if there are any errands that I can run for you. It won't be fun for either of us if you feel too much last minute pressure."

She smiled and gave him a quiet but pointed answer: "You don't need to lecture me. You know I'll be ready."

The weekend before the big trip, he was drawing water to boil corn, waiting anxiously for Lauren to come for dinner when the phone rang.

"I'll be late," Lauren said. "Ellen and I are having a drink before I come over."

"Okay, but please don't be long," Ted said, trying to keep any sign of irritation from his voice. He didn't want anything to upset their delicate balance with next week's trip pending.

When she finally arrived, he put the corn in the boiling pot and poured them each a glass of wine. As he handed it to her, he saw her looking at the floor.

"You haven't cleaned the kitchen floor!"

"No. I had planned to do it this afternoon, but didn't get to it. I have it scheduled for tomorrow or the next day."

"It's a mess!" Lauren said. "Why didn't you get to it today? I mentioned it to you yesterday."

"I said I'd do it tomorrow. I'm hungry. Let's forget it and get on with dinner. I've kept the chicken thighs bubbling in the cream of mushroom soup, the mashed potatoes are ready and I'm timing the corn."

He turned to check on the corn as her voice became almost shrill: "How can you invite me over as a guest with a floor as dirty as this? What kind of a person are you?"

"I said I'd do it tomorrow." Ted's voice was steely.

"Get me the mop. I'm going to do it now. Forget dinner. Where is the mop and pail you use?"

"You're not going to mop the damned floor now. This is my kitchen!"

"It's a damned pigpen! You don't expect me to eat in this room, do you?"

Ted was now shouting while edging towards the closet where he kept the cleaning materials. She was almost in his face. He gritted his teeth but made no response.

Reluctantly, he handed her the mop and mixed the cleaning solution. After turning off the heat under the chicken and corn, he stood at the edge of the hall, arms crossed, staring in disbelief while Lauren meticulously cleaned his kitchen. Not once did she speak or look at him.

Thoughts crossed his mind about cancelling their trip, but he dismissed those as a needless act of revenge.

They ate a reheated dinner in relative silence, with no reference to what had just occurred. Lauren thanked him for dinner and immediately went home.

On the day of the trip's first leg, to the San Francisco airport hotel where they were staying in order to catch their early flight the next morning, Ted saw Lauren's kitchen light come on a full hour earlier than he had come to expect as normal for her workdays. He wondered if she was so excited that little sleep had been possible. She responded to his wave through the window, and he went back to his morning paper and coffee. If sleep had been a problem, she didn't show any indication of it as she exited the house and climbed nimbly into her car. She backed into the street and rolled down her passenger side window. Ted had taken his position near the sidewalk.

"I called my mother in Wisconsin last night and we talked for forty five minutes. It was great. Three of my family members are visiting her and my dad. They all said you were wonderful for taking me to Cabo."

Ted nodded and smiled his approval from ten feet away. He imagined her family never knew what to expect from her, after she ran off with an old millionaire for a few weeks, and jet-setted between Mexico and the US with another guy, but he saw her as different now.

Lauren continued as the car began to edge forward.

"I've never told them how old you are. I've only mentioned that you're a little older than I am."

As her car sped away, she turned and gave him a whimsical smile and final wave. He shook his head and headed back into his house. How much did his age play a part in her thoughts? Lauren had mentioned the possibility of paying her mother's way to California for a summer visit. Would her mother be aghast to find out that he was older than she was?

He checked every detail around his yard and house, and added last minute small items to his packed bags. It took only a few minutes to talk with George and Irene in the house to his left about taking care of his mail and newspapers. Shortly after noon, Lauren called. She was home.

"I'll drive. Bring your bags over and we'll take my car. I'm going to have a quick lunch, and then I'll be ready."

She didn't wait for a response and hung up. Ted knew he had an excited companion. He packed a bottle of wine on ice in a small cooler for pre-dinner festivities in their motel room.

They left Sacramento on time and arrived at their hotel before dinner. They secured the car for the trip, checked into the hotel and laid out the trip brochures. Lauren pointed, as she had so many times before, at the close proximity of the hotel to the downtown shopping area.

"Ted, you just have to agree to spend a day shopping with me. You won't believe the great bargains I can get with my negotiation skills. I always find stuff I like."

He grinned. "Count me in, but only to look. There is nothing I need and have left very little room in my bags. I'm more interested in seeing the place, eating, and spending time on the warm beach with you."

They filled up on nuts, cheese and wine and by the time Ted had finished showering and shaving, it was later than he had planned. Lauren decided she was too tired to eat and he was no longer hungry. Even with the TV on, Lauren was sleeping within fifteen minutes.

It was a restless night for both of them. Ted welcomed the five o'clock wake up call and was up and dressed quickly. She continued to fall back to sleep until she had to rush, and kept the shuttle driver waiting, honking impatiently before their bags were out the door. She fell back to sleep in the van, which irritated Ted who suddenly felt that she wasn't appreciating all the hard work he had put in to make this trip happen.

Ted was relieved that her sleepiness seemed to vanish when their turn came at the Mexican Airline ticket counter. Her demeanor changed as she took charge, speaking Spanish with the clerk. He stood attentively and answered Lauren's relayed questions about seating preferences.

"She says the plane will probably only be half filled and is running on schedule. We should be in Cabo in about four hours. We're ready to go!"

Lauren squeezed his hand tightly as they grabbed their carry-ons and headed towards the boarding area. They were soon on the plane.

The attendant announced that champagne would precede their breakfast. His request for the morning paper was promptly filled.

"This is my kind of air travel. I might even get over being a nervous flyer," Ted said.

Lauren asked for a pillow after finishing her breakfast. She closed her eyes with her head wedged between the seat and the window. The middle seat was unoccupied.

"Don't try to talk to me. I sleep great on an airplane. Just wake me before we get there."

He watched with envy and amazement as she dropped off to sleep. Any changes in engine sounds and occasional messages from the flight crew startled him and broke his concentration on the newspaper. Lauren didn't flinch. After two hours of flight, she was awake and appeared to Ted to be relaxed as she watched the moving panorama below. She turned to him.

"Lean over and look at this. We're going along the beach for a while and then over what looks like deep, dry ravines. I can't believe they have that much water running off those low mountains at any time of the year. I've been looking for cruise ships, but only have seen one."

He looked out the window with her for several minutes and then settled back into his seat.

"They passed out forms for custom declarations and other information while you slept. One asked if we have any fruit with us. I think I'll ignore those two nice apples you tucked in and the banana I added for tomorrow's breakfast."

They filled out the paperwork and had a Bloody Mary with lunch, reading the airline magazine's section on their destination.

"There are twenty three flights full of tourists landing in Cabo every day."

"It's going to be hectic when we land."

An hour later, they stood at the top of the staircase following other passengers out of the plane and into the glaring desert sun. Ted glanced at her attractive photo gray sunglasses.

"How could I have forgotten my dark sunglasses and trusty straw hat?"

They stayed close together as they started their way through the banks of shouting condo salesmen lining the air terminal passageway. Ted was finding it almost impossible to hear the announcements coming over the loudspeakers. Lauren seemed unconcerned and held back to listen to some of the salesmen's pitches. He impatiently motioned to her to stay closer to him.

"I'm glad the travel agency warned us about these guys. They all say they want to give us something really nice for free if we spend time looking at the condos they're selling. It's enticing, but our time is so short here that I suggest we find our bus."

Ted found a porter while Lauren grabbed the luggage off of the carousel. He hunted for shade while they waited for their tour bus to load. It was hot, and crowded, but the excitement was catching.

Once underway, the smiling tour representative took a microphone and welcomed the group to Cabo, informing them that their ride would be about an hour. Lauren bantered with the tour guide and asked other vacationers about their prior experiences in Cabo. Soon she was the center of attention. Ted touched her wrist when there was a pause.

"How about telling me what some of the billboards are advertising? Except for the beer signs, I can't put anything together."

For a few minutes she concentrated on identifying key words on some of the signs, but soon resumed her social chattering with other passengers. He sat quietly feeling ignored and half listened to the chatter while watching the Mexican landscape whiz by.

Their guide pointed out a new golf course under construction. "It's very expensive, but a lot of people from your country like to play golf. The green fees here will be one hundred and fifty dollars."

Ted noted the dehydrated, barren look on both sides of the road and asked the guide about the water source for the course.

"It all has to be pumped down from storage tanks seventy five miles north of here," he answered.

During a lull in questions, the guide made one of his well-rehearsed remarks: "We have twenty two thousand people in Cabo and two thousand of them are condo salesman. He got the expected laughter and added, "One of them is my brother, and I hope you'll buy from him."

Each time the guide grabbed for the overhead railing because of abrupt lane changes by the driver, Ted held his breath. He was certain that often no more than twelve inches separated the bus from oncoming vehicles. He was tempted to ask the guide if the drivers were required to take courses in near misses but decided it would be rude. At each bus stop, Lauren oohed and aahed at the hotels where most of the other travelers disembarked for their stay. Theirs was the final of five stops the tour company made at hotels and condos. Only four other passengers got off with them, prompting Lauren's question:

"Could our place be so bad that only four other people are willing to stay here?"

Ted was looking at the simple but nicely manicured area in front of their condo-hotel. The place did seem almost deserted except for three porters anxious to pick up their bags. She had raised a logical question, but was she implying again that he was a cheapskate?

"Look at the bright side," he said, "We won't have to stand in a long registration line. Besides this is the only place the bus stopped where it's close enough to walk to town."

Their second floor room opened onto a small veranda with a spectacular view of the ocean. They stood next to each other listening to the splash of the surf and muted roar of watercraft. Music was coming from the direction of several low buildings on the beach below them.

Lauren began examining the room's amenities while Ted started to unpack. He was fascinated by the storage areas for their folded clothing, with no doors or drawers but open shelves made of rough mortar and painted a pristine white.

She called from the kitchen: "Look, we have a big refrigerator that seems to be working and an electric stove with an oven. I don't see a lot of cups or dishes but enough for the two of us if we wash them each time we use them. I love to have breakfasts in our room, and I even packed some instant hot cereal. Why don't we go grocery shopping right after we get everything unpacked?"

After walking for about half a mile towards what appeared to be the center of town, Lauren identified a sign attached to a warehouse.

"This is it. This is it! The sign says market."

As they entered, Ted could sense her delight in having used her Spanish to help them find their way around. The store was impressive. They walked slowly up and down the half dozen aisles of well-stocked shelves. They noticed only a few American labeled items. Everything was priced in pesos. Ted picked up a small jar of coffee.

"This is going to be easy. They guy at the hotel told me that today's dollar is worth about ten pesos, so we simply divide the price by ten. This coffee says 'thirty eight pesos' so it is three dollars and eighty cents. Why don't you grab what you think we'll need and I'll check the prices and push the cart?"

Lauren made all of the decisions about what would fit their four-day needs. Together they selected fresh sweet rolls from the bakery to go with their coffee. Lauren only voiced one complaint, that they sold gallons of milk but not quarts of milk. She bought a small can of condensed milk for her morning coffee.

Both knew they had bought too many things for the short stay when they were handed the four heavy bags. They broke into laughter. He had assured her they would be dining out every night and for as many lunches as fit their situations and appetites.

"Why did you let me pick up all this stuff? When I'm hungry, you know I get carried away!"

"Let's not worry about it," Ted laughed again. "The one thing I'm sure of is that we don't want to lug these bags to our hotel. Let me get a taxi. I noticed there are several over on the far edge of the parking lot."

"Let me do it please! I can use my Spanish to get one cheaper than you. You get embarrassed haggling over money. I don't. You watch our stuff, Ted."

She sauntered over to the line of cabs. He watched as she moved among the vehicles. After talking with three drivers, she pointed one over in the direction where Ted was standing with the groceries. She was in the cab when it arrived next to him. The driver emerged and put their bags into the trunk. Ted climbed in next to her and squeezed her hand.

"They wanted six dollars, but after the first two wouldn't go down, I got this guy for two dollars. Aren't you proud of me?"

"Yes, I am. But I'm afraid those other two drivers will want to cut this one's throat the next time they see him."

After putting away their groceries, they walked into town in the balmy air, and did some window-shopping downtown. Vendors were everywhere, accosting them in their effort to sell jewelry, T shirts, paintings and trinkets. He watched and listened as Lauren bartered with them, even though she had promised him that she wasn't going to buy anything this first day. He expected her to break her resolve any minute, the way she was going at it with these aggressive sellers. Several vendors followed them for fifty feet before giving up. Ted was annoyed, getting hungry and out of sorts, and did his best to distance himself from her as she bartered. Occasionally he looked at his watch. He wondered how she could be enjoying the hassle of the mostly cheap merchandise being pushed into her face.

He walked up to her: "It's getting about time to look around for a place to eat dinner. If you remember, we only snacked for lunch. I've been looking down some of the streets we've walked past, and I think there may be a couple of restaurants down that last one we just crossed."

She quickly agreed, and by walking rapidly and avoiding eye contact with the street peddlers, they were soon in what appeared to be a restaurant row. Ted was fascinated to discover pitchmen in the doorways of many of the restaurants. Just like the street sellers, they bragged of high quality and low prices.

"Hey amigos, come in here and look at our place! It's the best! A free margarita if you just come in and look!"

One man came out on the sidewalk and followed them a few steps.

"This is the best place in town, amigos! Two dinners for the price of one! We can serve you right now."

They walked up and down several streets before Lauren made the choice for them. Free margaritas, white linen tablecloths, in a place called Acapulco.

"I'm starving. Let's eat here," Lauren said.

There were only a few customers because it was so early, and they got undivided attention from the wait staff. Ted ordered the drinks while she studied the menu. They were served a generous order of chips and salsa. Lauren pointed out several possible selections for dinner. He assured her that her choice would be perfect for him.

They were enjoying jumbo coconut prawns and fresh cooked veges, when a trio of mariachis entered the restaurant. Lauren exploded with excitement.

"This is the Mexico that I remember, Ted. Thanks for bringing me!"

She was soon keeping time with her hands and feet. When asked if she wanted a song, she spoke in Spanish and requested one of her favorites. Then, to the delight of the musicians and the cheering approval of the diners at two nearby tables, Lauren sang along with the trio.

Ted was enjoying the music himself and wanted to hold onto the moment. He turned to her when the trio finished.

"Why don't you tell them we'll pay them five dollars for three more songs?"

Lauren easily conveyed his offer in Spanish to the men who smiled and nodded. Ted placed his wallet on the table. He stopped eating while the tunes were being played, including a repeat of her favorite. Two other waiters came to the table and joined in the singing. Ted was ecstatic to see his sparkling lover getting so much attention. His time would come later.

Although it was dark when they finished dinner, there was a bright shimmering moon, and they decided to make the long walk through town and up the hill to their hotel. He had at first suggested a cab, but she refused the offer. After arriving back in the room, Lauren ducked into the bathroom first and when Ted was finished a few moments later Lauren was already tucked in bed and her light was off.

"I'm so happy we're here. Thanks for a wonderful dinner. I'm really tired, though, and haven't enough energy for anything else today. Goodnight baby."

Ted, disappointed, resigned himself to the fact that they wouldn't make love their first night in Cabo. There were still other nights to come.

They breakfasted in their room and walked down to the downtown shopping area after washing up the dishes. Today Ted noticed that the salespeople were all looking at him and seemed to be asking her a question.

"What's the matter? Am I having a bad hair day or something?" he asked her when he saw the third head nod in his direction.

"The clerks keep asking me if you are my rich old husband. I wish they wouldn't ask, because I don't know how to answer them, especially in Spanish."

"Why don't you tell them right off that I am your lover? That would settle the question, and you could go on with your shopping. Is there a Spanish word for lover?"

Lauren thought for a while. "The closest word I can think of is *novio*. It really means boyfriend but sometimes implies an intimate relationship."

"Well, what's wrong with coming right out and telling these curious people that I'm your novio when they ask?"

A little reluctantly, Lauren agreed. Ted's spirits picked up and he walked with his chest out a little further as he watched the response of the store clerks to her new approach in defining their relationship. He couldn't help but tease her.

"Did you notice that the men scowl at your answer, but the women smile and wave at me?"

After another hour walking through the vendors, Lauren announced that she had had enough looking and would be ready to make her purchases the following morning. "I wanted to compare prices. I didn't want to pay ten dollars for something tomorrow and then see that I could have bought it for five in the next shop! I'd hate myself."

"Let's go back to the room, have a snack and go to the beach for an hour or two. I know you'll like the water as much as I will. Maybe we can check out the little cabanas on the beach. Are you up for that?"

She was, and after lunch they went down to where Ted had heard the music playing and got a drink at the bar. A man told him about a restaurant called "The Office" and gave him directions to this spot for dinner. They walked several hundred yards down the beach to get away from the crowds of swimmers and boat traffic, and the water was warm and clear with an easy surf very much to his liking. But Ted's desire to spend time in the water with Lauren was not met, as she kept leaving the water any time a stranger walked in the area of their beach blanket.

"I have all of tomorrow's shopping money in my purse, plus my watch. There are too many stories of people walking down beaches and suddenly grabbing stuff and running. Even those two vendors walking along there now might be thieves. Do you want your wallet stolen? We could never catch them once it happened, and our whole trip would be ruined. I'm not going to take that chance."

Ted was embarrassed that he hadn't thought about that and offered to take turns staying by their things, but she assured him that she'd had enough swimming. It wasn't long before they were on their way back to the hotel. The dry sand was delightfully warm on their feet. Ted took Lauren's hand for the walk up the steep dirt road that led to their hotel where they had a snack and got ready to go to dinner.

With no reservations, they were told by the maitre d' at The Office, they would need to wait ninety minutes for a table. Ted offered the maitre d' a ten-dollar bill, but still he insisted that they would have to wait. It was dark and the only lights were atop short poles driven into the sand. Ted could see what were probably fifty or sixty tables, mostly seating four, and most of them were occupied.

"What about that one?" Lauren asked him in Spanish.

"Reserved," the man replied.

Ted was ready to put his name on the long list, but Lauren had other ideas.

"Forget him! Just follow me around and watch me persuade these guys. I'm hungry and we're not going to wait any hour and a half!"

She led him casually through the crowded space, found the first empty table and sat down, motioning him to do the same. A waiter immediately appeared and advised them that the table was reserved. Lauren spoke earnestly in Spanish and smiled at him invitingly. The waiter nodded and left.

"I told him that I believe the reservation is ours, and he should check at the desk. I told him we're hungry and ready to order, and ordered two margaritas and an appetizer right off the bat. I hope you don't mind, it will help persuade him."

He smiled his approval and marveled at how far she would go to get her way. The table was ideally located on the edge of the seating area, and Lauren took her sandals off and buried her feet in the white still warm sand.

Halfway through dinner, a trio walked through the open dining area and played tunes for requesting patrons. When the men neared their table, Ted signaled to them. Lauren again sang with the men and waiters gathering to share in the fun. One of them grabbed Lauren and insisted on a fast, twisting dance in the sand. She tried to smile but Ted could tell she really wasn't having much fun.

She sat down when he let her go, and took a slow sip of her margarita. "That guy really hurt my feet. He must have stepped on them three or more times."

Ted looked at her attentively and sipped his margarita before speaking. "I hope he didn't bruise your feet too badly. He needed to impress you with how macho he was."

"I wish he'd left me alone."

"You don't likely realize it, Lauren, but in your enthusiasm, the smiles and looks you gave those waiters sort of promised them that there might be something more. You had to notice that they totally ignored me." He finished his second margarita.

"I didn't mean anything by it," Lauren snapped.

"Yes, I understand completely dear, but you can't expect them to."

She gulped the rest of her margarita and wiped her mouth with her napkin.

"Are you ready to call it a night?" Ted asked. "It's almost ten thirty. Been a long day."

She nodded. They soon joined the other weary travelers trudging up the rutted dirt street to their hotel. Little was said. Lauren reached for his hand when ascending the steeper stretches of the road. Ted's anticipation of completing their day with lovemaking was high. Once in bed, he reached over and caressed her hips. She rolled towards him, held their kiss briefly, then turned away.

"It's been another wonderful day, Ted. I'm terribly tired again. Do you mind? Good night."

Did he ever mind! Damn, he thought, I just can't believe this. He responded by getting up and making a trip to the refrigerator for a bottle of water, taking a sip before putting it back and getting back in bed. She was already asleep.

Lauren was up soon after he had the coffee water heated and set out another attractive veranda breakfast, already showing her excitement over the morning's plans.

"I can tell that I over-packed, but I have enough room for the things I have in mind to buy. I know you're going to find some things you'll want too. I looked at your bags. There's definitely some extra space."

Ted wasn't going to give ground easily, but saw no reason to close the door completely.

"I haven't seen anything yet that would fit in my home. I'll be glad to watch the action, though, and help carry what you buy."

They were only forty five minutes into Lauren's self described serious shopping when he first found himself caving into her appeals.

"You absolutely cannot go home without one of these beautifully painted metal parrots! I know I can get this guy down to nine dollars if I buy two. One for you, one for me."

Ted agreed it would look good hanging in his kitchen. And three shops later, he had a set of painted and lacquered papier mache vegetables, hanging in a roped strip of nine or ten for his patio to take home with the parrot.

"The avocado looks a little phony," Ted said as he examined it as they walked away.

He suspected she wasn't through when they left the open-air market. He felt their shopping so far had been interesting and fairly relaxed. He hadn't felt pressured to buy the two items; it was more like a game. Also, Lauren hadn't pushed him toward anything expensive.

They turned another corner when Lauren tugged at his sleeve and pointed to a low tan colored building with a large canvas flap covering the entrance.

"I saw this blanket manufacturing factory yesterday morning and I've always wanted another of these authentic Mexican blankets. I had one once, but it got misplaced in one of my many moves. The color combinations are really something."

His interest perked up when they pushed aside the canvas flaps to enter the small warehouse and found the weaving loom in operation. The young operator was drawing from several large spools of dyed, twisted fiber. Ted was startled by the loud bang as the unit pulled the threads together and reached the end of the long loom. Another piece of equipment automatically came into play and compressed the threads into the partially completed blanket. The weaving unit raced back for another run. Ted was fascinated.

He glanced over to where Lauren was examining the folded stacked blankets and then watched the operator for several more minutes.

A small muscular man came from another room and introduced himself as the owner He immediately excused himself to answer Lauren's questions about sizes and prices. Ted joined them, listened for a while, and then began looking at patterns and prices himself. They were impressive, but he didn't find a size that would fit his queen bed. The owner asked him what he couldn't find, pretended to make a thorough search for a larger blanket and then offered to sew two blankets together for him. Ted looked at Lauren.

She pulled him aside and said, "Even if it isn't exactly the right size, it will look striking on your bed, and the blankets are warm. I might even sleep with you more. I'll be nice and warm."

He knew he was going to buy the blanket. But how was he going to pack the bulky thing? Ted had visions of carrying it over his arm and entering the plane to the amusement of too many fellow passengers. He decided he'd figure that out later. He turned and addressed the owner.

"I'll buy it if you show us yourself how to run this loom. And let us photograph you doing it."

The man readily agreed, took a drink from an open bottle of liquor that sat next to him on the bench, and started the machinery. They watched for several minutes while he skillfully added rows of colorful thread to blanket on the loom.

"I'll photograph my novia with you, then she'll take a picture of you and me. Is that okay?"

The owner grinned, and soon the couple was in the bright sun each with a blanket and mementoes of their day.

They decided to use the afternoon to travel away from the big city to a village of San Jose del Cabo about 20 miles from their hotel. On their parcel laden walk back to their hotel, Ted decided he really wanted to observe some of the daily lives of the local people, so kept stopping to check signs on the main street for bus departure times. Studying the schedules, he determined that one passed the corner every thirty minutes on the way to the town. Lauren watched one bus pass and expressed some skepticism.

"I don't see any tourists on that bus. Are you sure it's a good idea? A cab would be quicker."

"Once we've unloaded our stuff in the room, had a snack and walked back down, I think you'll enjoy the bus. It won't be more than an hour ride. If you're tired at the end of the afternoon, we can take a cab back. Besides," he said with an exaggerated bit of persuasion, "the twenty mile bus ride is only one dollar each. I'll treat!"

Lauren agreed reluctantly to the bus ride. He was relieved to board the bus without incident, find the seats comfortable enough, and the courtesy and skill of the driver to be impressive. They enjoyed the view from the bus windows, but were uncomfortably warm. After several tries, Ted was able to pry open a window. They were the only tourists on the bus, and when they got off of the bus at what the driver said was the closest stop to the main street of San Jose del Cabo found that they were hungry and had an eight block hike ahead of them.

Lauren was unusually quiet as they walked. He figured silence was safer than defending his decision to ride the bus. He didn't push her into conversation and let her set the pace for the long walk.

Relieved, Ted spotted a big, old hotel almost hidden behind a grove of high trees as they entered town. He insisted they go no further.

"It seems deserted, but I'm so hungry and tired. Maybe we can sit down for a little while and you can ask where there is some place close."

But when they walked in the front door, a small but nice dining room was just inside. Lively Mexican music was coming through the speakers. They were quickly seated and handed menus.

They shared a giant margarita and ceviche. Lauren now seemed more relaxed and was back to being the delightful companion he so much admired.

"I would have never expected this place," she said. "Thanks for a lovely lunch. Are you ready to tour the town?"

Ted smiled, pushed back his chair and stood. They walked for almost two hours, taking turns choosing which short street to explore next. The quietness and lack of vehicle traffic and sidewalk vendors was a good contrast to Cabo san Lucas. Lauren stopped often to admire the colorful flowering shrubs in front of the small homes. It was a simple beauty.

"In a way, it reminds me of the older sections of Carmel, but just in a much warmer setting," Lauren said. Ted was happy that she was thinking fondly of their past trip together.

Finally, their walk took them into the small business district. Lauren entered some of the shops. Ted patiently stayed outside looking at the window displays. Their afternoon was to his liking, and he wasn't rushing her. She came out of a narrow shop and he took her hand.

As they walked past a shop window, Lauren showed an unusual interest in a simple dress on display. The colors, Ted thought, were striking, but he wouldn't have thought it matched her tastes and said so.

"I think it is attractive! It's so pretty and so Mexican, but not gaudy." She went in the store and chatted with the clerk about the dress. He followed and offered to buy it for her.

"Let it be my gift to you to help you remember our trip. We've had a good time together, and I really want to do it."

"Thanks, Ted, but you don't need to. I was going to buy it. I'll wear it for you the first chance I get when we're home."

They left the store and came to a stately old stone cathedral with a long, broad walk leading to stairs and huge oak entrance doors. Lauren was thrilled to have found this place, which she had once read about. Ted led the way. The heavy doors appeared to be fifteen feet high and required a strong push to open enough to peek inside. There was no sign of anyone.

They walked around the inside of the church, talking in subdued voices, marveling at the hundreds of stained glass windows reaching forty feet from the floor. They paused to stare at the unique pieces of religious statuary. Reluctantly, they again pressed open the heavy carved oak doors and left.

Ted shaded his eyes from the western sun. "I'm ready to go back. How about you? Should we find a cab?"

Lauren agreed, and they walked two blocks and found a group of cab drivers sitting idly in their cars.

"I understand from talking with people in Cabo that the drivers ask for twenty five dollars but will drop to fifteen if you push them enough. There's no one else waiting for a ride so it should be easy," she said.

She moved ahead to negotiate a deal, and the first driver she spoke with okayed the price. Ted opened the rear door for Lauren and climbed in beside her. The young driver spoke English quite well and seemed to welcome Lauren's questions about his family. Ted asked him about work. At the end of the trip, Ted tipped him the ten dollars they saved with her negotiations.

"I feel good, but am so tired I could go to bed now," said Lauren. "We need to start packing, too."

Ted mixed a vodka and orange juice for each of them and set her drink on the veranda table. "Why don't you sit out here and relax while I grab a shower."

When he emerged, her tiredness seemed to have left and she got up to get ready to go out. He mixed another drink and began piling his purchases and loose items on the small couch.

When she was ready, they decided to head back to The Office for dinner. Since it was earlier they were promptly seated and Ted hoped for a pleasant extension of the night before. Lauren's bare feet were once again buried in the warm sand. When a trio of musicians arrived, Lauren suggested that he pay them in advance just to come by often throughout the evening. He agreed, and she signaled them over and discussed the detail with the leader. Ted handed the man a twenty-dollar bill and they played a song before moving off.

"That's was lovely," Lauren said. "Let's order before they come around again."

But soon the trio had nonchalantly walked out of the restaurant without playing again. Ted and Lauren looked around for them and looked at each other in disbelief.

"Oh Ted, I feel terrible! I should have known how these Mexicans are once they get your money. I'm sorry Ted."

"I still think you had a great idea. I don't know what was wrong with that bunch of bandits, but it doesn't stop me. Besides, I want us to have lots of music during our final night here."

Within twenty minutes, another trio entered the sandy dining area. Most of the tables were filled. At Ted's insistence, Lauren propositioned this group with the same plan. With a flourish, nods and grins, the group played her favorite song. Dinner arrived and the musicians disappeared into the darkness. Lauren shook her head in dismay when she realized that they had been duped again.

"I've never seen you give away forty dollars so quickly for nothing. I'm sorry about my part in it."

They enjoyed their dinner and were oblivious to other walkers as they climbed the steep rutted road to their room. Ted held her closely most of the way and was increasingly excited to feel her body responding.

He wanted her so badly this last night in Cabo. They left the door on the balcony open and the music drifted in from the beach. The warm sea air caressed them as they held each other tightly. Their noises blended with the noise of the surf below. He thrilled to feel her surge and the wonderful sounds of her lips forming his name. They could pack their bags in the morning.

EIGHT   The Meeting

For Christmas, Lauren had been invited by her cousin Sally to spend the day with her and her husband. Ted was glad that she wouldn't be home on Christmas Day, when his children and grandchildren arrived for gift exchanges and dinner. He hadn't figured out a way to soften Kathy's stance on Lauren and their relationship, and it would have made him uneasy not to invite Lauren had she been home and viewing the holiday festivities through her kitchen window. He promised her that he wanted her to be included in his family, and that he planned to keep working on it.

Christmas Eve, however, he invited Lauren to dinner, and she accepted with a condition:

"This family situation gets to me, and I can't feel romantic while it's hanging over my head. I hope you understand."

He wasn't sure that he could relate the two, and although he nodded and smiled, Ted didn't like the implied pressure.

"I'll order pizza and make a salad. If you get here around six-thirty, I should have things set up and the fireplace going."

She arrived carrying a holiday tablecloth for the card table he had set up facing the fireplace. She also had a large Christmas candle and a wrapped package.

"It's Christmas Eve, Ted. We want to look a little festive. Other than those few nice things on the mantle, and the tomatoes and basil on the pizza, you don't look much like Christmas around here."

She set the three items on a lamp table and they embraced. Ted looked at her intently.

"You're not in a very good mood, are you?"

"No. And it's not likely to get any better. I miss my family and wish I were with them. You don't know how lucky you are!"

He watched a tear form, and pulled her tightly to him. What, really, could he say? Lauren had occasionally talked about her family. He had concluded that she was part of a large, loving family, but one that didn't always exhibit harmony. Everyone else had settled in or around Wisconsin and couldn't understand this renegade younger sister, Lauren, who left town after a failed marriage and seemed to be happy living a life of partying. Seldom keeping in touch, never holding a job for long, moving from place to place, these characteristics didn't fit the mold of an established Midwest family. They had applauded her decision to settle down somewhat and work towards getting her college degrees. She felt certain they thought she'd never stick with it. It was so contrary to her earlier decision to have fun while she was young and let tomorrow take care of itself.

Lauren had talked to him about going home for this Christmas, but had decided against doing so. Yes, she loved her holiday visit two years prior, the first since she had left the area many years before. Too, her father was experiencing critical health problems. But she remembered the constant bitter winter storms while she was there. Flights had been horrible. Ted had listened quietly as she was making up her mind. Several times he was on the verge of offering to pay half of her fare, but he had neither encouraged nor discouraged her. It was her decision not to go, but to instead accept this invitation from a cousin to join them for the day.

"Yes, I can imagine that it's tough. But I do hope you enjoy the day with your cousin tomorrow. They likely have something special planned." Ted paused and backed away.

"Why don't you put on that pretty table cloth and light the candle. I'll pour a glass of wine for us. The pizza is still hot. The salad is ready. Let's eat."

Their dinner was eaten mostly in silence with both seeming to concentrate on the flickering light from the oak logs. She declined a second glass of wine.

"I'm just not in the right mood, Ted. I'll stay until ten if you want to watch a movie. There's a pretty good one that starts at eight. Then I'm going home and look at old pictures, and maybe read for a while. Thanks for the nice dinner."

His answer carried little conviction.

"You're welcome. I'm glad you felt up to coming over. I'd like to watch the movie with you. I've got everything lined up for tomorrow except tidying up the house, which I can easily do in the morning. Why don't you stretch out on the couch if you like? I won't be but a minute with the dishes."

Ted walked into the bedroom and returned with her favorite pillow. Lauren was stretched out with the T.V. on. He tucked the pillow between the couch cushion and her head. She looked up at him and smiled.

Lifting her feet gently, so he could slide under them, Ted joined her in front of the television. No amount of caressing her feet brought any response from her. She excused herself during a commercial break and went to the bathroom. Ted resumed his position rubbing her feet and legs when she returned. A few minutes after nine, Lauren abruptly swung her feet off the couch and stood up.

"I'm going to watch the rest of the movie at my house." She picked up her package. "Here's my gift for you, Ted. Merry Christmas."

He thanked her, kissed her gently, and unwrapped the gift. "Wonderful, Lauren, driving gloves and slippers! I love this soft leather." He tried on the slippers and laughed. "I guess you noticed how mine have run over badly and the soles are starting to separate from the tops. These are beautiful. Thanks."

Ted disappeared into the study and returned with a small package and a card. "Here's yours. Merry Christmas."

She shook the package. "It's my favorite cologne, isn't it? You didn't forget. Thanks!"

"Aren't you going to open it? It, or the card?

"Nope. I'll do that later tonight. Thanks again for dinner. Have fun tomorrow."

She stopped for a kiss and opened the door herself. He could only offer a half-hearted goodnight as she was halfway down the walk, then watched until she closed her front door.

He turned off the TV and picked up a magazine, uncertain about his emotions. He was badly disappointed, puzzled, and almost angry. She could carry this family thing only so far! Ted had tucked three one hundred dollar bills in with the card with a note that read:

Get something especially nice for yourself. I know you love to shop, while I hate doing it. Wish we could be together for Christmas. -Ted

He noticed Lauren's car was gone at ten-thirty on Christmas morning. She hadn't called. He vacuumed, cleaned the bathrooms, and mopped the kitchen floor. Finally, Ted put the extension leaf in the dining room table and spaced three folding chairs between the six matching ones. Nine was a tight fit. He could visualize an almost impossible situation when all four grandchildren were adults.

The previous year, he proposed setting up a separate card table in the TV room for the grandchildren to give everyone more space, but had been quickly voted down by his son, who wanted the family to celebrate this once a year event at one single table.

The first carload arrived at almost exactly two. Ted was right out front to greet them. Matt, his wife, Susan, their son Chuck and fourteen-year-old daughter Julie, lifted bags from the car and embraced Ted warmly. They were no sooner in the house when the second car arrived. Everyone piled outside.

"Come on in everyone! There's lots of places to sit in the living room and the fireplace is going. You kids can turn on the TV if you want, but you'll have to use the one in the family room. I'm sure you remember that soft drinks are in the fridge in the garage. Pick out anything you like."

Ted turned to the boys right behind him. "Remember my rule, though. I don't want things wasted. Share a can if you don't want a full one. The glasses are in the cupboard to the right of the sink."

The adults settled into chairs near the fireplace. Ted could hear a college football game broadcast coming from the family room. He made sure the door was tightly closed and then suggested they start the afternoon with a Christmas toast. He filled their requests and then stood, glass in hand.

"I'd like to toast my good fortune again this year: Having two beautiful and healthy families. Merry Christmas to all of you!"

The door opened and Julie entered the room, frowning.

"Why do boys have to watch that dumb football? I'd rather be bored listening to you guys!" She sat down to the cheers of the two women.

They visited thirty minutes before the boys burst into the room.

"Half time Grandpa. Time for our touch football game on your front lawn."

"Chuck talks about this game all year, Dad." Matt said.

"We need you to make the teams," said Chuck.

"I pumped the football yesterday. Matt, I'm going to light the briquettes. They'll be ready in twenty minutes. Will you handle the prime rib roast like you did last year? If we get it on the barbeque within the next thirty minutes, we'll eat around six."

Matt shook his head. "Dad, you'll never grow up. Just try not to overdo it. I'll take care of the roast."

The boys piled out the door with their grandfather towards the front lawn for their traditional Christmas Day game. Forty-five minutes later, when it was over, they tumbled in talking excitedly about the great catches and the tie score. Ted went out to check the roast and Matt followed him out.

"I can smell it cooking, Matt. You've got it positioned just right."

"Yes, we've got the timing down too." Matt looked at his father and tapped him on his elbow. "By the way Dad, did you and Lauren have a nice time in Cabo? Everything still going well?"

"Well, Cabo was lovely, and we had dinner together here last night. She had an invitation to spend today with her cousin here in town, so I haven't seen her all day."

"Kathy called me and gave me an earful. Have you talked with her about Lauren recently? Kathy says she doesn't want Lauren at any of our family functions. I guess that worked out today, but what about the next one? You know it's going to come up again."

Ted considered his answer.

"I'm not going to push things at all until Easter. Then I plan to invite Lauren to join Edward, Kathy, the boys and me for our Easter brunch. I honestly feel that your sister won't make a big issue of it. She may not like the idea, but it's my party and I'm confident she'll do her best to make Lauren feel welcome. I think time is on my side."

They turned to walk into the house.

"Well, Dad, you amaze me with your energy. I'll probably be watching soap operas at your age. If the subject comes up again in our phone conversations, I'll encourage Kathy to bend a little and try to focus on your side of the picture."

Gift exchanges and dinner completed the day for Ted. Susan and Kathy insisted on cleaning up the kitchen before they left. Julie put on an apron and did the drying. Ted stood under the streetlight and waved goodbye as each car left. He then sat in his rocker after putting in a Patsy Kline tape. The phone rang before nine. He was relaxed and considering going to bed. It was Lauren.

"I just got back and saw that most of your lights are out. How did the party go?"

"I really couldn't have been much better. I'm lucky that my family all get along so well together. By the way, I hid your gifts. It was just as well because Kathy gave me a pair of slippers, too. How did your day go, Lauren?"

"They had a bunch of Christmas music tapes going most of the day. We watched a movie they rented and had a few drinks. Then we went out to dinner. My cousin didn't see the point of taking time to put together a big dinner. It was good, but not like I remember with my family. The whole atmosphere is different, of course." There was only a slight pause. "Oh, yes, and thank you for the cologne and all that money. I'm not going to spend it though, do you mind if I put it in my savings account?"

"It's yours to do with as you want. Will I see you tomorrow?"

"Yes," she said, her voice brightening. "Let's do something together. Call me about ten."

Ted's morning routine was interrupted before nine by Lauren's call. His plan had been to suggest lunch and a movie. Both would fit the chilly, damp Sacramento day. Her news was a jolt; her father had died unexpectedly. The funeral was in three days. She had told him earlier that her fathers' health was deteriorating and that she planned a short visit when the Wisconsin weather was more pleasant. Now she tearfully told him she was going to use his three-hundred dollar gift to help pay for this urgent trip.

Ellen was going to help arrange her flights and would get her to the airport. Lauren asked Ted if he would pick her up upon her return. She would get the details of the return flight to him the next morning. He had hardly said a word. What was there to say? Thank goodness for Ellen.

He phoned the airline an hour before the prescheduled arrival time. There had been no weather delays. It was well past dark when he met her at the baggage carousel. Lauren's wan smile and tight embrace was accompanied by a reassuring: "Thanks for coming out this late to get me. I'm so tired!"

She snuggled up as close as possible in his SUV. They held hands tightly, letting go only when two-handed driving was necessary. Ted felt complete again. His offer to fix something hot for a late snack was declined; all she wanted was sleep.

His mid-morning call found a refreshed Lauren agreeing to have lunch with him about eleven. A bright winter sun was warming his back porch. They sipped glasses of wine and ate Ted's carefully prepared tuna salad sandwiches.

The funeral had been a widely attended ceremony. Dozens of relatives and friends she hadn't seen in twenty-five years clamored to hear about her life in California. Ted understood her comment about the irony of the situation. Her marriage a quarter century before had attracted many of the same people. Now they wanted to learn of her life of independence, unencumbered by a husband or children.

As Lauren stood to leave, he handed her an envelope. "I know it's untimely, but do try to fit in a merry Christmas when you feel up to it."

After she got back from the funeral, she seemed to have lost some of her enthusiasm for life in general. Few visits escaped her bringing up the topic with brief periods of tears. Ted watched as early spring also brought an added workload to Lauren's teaching schedule. While dinners and lovemaking by the fireplace lessened in frequency as winter worked towards spring, Ted tried not to take it as a rebuke. She seldom failed to find at least once a week to stay overnight at his house, even if the event wasn't preceded by dinner. As each week progressed, he felt an anxiety that would only end with her in his arms.

Sometimes he wanted to scream at her, "How can you take our relationship so lightly when my life depends on it!" Then he would jerk himself back to reality and tell himself to quit acting like a teenager in love for the first time. He knew Lauren had a life and special needs of her own and that he was only part of it. He tried to shake off the low confidence. He was stronger than that.

Each weekend of increasingly warmer weather did find the neighbor lovers more frequently together. Her yard needed attention. Ted was certain that it had never had a vegetable garden and loved her determination to change that. He mostly welcomed her need for him.

"Here are the four stakes we pounded in last fall. Remember? I just know things will grow here."

It was mid morning. He looked at the areas now covered with full sun and those still shaded. Grass and weeds completely covered the area she was indicating.

"Look at that! We didn't do a bad job of choosing a site. Let's get started. I'll get the tools from my garage."

When Ted returned with a large double bitted axe and heavy-duty pruning shears, two shovels and a rake, she laughed at him. "Just what in the world will we need all that for?"

He handed her a shovel.

"Just wait until you see what's underneath this innocent looking ground! It'll be a jungle of roots because of the shrubs and that huge tree. Why don't you begin spading in that corner and I'll start over here."

After about an hour of work and good-natured teasing, they had accumulated a wheelbarrow full of large and small roots. They threw clumps of grass into a small compost pile she had started during the fall in anticipation of the garden. Ted was visibly sweating from swinging the axe.

"Now you can see what we're facing! We've only finished half and look at that pile of roots. Nothing will grow well unless we clean the rest of them out. Whatever we plant wouldn't be able to compete."

After they agreed that enough had been done for one day, Lauren didn't appear to him to be tired, although she had worked steadily with the shovel and rake. She was obviously anxious to move the garden along.

"I always helped my dad with his big garden. It was never like this! Thanks for helping with the tough part. When can we finish and get something planted?"

Ted thought for a moment while gathering up his tools. "We can work together next weekend and maybe even get some tomatoes planted and the peas seeded. I noticed the plants have been in the nurseries for several weeks. I can even put in a few hours this week while you're teaching and dig out these remaining roots."

She smiled and nodded, assuring him that she welcomed the offer. He loved spending time gardening with her. She worked at a pace almost equal to his. It was an atmosphere where neither seemed to find a reason for disagreements. The weather didn't entirely cooperate, however, and the winter-like storms returned for several weeks, delaying their gardening plans.

"I know you're impatient to have things happen," he said during one afternoon between storms, when the ground became sufficiently dry. He looked up into a group of thirty-foot high trees. "Listen to those happy birds. I bet they're impatient too. They're no doubt mating and building nests. It has to be their favorite season. Don't you think that we're like them?'

"Yes," she teased. "And you're a lucky bird who doesn't have to wait for nature to dictate the season."

Soon, the ground was ready. Once the tomato and pepper plants were in and the pea and cucumber seeds buried in the warming soil, Ted watched Lauren's demeanor change. Her spirits rose with each emerging plant. He was delighted and reassured. His own spring garden had each season affected him the same way.

When Easter neared, Ted confirmed a table for six for the eleven o'clock seating at the Las Casuelas restaurant, located about halfway between his home and his daughter's. His custom of treating them to the Easter Sunday brunch had begun two years before his wife died, and he'd insisted that it continue. It was a Mexican buffet, and a small mariachi band circulated between the tables. The twins loved the unlimited supply of desserts allowed them after they ate their plate of fruit, their favorite omelet and freshly made waffles, hardly Mexican fare but suiting their tastes exactly.

He arrived at Kathy's house for one of his alternate week visits fifteen minutes before the kids got home from school to tell her the plan. "I've lined up a table for six at the same place we always go. We eat at eleven."

"Six? Oh, no, Daddy, do you really have to?"

"Yes, I plan to ask Lauren to go with us."

Ted saw the disappointment reflected in her face. He steeled himself and waited.

"Daddy, it's just that our family being together has been so special. Do you have to bring this woman into the picture? I can't imagine that it would do anything but make everyone uncomfortable."

"I think you'll be surprised, Kathy. Lauren is really an outgoing person. She seems to like young people. Besides, she's a teacher, and you'd find interesting things to talk about. It's important to me that you and Ed meet her. I know she wants to meet you."

"I just don't like it! The boys remember you as always being with their grandma. Now, you're with another woman. It isn't fair to them. They'll think you've forgotten their grandma."

"Honestly, Kathy, I don't think it will bother them nearly as much as you think. Glenn and Greg look up to me now. They will want to be friends with whomever I'm with. They know I haven't forgotten their grandma. We talk about things we all did together many times when I'm there. They'll like Lauren."

He heard the school bus pulling up and then the twins coming up the front porch step. Kathy headed for the door to let them it. "Okay, Daddy. But I'm not looking forward to it."

He called Lauren as soon as he reached home.

"It's all set. My family is looking forward to meeting you on Easter. I'm sure that Kathy's a little uneasy, but she didn't voice it. I guess if your father, under the same circumstances, had told you he was bringing home a date six years younger than you, there'd be some uneasiness in your mind."

"I'm glad you set it up. I know that Kathy and I will get along fine, and the boys have always sounded like fun. You just had to make the effort to put something together and quit being afraid of your daughter's reaction."

He changed the subject by asking her about her workday, and then discussing plans for their next dinner together at midweek. Around nine o'clock Lauren called back.

"What's Kathy wearing on Easter? I don't want to be underdressed and have her think I'm a slob, but you know how much I prefer casual stuff."

He put down the magazine he was reading and thought for a minute.

"If I remember, last year she had on a rather plain but nice dress. The boys had white short-sleeved shirts and ties. Ed wore a tie and jacket. I didn't; I wore and open shirt and slacks."

She didn't respond immediately so he added, "I noticed that a lot of people were very casually dressed, especially the men. Jeans and short-sleeved shirts. I wouldn't be too concerned."

Lauren laughed. "You're not much help. If I knew Kathy, I'd call and ask her. I'll think of something."

On Easter Sunday, Lauren wore a nice skirt and bright blouse. Ted complimented her choice. "I'd use the word classy," he said.

"Thanks. I didn't want to look too young. I'm going to be enough of a jolt on your daughter anyway."

They walked to the restaurant entrance and he touched her arm. "Why don't you wait here in this nice sun. We're fifteen minutes early, but I want to check in and let the hostess know we're here." He was back almost immediately and pointed to his family's car pulling into an open parking space.

"Right on time," Ted said as a wide smile crossed his face.

They walked between the rows of cars to meet his family. He got an enthusiastic hug and kiss from his daughter and hugs from the grinning boys. Ed held out his hand.

"Happy Easter, Ted. We all sure look forward to coming here."

Ted introduced Lauren to each of them in turn. She offered her hand to each and smilingly acknowledged them with a hello and their name. He watched his daughter's face and was relieved not to see a hint of displeasure. Soon their party was paged.

The seating happened so quickly. Lauren took a corner seat. Ted had planned for Kathy to sit across from her, but Ed moved into that seat with Greg immediately sitting down beside him. Kathy's seat was at the farthest point from Lauren. A big vase of lilies filled the center of the table. Ted seated himself next to Lauren and Glenn took the final chair, next to Ted and across from his mother. Ted was disappointed with the seating.

Kathy and Ted had complimentary champagne, but Ed ordered soda. After hesitating, Lauren too ordered soda, "I really don't care for champagne," she said. Ted offered to order her a glass of wine, but she declined.

The hour passed quickly. Their table was alternately full, empty, or partly occupied as individual trips were made through the various buffet lines. Other diners were in a festive mood aided by the champagne and the noise level was high.

When at the table, Kathy talked mostly with her two sons, with an occasional bright comment addressed to Ted. He caught parts of the amiable conversation between Lauren and Ed, but agonized over the fact that Lauren and Kathy could barely see each other, much less get to know one another.

The musicians arrived at their table when they were completing lunch. Lauren beamed and greeted them with a few words of Spanish. Even Greg and Glenn sat back and gave the trio their full attention. Lauren did not sing, however, as she always had in Mexico. Ted was disappointed. He should have suggested it. It would have been a wonderful way to break the ice.

The six paused outside the restaurant under a sun partially obscured by broken clouds. Kathy held out her hand to Lauren.

"It's been nice to meet you, Lauren."

"Likewise, Kathy. You have a lovely family."

They watched as his family drove away, Ted returning the boys' waves until the car rounded the parking lot corner.

"Well, Lauren. How did you enjoy lunch?"

"It was fine." They sat in the car and rode in silence for several minutes before Lauren spoke again.

"Why did you seat us like you did? My reason for coming was to have a decent conversation with Kathy. I could barely see her!"

Ted shook his head. "It all happened so fast, Lauren. I almost asked Glenn to trade seats with you but it would have been awkward moving you away from Ed. I didn't want him to think I didn't want you to talk to him."

She didn't respond, and he added, "Ed's a serious guy, isn't he? From what I heard of your exchanges, he had to be impressed by you. The boys were comfortable with you too. I told Kathy the boys would be at ease around you."

Lauren gave him a wan smile.

"Maybe I expected too much. I want your family to accept me. It's kind of as if I don't exist, otherwise."

He reached across and touched her knee.

"I understand how you feel. There will be other opportunities." He turned on the radio and adjusted the music to a low volume.

"What if you should have a heart attack and die while we're being romantic?" she asked him one evening after a light supper and a glass of wine. "I'm sure that many older men do. How am I going to explain it to your family? They would have to think that I was at fault!"

At first, Ted tried to make light of her expressed concerns, but unexpectedly generated anger.

"Why would you care? You'd be dead, and I'd have to face all of their questions and accusations by myself!"

He pooh-poohed Lauren's suggestion that he talk with his son and daughter, and she went home angry, leaving him alone and unfulfilled. And though he tried to avoid the conversation when they met again the next day, it was a repeat of the first night she mentioned it. He began to worry that her concern would affect her willingness to engage in strenuous sex activity with him, if it already hadn't.

He decided to write her a letter.

> Dear Lauren,
>
> On too many recent occasions you have expressed your concern about my children's reactions in the event I should die when in bed with you. You felt they would blame you personally for their loss and perhaps conclude that you were the aggressor, showing no concern for my age.

This letter is in response to those often-voiced concerns. In the unlikely event that I should suffer a heart attack during our love making, you may show this to my children if you feel it would help.

I have found you are an exciting woman to be with in bed and out. You are a very social person where as I might be viewed as a sort of recluse. Some could say you have brought me out of my shell. At any rate, I like the new me!

Where intimate relationships are concerned, we share an understanding. You hold to the idea of being a one man woman and I equally hold to being a one woman man. This hasn't been difficult for us. The commitment removes an immense amount of anxiety in our personal relationship, especially for me.

Sex has proven to be a most important and fulfilling part of this relationship during our first year. I'm sure we both hope it will continue to be so for many years.

You have always let me set the pace in our lovemaking. You have never pressed me or voiced an objection to our just being close together in bed and getting an early sleep. I do find your nearness very exciting. This likely affects my heart in a positive way. Although I feel pleasantly relaxed and momentarily tired after a love making experience with you, it is certainly never close to a situation of exhaustion. There is always this wonderful feeling that each episode holds us a little closer together as a couple. Ted

NINE   A Bargain Price

Soon the garden was growing beautifully and the weather was warming.
They began to talk about what they might expect on their first summer
trip to his mountain place. For him, it had been a pleasant anticipation
every June for many years. He promised her that this year she'd see the
goslings, the size of teacups, swimming between their parents while snow
lay still melting on the ruddy earth. But heavy late snowfall at higher
elevations delayed their trip, closing out much hope for an early trip to his
lake and certainly eliminated an overnight stay. Although Ted was content
to wait, he sensed a need on Lauren's part to get away from the routine and
structure of the classroom. She confirmed this when they shared dinner
one night.

"Why can't we spend a weekend in Carmel soon? Ellen and I bought
a discount book that we could use. We could stay at a less expensive place
than last fall. From the description in the book, we could make two trips
for less than the cost of the one last year."

He thought about her suggestion for several days. Yes, it would be a
lot less cost, and she seemed sincere in wanting to save him money. Ted
ruefully remembered though, the several times he had taken his wife's
suggestion that they really should look at alternatives to the expensive
Carmel lodging they favored. Afterwards, she hadn't complained directly,
but the casual negative observations his wife had expressed had convinced
him that some of the specialness of their limited number of seaside trips
had been lost. Lauren persisted on the saving issue and he tried to show
enthusiasm.

As summer officially arrived, Lauren took on a summer teaching assignment four days a week. Ted encouraged this as a way for her to have a more steady income even though he recognized that a summer work schedule might get in the way of time with her. Fortunately, though, she had Fridays open, and they planned to make that trip to Carmel, and despite his hesitancy, use the coupon book.

When Ted called to book a room, he found that all the choice accommodations at reduced rates were taken. He was both surprised and dismayed. When he told Lauren, she was angry.

"Why didn't you call when we first talked about it? You always think we can do things at the last minute. You know it's summer. How dumb can you be?"

He glared at her, throwing his arms apart, palms up. "Come on, give me a break, for pete's sake! I'm not sure two or three days would have made any difference. There are just so many rooms that the upscale places are willing to offer at reduced rates."

He lowered his arms and softened his tone. "It's not a big deal. I'd be happy to go ahead and get us the same place we liked so much last summer. They have rooms. I checked."

"I don't want you to spend the extra money knowing how tight you are."

He bit his tongue. Hadn't he always treated her well? Paying for her travel and dinners and even helping her with her bills from time to time? Why does she always bring this up?

It wasn't that he didn't get up early enough to prepare for their departure; He thought he could get out an overdue letter to a friend. Then, he noticed the garden needed watering. Suddenly he saw their nine-thirty departure was upon him and he had only begun to pack the car. Lauren's kitchen light was on, the one time he was desperately hoping that she would oversleep.

Within a few minutes she placed her overnight bag on her front porch. It took an additional forty minutes for him to ice up their bottled drinks, get himself packed, and prepare the house for the planned three days away. He couldn't believe he had underestimated the trip preparation time so badly. Why had he even stopped to read the paper? He could have taken it along.

At ten-fifteen he parked in front of her house and carried her things to the car. He was anticipating some caustic remarks and hoped his answers would be adequate. She immediately came out of the house with her water bottle, purse, and a small backpack. Lauren turned after locking her door.

"What the hell is wrong with you? You're almost an hour late!"

"Yes, and I'm sorry about that. It seemed to take extra time to get things ready. I did a little watering too. We'll still arrive by check in time. They don't want us early."

"Did you check to see if this motel is within walking distance of the town?"

"No, that didn't seem important to me. I doubt that it is close enough to walk. We can always take the car."

"You could have at least made sure the place you chose was within walking distance!"

"Well, I didn't. So I don't know!" Ted knew he was totally at fault, but hadn't he apologized and explained his mistake? His irritation mounted and he couldn't hold back his response. "The next time, since you're so perfect, you make the arrangements."

"Well, fuck you. I'm not going to talk to you the whole trip." She slipped into the passenger seat, fastened the seat belt and stared straight ahead.

"Screw you too! I try to put it all together right, and all you do is find fault. What the hell is wrong with you?"

Instead of getting into the driver's seat, he opened the rear door, grabbed Lauren's bag off the seat, strode to her porch and slammed down the bag. Coming back to the car, he jerked open the passenger door.

"If you can't act like a human being, we're not going. Get out, please!"

After sitting for a few minutes staring straight ahead and chewing slowly on a piece of gum, Lauren got out of the car and let herself into her house. Her bag remained on the porch. Ted backed the car across the street into his driveway, opened the garage door and finished unloading the car. He shrugged his shoulders. Lauren had to be taught a lesson.

Shortly after lunch, Lauren knocked on his door. He let her in. She was hardly through the door when she blurted out, "I didn't intend for this to happen, Ted, and I'm sorry. But you know how I am. My father had a big influence on me," she said. "My sister is the same way. We're just like him. He always said: 'Don't take anything from anybody! Get right in their face.'"

He listened to her excuse for the unpredictable flare-ups that had too often rocked their relationship. His silence prompted a further defense:

"You have to remember that I face things right now. I don't let problems build up. You, on the other hand, let them build up, and then you explode."

Ted acknowledged that she was no doubt correct, but inside he wanted to remind her that her mean words, uttered even under defense of wanting to get things out in the open, were hurtful and difficult to forget. Instead, he said, "I've never handled conflicts well. My way is to work hard at avoiding them in the first place."

Neither had given ground, and he continued to think not just about this most recent flare up, but others, including when she had berated him for inviting her to dinner when his kitchen floor needed to be mopped, the continuing friction surrounding Kathy, and worse yet Lauren's demands that she move in with him. Then of course, there was the incident with the freezer. He thought over that chain of events, and then this conflict today. All that they were trying to do here was save some money. It had actually been Lauren's suggestion. He smiled inwardly as he resolved not to again agree to a money saving suggestion where Carmel and she were concerned. The price again might be much too high.

"Let's go grab a bite downtown for dinner. May I pick you up at five?" he asked.

"If you promise to make the reservations," she said.

TEN   Sex And Pressure

A week after their failed trip to the coast, Lauren accompanied Ted up to the mountain place to open up the trailer for the season and clean up any small winter-related problems. Patches of snow still lay on the surrounding mountainsides, but the sky was a brilliant blue. While Ted had been surprised by Lauren's eagerness to make this trip, since she often complained about tramping through snow and mud, he welcomed her help. Together, the work was easier. They quickly removed the plywood, dealt with some dead mice, and then headed up to the lake to take down the boat.

"I hope it survived the twelve-foot snow pack! I'm bringing my rod just in case. Bring your book so you can read."

He wasn't prepared by her change of attitude when they reached the lake and viewed the boat, still roped tightly to a thirty-foot evergreen in a small grove at the lake's edge. She said: "The only reason I came is because you don't use good sense. How the hell is a man who is nearly eighty going to get a huge rowboat out of a tree? I don't know why you persist on doing this each year by yourself. You think your age doesn't count! What's wrong with your son or Ed? They don't give a damn about you, or they'd be here to take the boat down."

"Whoa." He said. He was dumbfounded. "They could have, and would be happy to help if I ask them to. I never saw the point of suggesting they make this long drive when we were coming up. It's a simple job for two people."

"If it's so damned simple, do it yourself and I'll watch! Break your back if you have to."

93

He quickly untied the ropes, steaming despite the chilly breeze, while trying to steady the boat. Ted was edging his way around the teetering boat when he realized that Lauren was in position and helping.

"Hi. I thought some elf must have stepped in. Thanks."

"I'm sorry, I don't know what came over me to act like that. Be careful now, because this thing is heavy."

They safely lowered the boat and dragged it to the water's edge. Going back to the truck, he grabbed a coat and his rod. She embraced him and insisted on a prolonged kiss.

"You fish as long as you like. There's lots of time between now and dinner, and I'll stay in the truck and read. I'm loving this book."

Ted spent an hour fishing but only had two trout to show for it. They ate a simple dinner and went to bed early to escape the chill. They cuddled under the covers and soon fell asleep. At barely sun up, she climbed over him on her way to the bathroom, saying provocatively, "Why don't you follow, brush your teeth and wash up a little too?"

After rushing through the thirty eight degree morning and returning to the sleeping bag, they kissed, touched and caressed until their entire bodies were tied up in the rapture of complete lovemaking. Here was the same woman who had angered him the previous afternoon, now showing him she loved him completely and without reservation. They finally settled into each other's arms, almost returning to sleep, until Ted got up and made them coffee.

Their work was done. Initial plans were to leave for home right after breakfast. But the direct sun on the deck quickly warmed their backs as they sipped the last of the coffee. Ted thought about how he would have liked to take home a better trout catch. The two fish he had caught were barely enough. As if she knew what he was thinking, Lauren suggested that they stay.

"It's only ten, and I'm not finished with my book. If you'll fish from the bank, I'll sit in the warm car and read."

Ted held her hand as they wound their way along the dirt road leading to the highway. He packed in three more nice trout before they left. He didn't feel old or unappreciated at all.

An entire week passed before her next visit, and when she arrived, she brought news of her long time friend, Pat, coming for a four-day visit. Ted was happy for Lauren. As he saw it, both women would benefit from an uninterrupted visit. Confidences would be shared.

"Why don't we plan to have two dinners over here? Invite Ellen too, if she's around. The weather's so nice, we can dine on the patio."

Lauren embraced him enthusiastically. "What a wonderful and thoughtful idea! It would be a chance for Pat to meet you. She's not the kind of person to be judgmental about our age differences. I know you will like her."

"Done. Let's get together and plan two good dinners. I have a London broil in the freezer for one of them."

She wasn't, apparently, planning on staying for the evening, and Ted was disappointed. As he walked her to the door, she leaned to him and said, "I'll come over to sleep with you on Thursday night. Pat won't mind a quiet evening by herself after a busy couple of days."

Ted was elated. He loved the anticipation of her overnight stays with him. He walked out onto the patio, already visualizing where he could reposition some of the potted plants for a better effect at the dinner party. The screened patio would get a special scrubbing. He wanted his place to be worthy of compliments.

Thursday was the second of the two dinners at Ted's. The first dinner had gone well. Ellen joined them the first night, but not for this one. Much of the conversation the first night, while he consciously refilled their glasses of wine, centered on men's and women's relationships. The three women offered a cheery "goodnight" around ten, leaving him with a stack of kitchen dishes and, as he told the ladies in jest as they departed, a lot of comments about his gender to digest.

He could hardly wait for Thursday evening to come. It didn't bother him at all that he saw only glimpses of Lauren during the day. This night was to be very special. During the hour preceding his London broil dinner, Ted was especially attentive to the women's wishes for drinks and snacks. In between checking on the barbecue and other last minute preparations, he joined in the conversation. Pat was effusive with her compliments.

"The meat smells fantastic! Where did you learn to cook? Can't we help you with anything? You make me feel completely spoiled."

Ted beamed. He sensed that the evening was going well. Lauren's affirmation of his cooking talents and her frequent smiles confirmed that feeling.

"I've always done the outdoor cooking. The rest of it I had to learn after my wife died. Lauren is an excellent cook; she helps me sometimes."

Shortly after nine, Lauren and Pat excused themselves with compliments on a wonderful dinner. Lauren held back as her friend started across the street. She and Ted shared a hug and kiss, followed by his whisper that he was so excited about her coming back later.

"What are you talking about? I'm not coming back."

"But you said you wanted to stay with me on Thursday night, and this is Thursday. I've been counting on it!"

"That's ridiculous. How can I possibly leave my guest alone? You know better than that. Good night. Thanks for making dinner, Ted. We'll see you tomorrow."

After returning her goodnight, Ted walked into his kitchen and looked sadly at the stacked dishes. He felt cheated, and his anger was increasing. Here he had devoted time to putting together two special dinners for Lauren and her friend and she blatantly broke her promise. His overtures were dismissed as nothing!

He saw very little of the two the next day, as they went to visit a mutual friend and then went to dinner and a movie without him. Ted tried to go on with his own plans for the day but couldn't shake the feeling of unease. While he caught up on personal letters and did three loads of laundry, the day dragged by. He did yard work and read magazines. He became very impatient to see Lauren and talk with her. They arrived home after he was in bed. He heard their voices through his open bedroom window. His phone didn't ring.

The next morning, Ted was watering his front shrubbery when Lauren returned from taking Pat to the airport. She walked up to him and had apparently also been dwelling on the state of their relationship.

"I don't like being pushed into sex. Besides, my period started this morning, and it might be two weeks before I go to bed with you again."

Ted's anger was difficult to disguise. How could he respond to this most unwelcome statement made almost as a threat? Anything he said would likely make matters worse.

"I'm glad your visit with Pat went well," he said, turning back to his watering. Inside, he was seething, and she walked away without saying anything else.

His mood didn't improve as morning became afternoon. All of the yard watering was finished, and he watched through his kitchen window while fixing lunch. Only twice did his neighbor come into her front yard and then only briefly to adjust water settings. Was her life going on as if everything were fine between them? How could she react the way she had?

He held hopes that Lauren would call and suggest a light dinner, but the phone remained silent. Even his two pre-dinner drinks failed to change his depressed feelings. Finally, he prepared a late soup and salad dinner and ate while listening to an old Roger Whittaker tape. At nine o'clock, Ted picked up the phone and pushed the auto dial button for Lauren. When she answered, his tone was uncharacteristically blunt.

"I have all your stuff packed and in bags. It will be on my front porch. You can pick them up in the morning, or I'll put them on your front porch after Ellen is gone."

"Why are you doing this awful thing to me tonight? Couldn't you at least wait until tomorrow?"

"There's no point in waiting. It isn't your fault, Lauren. I simply can't handle what's happening and I'm bowing out. Goodnight."

He hung up the receiver without waiting for a reply. The three paper bags with her personal belongings sat on his porch all morning. He never saw her. Shortly before noon, he left to do a number of errands. When he returned, the bags were gone.

Ted now had the entire afternoon to reflect on what he had done. He was free of this woman who, on occasion, had caused him so much pain. In a way, he felt a new sense of freedom. No longer would he get those afternoon calls from her inviting herself for dinner. How many times had he jumped into his car and headed for the local market for something that would spice up his planned simple menu? He could now go back to his own meal planning again without last minute changes or interruptions.

Ted found himself smiling ruefully when recalling her abrasive remarks about his diet:

"What do you mean you had a half banana and slice of toast for breakfast? Where are the eggs? Look at you, you're losing a lot of weight." He had hoped she was joking, but soon realized she wasn't. "Soup and salad is no dinner for a man. You at least need some potatoes. Don't you care about yourself?" Ted had to admit to himself that she was partially right, and had purposefully added items to his menus.

He imagined more trips to his mountain place with friends. Some he had been neglecting could be called again. He knew that his neighbor, George, must have been especially disappointed. For each of the three years before he met Lauren, he'd made it a point to take George out fishing half a dozen times each year. Since Lauren, they hadn't gone once. It bothered Ted that he let this happen.

But then despair set in as he reminded himself of what he had just given up. There would be no more nights or afternoons of their spectacular lovemaking. No longer would he waken with this teasing, lovely woman beside him. Who could possibly replace Lauren at his mountain lake, holding hands by the fire pit, confident of the bliss that lay ahead? Would there ever be another Lauren to share his favorite Carmel with?

His afternoon of reflection turned into a weeklong painful assessment of what he had accomplished with that brief nine o'clock call. Ted simultaneously congratulated and hated himself for his abrupt dismissal of this woman who had become the focus of his every day.

For nearly two weeks, she came and went with barely a glance his way. Only occasionally did eye contact force half-hearted waves. Not once did she volunteer a good morning wave from her kitchen window. He thought several times of drawing his kitchen curtains to avoid having to think about it.

But, he found himself taking advantage of his new independence, and did call George one evening after twice hanging up the phone before dialing.

"George, this is Ted. I've got an open day tomorrow. How about going fishing? Can you fit it in on such short notice?"

"Hell yes! I thought you'd died. What time do you want to leave? I'll fix up a couple of sandwiches."

Ted forced a laugh.

"That's great. No, I haven't died. You know how it is when you get hooked up with a woman. There always seems to be something she wants to do. Let's figure to leave at six thirty. That'll get us fishing before ten. The truck's all gassed up and ready to go."

On the drive up, Ted side-stepped George's immediate question about how things were going with Lauren. He changed the subject to some improvements he planned for the wilderness property.

"I think I'll have a small storage shed built," he said.

They talked about the stock market and politics and the remodeling George and his wife were doing in their kitchen. They made their usual wager of a dollar for the first fish caught over thirteen inches, and another dollar for the largest trout over fourteen inches, but fishing was slow. By three o'clock Ted had a fourteen and a half inch Rainbow and George had topped it with one over sixteen inches. They had five fish between them when George suggested they pack up.

Ted was ready. He loved the gentle rocking of the boat while looking at the splendor of the rocks and trees banking the huge basin containing the lake. Too often though, today his thoughts had turned to Lauren. Suppose she called? He pulled up the anchor and climbed onto the center seat to row back to shore.

There was only one phone message when he got home; a call from his daughter, Kathy, reminding him that this upcoming weekend she and her family were going to be with him at the mountain cabin.

The high mountain temperature was lovely for his daughter's family's campout. His son in law, Edward, laid out the foam rubber pads on the redwood deck and tossed their four sleeping bags onto the pads. Ted placed his bag between the two boys. This had become a ritual since his daughter's family had first visited his place when the twins were five years old. During those early visits, Ted had never slept comfortably, and had found himself waking each time one of the boys said something in his sleep, or complained of being cold. He had felt needed. He would adjust the pillows, push his stirring grandson deeper into the bag, and then rub the wakened boy's back for a minute until his steady breathing indicated he was again sound asleep. Ted had loved his role. He wouldn't consider taking one of the more comfortable beds inside the trailer.

Kathy and Edward prepared their breakfasts of hot chocolate for the twins, a pot of coffee for the adults, with cereal and sliced melon for everyone. The boys dressed quickly and challenged him to games of cribbage on the stumps by the fire pit while sipping the chocolate.

"I have a new project for you today," Ted said to the twins, Greg and Glenn. "How good are you at rowing a boat on your own? I'm ready to give you lessons."

The boys raced down to the water and grabbed their life jackets from the bottom of the rowboat. "Grandpa, can I be the first in the boat?" Greg shouted up the hill as Ted walked down.

"Yep. You guys each have to show me today that you can handle the oars. One at a time in the boat. I'll ride with you."

Ted gave a rowing lesson to each of the two grandsons while the other fished or explored the woods with Edward and Kathy. He was pleased that after an hour both boys were able to keep the boat moving steadily on a fairly straight course.

Ted then suggested a hike up the Prosser Creek gorge. It was his own favorite walk. He had hoped it would become Lauren's. His grandsons scampered up the trail ahead of the adults, seeming to never tire.

After the hike, Edward and the boys went fishing, and Kathy and Ted stayed at the camp to put things in order for their departure. Kathy didn't ask about Lauren, and he felt comfortable not bringing her into the conversation. They talked about the boys' summer activities and their gardens, inspired of course by their grandfather. Five nice trout were brought back, cleaned, and packed on ice. They packed their van; goodbyes were shared, and they preceded Ted out of the valley.

The drive home gave him a chance to reflect on his fortunate family situation. They would always be there for him. He wished that some of Lauren's immediate family lived close by. It would give more balance to her life. Ted knew she envied his ability to have almost weekly visits with at least some of his close family members. He turned on his favorite radio station, changing it only once to pick up the day's closing stock market report.

As he drove the car into the garage, Ted began planning activities to fill the afternoon. He knew his four backyard fruit trees needed some deep watering. He had been thinking, too, about trying a late planting of green beans, hoping for a mid-October harvest if the fall temperatures remained high enough. He decided to make that the afternoon's main project, and then to fill in with some reading. With a glance across the street, Ted saw that Lauren was home; Her car was parked in the driveway next to Ellen's.

He cleaned up and shaved after completing the gardening, then relaxed with a drink and Lauren's Kenny G tape, which he didn't, until that moment, realize he had forgotten to give back to her. Dinner was a thawed-and-reheated pint of beef stew from a batch he had made more than a month ago. It was one of his favorite uncomplicated meals when combined with a tossed salad and a slice of sour French bread.

Ted looked at the clock. After washing the few dishes he would still have almost two hours before bedtime. Another empty night faced him. He was startled by the phone ringing. It was Lauren.

"Why don't you come over tomorrow morning about ten, Ted? Ellen will be gone to some meeting by then. We need to talk. I haven't unpacked those paper bags since you threw me out. You'll find me working at my table on the back patio."

She didn't seem to want or expect an answer, but he said he'd be there.

His overwhelming relief turned quickly into excitement but with equal feelings of concern. What had she been thinking about for the last ten days? Could she have reached a decision that she needed and wanted him? He felt some hopeful significance from her comment about having not unpacked the three bags.

Ted thought of Lauren during the night. Was she suffering as he was? He hoped so. Maybe she hadn't been able to brush aside their relationship so easily.

When Ted arrived, it was as if she hadn't completed their conversation from the last time they were together.

"I love you Ted, and I want to have sex with you. But I keep feeling this pressure from you and it makes me stressed out. I don't want to have to promise you when I'm going to be intimate with you. If I change my mind, you get mad or upset. Do you understand how I feel?"

"I don't believe you have the slightest idea of what is going on inside me when I respond the way you say I do. Yes, I do get upset when you ignore your promises. You're forgetting that I'm an older man. Younger men don't have this problem. They have more time and more confidence."

He looked away for a few seconds to gather his thoughts, and then returned to meet her gaze.

"The best explanation I can give you is that I need constant reassurance that everything is okay between us. The best way I get this from you is through our lovemaking. When we make love, it tells me that you're my girl totally and completely."

Lauren nodded.

"I know you're not out with other men, but because I'm older it's the regular attention I seem to need. If that seems strange to you, I ask only that you try to understand. When you told me you might not be sleeping for me for two weeks, I just crumbled. I know you wouldn't have been that blunt if you'd taken a minute to think about how it would bruise me. I'm asking that you do understand that for me, making love with you isn't simply sex for the sake of sex, no matter how nice it is. It goes much deeper than that. Does what I've said make sense?"

Lauren continued to look at him intently after he stopped talking. She seemed content to let him finish, to allow his feelings to spill out. He usually wasn't that long-winded. Ted wondered if he looked as forlorn as he felt. Could she, a much younger woman, begin to understand? Would she accept his explanation, and would it make a difference? He watched and waited.

Lauren began to cry and said, "You dumb shit! This has been as bad a time over here for me as it was for you. What do you think I've been doing, celebrating? Why did we do this to one another?"

They embraced, and held each other for a long time. Ted knew that this beautiful and desirable woman wouldn't withhold herself from him much longer.

Lauren gently pulled away.

"Why don't you relax here, Ted, while I fix us each a cup of coffee. Don't go away!"

She flashed him a smile, which he returned to assure her he would go nowhere.

They visited quietly for twenty minutes. She mentioned several times that she wanted their lovemaking to be spontaneous, not a planned event. She got only half-hearted concurrence from him. Ted felt a need to restate his position.

"You've mentioned this pressure thing before, Lauren, and while I suppose I can understand your feelings, I must tell you that if you don't feel the desire or need or pressure or whatever that it takes to remember that I'm in the picture too, I worry that our relationship won't hold together."

"Don't worry. I won't forget you. Shall I bring the bags back over tonight? Do you promise not to throw them back out?"

Ted promised, and his steps were light as he walked back across the street. His exuberance was tempered, however, with a slight feeling of guilt. He was sure he had made his position clear that regular lovemaking was critical to sustain their relationship. Lauren hadn't indicated that she felt that statement to be an added pressure. Maybe it was just the right amount. He hoped so.

"What are we having for dinner?" Lauren carried a bag in each hand and greeted Ted with a kiss on the mouth.

"Green beans, salad and a trout I brought home from camp this weekend."

"How was your weekend with your grandchildren," Lauren asked. "I'm sure it was fantastic, wonderful, and perfect as usual!"

Ted cringed and tried to ignore the sarcasm in her voice.

"It was a good weekend. Tiring. Young people want to keep doing different things, and they like me to be a part of it. We played darts for over an hour."

"I suppose you slept out on the deck?"

"Yes, we did. We even saw a coon up on the deck exploring the garbage bag. I shined a flashlight on it and almost everyone woke up. It was a big coon, and the boys were excited."

"Why don't you sleep in the trailer? You have a good bed in the trailer, and you don't use it! That's just silly."

Ted realized that part of the cause of her harangue was concern for his rest and health. He also realized that she had no family close like he did, and couldn't help her feelings of jealousy. He felt a need to protect and comfort her, so throughout the evening remained the perfect gentleman, ignoring the things she said that might have otherwise provoked a response from him.

After they washed the dishes, she turned to him and said, "I've decided to spend the night with you."

"Wonderful!"

"Do you want to go to bed now?"

"Hey, I'd like that. Let's not let another minute go by." Ted couldn't hold back expressing his feelings of relief. Their lovemaking was prolonged and reassuring although neither reached a climax. His lovemaking didn't equal his desire, but he knew what part of his problem was: You don't have much energy left after you spend two days in the mountains with active grandchildren.

They talked quietly afterwards about their intense feelings for one another, assuring each other of their deep love. Lauren seemed to want to make certain the tension was over. After a long period of silence in a loving embrace, Lauren whispered,

"I'm happy we're together again."

Ted's response was a barely perceptible squeeze of her hand and a sleepy "goodnight."

In the morning, Ted woke first to the sound of the paper being thrown on the porch. He quietly slid from under the covers, but Lauren stirred. He leaned down to kiss her and whispered that he was getting up to make coffee. She pulled him down and put a leg across his thighs.

"No, you're not going to get up and make coffee. I want you right here with me. Why are you always in such a rush to get up in the morning?"

"Let's say it's a habit. Maybe a carryover from milking cows as a boy."

"Well, today, Ted, your day is going to start with staying in bed with me. You're constantly rushing, and we don't get to do this very often. I don't like it in bed alone."

She changed positions and her bottom was nestled into his groin. Suggestive movements against him eliminated any thoughts of coffee and the morning paper.

"Let me go and brush my teeth! Don't go away!"

He was gone only a few minutes and climbed back into bed, tossing his pajamas onto the floor.

"It's your turn now! Don't be long."

Morning love sessions were different. Perhaps it started with the almost fully lighted bedroom. Only the sheer curtains acted as a sun filter. Ted was full of energy. Her eyes expressed her sincere devotion as he touched her face and the errant strands of hair. "You are so exceptionally beautiful in the mornings. There aren't any signs of stress after you've had a good night sleep."

"Maybe it's because I can't imagine another man I'd rather be with right now. You make me feel so wanted and complete."

For a few seconds he was concerned about his white hair. Was she even aware of it now? Ted had no question that her expressions were honest and deeply felt. Both reached fulfillment. Now they lay quietly together, bodies and hands still touching. Very little was said, and then nothing. He felt her body and hands completely relax. Ted raised himself on one elbow and peered into her face. She was sleeping soundly.

He edged himself quietly out of bed and dressed. Now it was time for coffee and his newspaper.

ELEVEN   Whalers' Bench

Ellen often joined Ted and Lauren to watch a movie after dinner when they dined at her house that summer. They enjoyed each other's company during muted commercials. One evening, Ted was encouraging a discussion about vacations at the coast because he hoped Lauren might want another ocean trip before the summer was over.

He wasn't complaining that they weren't doing enough together. Since their separation after Pat's visit, Lauren had been especially attentive. They had taken one weekend trip to his mountain hideout since then, and though the mosquitoes and gnats were terrible, they enjoyed wading across the two small creeks that crossed a hiking trail, seeing the huge variety of wildflowers, and watching the wildlife.

But soon another summer would be over and Lauren would be back at school. She agreed to another trip. "Point Lobos," she decided. "The scenery is supposed to be spectacular and I hear that the hiking isn't overly tough."

He was able to get reservations at their favorite Carmel motel.

Coastal fog was still shielding the sun when their continental breakfast was delivered to their room. He was looking at the morning paper. Lauren began to stir.

"It says here that we're going to have morning fog, followed by bright sunshine. We may be lucky. Do you think we could plan to be at Point Lobos by ten?" he asked.

She pulled herself up drowsily and sat on the edge of the bed.

"Gee, is it time to get up already? I did have a great sleep. If the park entrance isn't too far from here, I guess we can be there around ten. I'd like to finish our hiking before it gets too warm, anyway."

Even at ten, traffic at the park fee-collection kiosk was backing up. They parked in one of the last three remaining parking spaces in the boulder-lined area adjacent to a small bay. Ahead of them lay the trailhead.

Ted watched the activity around what appeared to be a small boat launching ramp.

"Now I see why the parking spaces are scarce. Look at all those people in wet suits. They must have gone out early for scuba diving and are now coming in with their boats."

They watched the water scene for a few minutes before following the signs and arrows and heading for some rock stairs. He adjusted the straps on Lauren's backpack and they began their climb.

Halfway up the hill they met a park employee resetting stones on one of the steps. He stood aside with a smile and pleasant greeting.

"You've picked a great morning for a walk. The sun has already taken care of the fog. We're not expecting much wind today, either."

At the top of the stairs, the trail circled back and overlooked an almost vertical drop to the bay. Lauren called for Ted to stop and sit on a two foot high rock wall.

"Get ready to smile because I'm going to take a picture when the next big wall of water crashes into that tall rock jutting up out of the bay behind you. I'll try to get you back-grounded with the spray."

They exchanged positions and he asked which button to push and finally announced that he was ready.

"There are two big pelicans about ready to light on the same rock. I want the picture to look like they're almost sitting on your shoulders."

The trail sometimes bordered other abrupt cliffs to the sea. At another time they peered into a quiet pool to watch several harbor seals. One was pulling itself up on a low rock ledge for sunning.

They were surprised to see an elderly woman docent waiting on the trail with a tripod and viewing telescope. She welcomed them with a warm smile.

"You're some of the first hikers this morning. I have the telescope focused on a nest on a limb hanging out over the water." She pointed to a cypress about two hundred feet away. "That nest is used every year. We have regular hikers who come each year to watch the parents feed and look after the little ones. If you look closely, you can see one adult perched not far from the nest."

They took turns looking through the telescope. The adult bird finally hopped off the limb and soared out over the bay. Ted knew his partner had an acute, sensitive feeling for young life. He listened intently to her questions and the docent's responses, and thought back to earlier discussions with her. He was convinced that she would have made a very loving, successful mother had fate not intervened and taken her only child a few weeks after his birth.

They heard voices and another couple rounded a bend in the trail and approached the docent. Lauren and Ted thanked her, and Lauren led the way up the path. He marveled at how effortlessly she climbed the carefully placed stone steps. She was wearing his favorite shorts with a sweater tied around her waist. It excited him to watch the smooth motion of her body. Ted was glad that he'd jumped right in and lined up this trip, probably the last one for the year. His thoughts moved ahead to what might continue to delight her for the balance of the day.

They stopped to observe the contorted shapes of a few Monterey cypress trees. Twisted, gnarled branches told the story of the coast's often brutal winds. Dead trees, unless they had fallen across a trail, had been allowed to decompose where they fell.

Ted commented about the ever-present knee-high cable lining both sides of the trail.

"These park people must be really serious about us not even stepping a few feet off the trail. I've noticed the little signs hanging from the cables almost every hundred feet reminding visitors not to disturb anything,"

They stopped to admire the fern growth, seemingly spurred on by the rotting fallen trees and the regular fog. Lauren pulled him to a stop several times to point out bunches of flowers with vibrant colors.

"If it were allowed, I'd climb over the cable and pick ups a little bunch for our room tonight."

Often they would find themselves standing with their arms around each others' waists, saying little.

Another hundred yards up the trail, a small sign showed a cutoff to a place called Whalers' Lookout. Ted said, "As an old seafaring man, I'd say we have to do this. I'd forgotten, but I guess whales were hunted off this coast many years ago. I still read about whale-watching excursions here during the migration season."

The trail segment turned sharply left with a steep grade upward. Both were breathing hard when they reached a more level area. Ahead, on a knoll, as if planted to fill an open space, was Whalers' Bench, identified by a small metal plaque.

The sun hadn't completely dried the plank seat from the nightlong fog. Lauren spread her sweater over the boards, and he followed her lead.

"Can you believe a spot like this? I'm so glad Ellen suggested we go to Point Lobos. Do you think this can sort of become our trail?" he asked.

She answered by leaning over and giving him more than a causal kiss, then sat back immediately.

"This is a great time to eat our apple. Get out your knife, Ted. I brought a few cookies in my backpack, too."

Soon, Lauren began a serious discussion about her future. The words mirrored several earlier discussions they had had. Her mood no longer matched the splendor of the mountaintop sunshine. He was disappointed because he had anticipated a more romantic turn, but saw no way of re-directing the conversation. He waited.

"My job isn't going anywhere! I know I'm never going to get a full time college teaching position. The other part time instructors are in the same boat I am. Here I've worked at this community college for five years, and where has it gotten me? I'm almost where I started!"

Ted nodded without answering. He knew that he had encouraged her to apply for all of the few permanent openings in her field and that nothing had materialized.

"I need a full time job if I'm ever going to get anywhere. You know that I don't even get medical benefits now. I have to pay extra for the coverage. Here I have two degrees and can't get a decent job. I'm almost living below poverty level."

He was relieved that Lauren no longer talked about bankruptcy as a quick way out of her financial hole. This had disturbed him during the first few months of their relationship. He had openly scorned any inkling of that idea, reminding her that the burdensome student loan was an honest debt that she owed and must repay. Ted hoped he could lean on her strong sense of honesty.

He felt he had closed off the bankruptcy thoughts by offering to add a thousand dollars towards payment of her student loan that December, providing she made the scheduled payments for the year. Ted wanted to give her an even greater incentive.

"I'll double that the following year, if we're still hanging together, and if you make those payments." He was relieved when she'd assured him two months earlier that the payments were being mailed regularly.

Other than an occasional observation such as "that's true," he said nothing. Today, as always before, Lauren reached her own conclusion without his intervention.

"I want to stay in my field. It's what I studied for, and I want to continue teaching at the college level. I'm good at it, and I truly enjoy working with older students."

She shifted and re-crossed her legs on the wood bench and gazed off in the direction of the retreating fog.

"I'm a survivor and always have been. I don't need a lot of money to live on. So what if I don't have anything when I retire?"

Was she looking for more money now? What was the purpose of this conversation? Ted wondered. Was Lauren looking for him to provide a permanent escape from her financial and job woes? He tried to sift through her words for an answer.

Ted knew he could help her gain a stronger financial base if he chose. Too, hadn't he fantasized about asking her to live with him? The idea of marriage to this sensuous and intelligent woman was enticing until the memories of too many bruising arguments snapped him back to reality.

Did he love her now just for what she could give him? What was she giving him besides sex? She had hinted at a need for a commitment from him, but how would she define it?

Her temporary dark mood subsided, she turned to him with a bright smile and edged closer. Lauren's hand covered his when it was gently placed on her thigh. Together they listened to the songs of the birds around them. A light breeze came and went but had little effect on the warm summer air. The two said nothing but gazed at the beauty and serenity surrounding them.

She glanced at him as if asking what was on his mind. Ted's thoughts turned back to an idea he'd been considering earlier while slicing the apple for lunch.

"Do you see that big grove of trees down that side hill? Wouldn't you agree that our two sweaters would make a perfect blanket? There is only one trail nearby."

He looked at Lauren expectantly and was answered by her immediately standing and picking up her sweater.

"What's holding you up? I can't wait."

He reached out and brushed her hand as she walked past, leading the way down the slope to the spot. Together they cleared away twigs and pebbles. Ted peaked over the top of a bush every few seconds to make sure there were no hikers at Whalers' Bench. No sounds of voices challenged the chirping of the small birds. They laid their sweaters out; folded his jeans and her shorts into makeshift pillows. They quickly dropped from the potential sight of others. Lauren seemed unable to avoid teasing.

"This is almost like the rug in front of your fireplace. Do you think your butt will get sunburned here?"

"Not a chance! With the state of mind you have me in, lightning may strike awfully fast."

All of the myriad emotions that had build up on the trail and bench seemed to envelop the two lovers. They spoke in whispers. If there were irritating stones or twigs beneath the sweaters, neither appeared to notice. Ted saw that her eyes were closed against the midday light, and marveled at the intensity of Lauren's expression as she moved her body with his. He wished these passionate moments could last forever. He reached a climax with her only seconds later amid his hoarse whispers.

There seemed to be no need for words as they climbed back out of their secret spot.

TWELVE   Damn Those Margaritas

"Here's to a great summer garden! We did it together and I pronounce it a big success!" Ted and Lauren clinked their margaritas and drank them down.

Ted refilled the glasses from the pitcher and turned toward the salad preparation. She stood beside him, washing and snapping the beans. Once she teasingly flicked water in his face. It seemed to Ted that her mood was just right.

Unfortunately, once the medium-rare steaks were pulled from the barbecue and the Elton John Love Songs tape inserted in the player, Lauren abruptly turned the conversation.

"You say you're close to Kathy, but you can't even talk to her about us."

"I do tell her what we're doing together. She doesn't always respond, but I'm direct with her."

"That isn't good enough. You have to confront her with the fact that I mean a lot to you and that she has to accept me as part of the family."

Ted didn't know what he could say to placate her. He knew if they were lucky that time would lead to his daughter's acceptance of her father having a woman friend younger than her. "She has nothing against you personally, Lauren. Kathy made it clear to me right off that she was against our relationship. It wasn't a personal thing. I'm sure she'd have reacted differently if you were seventy years old. You've brought this up before, and I can't give you any different answers. How's your steak?"

"You have to do something about her. You say you care for me, and you let your daughter ignore me. I think your relationship with Kathy is superficial."

"That's a bunch of bunk. There's nothing to be gained by continuing to raise the issue. She's five years older than you are. Why do we have to beat this issue to death?"

"I don't want to go on this way. I feel comfortable with the rest of your family, and the few of your friends who I've met, but you have to do something about your daughter."

Both had ceased to eat, their plates still half filled with dinner. Ted absentmindedly sipped on the glass of wine he had served with dinner. He had been through Lauren's agonizing over the family not accepting her on several other occasions and had found that none of his responses seemed to reduce her frustration. He knew there was nothing to gain from further trying to justify his position. He cut a small piece of steak and waited.

He wasn't prepared, however, for Lauren's next shocker.

"I want a signed contract for one hundred thousand dollars. That's fifty thousand a year for two years." Lauren placed her knife and fork on either side of her plate and folded her hands in front of her on the table.

"What are you talking about?"

"Everyone says that you're taking advantage of me and that all you're after is sex."

"Who are you talking with about our personal affairs?" Ted asked, leaning towards her and tilting his head. "I think that's our private business."

"Oh, Ruth, and a couple of other friends. They all tell me that I need to get a commitment from you because I'm wasting my life. They say you're just enjoying sex and that I need to get something for it." She waved her hand around in the air in a wave meant to include everyone with an opinion.

Ted abruptly straightened up. "Not Ellen! I can't believe she feels that way. In none of my conversations with her has she ever hinted that I was taking advantage of you. It's the opposite. Do you remember when she said that I was the best thing that has happened to you? You were there!"

Lauren nervously placed her hands in her lap. She found it hard to meet his glare.

"Yes, you're right. Ellen didn't agree with the others. She stuck up for you. She said you deserved someone to love you."

Ted felt some added strength to his defense.

"I thought we had something a lot better than that going for us." Ted covered his mouth with his hand and shook his head in silence for a moment before continuing. "It also seems to me that our time together has been fair to both of us. It's been a equal shake. Haven't you felt the same way?"

"Yes, but I'm getting older. What if we keep on like this and you die? What will I have?"

"You've told me dozens of times that my money meant nothing to you. You always bragged that you were a survivor and completely able to take care of yourself since your marriage broke up. Have you changed your feelings?"

"No, I haven't changed. I just want to know what's going to be there for me if I continue with you. My friends tell me I'm a fool to let you keep having sex with me getting nothing for it."

"Whoa," Ted said, as he pushed his chair back from the table making a loud grinding sound on the floor. "Let's look at how we got started with lovemaking. You announced, out of the clear blue sky that you were horny..."

"Yes, I did," she interrupted. "But you have to remember that your situation as an older man is very unusual. Young women just don't look at old men romantically. I regret that I got involved with you. I wasn't thinking it out. I let myself fall in love with you." Lauren said, and added more softly, "I don't want to walk away, but I want to know what's in it for me if I continue with you. My friends tell me that if I meant something to you other than sex, you would do something to take care of my future."

"I don't like this business of your talking with neighbors and friends about our personal lives! Why do you do that? What concern is it of theirs!"

"Well, they asked me how things are going between us, and I told them. They said they're worried about me. I can talk with them if I want to."

"Okay then, I can't stop you from doing it, but we need to get something clear so there will be no misunderstanding between us." Ted sensed a need to be very deliberate and continued after a few second's pause.

"After one of the money gifts I gave you earlier, I told you there would be nothing for you in my will. What money I give you will be before I die. It's not fair that you should look forward to something after my death and then be disappointed."

113

"And besides," he added with as much humor as he could muster up, "I never want to be worth more to you dead than alive. I feel that I've been reasonably generous, and you've indicated you felt that way too."

"Yes, you have, but our situation is now different. I'm getting older, and I need a good reason to spend more time with you. Thanks for dinner. I'm going home now. Goodnight."

Ted walked across the street with her. There was no kiss as she unlocked the door and disappeared. What a disaster this night had turned out to be. It had been almost a week since their last lovemaking. Lauren had doused his hopes almost on arrival.

"Damn those margaritas!" he said to the dark sky.

He threw away the uneaten dinner except for the steak, which he packaged up for use later in a stew. He found no relief in sleep. His thoughts went back to several weeks earlier when they'd been on a single overnight trip to his mountain cabin. The money talk had suddenly surfaced briefly then too, and had both puzzled and upset him. He remembered Lauren being surprisingly casual in her remarks, then dropping the topic. How long had she been thinking about equating money and sex? Was she serious about it? There was no doubt about the intensity of her demands during this evening's dinner.

Thinking back to that overnight several weeks ago, Ted remembered that she was a little testy as they completed loading the Explorer that morning before leaving. She had originally wanted a three-day weekend, but her own work circumstances had called for a shortened trip. He knew she'd been disappointed. Friction about precise packing for any trip was not unusual. Ted had always asked that she give the ice chests a final check. He found Lauren to be practical and adept, and he would promptly reorganize the food and drinks the way she directed, though not enjoying her criticism. The start of this trip had been no exception.

"Why didn't you put all of the salad stuff together? You know how much I hate to have to dig around. The cheese can't be near the bottom; it might get wet. Why didn't you put more things in Zip-locks? You could have put the milk and orange juice in smaller jars and saved room. We don't need a full quart of either."

As he remembered, though, she seemed to enjoy her part of the morning drive. Ted had played several of their favorite tapes. They said little, but touched hands occasionally. Lauren had at one point said:

"I love these songs. So many of them seem to have been written just for us. I never have a doubt about our love though sometimes we stumble."

On the lake that day, Lauren had insisted they follow the two geese families who seemed to be willing to cooperate and let the boat get within fifty feet. The goslings were almost of flying age which must have increased their parents' confidence. They had been able to lift off the water for short distances when the boat got too close.

Their planned two hours on the lake had been cut short because of increasing winds. Ted had seen no reason to suggest fishing. There would be ample time the next morning. Chairs had been left in the truck and the wind had been too brisk for reading so they had decided to return to camp early.

She had marinated slices of chicken breast for their evening meal. He had made certain that nothing interfered with the complete attention to the basting and turning of the delicate meat on the hot barbeque. Yes, he remembered that dinner was a success, where some others had not been.

Their showers had been squeezed in before starting dinner while the sun was still fairly high. Ted had fixed himself a drink while the charcoal was heating. Lauren had accepted a glass of wine and suggested the toast: "To us and our lake."

He loved outdoor toasts, made while standing by a set table, and the added romance of a kiss to go with the clinking glasses. Yes, he remembered too a shortened but pleasant time by the glowing fire pit that particular evening. She always brought marshmallows and chocolate bars. He kept an array of sharpened sticks handy because his grandchildren never felt an evening in the mountains at all complete without the treat. Lauren had insisted that they were absolutely correct.

"How can you say we're camping out in the woods and not toast marshmallows over those great coals?"

Eventually, the added chill from the wind and their need to constantly move their chairs to avoid smoke brought the evening to a close.

"Why don't you go get your things together for the bathroom, and I'll get our bed ready."

She passed by him with her towel, washcloth and toothbrush and tapped him on the shoulder. "Would you hand me a flashlight? And don't forget to douse water on the coals when you finish with the bed."

He vividly recalled that there had been no hesitation on her part about engaging in love making. How could he forget her expressions of devotion and exclamations of ecstasy? It had ended in a wonderful, deep sleep for both of them.

Now, as Ted lay in his own bed, still disturbed by the abruptly terminated dinner, his mind continued to follow the events of the following morning in the mountains. She'd been standing on the deck flooded with the welcome morning sun, sipping a cup of coffee. They had finished their breakfast of cereal with strawberries and melon slices. Ted had rolled up the double sleeping bag and converted their bed back into kitchen seats. He was seated in the semi-shade under an overhanging limb with coffee. Her voice had startled him with its sharpness.

"My interest in you is money and sex. And your interest in me is sex and having a young woman as a companion."

"Well," Ted replied to her matter of fact statements, "if you say so. But I don't believe what I'm hearing."

She had turned without further comment and deposited her cup in the kitchen. Ted was standing as she came through the trailer door. He needed to change the subject.

"How about a hike up the creek? It will take less than an hour and a half."

"No, I don't think so. Why don't we drive out to the lake and take a shorter walk there? Isn't there an old logging road that leads over the mountain? We could explore it. I'd also like to go out in the boat if the wind isn't too strong."

He had quickly agreed, almost desperate to do something physical. Maybe Lauren would recant her blunt statement about money and sex.

Lying in bed now, he tried but couldn't remember much of the discussions during their forty-five minute walk up the rock strewn, rutted remnants of a road. He did recall how delighted she had been with the wild flowers, and how she had stooped to examine many tiny blooms.

The small streams passing through broken culverts under the road had seemed to fascinate her. They had challenged each other in throwing rocks at a dead tree stump, and finally reached the level where they could have an unobstructed view of the lake. He had put his arm around Lauren and momentarily drew her close to him. She did the same and added a reassuring smile.

"Let's forget the boat ride. We can take our lunch back to camp and eat it there. In a way it will help me if I get home early enough to do some work. Do you mind?"

Truthfully, though he wouldn't say so, he had felt relieved.

Mornings, even with limited rest, always seemed to give him a clearer outlook. Difficult situations felt less ominous in the light. Ted's spirits were buoyed with some coffee, fruit and toast, along with half an hour with the morning paper. He couldn't shake the feeling of being unfairly pressured the night before, however. How would he best handle her ridiculous demand for a hundred thousand dollars? He thought too of what she had said in the mountains: "My interest in you is money and sex."

Around mid-morning, with no call from her and no wave from her window, he walked across the street and through the side gate into Lauren's back yard. He found her working at the patio table as he had hoped. She welcomed him with a smile. After casual greetings she was the first to approach last night's touchy subject.

"It won't be necessary for you to leave me something in your will. That was dumb of me."

"Thanks. I'll admit I was floored when you brought it up last night. You've always been reluctant to accept money from me, but also delighted when I've surprised you with little gifts of cash. You almost knocked me off my feet with that high-powered demand."

Without waiting for her response, Ted continued, "If our relationship continues, I'm sure you'll know that I'll give you some help and some surprises through the years. There can be nothing concrete because neither of us knows what lies ahead. I may die or become incapacitated. You may run across a younger guy who you just can't live without."

"I've told you before," Lauren said with a smile at him, "I'm not looking."

He wasn't sure how to feel. It was a relief to have this potential crisis behind them. Every slight disagreement recently, though, seemed to include a reference to his age. She had to be dwelling on this issue more and more. Ted wished so badly that he could look young in her eyes. He knew he felt young when he was with her.

Neither held back with a deep kiss and warm embrace. She sat down and picked up a pencil, looking expectantly at him. It was her signal that the conversation was over. He knew he had a lot more to say, but she would have to open the door.

"I'll let you get back to work. Maybe you'll be up for having dinner this week. Let me know."

THIRTEEN   A Special Friend

"The only reason I'm going is because you're pushing me."

Lauren wasn't smiling as she buckled her seat belt in Ted's Explorer and prepared to start her half of the two-hour, thirty-minute drive to his lake and trailer. They had made plans more than a week earlier to spend an overnight. She had suggested it be a Friday-Saturday trip, leaving her Sunday to prepare for the next week's classes.

Now they were down to a single day. Lauren's Friday work had been pushed so late that night travel would be necessary. Ted could visualize only four hours for them to be on the lake or enjoying the camp. He had settled for that because he felt a need to have some uninterrupted time with her.

"I think you'll be glad you took Saturday off. You shouldn't have to work all weekend! Besides, we need the time to talk about a number of things."

Up until the moment Lauren showed up with her final bag of travel items, he was fearful she would back out. She had been visibly upset and depressed during the week, and had told him it was because her fall classes were changed at the last minute; she went from a schedule she liked to one she didn't like; and, she had an argument with her department chairperson when she accused him of favoring other teachers.

Ted tried during the week to keep their conversations positive, but hadn't succeeded. She was stressed and told him she had cramps, which made him wonder if maybe they should postpone the mountain trip. However, he reasoned he would have few other opportunities to discuss their fading romance. He wasn't ready for it to collapse even though he saw signs of this happening. There had to be something Lauren would respond to favorably unless she wanted to drop everything and just return to being neighbors. He doubted that she wanted such a drastic change.

For the first hour, neither said much. He changed tapes without her prompting. The Harry Belafonte tunes were favorites of both of them, as was the Kenny G tape. The latter had almost played through by the time they reached the half-way point and stopped to change drivers.

Lauren turned off the engine and turned to Ted.

"We need to talk about our relationship before we get there. I don't want to ruin our time at the lake."

Relieved that Lauren wanted to talk, but timid from memories of sharp exchanges that had raised his doubts if any future with her could be worked out, he responded immediately to her request.

"Yes, I want that too, Lauren. I have a couple of ideas that I need to run by you. If you like any of them, it might keep our relationship going."

"That's good because I thought you were going to tell me you wanted to end it."

"End it? How could you think I would do that? Surely you know that I cherish you far too much, unless there's no other answer."

He didn't have to wait long for her rejoinder. Lauren apparently wanted something resolved as much as he did.

"Let me tell you what I think first," she said.

He made a quick resolve to hear her out and not to interject his own thoughts. Maybe she would open the door for him to express an idea he had considered proposing.

"I think we're seeing too much of each other. It seems that every time we have dinner together, it ends in a fight. I need to spend some time with other friends and get away from you more. I need more space," she said. "For example, when Ellen and I are talking about going to a play or a movie, I always feel that I have to ask you. You don't have friends to pal around with, and we don't want you to be left out, so we ask you to join us."

Ted was so puzzled he felt he had to interrupt.

"Let's clear up one thing, Lauren. It never occurred to me that you asked me to join you because you didn't want me to be left out. I enjoy going out but would sometimes just as soon not go. For gosh sakes, if you want to do things with your friends, please do them. You need a social life too."

She continued as if she hadn't heard him. "Ellen and I have talked about going to the mountains in December for a ski weekend, but worried that not asking you would hurt your feelings."

"Just to reassure you, Lauren, I can't think of much I'd rather not do than drive over icy roads. I'm not even a skier." Ted started up the car, left the rest area and began the second half of the drive.

"I want to come over sometimes and have sex with you and travel to places with you, but we're spending too much time together. We don't need to have dinner at your house so often. It stresses me on top of the stress I already have. These last few days, when we haven't seen much of each other, I've been more relaxed."

Ted continued to drive and listen as she covered much of the same area over again. At times she seemed to be pleading. When he thought she had fully expressed herself, he waited another minute while gathering his own thoughts. Was she really telling him she wanted to see less of him? Or was she under more stress than he had realized, and this was affecting her decisions? He knew it was now his turn to speak.

"I want to go through a couple of options I believe we have, even one that's rather far out."

"Far out? That's a nineteen sixties expression. What are you talking about, 'far out'?"

"Patience, patience; please give me time. Probably it isn't far out, but just unusual. You've told me often that I don't always choose the right word."

He sensed a spark of interest as well as evident concern over what he was about to propose.

"We've been on a sort of day-by-day basis in our relationship since the last bunch of arguments. My suggestion is that we try to look ahead for a definite period of time. I was thinking of six months. That would put us at the end of February after Valentine's Day and my birthday."

Ted concentrated for a minute until he cleared a section of heavy traffic and then glanced sideways at her. Lauren appeared to be studying him but said nothing. He continued:

"As I explain my idea more completely, I would ask that you accept as being true that I'm not a man to make casual remarks about money. I'm sure I've proven that to you."

"Your mentioning money doesn't make me feel good. I don't have to have money from you."

Ted nodded and continued. It was a denial he had expected.

"Please hear me out. I have to remind myself, and you, that feelings may have changed between us. Yes, you assured me repeatedly during our first year together that you had no interest in money. You wanted to make sure my children understood that too. I loved and respected you for that strong feeling you had about your independence. I am sure your feelings were genuine, Lauren. This made it easy for me to give you those few money gifts I've surprised you with. You know my feelings about people who ask for money. They're very negative.

But now I have to consider our new position on this. You jolted me hard about a month ago when you announced that your interest in me was money and sex."

"I regret ever having said that!"

"But you did, and neither of us had been drinking, even. We were having what I felt was a very special morning." He continued with a hint of sadness in his voice. "We were standing on the mountain deck after breakfast. You followed that statement with another that really bothered me. You said that my interest in you was 'just having a young woman as a companion, and sex.'"

Lauren nodded slightly but said nothing.

"I was taken aback and didn't know how to respond. But that is behind us now. In looking ahead, I don't have anything but good thoughts about being able to help you out with a little money. I'm determined to do something that helps us look ahead and know what to expect. Both of us need to feel that we come out as winners if any relationship is worthwhile. Right now, both of us are frustrated, at least I am." Again she nodded but remained quiet.

"My proposal is that our relationship terminate at the end of six months. It may not last even that long, because we aren't getting along well. But if it did, and for my part I surely hope it does, our deal will be over, allowing each of us to take a fresh look."

Lauren almost exploded.

"That's no good at all! It can't work! Supposing we're very much in love, and then you say we suddenly would mean nothing to each other? I don't like it one bit!"

"Who said we'd have to stop meaning a lot to each other? I said the relationship would stop after six months so we could both look at what we had. We could renew it for another period. We could change the rules. It would give us the break needed and the chance to review how we feel." Ted was beginning to feel strength in his argument. "What in hell is wrong with that? It would end this crap of dragging along, each of us wondering what the other really wants. It's been awful for me and I know you've lost a lot of sleep too."

"I think you're talking about sex. That bothers me. You know I like to have sex with you when I feel like it. I don't like your idea of having so many things planned and on a schedule."

"Of course I'm talking partly about sex. Why shouldn't I? It's been a wonderful part of what's held us together for these two years. Why shouldn't it be part of any plan we talk about now?"

He took her silence to mean that she wasn't cutting off his entire proposal but at the same time not endorsing it, so he continued with his plan.

"The other main part of the plan deals with those continuous arguments that keep tearing us apart. If we don't find a way to stop or change these discussions before they become bitter exchanges, nothing is going to work. If these outbursts continue, all of the sex you could give me will be worth nothing. I'll walk away if we can't resolve them."

"You start some of the arguments too! It's not all my fault." Lauren almost exploded and then settled back, adding, "It's especially when you drink hard liquor. You change, but you don't know it."

He'd heard this argument before. He always assured her that he spaced his two pre-dinner drinks over an hour or two period and that they couldn't possibly figure into a belligerent attitude change. He saw the slight buzz as a pleasant atmosphere while he was reading, writing, or starting preparations for dinner. Ted knew that his use of alcohol probably much exceeded hers, but had observed that when Lauren did drink, she crowded the drinks into a short period of time. This situation often had preceded some of their worst arguments. He saw nothing to gain by reminding her of this, though, and decided to take a different approach.

"Look, Lauren, as much as I don't agree that two drinks spaced over a reasonable time is a factor in our arguments, I'll cut it to one or even none if I know you're coming over for dinner. That would be no chore at all. I'm just forced to tell you that my interest in any relationship with you will end if those arguments don't stop."

She picked up with off-handed remarks about his buzz being a sign of alcoholism, then hesitated and seemed to want to lessen the impact of her attack.

"I know I completely change with a little too much alcohol and become a very difficult person. Have you noticed that I've hardly had anything to drink at your house since our last big argument?"

He acknowledged this, and added a compliment about her great job quitting smoking as well. Ted knew she had more to say so drove in silence and waited.

"You don't know how much pressure I'm under with all of these situations coming at once, including the pressure I'm under with you."

He assured her that he understood that some of the difficulties she faced, especially with her job, could be stressful to her. They were approaching Donner Summit.

"How often do you want sex?" she asked.

"I'd like to think that once a week would be just great. Once in a while we might choose to make it several times. We have before, when you get those nice horny urges. Just being with you makes me want to play with you. You know how desirable I find you to be."

He glanced at Lauren expectantly but found her gazing at the high mountain scenery. He decided to continue.

"We've talked before about our time together being a fair shake for both of us. I realize that a couple of your friends have pressured you to look at your future with me differently. My hope is that you would feel a little more at ease, especially as you handle your job, if you were able to count on me for a little financial assistance on a somewhat planned basis. That assumes our romance hangs together, and I surely hope it does. I see the fights as the big hurdle. We will both need to figure out a way not to let them happen. They alone have almost ruined our nice relationship."

He drove in silence again. She inserted a Garth Brooks tape in the player but seemed to purposefully keep the volume down. He reached over and rested his hand on her knee for a few seconds.

In another fifteen minutes they had reached the final three-mile stretch of dirt road. Lauren looked across and smiled slightly. This time he squeezed her hand but couldn't think of anything appropriate to say. He didn't want to reopen the discussion. He opened the locked gate and began the half-mile drive through his club's property. She rolled down the window.

"Everything smells so good. Why do all of the little evergreens look so healthy?"

"They react well to lots of winter rain and snow, and we've had plenty of both for two years now. That's the most likely reason. Don't you just love that warm sun coming through the open areas between the trees?"

"Yes. And that's going to be welcome out on the lake. I can see some breeze moving the tree branches. Will we see any deer?"

"It isn't likely, not unless they come down to the edge of the lake for a drink later this afternoon. Most deer are bedded down in the shade somewhere now."

They stopped briefly at the camp. He unlocked the trailer door.

"We only need two folding chairs and a couple of life jackets. If you'll get them I'll get the table and my fishing rod. Your suggestion of having lunch out in the boat is sounding better all the time. I'm getting hungry."

Fifteen minutes later, they were parked within fifty feet of the lake. Ted headed for the row boat with the ice chest in one hand and the life jackets under an arm. Lauren stopped at the water's edge.

"What an absolutely perfect day! I can't see a person around. We're going to have your lake all to ourselves." Then, looking at Ted as he turned the boat over, "Why are you in such a rush? I want to enjoy myself in this warm sun or a few minutes, and then I'll help you. Besides, you have to rub some sunscreen on my shoulders and back. I want to take advantage of being here by ourselves."

He obediently took the proffered tube of sunscreen and waited while she removed her blouse. He pretended to accidentally touch her bra-covered breasts, which brought a teasing rebuke:

"Come on now, Ted, pay attention to your work."

They set up the table and chairs in a shaded area. Together they lifted the boat to the water's edge and then pushed it partway into the lake. He held the boat steady while Lauren climbed in and seated herself. He then hopped in and at the same time pushed the craft into deeper water.

They quietly rowed to the center of the lake. She removed her shoes and socks and held her feet out to him to apply sunscreen. Ted rinsed his hands in the clear water and dried them on a paper towel. He pulled a small carafe of wine from the ice chest.

"Would you like a cup of wine?"

"No, thank you," she said. "Would you fish out a soda for me from the ice?"

They ate their lunch while rowing slowly or drifting. Talk was limited to comments about the surroundings. They made a game of traveling close to the shore for a glimpse of the family of ducks. They saw only one.

"We'll have to use our imagination," Lauren said. "That duck scrambling up the bank and into the grass had to be a parent following her family into a safe hiding place."

"I've been watching these families of geese for about twenty years," Ted said, "Even when this lake is accessible in early June, the geese are always here ahead of us. There's snow all around, but it seems to have no effect on them. That means the adults had to fly in while the snow was still heavy. Can you imagine them having to build nests and protect their eggs under those awful conditions?"

They continued to row slowly and explore some of the more hidden inlets around the lake. "Your shoulders are starting to get pink," he teased.

"What time is it?"

He glanced at his watch. "It's about three. We can go in anytime you'd like. You did say that you didn't want to get home late because there is still work you need to do."

"This is too nice. I'm not ready to pull the anchor yet," Lauren said. "Let's travel completely around that part of the shoreline over there." She pointed to a shallow part of the lake with tall pines coming almost to the water.

Ted rowed slowly, carefully avoiding the overhanging limbs along the lake's edge. Finally, she was ready to stop. They pulled the boat up on the beach, unloaded it, and then turned it upside down. She put on her blouse, moved a chair to a semi-shaded area and soon was engrossed in reading the morning paper they'd brought along.

Ted baited a hook, cast out to where he knew there was a fairly deep channel and joined her. Lauren continued to read for almost an hour with no interruption from him except when he jumped up to respond to a savage jerk on his rod.

"Looks like we're going to have trout fillets for dinner one day next week!"

An excited Ted noticed that she kept her face buried in the newspaper each time he drew another exhausted fish up onto the gently sloping beach. What a contrast, he thought. My grandsons gather around and insist on helping to clean the fish. They want to know what each part is and want to feel it. This time he took his four trout into the woods, cleaned them, rinsed them in the lake and then stowed them in a tightly closed bag under the ice in their chest. Lauren agreed that it was time to go home.

They quickly reloaded the truck and made the five minute drive to the camp. Ted unloaded the few items and locked the trailer while she made a trip to the bathroom. He climbed into the driver's seat. "If it's okay, I'll take the first half of the drive home, and we can change at the rest stop," he said. "No, I want to take the first half. That way I can get it over with!"

He was surprised and puzzled. Lauren had driven the more sharply graded half of the drive only once and had declared she was uneasy and didn't want to try it again. However, he saw no benefit to quizzing her. It was an uneventful first hour. Ted observed that she seemed to have overcome any nervousness and handled the heavy Saturday afternoon traffic well. He found himself enjoying watching the familiar sights and landmarks along the highway. He suddenly remembered that he had purposefully brought along a small book that Lauren had given to him early in their romance, and wanted to read some of it to her. Now, with only thirty minutes left of her drive time, Ted felt a sense of urgency, and quickly took it out of the glove compartment.

"I brought along your friendship book and want to read some of it to you. Would you like that?"

"Yes, what a thoughtful idea."

He opened the book, glanced at Lauren momentarily, and then began to read.

"'My friend, you never expect too much from me. You are glad when I succeed, but failure makes no difference to you. You give me all the help you can, but more important, you are simply there.'"

"And here's another one from the same author: 'A friend never says I told you so even when she did.' Do you remember that you underlined the word 'she'?"

Lauren's quick smile was enough, but she added, "I surely do."

Ted turned to another page: "'Friends stay friends because they don't mess about in each others' lives.'"

"I don't like that one very much."

Ted felt he could understand why. She had a habit of wanting to give solutions to everyone else's problems whether asked for or not. He couldn't help but chuckle to himself but made no comment.

"'Silences make the real conversations between friends. Not the saying, but the never needing to say is what counts.' Margaret Lee Runbeck is that author. There's no indication of the years she lived. You inserted a check mark and wrote in the margin. It says 'that's you.' I appreciated that you did that." Ted paused and then asked, "Do I really?"

A faint smile crossed her face, but she didn't respond. He reached across and softly brushed her knee.

"Friends do not live in harmony merely as some say, but in melody'. That was way back by Henry David Thoreau, who lived between 1817 and 1862. His wasn't a very long life. You put two musical notes and a smile sign next to this one. We were making lots of nice music together then, weren't we? Do you remember all of those wonderful nights by the fireplace?"

"Of course."

Soon they changed drivers, and in an hour they were home. Lauren reached over and squeezed Ted's hand.

"Thanks, you're nice."

They parted, agreeing not to have dinner together. She wanted the extra hour for school preparation. Ted was relieved. He wanted time to think through a written proposal he might lay out to convince Lauren that it was worthwhile to try and rebuild a closer relationship with him.

She seemed to bristle at money suggestions coming from him, but at the time his gifts, sometimes generous, had been given, she seemed to welcome them enthusiastically. Yes, he was sure he could put together a timetable of relations and at least reference money that she could anticipate getting.

Finally, before he went to bed, Ted had it mostly planned. He would put it in writing for Lauren. It would be a plan, an outline of his dreams involving her, all carefully squeezed into the six month period ahead. It had to be worth the effort because she hadn't directly said No.

It took only an hour the next morning and the letter was completed. He had to wait for the florist to open, but was there to select a fresh bunch of carnations when the clerk unlocked the door.

When he walked over to deliver his letter and flowers, she told him that she feared his letters, sometimes waiting hours before opening them.

Don't be afraid of my letter," he said. "You will enjoy this one."

After an embrace and a kiss, he left as she poured another cup of coffee and began to arrange the carnations.

> *Dear Lauren,*
> *I wouldn't write this letter except that I'm desperate*
> *to find a way to make our relationship run more smoothly.*

I don't want to lose your affection but I can't stand being bruised so often.

I'm not certain what you want. You send mixed signals. You first brought up money and sex some time ago at my mountain place. Then you came on with that high-powered demand a week or so ago. I appreciate the fact that you tempered those remarks the next day and told me you had been pushed by your well-meaning friends.

I care for you a great deal, Lauren, and your financial comfort has become important to me. You know that. I like to support winners, not losers. You've proven to me that you can be a winner. I like your style! You need to keep as many doors open as you can in your quest for full- time work in your educational field. I know you'll make it.

As long as you're thinking in terms of money, I want you to know that this doesn't really bother me. We just need to be honest.

I'm planning to give you two-thousand dollars around Thanksgiving. It's my way of telling you that I'm very thankful that you came into my life. Please don't forget that.

You said a few days ago that you regretted ever allowing yourself an intimate relationship with me. How can you say that? It's been wonderful, I believe, for both of us. We know we'll eventually have to accept the pain of separation, however it occurs. In the meantime, don't you agree we both need something nice to anticipate, to look forward to?

I want to take you back to Cabo for a week around Christmas if we hold together that long. You have asked several times about my getting reservations, and I've held up until now because I was scared you might suddenly walk out of my life. I need to feel your commitment.

Valentine's Day has come to be special in our lives. Something nice seems to happen between us at that time. I dream of giving you a little surprise then.

One gift that won't depend on our continuing to regularly make love to each other is a two-thousand dollar contribution towards your student loan. That will be yours around year-end as long as you have kept up paying your loan payments each month. I realize that this loan hangs threateningly over your head, but you needed it to get your degrees. I love and admire you so much for the effort you put into completing college. I know you have to save elsewhere to make those payments, and I do insist on helping.

You have said a number of times that you like a man with a plan. I am such a guy, Lauren, and I hope I can continue to be that man in your eyes.

I believe our best chance of getting through these next six months was your suggestion that I intervene forcefully and early when an argument seems imminent. I will also, as you suggested, remind you that you wanted me to do so. I too, promise to stop short myself rather than add fuel to an already tense situation. ~ Ted

FOURTEEN   Bittersweet Holidays

Ted wasn't at all sure about Lauren's response to what he had come to call his six-month letter. She had made no reference to it at any of the meetings since, but he felt that curiosity alone must have prompted her to read it. He was still uneasy about Lauren's spur-of-the-moment demand for one-hundred-thousand dollars for two years with her, but he was trying to regain confidence that their romance had more going for it than just money and sex. Hadn't she also said she regretted the situation only because she had fallen in love with him?

He saw no point in crowding Lauren for a response to his letter. If she concluded that she was being pressured, he was certain of a negative reply, which would be worse than none at all. It was much better that he wait for her to mention it. Ted complimented himself on his patience. He rather liked the expression, "the ball is in your court."

Lauren was on a regular early class schedule, and he didn't miss an opportunity to be out front to blow her a kiss as she sped off to work.

One Wednesday morning, Ted left early for a single day of trout fishing with a long time friend, Carl. Their friendship dated back to their work for the same company. It had become a firm tie, and a relationship that his wife had enjoyed with Carl and his wife.

Ted had taken Lauren for a dinner visit with the two on one occasion about six months earlier. He had viewed the meeting as a success and a good indication that his older friends would accept her role in his life. He recalled having written to Carl within a few months after meeting Lauren, and referring to her as "His Polish Bombshell."

Today he met his friend at a local restaurant parking lot. They transferred Carl's fishing gear, warm jackets and lunch to Ted's Explorer. It was almost seven-thirty when they had completed a light breakfast and were in the truck headed for the Sierra.

Ted expected Carl's first question: "How are you and Lauren doing? We only met her that one time in Stockton for dinner. Ida and I thought she was sharp, pretty, and a lot of fun."

"I guess you could say we're doing okay. She's sometimes a little unpredictable. Right now she's teaching several new classes and I have my speeches to give, so we won't see as much of each other as we did during the summer."

Carl looked at him questioningly.

"I don't mean to pry, but you sound a little hesitant. She's not wearing you out, is she Ted?"

"Not in the way you might think, but she does wear my patience thin sometimes."

They were at the lake by ten-thirty. Ted rowed the boat to a spot where he knew the water was quite deep. He threw out the bow anchor and instructed Carl to drop the stern anchor once he saw the one off the bow was holding. A brisk wind made Ted glad they both had warm jackets.

He was delighted to find trout start almost immediate action on both rods. This wasn't going to be a day of being skunked.

"This is terrible," Ted said. "They won't even give us a chance to open a can of beer!"

His friend was equally ecstatic as he carefully led a tiring trout towards Ted's waiting net.

"You'll spoil a guy. I only fish this one time each year, but have always taken home a nice limit."

By two o'clock, the five-fish limits were cleaned and iced. They set up a folding table near the water. Carl laid out the lunch Ida had made for the two men while Ted brought two camp chairs from the truck.

"You can see why I always eat a light breakfast. Be sure and tell Ida how much I enjoy her lunches," Ted said.

Carl held up his glass of orange juice and proposed a toast. Ted followed with his.

"Here's to friendship, without qualifications."

Thanksgiving Day dinner was scheduled for his son's house. When Susan asked if Lauren would be attending, Ted confidently assured his daughter-in-law that she would be. He tried to be as casual with Kathy during his next visit, now only three weeks ahead of the big family holiday.

"I meant to mention it earlier, but I've asked Lauren to join us at Matt's for Thanksgiving. She's excited about going."

His daughter didn't protest. Instead, she said, "I love you Daddy, and I'm not going to make an issue of this. You know how I feel, but if Matthew says it's okay, it's his house. I just wish Lauren could have her family close by to spend this special day with."

He called Lauren as soon as he returned home and fixed a drink.

"We're all set for Thanksgiving. We'll be driving to Matt's. I took the liberty of accepting the invitation for you. I hope that's all right. Are you still free to go?" He continued without waiting for an answer. "They're planning on an early dinner so we can drive home that same night. Kathy's family will be staying over. It's only four hours, and we can stop at a motel if we find ourselves too tired to drive all the way home."

"I can handle that. I'm looking forward to seeing your son's place and meeting his family. Let's just make sure we don't drink very much so we can both share the drive home. I don't know how you handled Kathy, but thanks. I know she'll like me if she just gives us a chance."

Ted's relief was apparent.

"That's great. I know she will, too. I mostly wanted you to know that I've been working on this the best I can. I'm so glad you'll be a part of my family for Thanksgiving this year."

Their drive south to Delano, located just a few miles north of Bakersfield, was uneventful. Thanksgiving morning traffic was light. Lauren seemed to be at ease driving the heavy car as far as Merced where they stopped for lunch. They arrived ahead of Edward and Kathy's family. Ted took advantage of the half hour to make sure that each of his son's family had a few minutes with Lauren. His grandson, Charles was shy at first but soon became more responsive when she asked him several questions about school sports.

Julie welcomed her openly, and they were soon sharing opinions about hairdos and boys. Ted enjoyed half-listening to their patter and laughter. He sensed that he had more than one sure ally.

Lauren welcomed Susan's request that she take charge of setting the big table. Stacks of dinner, salad, and bread plates were at one end.

"You've now met everyone, Lauren, so I'll also let you decide the seating." She pointed to a tray of black and orange cardboard turkeys with a family member's name printed on each.

"Just put Matt at one end of the table and Grandpa at the other." She thought for a moment. "Oh, yes, don't put all of the kids together. They will have plenty of visiting time after we eat."

Ted excused himself from visiting with his son to take a quick tour around the long table. Lauren's nameplate was directly across the table from Kathy's. He gave Lauren a smile and a thumbs up. Susan came in and took Lauren away into the kitchen asking her another favor.

As soon as they were all seated, and after Matthew's welcoming toast, Lauren spoke:

"What lovely nameplates. Did you have an artist make them for the family?" She smiled at the children. Kathy smiled at Lauren and winked.

Charles and Julie smiled bashfully before Julie spoke: "We made them."

"My, aren't they professional looking,' Lauren said. "Great job."

Ted began the drive back to Sacramento about eight. He was mentally comparing this holiday with so many others shared with his son and daughter's families. He felt good about Lauren fitting in so well during this first real opportunity she had had to be in the group as his partner. Even Kathy had seemed relaxed during the several conversations he had noticed her having with Lauren.

After thirty-five years, his wife had given up hosting Thanksgiving dinner for her family. Their two children had volunteered to alternate having the event at their homes five years prior to her death. He smiled as he recalled that his wife always had insisted that she furnish the turkey, or at least pay its cost. He had privately handed his daughter in law a check and had the usual honor of being asked to carve the succulent bird. Yes, it had been a good day for the patriarch of the family.

Ted slept soundly after their midnight arrival home, and was up at seven to pen out a special note to Lauren. Shortly after nine he entered the bank to pick up a cashier's check for two thousand dollars. He stopped on his way home to select a small bouquet of carnations from the florist. Then he tried to be patient while he waited for Lauren's kitchen light to show. At ten thirty the light had been on for fifteen minutes. He walked across the street with the flowers and a card with the note and check enclosed.

"What a wonderful surprise— flowers to go with that nice Thanksgiving trip! I had a great sleep."

She dropped the card on the counter and began arranging the flowers. Ted winced.

He accepted an offer for a late cup of coffee. They talked about reactions of his family and the enjoyable feast for at least fifteen minutes. Then, he excused himself and left. His note had read:

Dear Lauren,

I want you to know that I'm thankful you came into my life when you did. I'm thankful too, that you're still here, almost a year and a half later. I hope you feel the same way.

You told me you had read my letter with its six month timetable, but you haven't indicated whether you saw it with favor or disfavor. Do I dare ask?

I'm thankful that we've done better where arguments are concerned. They're still painful when they happen but there have been fewer.

Am I thankful that you have continued to find time for our lovemaking? What better time is there than thanksgiving to assure you of this?

In my letter, I promised you two thousand dollars at Thanksgiving. Here it is with my blessing. -Ted

FIFTEEN   Mexico Revisited

As he had promised in his six-month letter, Ted had put all the plans in place for a second trip to Cabo San Lucas. It was scheduled for the day after Christmas, but the holiday began badly. On Christmas morning, Lauren's cockatiel, Buddy, squeezed by her through a partially opened front door as she leaned over to pick up the newspaper.

He had suddenly noticed her through his kitchen window, standing in the middle of the street, and then heard her frightened calls.

"Quick, Quick! Buddy's flown away."

As he rushed to the door, she was pointing down the street. Ted saw nothing in the sky, only this lovely woman, now sobbing quietly. What an awful way to begin Christmas! As much as he wanted to stop and console her, he reacted quickly.

"Why don't you watch for him on our street? I'll take the truck and drive over to the next street. It was the direction you were pointing."

He ran into his house for a jacket, jumped into the truck, and was away in the icy morning air, seeing only Lauren's frantic, hurt expression.

Ted's thoughts were in turmoil. How could this happen? Why did it have to happen on Christmas morning, just a day before leaving on their trip? Things seemed to be going so well between them, and now this! His thoughts weren't focused on the lost bird, rather, he was concerned about her and how it would affect their plans.

Two hours later he drove back into his driveway. Ted had walked slowly up and down the length of the adjacent street several times, occasionally whistling a sound that Buddy always seemed to respond to at her house. In between whistles he had listened intently. Even a further walk up and

135

back on the short street alongside their area park had produced no sign of her bird. Lauren was still standing numbly in the street when he drove up. She walked over to the truck.

"I should have known Buddy would follow me to the door. Now, he's gone! I knew it was past time to have his wings clipped," she said.

Tears welled up again. Ted put his arm around his neighbor and quietly outlined the route he had taken in the search.

"I haven't a clue about where else to look unless we go on a backyard search of every home within a quarter mile. Buddy may well be in one of those yards. He couldn't stay in the air very long. I'm so sorry your Christmas Day has been ruined like this."

He handed her his handkerchief. Lauren thanked him and wiped away the residue from the tears.

"I'm not going to be able to join your family this afternoon when they come for Christmas. I'll be all right, but want to be by myself. I know they will understand."

"Yes, they will, but I'll count on you to come over and have a little to eat with us later on. Dinner is usually about six. I'll call you."

Ted went to his house and she slowly entered hers, seeming to hate getting out of her cockatiel's possible sight.

Early in the afternoon, he again saw Lauren in the street, now pointing up into a high tree two houses away, on his side. She was alternately calling for him to "come quickly" and then repeating a series of whistles.

"There he is! There's Buddy! Can you see him in that tall tree? He's answering my whistle."

There was no question that it was her pet. Although the bird could be seen cocking its head in response, it never moved from its high perch. Ted joined in, and their efforts continued for ten minutes. Somehow he knew that Buddy would hop from the limb and come gliding to their feet.

Then suddenly, her bird did leave the tree but flew high and rapidly east down their street and was soon gone from sight.

That was the last they saw of Buddy. Ted made another careful search among the trees in their nearby park in the direction the bird had flown, but it netted nothing.

He returned home a few minutes ahead of the arrival of the first carload of family members. Lauren wasn't in sight. He knew she was in her room crying. He was also sure that she loved him for trying to help. Ted decided there was nothing to gain from injecting himself into her misery.

She did join his family for dinner but ate little and excused herself shortly afterwards. His family listened to her story but could offer little support.

She called him after everyone had left. "Thank you for spending so much time trying to find Buddy. If you don't mind, I won't be coming over. I'm expecting some calls from my family and still have quite a lot of stuff to pack."

The morning after Christmas, Ted spent two hours walking through the park and the playground area trying to identify Buddy from among numerous other birds enjoying their morning in the tall trees. How could this disaster possibly have happened to her? Why did it have to come just before a trip she was anticipating so much? They would be leaving in a few hours.

Their plans were to drive to San Francisco that afternoon to be ready for the early morning flight to Mexico. They were to take Lauren's car, and she was to do the driving. Ted had taken the car down for a tank of fuel. He was packed and impatient to go.

She emerged from her house with four cardboard sheets in her hand.

"Can we take time to put these up on posts around the neighborhood? I've marked them with Buddy's description and my phone number. The message machine will take any calls. I've also put an ad in the paper. I know that Buddy is lost and probably froze last night, but there might be a chance someone will find him and see the posters or the ad. I just can't leave without doing something. I feel terrible about is as it is."

"Absolutely, Lauren. Let's go! I'll grab a hammer and some small nails. Will you get a roll of tape? It's a good suggestion and won't take us but a little while, and then we can go."

They toured the neighborhood and selected prominent wooden electrical poles or metal light standards. She held the posters in place while he pounded in the short nails or applied strips of tape. Then they quickly loaded luggage and made final checks of their houses. Lauren climbed into the driver's seat and gave him a warm smile through glassy eyes.

"Thanks for doing this with me."

He responded by gently touching her knee. They said little during the two hour drive until the question arose about which turnoff to take from the freeway to reach their motel. Ted smiled at her humorous directive and hoped she had relaxed somewhat with the drive.

"Give it to me right, this time! I'm sure you remember you had us heading back home last December."

He almost wished they were going home. He had made the reservations primarily to please Lauren. She seemed to love the idea of the entire trip, the overnight stay in San Francisco and even the long flight to Cabo San Lucas. He could understand her desire to live in the Mexican culture for another four days, but how pleasant it would be to be seated on his couch facing the glowing fireplace this evening. Lauren could be stretched out with an extra pillow to better see a favorite TV show. Her feet would be across his lap. He would be able to caress her feet and comfort her over today's loss.

She broke his reverie as she pulled into the motel entrance.

"Let's plan to eat early. I don't feel like much, but maybe they'll have some good soup and a salad. Is that okay?" Lauren looked sadly at Ted as he climbed out to register, and continued, "I feel so awful about poor Buddy. I know he'll freeze tonight if nobody finds him. I hope he dies quickly. I almost wish we hadn't left."

Ted knew some response was required.

"It will only take us a few minutes to get us all set here, then we can talk about dinner. I understand how broken up you are about Buddy, but we did everything we possibly could."

He reached across and squeezed her hand. "Wait right here."

They ate their dinner quietly at the restaurant bordering the motel grounds. She dressed for bed almost immediately afterwards. Ted propped himself up beside her but soon tired of watching the TV movie. He settled down onto a single pillow. "I've asked the desk to give us a five o'clock wake up call. Don't stay up too late. Goodnight."

She responded by touching his shoulder.

"Goodnight Ted. I'm not sleepy yet. See you in the morning. Make sure I get up."

The next morning, as they boarded the plane, Ted could see that a crowded charter plane had been substituted for the comfortable plane provided the year before. He sat in a narrow middle seat where there was no elbow room to turn the pages of his newspaper.

He envied Lauren's seeming ability to adapt quickly. She read her book by the window.

He read most of the short articles in the airline magazine. The man in the seat to his left busied himself through most of the flight studying what appeared to Ted to be a course in finances. Ted wished he'd thought to bring a book.

Two hours later, they were being escorted to the fourth floor room of their condo hotel.

"I thought you paid for a room with an ocean view and a veranda just like last time! The view's fine, but there's no balcony," she said. "Wait here. Don't unpack. I'm going to get this changed right now." She disappeared down the corridor.

Ted opened the sliding glass doors and listened to the sounds of activity several hundred yards away on the beach. He knew Lauren would use her Spanish effectively to get a room more to her liking. She wasn't one to easily accept refusals. Within minutes she was back followed by the porter.

"I got a change. I think it's exactly the same room on the second floor that we had last time. Let the porter take the two heavier bags. We can handle the others."

It was the same room. Ted immediately moved the small leather-covered table onto the balcony and then followed with the matching chairs. Lauren was examining the kitchen items.

"This coffee pot has a broken handle, and I see the candle in that nice chimney is all burned down. We'll want to use that tonight."

He was looking in the bathroom.

"The towel situation looks good," he said. "It will only take me a few minutes to track down a maid. Why don't you go ahead and start unpacking." He picked up the damaged coffee pot and candle stub and opened the door to the hallway.

"Don't worry about the maid not understanding English. She'll get the idea when I show her these."

When he returned with the replaced items, Lauren was playing a tape from the selection she'd brought. Ted could hear her humming softly as she arranged her clothes on the shelves. The cabanas along the beach hadn't begun their music. He relished the idea of a walk after sitting so long on the plane and shuttle bus.

"Do you think we have time to go shopping for the things we need for our stay?" He asked. He was a little surprised, though not disappointed by her response:

"Yes, but I'd rather not. I heard music coming from the bar down by the pool. We could have a margarita there before dinner." She looked at him for approval.

"Gosh, that suits me fine. Would you like to try out our hotel dining room afterwards? I was surprised to see it listed last year as a top place to eat here in Cabo. We just never got around to trying it."

Lauren grabbed him for a quick dance around the room to the beat of the music.

"I'm liking this already. Let me take the shower first."

Ted's voice followed her: "And we'll go down to The Office after dinner."

He was impatient to start their walk down the hilly dirt road to the beach. It was almost eight but there was a sparse crowd when they arrived. They were promptly seated. Ted tried to be philosophical.

"Maybe both the locals and tourists have exhausted their money and energy during Christmas."

The sand under their table was warm, and Lauren soon shed her footwear. After ordering their margaritas, he looked around, hoping to spot a trio of Mexican musicians. There were none in sight. He reminisced about the prior year's experience. Several times after returning home they had tickled friends and family members with their story of being conned by the two threesomes.

"You just don't understand Mexico!" was the unsympathetic response he'd received when relating his story. "They love to trick you Gringos with the fat wallets."

This evening none showed up at all. They found it pleasant, though, and enjoyed the music from a group on the stage. Lauren quickly struck up conversations with guests at the tables near them.

She seemed to love to identify herself as a Wisconsin Cheesehead. Ted felt relaxed and responded amicably when questions were directed to him.

She surprised him by wanting to cuddle and make love when they returned to their room. She had to be tired after being up since five that morning. Could she be doing this just for him? She couldn't be very upbeat with fresh memories of her lost cockatiel. Maybe it was her way of saying thank you to him for his effort at helping her through a personal crisis. Ted didn't ask. He sensed she knew, as a woman, when it was time to tailor her lovemaking to match special occasions. Did it really matter? He slept deeply.

He was the first to open the sliding doors to the veranda letting in the distant noise from the morning surf. They could very clearly hear the sounds of occasional small trucks and vans passing beneath their window. Lauren joined him, and they watched the increasing activity as workers, mostly women, joined the few vehicles on the narrow street.

"If I listen carefully, it's easy to get the gist of what they're saying. Some are talking about the work to be done today. One was telling the other about her boyfriend. I don't think he was very nice to her."

Ted pointed out a small cluster of birds in a tall palm tree across the street. They were chirping excitedly.

"Do you suppose they remember us from last year? Those cracker and bread crumbs we dropped didn't last long."

He put his arm around her, and together they watched the morning activity. He was thinking of the night before. Lauren turned and kissed him. They moved into the kitchen area together. Ted picked up a folder from the counter.

"I was looking at this menu from our restaurant downstairs. How would you like this Mexican egg dish for breakfast? I can go get it while you're having your cup of coffee and dressing."

"Wonderful! I'll share one with you. Will you get a couple of muffins while you're there and a little milk for my coffee? I can see we'd better do some shopping this morning."

Ted took the menu and called back as he opened the door: "I may not be able to say a word in Spanish, but I can surely point. They'll understand. I'll be back in about fifteen minutes."

Their grocery shopping was much simpler than before. Ted checked off the list as they loaded the cart. He was about to pick up the bags from the checkout counter when they were grabbed by a boy no older than ten, who then carried the bags to the door. Ted turned to Lauren.

"There's a hustler for you. Did you see the determined look on his face? And this is a school day. I just had to give him a couple of quarters although I hate to encourage truancy."

They carried the two bags to their room, agreeing not to take a cab, Ted found himself falling behind Lauren's brisk pace and wished silently that she would slow down. Instead, she stopped and waited each time for him to catch up.

His energy level rose upon their arrival in the room. He opened up a can of tomato juice and a beer for her and a can of beer for himself. "Red Beer" was a new term for him, but Lauren had assured him it was a standard beverage in Wisconsin.

She cut up a plate of fruit and cheese and added a stack of crackers. Ted was soon ready for more activity.

"Are we going to the beach this afternoon? This might be our best day because the snorkeling trip we looked at for tomorrow will pretty much fill that day."

They checked out some beach towels at the desk. Her enthusiasm seemed to match his.

"This will be a wonderful day to get some sun. Look at that sky! There isn't a cloud in sight."

They were soon tracing their steps of the prior year, moving down the beach a full three hundred yards from the noisy crowd. Ted rented an umbrella along the way. The sounds of the summer visitors and the constant flow of trinket vendors were soon behind them.

Lauren was first in the water while he positioned the umbrella and applied sunscreen to his shoulders and face. She was an accomplished swimmer and soon was churning through the buoyant salt water. Ted was surprised when her stay in the water lasted only a few minutes.

"It's really too cold for me. I'm going to stretch out on a towel and get a big dose of sunshine. Will you put lotion on my back?"

She handed Ted the plastic bottle. He carefully rubbed lotion on the areas Lauren indicated, gave her a pat on the bottom and announced that he was off for a swim.

Ted also thought the water was much colder than he remembered it and soon stretched out beside Lauren. He angled his body so that only his head was in the shade of the umbrella. The warmth was welcome. He ignored the likelihood of burning.

Lauren read all afternoon. He closed his eyes and stirred only when she asked that he apply lotion to her. He brushed off her suggestion that he do the same.

At the end of another hour they were underway on the long beach walk back to their room and welcome showers. He expected her to suggest another walk downtown, but Lauren had other ideas.

"Let's go down to the pool again. I met several couples yesterday but barely got to say hello. After all that nice sun, I'm also ready for a drink."

The chairs and lounges in the pool area were almost filled, but they were able to find a perfect spot with two lounge chairs, an umbrella, and a small circular table. Ted signaled the roving attendant and placed the order for two margaritas while Lauren went up to the bartender and asked him to turn up the volume of the music. Ted watched her at the bar talking with the young man behind it. She looked so youthful in her tropical island clothes. He moved his eyes from her to take in the other hotel bar patrons; other couples sat in pairs of chaise lounges around the ones they had selected. Young men and young women who looked mostly under forty years old. No one had white hair; everyone had smooth, evenly tanned skin. He was almost shocked to realize that he was the oldest man there by at least fifteen years. He shifted in his chair and smoothed the hair over his ears before scanning to find Lauren who was no longer at the bar. It took him a moment to find her, a moment where he almost panicked. She was chatting with a couple on her way back to their spot. She arrived back in her chair just ahead of the drink order and soon was in an animated conversation with the couple her age on the adjacent lounges.

When the margaritas arrived, she introduced Ted as her friend and neighbor. He responded cordially but with no added description about their relationship, although he wondered at Lauren's aloof way of introducing him; not as her boyfriend, which he supposed at his age would seem silly, not man-friend which, while more accurate, sounded awkward. What would he have had her say? My lover, Ted? That would have been too personal. In any case, Ted enjoyed watching the couple's obviously curious glances as they tried to decipher more about the relationship between this white haired man and young blonde.

Although little of the conversation seemed directed at him, Ted joined in with some of the humor when it seemed appropriate. For the most part, he listened and concentrated on looking pleasant and interested.

Two other guests joined them. Much of the talk revolved around hometowns, family sizes and make-ups and vacation experiences. When the conversation momentarily settled on where and when they went to high school, Lauren quickly changed the subject. Ted sensed that Lauren was becoming uneasy about their obvious age difference. He wondered how much it might further bother her as the afternoon developed. He almost wished she had suggested shopping. He made certain they had drinks to sip on and gave an affirmative nod to the circulating bar attendant to bring a tray of snacks.

Lauren had easily become the center of attention. Ted was content to lie back on the comfortable tilted lounge, enjoying the warmth and listening to the chatter. He fielded the occasional questions addressed to him but tried not to divert attention away from Lauren. He knew that she missed similar levels of social life at home. Her close friends were few, and his were a part of her parents' generation. Ted wished he were much younger.

Quite a few of the pool guests were gathering up their towels and personal items and leaving. He saw his opportunity to ask Lauren if it was time to go.

"If we leave within an hour, we can avoid walking to town in the dark. There's that place we enjoyed so much last year, the one that had the coconut prawns and some live music."

"Why can't we eat here? I think we can order hamburgers and fries from the hotel restaurant. I saw someone eating at the bar. Besides, I asked the bartender if I could bring down some of my music. He agreed to play the tapes."

Ted saw no reason to disagree. It would simplify their night. He nodded.

"Good idea. Let's go up to the bar and ask. We haven't had French fries in a long time. I'm not really hungry after all those snacks, but we could share a burger."

He climbed on a barstool and waited to get the man's attention. Lauren stood beside him.

"You go ahead and order our dinner while I run up and get some tapes. Tell them to bring lots of catsup. And I think I can handle one more margarita."

The bartender finished with his customer and turned pleasantly to Ted to receive his order. After ordering, Ted turned to face a man who had just occupied the stool to his left. He had remembered the man because he had thought the woman with him was physically unattractive. Ted had a close look at her as she flitted around the pool in very tight fitting shorts. He also thought the woman was drunk. He had avoided looking directly at her.

Ted smiled and introduced himself with an added observation that it was great to be in such a warm place in December.

The response was a grunted, "Hi, I'm Larry." The man turned and stared straight ahead tapping the bar with his fingertips.

Ted turned the other direction as a young woman climbed onto the stool to his right. He was about to tell her the seat was taken when she held out her hand.

"Hi. I'm Caroline. I've been noticing you and your friend. She's awfully pretty and seems to be having a lot of fun. My husband, Randy, is standing over there." She pointed to a dark haired man standing back alone at the other end of the bar, holding a drink. The light was dim, but Ted estimated the man to be in his mid-thirties. She smiled at Ted and shrugged, "He sometimes isn't very sociable."

Ted grinned back. "Well, hello. I'm Ted. My friend's name is Lauren. She doesn't have any trouble being sociable. Right now she's up in our room getting some tapes for the bartender to play. I think she plans to bring down Elton John, Linda Ronstadt and Kenny G." He paused. "Lauren is having a good time." At that moment, Lauren arrived with a handful of tapes.

"Hi. I see you've met my friend, Ted. I saw you by the pool. I'm Lauren."

Caroline slid over to the next stool, and Lauren climbed up between them. The bartender set down the pair of margaritas. Ted turned to the young woman. "May we buy you a drink?"

"Thanks, but no. My husband and I stayed here last night until the bar closed. I've had more than enough. But if it's okay, I'll just stay and visit for a little while."

The two women exchanged information about their jobs. By coincidence, it turned out that Caroline and her husband had recently moved to Sacramento within ten miles of Ted and Lauren's homes. The two exchanged phone numbers. He provided pages from a little notebook and a pen from his shirt pocket. Caroline excused herself when their dinner arrived.

Ted carefully divided the hamburger with the plastic knife. Lauren was already eating the French fries. She ate quickly and excused herself before Ted had finished. She picked up her drink.

"I've met some really nice people here and want to get back to visiting with them. Don't forget to eat all of those French fries. I won't be gone too long."

She gave Ted a quick kiss then was gone. He toyed with the potatoes, occasionally getting a glimpse of her eager face in the group at the end of the bar. He was surprised to find Caroline back on the stool beside him. Her smile seemed genuine. She touched his hand.

"I saw you were alone again. Do you mind if I visit with you?"

Ted offered again to buy her a drink. She again declined. He wasn't sure how to proceed but pushed back the residue of dinner and signaled for the bartender to remove the plates. He found Caroline to be a very attractive and easy person to talk with. It was her husband's second marriage and her first. He was happy to have the conversation centered around her.

"It isn't that we aren't getting along well. My husband just isn't one who likes to sit and talk about us. He's so preoccupied all the time, I almost get lonely."

"What brought you to Sacramento? It isn't considered the most exciting place to live."

"My husband is a computer technician and very good at it. His company transferred him to Sac. I was able to get a part time job as a librarian and still sell real estate on the side."

He sensed that Caroline would be good at both. He then reluctantly responded to her question about his relationship with Lauren. How could he project himself in a positive way and still be fair to Lauren? It was apparent that Caroline felt Lauren was a refreshing addition to the group at the bar.

"Probably my greatest deficiency is that I can't provide the entertainment that she wants and needs as a young woman. It might surprise you to know that we enjoy a nice romantic relationship. But, she wants to travel more and even have me take time off from what I'm doing. This short trip has been nice, but I don't relish long flights and being away from home for more than a few days."

He looked at Caroline for approval and welcomed her smile and nod.

"But Lauren is very unpredictable. She gets pushy about wanting to move in with me and then shortly afterwards tells me she needs space from me. I'm not sure where I stand and worry that she might look for a younger guy."

Lauren's voice interrupted: "I'm going to our room, Ted. Come on up when you're ready."

She disappeared and Ted and Caroline slid off the bar stools and stood facing each other. She suddenly embraced him and held the hug for a long time.

"Don't worry about it Ted. I know everything is going to work out for you two. Just don't do anything hasty. Can I give you my phone number just in case Lauren loses it? If you'd be agreeable, I'd like to take you to the Sac Zoo, and we could have lunch afterwards?"

"You should have my number as well," Ted said. "I hope you'll call."

He found Lauren almost ready for bed. She didn't seem annoyed or amorous.

"It makes me feel alive to be around so many young people," she said. "I've had too much to drink, though, and I'm drowsy. I love you. Good night."

The next day, their one special side trip was a mid day snorkel party on an off shore island. Ted had seen it advertised on the hotel activities board. Lauren had shown excitement over his choice for the day.

He moved quietly around their room that morning and watched the town's early activity from the veranda while sipping coffee. He saw no point in waking Lauren until almost nine. Their excursion boat didn't leave the dock until eleven. Ted estimated the walk to be about a mile. It was almost visible from their hotel room.

Lauren finally stirred and then sat up in bed.

"Boy, did I sleep! I'm sorry if I was abrupt last night but I was almost out on my feet. One guy absolutely insisted I have a drink on him. He said I was the life of the party."

Following a lazy breakfast, they found that their walk to the dock took longer than he had estimated. The direction towards the dock was accurate, but a lagoon separated them from the excursion boat dock. He was annoyed with himself.

"We can wait our turn for that little boat that's ferrying other people across, or we can walk the long way back around. It would take less than half an hour and still wouldn't make us late. Ted looked at Lauren for her input.

"I'm tired of walking! I'm surprised you didn't see this water problem in the first place. We could have saved all of this by walking the other way around to start with. We'd have been there by now!"

Ted saw no point in making any defense.

"We'll wait right here, then. Yes, I guess I should have noticed earlier that there was no walkway across from this end."

The small open ferry returned within ten minutes, and there was room for them on the next crossing. Ted hurried to the ticket booth.

"You get in line for boarding, Lauren. It looks like there are about a hundred people in line already, and that isn't an awfully big boat."

Soon they were onboard the snorkeling trip boat. They were able to get a good seat on the lower deck, and after a forty-five minute trip were soon anchored nearby the island. They stood back as the crowd surged to get snorkel equipment from the bins. Before long, most had dropped into the water for the swim to the beach.

Ted wished that Lauren wasn't such an accomplished snorkeler. His use of the equipment had been limited to one successful try three years earlier off Grand Cayman in the Caribbean. He didn't want to look amateurish.

"I seem to have a pair that fits me," he said as they fished through the limited selection of facemasks left in the bin. He then helped Lauren adjust straps on the masks she had selected. None fit, and she was becoming irritated.

Ted pulled off his mask. "Why don't you try on mine? There's nothing to lose."

She gave him a quick smile. "This fits great! Find yourself one. See you on the beach!" Lauren headed for the rope ladder to the water.

Finally he climbed down the short ladder and into the less than warm water. Finding another suitable mask had taken time. Ted had broken the strap on one that seemed to fit, and he had to search for the attendant to get a replacement strap.

It should have been a relatively easy swim for Ted, but he felt very tired when he stood up in the narrow band of shallow water adjacent to the beach. He removed his flippers and looked around for Lauren. He saw her wave.

After a few minutes with their faces in the water, Lauren announced that she was too cold. She stretched on the warm sand nearby what seemed to be fully half of the party. Ted's attempts at snorkeling lasted less than fifteen minutes. The water around the rock out-cropping was immediately deep, and constant swimming was required. He got some good looks at the many multi-colored fish, but tired quickly and was soon lying beside Lauren.

"That water was too cold for me too. I had counted on there being some shallow places to stand on and rest, but I didn't find any. Those little fish were beautiful, and I hated to give up so soon."

They spent the balance of what remained of the advertised two hours relaxing on the beach and enjoying the warm sand. Ted was reviewing in his mind the pluses and minuses of their brief winter vacation. Lauren broke into his thoughts.

"I want to spend some more time by the pool after we get back. For one thing, I promised myself I'd do ten laps while I was here so I don't lose muscle tone. After that, I do hope we can walk downtown for dinner."

He agreed that the two activities would fill the day beautifully. He looked around at the few people remaining.

"It looks like it's time to get back to the boat. Most everyone has gone ahead of us."

Lauren was away quickly and swimming towards the boarding ladder. Soon Ted found it difficult to identify her among the other swimmers.

The almost football field distance looked imposing to him. Ted knew that the side-stroke was easy for him and usually less tiring. He adjusted the snorkel strap to make certain he didn't lose the mask.

He glanced again at the distant boat. Why hadn't he asked for some sort of float from the attendant? The man would have looked at his white hair and not raised an eyebrow.

He swam slowly but steadily, now and then looking to make sure he was heading directly towards the boat. He was making little headway. Feelings of semi-panic came and went. Ted still had half the distance to go after what seemed like fifteen minutes. He saw no one close to him, and no one seemed to be watching from the ship's rails. A few stragglers passed him as they seemingly covered the distance easily. Ted thought about crying out for help but feared he'd take on a mouthful of salt water.

He was now frightened. Swimming at all became difficult, and it was hard to get any breath. He just kept taking one more stroke and hoping.

Finally, he saw the ladder just feet in front of him. Ted had never felt so thankful or so old in his life as he grasped the guide ropes.

Lauren was nowhere in sight. He felt an overwhelming sense of relief. He didn't want her to see him this way. When he recovered some energy, Ted gathered up his clothes and towel and headed down the ladder to the men's change room. When he returned to the deck, she was waiting.

"I see you're back and dressed. I'm kind of hungry. Let's get in line for some snacks." Ted made no mention of his struggle and the potential disaster.

As they stood quietly in line, his memory went back to when he was twenty-four and in Leyte Gulf in the Philippines during World War Two. He and other officers on his ship had accepted the challenge for a night basketball game in the empty hold of a similar ship anchored in the harbor.

On their return trip, the basketball had been accidentally dropped into the water as the skiff neared his ship. Ted had offered to strip and recover the ball, allowing the others to go ahead and board the ship. He dove into the warm water.

The breeze was stronger than he realized and the ball was soon blown out of sight. Wartime rules dictated that no outside lights be visible from ships.

Ted wasn't an endurance swimmer. For twenty-five yards he could match any of his friends. He knew that was deceiving. His fellow officers no doubt assumed he was a master swimmer.

Now he was in the middle of the harbor. Only the dark outline of his ship was visible. He had expected to use the basketball for buoyancy. After a few minutes of swimming downwind, he had abandoned his search for the ball and turned back towards the ship. Now he faced the choppy waters caused by the breeze he was facing.

He remembered then thinking that only a miracle could save him from drowning. He wondered how he could have been so unthinking. For what seemed like an hour he sucked in what breaths he could and slowly labored towards the ship. He felt no ill will towards his shipmates for not looking for him, only despair. He knew that taking one gulp of seawater would cause him to drown.

Finally, completely exhausted, he grasped the propeller structure at the stern of the ship. Until then, as today, he could have slipped beneath the water, and no one would have noticed. His family would have grieved when they received notice of his 'accidental drowning'. Ted knew he'd been lucky, twice.

It was almost four when they arrived at the hotel pool. Ted had agreed to wear his swim suit.

"But don't count on me for much swimming. I'll do a great job, though, of keeping track of your ten laps!"

Lauren moved ahead of him when they reached the pool and smilingly responded to the waves and calls from couples she had met. Ted took off his shirt and dived into the pool. He did short bursts of swimming for a few minutes before climbing out and picking up a towel.

"The water's great once you get used to it. Would you like a margarita, Lauren?"

"No thanks, not yet. I promised myself to get serious about today's swimming, and it comes first."

He joined in the conversation with the other guests. Lauren entertainingly recounted their mid-day boat ride and snorkeling experience. After a few minutes, Ted excused himself.

"I need to dry off and get warm." He turned to Lauren. "I'll be watching for your plunge into the water, but I'm not betting on it."

Once dry, Ted covered his face with the towel and let the afternoon sunrays warm him.

He was wrong. Within minutes, Lauren tapped his foot.

"I'm ready. Sit up and keep track. I don't promise to do ten laps all at once though."

Ted sat on the edge of the lounge and watched as she dove in and swam two lengths of the pool. Several of her new friends applauded. Lauren alternately swam another lap and frolicked in the water. He joined her to do the seventh lap and found he was quickly left behind and barely able to finish. After drying off, he watched the balance of her workout from the comfort of the lounge.

She smiled acceptance of the congratulations of some people and nodded when Ted made another offer to get her a margarita. Lauren took her drink and left. He sipped his and watched while she flitted among couples, seeming to thoroughly enjoy the social atmosphere. He moved to the bar and engaged in short conversations with other customers.

Lauren showed her readiness to leave after an hour. "I've had enough. Let's go up and get ready for dinner."

Ted was relieved. He didn't relish another night, their final one, of strictly bar activities. He led the way upstairs and into their room.

"Let's have a drink before we dress for dinner. We'll have more than enough orange juice left for breakfast and have hardly touched the bottle of vodka. Besides," he squeezed Lauren playfully, "we can leave most of the alcohol for the maid like we did last year. If she's a drinker, she'll be bidding to take care of our room if we come again."

They sat on the veranda with their drinks. It was almost dark, and the birds were silent. Activity at the beach was winding down.

Ted knew that Lauren was picking up the increasing sounds of music coming from the cabanas. He turned to her. "I guess we'll have to say goodbye to 'The Office' from up here. I'd like to make a toast." He paused and picked up his glass. "Here's to warm sand and bare feet, yours!"

Her glass touched his.

"I do love the feel of it. There's nothing quite like it. We came a long way but it's something we wouldn't find in Sacramento at Christmas." She stood and kissed him.

"Let's get ready for dinner!"

151

Ted was just finishing shaving when Lauren called. "Do you mind if we don't go downtown to eat? We've done a lot today, and a long walk suddenly doesn't appeal to me. I've been listening to the music coming from the beach. 'The Office' does have good food, and it's only minutes away."

He took only a few seconds to consider her request.

"Sounds fine. That other place will have to wait another year to get our money. I'm about ready when you are."

A musical group was playing on stage when they arrived. Seating was prompt. Ted was a little reluctant to order drinks but justified doing so by thinking, why not? This is our final night here, and it's a short walk back.

Lauren pointed out the choices for dinner and placed their order. She looked around in the muted lighting.

"There's somebody we know!" She jumped up in her bare feet and bantered with the couple at a table ten feet away. When she returned, her margarita and his beer had arrived.

By the time they were almost finished with dinner, Ted was joining her in lively exchanges with diners at two other close-by tables.

The music stopped, followed by an announcement from the stage.

"We're going to have a dance contest, and we need six beautiful women! Don't hold back, ladies, there's a nice prize for the winner!"

Ted looked at Lauren.

"Hey, that would be made to order for you! You love to dance, you dig this fast Mexican music, and you have the energy."

Three women were now lined up on stage. The master of ceremonies was pleading for three more.

Ted turned to the tables near them. "Don't you think Lauren would do great? I've seen her dance, and she could win this thing!"

Their cheers seemed to be the final prompting she needed.

Lauren slipped on her sandals and walked to the stage to be greeted and embraced by the smiling emcee. Two other women immediately followed. The six were then lined up to face the audience and to get instructions. The fast music began.

Ted was initially pleased with himself but soon questioned his decision. The emcee was pushing straight shots of tequila onto the women during each break in the twenty-minute show.

When Lauren's turn came to receive the applause that was to determine the winner, Ted led the cheering. A local woman was declared to be the best dancer and was awarded a fifth of tequila.

Almost immediately, Lauren pleaded to return to their room. "That tequila was awful, but I was afraid if I didn't drink it, that jerk wouldn't give me a chance to win. These sandals made it hard to dance to that really fast beat. I'm exhausted!"

They excused themselves and left. Ted steadied her in the hurried walk up the dirt road. She dressed quickly for bed.

"I'm sorry, Ted, but I'm still nauseated from all that alcohol. I wanted so much to make love with you tonight, but you'll have to excuse me. I'm done! Goodnight."

It was a relaxing morning with their departure time scheduled just before noon. Lauren professed to have had a good sleep and to be over the effects of the night before. She applauded Ted's suggestion that they order the same tasty Mexican egg breakfast they had shared the first morning after their arrival.

When he returned from the dining room with their order, he saw that she had sliced up the last of the oranges, the only remaining banana and was heating the final sweet roll. He prepared each of them another cup of coffee while she carefully laid out breakfast on the veranda table.

"I want this to be kind of special. Then maybe you'll bring me back again."

Although he was enjoying the nicely laid out breakfast, he was anxious to be home.

Lauren's thoughts had to be far from his. He had to realize there was no desire on her part to return to work.

"Do you think we could come back here next time, or would you rather we go to Puerta Vallarta?" she asked.

He shrugged and said, "We'll think about it when next winter rolls around."

She gave him a warm smile as she pulled her car into the driveway and unhooked her seat belt.

"Thanks for a great trip! I'm going to run in quick and see if there are any messages about Buddy. You can start the unloading."

SIXTEEN

To The Dance

Ted was hopeful that she would find a response to her ad about Buddy, but there didn't seem to be one. He carried her two bags into her house and placed them on the bed. She was listening intently to the recordings and barely glanced up when he left.

She called about nine to say goodnight, and added, "Tomorrow night is New Year's Eve. Why don't I come over? I'll help you make dinner and we can watch New Year's come in around the world on TV. I probably won't want to stay up until midnight, though."

Ted's spirits rose. "I'd like that. We'll talk tomorrow about what to fix. Shall I get a bottle of champagne?"

"Not unless you want it. It's not my favorite. I'll just have a little wine with dinner. Have a good sleep!"

Ted laughed. "We'll scratch the champagne, then. Goodnight."

They settled on spaghetti and a salad for dinner. He had the fireplace going and the salad made when Lauren arrived with a container of her homemade spaghetti sauce. It took only fifteen minutes to boil the noodles and set the table. He sensed that she seemed withdrawn and missed the banter that usually accompanied their preparation of dinners together. Her response to his toast, "To our new year" seemed reserved.

They alternately watched a network movie and cut into different stations during advertising to watch scenes of celebrations throughout the western world. She left before ten. "I'm still tired from our trip, and I'm a working woman you know."

Lauren didn't have time to talk during the week, but she called each night to say goodnight. "I'm behind and have too much work to do to chat, Ted," she said.

Ted's annoyance raised a notch when she had told him on Wednesday, almost immediately after such a claim, that she had just completed a forty-five minute conversation with a woman friend. He was tempted to remind her that most people found the time for what they chose to do but backed off. Maybe Lauren was unduly stressed. Her temper would likely flare up.

He had waved to her each morning about seven when her kitchen light first showed. He hadn't missed being out front to blow her a kiss as she left for work and had received a quick smile and wave in return. He chanced a call on Thursday evening.

"Would you like to have dinner on Saturday? I have a small pork roast in the freezer and could have it thawed and ready."

Lauren's voice was enthusiastic.

"I'd love to. I'll make up some coleslaw and bring the potatoes already mashed. We can make gravy from the drippings after I arrive."

Ted's uneasiness began to fade. Her less than normal warmth during the week had been both puzzling and disturbing. She was usually an easy person to talk with. Maybe she would open up to him while they were enjoying dinner.

He watched the clock on Saturday afternoon and made certain he had the roast thawed and in the oven in time to match their agreed six-thirty dinner hour. Then Ted busied himself with a load of laundry, showering and reviewing the afternoon mail. The roast was done and he had already poured off the gravy makings when he saw Lauren crossing the street, carrying two bowls. He opened the door and welcomed her with an exaggerated bow.

"Come on in, stranger! You're a beautiful neighbor, and I've been waiting to meet you!"

She had barely stepped through the door when it poured out.

"We need to have a discussion about ending our relationship." Then without taking time to put down her armload of food, she said, "I'm totally frustrated and want to get out!"

Ted stood up straight from his low bow and stumbled back a few steps into the corner of a side table. Rubbing his leg, Ted exploded, "What do you mean, a discussion? You seem to have already made a decision!"

"I meant to wait until after dinner, but I had to get it out. I feel better already."

Lauren walked into the kitchen, placed her containers of food on the counter and turned to face him again. Ted, who had unconsciously followed her into the kitchen, stared at her and said nothing but felt his eyes burning. What was there to say to take away the horrible, empty feeling?

"I made the decision while we were in Cabo. It was so frustrating and embarrassing. All of the people I visited with around the pool kept asking me what future I could possibly have with such an old man? I felt awful and had no answers. One person even commented on how skinny you were and asked if you had cancer."

It was difficult to hold back his own tears. He regained some of his composure and almost began to feel concern for her. He'd thought about their age difference often enough through their hectic romance. Were the threatened tears for her or for self pity? He knew he had to say something, but was afraid to open his mouth for fear a cry of agony would escape.

There was no hint of an embrace or anything to take away the horror of what was happening. Lauren seemed determined to stand her ground and not let emotions sway her decision. Seemingly oblivious to his feelings, Lauren took two plates out of the cupboard and two forks out of the drawer before opening her food containers and turning back to him.

"Well?" she asked.

"Maybe you're right. You obviously will find a younger partner at some point, and maybe soon," he said. He glanced out the window and saw Ellen making dinner across the way. "It kills me to lose you."

Dejectedly, he set up the card table in front of the fireplace. He had built the fire to surprise her. It had always added a nice touch to their romantic dinners. Ted could hear her in the kitchen beginning to make the gravy. He joined her.

"I love you too much to stand in your way. You have to run your own life, Lauren." She did not respond, except to ask for the salt. He left the kitchen to arrange plates and napkins and stood for a minute staring at the fire.

Lauren surprised him by bringing in and lighting a large candle that had often graced their table. He knew she loved to have the room lights turned way down or off. How often had she said, "Candles and the fireplace just make the perfect setting for a romantic dinner."

Together, they carried the food to the table. Ted excused himself and returned with a glass of wine for each of them.

"Well, here's to a cold dinner," she said, lifting her glass.

"While I understand that we've kind of let dinner slip, I can't possibly toast that!" Ted said. "Our toast tonight needs to be, "To the dance!""

Her eyes brightened. Lauren seemed delighted that he had remembered. She smiled and raised her glass again. "Yes, to the dance."

She had reminded him so many times, almost from the start of their love affair, that the Garth Brooks song, 'The Dance,' was their song.

He, too, had used the expression many months before when his daughter reminded him that she didn't like his and Lauren's relationship one little bit. Thinking back, he remembered that they were standing in her kitchen following lunch. He asked Kathy if she was familiar with Brook's tune that included the line, "I could have missed the pain, but I would have had to miss the dance."

"I don't recognize it, Dad. But aren't you a bit old to match song lyrics to real life?"

They had been snipping at one another, and his eyes followed her as she cleared the table. "Well," he had said, "regardless, I'm not willing to miss the dance."

He now was so deep in thought that it startled him to have Lauren's voice break the silence. "It isn't that I've quit loving you. My heart says to stay with you, but logic says I have to end it. We can't continue like we are. It hurts too much to think you're going to die soon, and then I would lose you. Don't you think it's better to face the pain now?"

He shook his head because he didn't feel like he was on death's doorstep. "I guess I knew this had to come, but I just can't accept the fact that it's here. Your decision is tearing me apart. It isn't that I question your reasoning."

They both continued to eat slowly keeping their eyes away from each other's as much as possible. Ted found it helpful to concentrate on the flickering orange flames. She was the first to speak. "You've given me a lot, Ted, and I appreciate that. I've never known anyone like you. I've told you that before."

"Yes, you have. You, in turn, have given me something I never had a reason to expect. What older man ever had an exciting, beautiful woman jump into his life so suddenly and unexpectedly. I don't believe you can imagine the pain now that you're telling me its all ending."

Lauren wasn't to be stopped. Did she even hear him?

"If we continue as we are, I will have to make the same decision later when I will have grown to love you more. Don't you agree that we'd better quit now?"

Ted pondered a minute before answering. Here she had posed the same question twice about the timing of her decision, Was she really asking if he had an alternate suggestion to their breaking up now? Was there a ray of hope for him?

"I guess it's a matter of how we look at our thirty-year age difference and what will be the real effect if we take this action now or later. In two years I'll be eighty. I find two more years with you wonderful to contemplate. We now seldom have those awful arguments. I like to think of two more summers at my mountain place and a bunch of Carmel trips. We just love those Point Lobos trail hikes, and I've heard good things about the trails around Big Sur. I question if giving those things up now really makes sense. It would be different if our feelings for each other weren't still strong."

Lauren seemed to be watching him intently. She said nothing so he resumed speaking. "I realize that I'm looking at how I am today. My health could go downhill, and then I couldn't fill your needs as a young woman." Now she seemed anxious to respond.

"You've been wonderful! Our sex life is great! I've always told you that you are the best man I've ever known."

"Yes, and you've kept me on cloud nine by reassuring me of that fact." He smiled at her, but she dashed his faint hopes for reconsideration.

"But we both know it can't stay that way. I wish it could. I just can't stand the thought of something happening to you. My logic says I have to find a younger partner now. I have to find someone while I'm still attractive to men. I can't allow my heart to convince me to stay with you."

Ted had a sinking feeling that he had lost out, but even the slight hope of keeping her in his life prodded him to continue. There might be an argument she might respond to. At least she was listening.

"Maybe we haven't thought this through entirely. In two years you won't yet be fifty. There will only be changes for the better where your appearances are concerned. You've quit smoking. You've changed your diet some and have done a fantastic job of sticking with your exercise routine. It seems to me that you're keeping in great shape."

"Thanks for noticing. I do feel better about myself than I did even six months ago. I've accepted the fact that I'll always need these workouts if I'm to look good."

She looked at Ted with tears in her eyes. He realized that he must look awfully old just now and that her feelings were those of both love and sympathy. He was certain that she felt an intense sadness about what was happening. Lauren would never purposefully hurt him, he was sure of that. A predictable situation had come to a head, one that both should have known was inevitable from the start. Yet, here they were nearly two years later fighting to postpone the hour of separation.

Lauren shrugged her shoulders slightly.

"I hate to do this to you now. I should never have allowed myself to fall in love with you."

He brightened and responded quickly.

"We didn't plan what has happened. That first night on the pad in your place wasn't love. Our loving each other began to develop and then grew over a period of time. I don't want to let you go, Lauren. I don't want to accept what you are telling me is happening."

He sensed a hint of compromise in her next words.

"I still want us to be good friends. I'll even come over and sleep with you now and then."

Ted shook his head.

"We talked about this earlier, Lauren. I've told you in as many ways as I know how that I can't be near you without wanting you. Never knowing when that now and then might come along would kill me! I'd rather return to just being neighbors."

She brightened momentarily, but then a frown covered her face. He knew she was recalling some prior conversations. Was he making his point too strongly? He waited.

"I suppose you want sex every week!"

"Yes, I don't want any relationship without it. Neither do you. You've told me that whenever the matter has come up," Ted stood up and gave her a light kiss on the forehead. He remained standing, looking at her thoughtfully, and then grinned and quietly added, "All too soon you will find a new guy, and then I'm out. It will be one of the toughest things I've ever faced, but I'll try to handle that situation when it does come. In the meantime I'd love you for understanding. Come over when you feel like spending time with me. It isn't the kind of pressure I feel good about putting on you, and you're probably hating it. I ask that you try to see my side."

"Maybe I won't find a man who likes me."

"From a selfish viewpoint, I like to hope that would be the case. But I find you so very beautiful and desirable that I know dozens of men will want you. You only have to open the door."

Lauren stood and picked up her dishes. Ted followed her to the kitchen with his. Then he wiped and folded the card table while she reset the candle on the low marble table in front of the couch. She reached for the remote control.

"I'm gong to watch TV for awhile. Why don't you come and sit down?"

"No thanks. If I don't do the dishes now, they'll still be a big mess in the morning. Besides, I've talked a lot, and it will give me time to think."

He finished the dishes, half listening to sounds coming from the TV, but never taking his mind off the discussions that had filled their dinner hour. She said nothing when he completed brushing his teeth and sat down. Both looked straight ahead. Ted hoped she would stretch out on the couch as she almost always did, allowing him to cradle her feet and lower legs across his lap. Lauren had told him often how much she loved to have him caress and rub her feet. She seldom withheld her lovemaking.

But she made no move to change from her sitting position. Both of them remained almost motionless. Their only conversation was an occasional brief comment about the show on the screen. She responded once with a smile when Ted reached across and squeezed her hand but made no move to indicate any desire for further closeness.

The show ended and she turned off the power. Both were standing. He made a final plea.

"Would you like to stay over tonight? I had hoped you might."

Her answer was a simple "No" followed by, "Thank you for dinner."

"Well, okay, and thanks for your part. The mashed potatoes and coleslaw were really good."

They walked across the street to Lauren's house, and with a brief kiss and casual goodnights their evening was over.

Ted entered his house, looked at his watch and picked up a National Geographic. It was only ten-fifteen and he was wide awake. He chose a K.T. Oslin tape from among a group Lauren had loaned him and inserted it in the player and set the volume at a low level.

He read for thirty minutes, getting up only once to turn the tape. When he sat back down he closed the magazine and pushed the chair into more of a reclining position. The music was soothing. Ted tried to put the evening's events out of his mind.

He awakened from a dreamless sleep to find it almost midnight. He felt chilled and crawled into bed, first glancing across to Lauren's darkened bedroom window. He wondered if she was suffering like he was. Sleep finally came.

SEVENTEEN   Goodbye, Blown Kisses

Ted awakened to find a light rain falling. He could hear the patter of drops striking the metal awning outside his bedroom window. He was glad that he'd already stacked his winter needs for oak logs and kindling under cover in the patio.

Then it came back to him. Lauren wasn't his anymore. There would be no reason for a bright fire unless he was willing to enjoy it alone.

He went through his normal morning routine and occasionally glanced across the street. Ted didn't expect a call and none came. He ran two loads of laundry and vacuumed the bedroom and family room carpets.

At eleven o'clock her car was gone. He vaguely remembered Lauren telling him she was having lunch with a fellow instructor. They were teaching similar classes at different community colleges and planned to share grading techniques during an afternoon meeting.

His day passed uneventfully. He felt fortunate that the professional football season was still on, and watched parts of two games. He was fixing a drink when her car entered the driveway about four-thirty. Lauren moved quickly through the rain to her door without glancing his way.

He finally prepared dinner and cleaned up his few dishes afterwards. His only call was from his daughter. Kathy talked about the boys' week at school. Ted confirmed that he planned to drive up for a few hours visit on Monday afternoon. She didn't ask about Lauren and he purposefully chose to not open the subject of the change.

The first Monday since her announcement that she was ending their relationship was facing Ted. Sleep had been fitful, but he was up soon after five, made coffee and read his paper for forty-five minutes. He saw no reason to change his routine, and concentration on reading took his mind off Lauren.

Next, he carried the word-processor from the study and positioned it carefully on the kitchen table. It was almost daylight and time to open the curtains. There were two personal letters to be typed. That was often his early morning routine. While writing, he would enjoy watching his neighbors' vehicles passing on their way to work and always responded with waves to those who looked his way. Today, they couldn't know the stress he was under.

Ted liked to amaze his friends and family by informing them his postage costs sometimes exceeded a hundred dollars while his long-distance phone charges were seldom that level. He had taken journalism in high school, came to enjoy writing, and found it easy. He knew that few of his friends or family members shared his interest in writing, but knew they respected and admired his ability. He watched for the light to come on across the street.

It did, a few minutes after six. It signaled that Ellen was up, as usual on weekdays, to be able to make her seven o'clock departure time. Her classes were at a high school about twenty miles away, and Ted knew that traffic conditions weren't always favorable.

He continued his typing, still half-numb from the realization that he was no longer Lauren's 'guy'. Everything around him was right on schedule, but his romantic world had died. She had said that she was ending their intimate love affair! Had he correctly heard her say she was relieved about her new independence?

His final letter was to an old military friend who lived in the mid-west. They had corresponded for close to forty-five years. Once, Ted and his wife had visited them. Twice, Dale and his wife had driven to California to see them. Dale wasn't as fortunate as he was and Parkinson's disease was causing his letters to be brief and the handwriting shaky.

Today, though, writing was an effort. Ellen was gone and the kitchen was dark. As he watched for the light to come on again, nothing else seemed too important.

The next time Ted glanced up from his typing, the light was showing from across the street. Soon Lauren's silhouette appeared, and he could see her hand waving. He returned the wave. She disappeared from sight, and he continued his writing, wondering what emotions she might be feeling.

Forty-five minutes later, she emerged through her front door, loaded with 'teacher' things. Although Lauren glanced at his kitchen window, he chose not to wave but instead walked out and took his normal place in front of a row of low shrubs that bordered a three-foot high painted picket fence.

For almost two years, with rare exceptions, Ted had stood there waiting to blow a kiss to her as she left for her morning job. She seemed to love the ritual from the start although occasionally she had motioned with her hand as if to say, "Cut out that silliness!" He knew that Lauren would be waiting to see him. His reward had been a saucy smile and a quick wave.

Today, there was no blown kiss, just a casual wave. She wasn't his anymore. She needed a younger man, someone who could give her decades of companionship and devotion, maybe even marriage. He cringed at the thought of what she had said, "Ted, you are old and going to die soon."

He knew that Lauren would be looking for commitment that was realistic, something that he was sure from experience she would be eager to give to the right man. She waved back, smiled, and was gone. Dejectedly, he returned to his kitchen table.

He could develop no enthusiasm for further writing. He began to think about what might have been with her. He desired her terribly. He was jealous of other men who paid attention to her. His life now seemed empty. What had gone wrong? Had anything gone wrong, or had he just grown old? He obviously had in her eyes.

Ted brushed aside the possibility that the blame might be at least partly his, but the thought nagged at him. Would Lauren have reacted differently if she had felt a firm commitment about a future with him? He knew he felt honest when he assured her of his devotion and loyalty.

But he had always stopped there. There was something about her when she was angry that made him afraid to seriously talk about a long-term relationship. Ted remembered her having asked him once, on the day following a rather bitter exchange, if he was afraid of her.

"Yes, in a way I guess I am. I sometimes fear that any answer I give you when you're upset will anger you more. You know how these personal conflicts tear me up. You seem to be able to take them in stride. I can't."

He recalled several times when Lauren had suggested that her situation was such that she ought to move in with him. It had seemed to be more than a casual observation on her part, and he had quickly brushed off the topic. Had she been looking for an affirmative response from him as a desired level of commitment? Ted was wary of making such a commitment.

It had crossed his mind at those times that he ought to write a letter to Lauren outlining the basis of which he would be desirous of their living together. Each time he had dismissed the idea. How do you tell a woman you profess to love that you wouldn't be able to handle her often domineering and sometimes confrontational personality? Yet, there was no way he could see them living together unless she could change because he knew it would be hopeless otherwise.

Too, would writing be only a wasted effort? She hadn't responded to his letter written several months earlier suggesting a six month plan.

Ted saw their lifestyle differences, some age-related, as posing an almost equal hurdle. She loved to stay up late, watching rented or TV movies, and reading for a while afterwards in bed. Rising early was torture for her. On weekdays, Lauren crowded the clock, sometimes allowing herself only thirty minutes between arising and entering her car for the drive to her workplace. Holidays, or non-workdays called for late sleep-ins often as late as ten.

By contrast, his day usually began around five with coffee and the morning paper. The days of the week made no difference. Ted's philosophy was to fill sixteen hours each day doing something partially useful but always interesting. His TV would remain off for days at a time, a situation usually changed only when Lauren was visiting after their dinners together. His exceptions were professional football broadcasts that he selectively watched. Ted required little outside entertainment though sometime welcomed music as a background for his work.

By nine in the evening, his eyes and mind were tired. Unless he had infrequent visitors, or a compelling interest in a book or magazine, it was time for bed. True, he could easily change for Lauren, for her special evenings or sleepovers, but her living with him might bring demands for a permanent change in his routine. He saw that as not acceptable.

He had loved the few times she had coaxed him to stay beside her, sometimes until after eight in the morning. He then saw her beauty as that of a happy woman with the stress of the day prior gone. This closeness, coupled with touching, talking and caressing, often had climaxed in love-making. He smiled at the memories.

On other mornings, Ted had slipped out of bed, tucked her in, given her a light kiss on the forehead, gently squeezed her foot through the blanket, and was gone. He would hear a murmur of content. His early morning activities would have been completed, and he would be working at the kitchen table when her footsteps were first heard. So, why was he resisting the thought of his making some changes if he truly loved Lauren and wanted her as a permanent part of his life?

Another concern wouldn't leave his mind as he sat at the kitchen table, staring out at the street. Would there be a reduction in Lauren's desire to improve her job situation if she were living with him? Would he be a part of defeating the very hopes he had for her success in a job? With no rent to pay, and a minimum food bill, what would stimulate her desire for improvement? He feared she would even begin suggesting that staying home and taking care of his house and yard was fulfilling enough and drop work entirely.

Still nagging in the back of his mind was a surprising proposal she had made sometime during the first year of their romance. The words had made a permanent impression. "I want you to take off five years from what you're doing and just hang out with me. We love each other. We could travel all over the world and enjoy ourselves while you're healthy! You have the money. Why not spend some of it while you can enjoy it?"

Lauren had concluded her proposal as if she were suggesting a walk around the block. "Then I could resume my job and you could go back to enjoying your retirement."

Still at the prime of her life, he could readily visualize her excitement of doing little but pampering and enjoying herself for five years. It would be a complete escape from a work routine that had so far proven to be more challenging and far less rewarding than Lauren had anticipated or wanted. She would be grabbing five years of luxury, most times reserved for wives or widows over sixty-five.

But, wasn't she looking at the excitement through her eyes and not those of a man in his late seventies? There was no fit! Was she seeing his life as fulfilled with the promise of sex and the companionship of a highly sensuous young woman? Ted grimaced at the thought of her being equally attractive to dozens of other men, many wealthy and unattached.

He saw himself as being exhausted after the first two-week trip involving long flights and dragging luggage around. She, by contrast, would be at the travel agency excitedly booking the next leg of their five-year adventure. Lauren wasn't one to let up, and he was certain her proposal had been genuine. He saw no better way than being direct even if it meant hurting her feelings.

He had told her he saw no chance of that working. That he hated the thought of long, tiring trips, and it wouldn't be good for her career.

The fault had been partly his. He had consistently tried to project himself as youthful. Ted was sure she had interpreted his physical ability and endurance during mountain hikes and ocean trips in a positive light as he had wanted her to do.

His thoughts turned to the past December just before their Cabo trip. Lauren had made a specific request that she move in with him. He had acknowledged that he, too, had been thinking how this might fit into cementing the future of their relationship.

The evening had been pleasant, starting with dinner. She had rented a movie and announced her plans to stay over. The issue of her moving in with him was broached while they were clearing the table.

"I want to move in with you. It's ridiculous for us to live across the street from each other. You've got this beautiful house and a lot of space going to waste. And since Ellen's gotten interested in this guy, I hardly see her at all. I need to get out!"

His initial comment had been that he couldn't think of any feeling more wonderful than waking each morning with her beside him. Ted knew he was sincere about that. Always the first indication that she was awake would be the feel of her toe lightly moving over his feet. When he responded, next would come a musical "Good Morning."

Soon she would be on her side, with her bottom snuggled into the curve of his body.

Ted hadn't discouraged further conversation about her moving in with him. He introduced a related topic while the dishes were being washed.

"You would need to have the entire guest bedroom converted into an office for you, Lauren. I would want to keep one of the single beds there, though. We never know when one of us might be sick and need a separate bed. The other could go into storage." He paused a few seconds while fitting several plates into the dishwasher. "I do wish the window in that room was low enough so you could see outside while you worked. You know how much I love my big kitchen window. I moved my office there right after my wife died."

Ted had seen the excitement in her expression. He thought he would allow her to complete a mental picture of what he had in mind if they were to live together.

"I would have another ceiling-high cabinet built in the study. You have lots of books and manuals that need dry, inside space. Some stuff would have to go into storage, Lauren. I'm sure you realize that. Your bed would be one thing and my big dresser in our bedroom would have to go, too.

I know how much you treasure your antique dresser so it could replace mine."

He knew she would balk about giving up her own bed, and she did.

"But I want my own bed! I've moved it with me each time for years. What's wrong with storing yours?"

Ted had wanted to close out the discussion and saw no reason to make an issue about whose bed would be slept in. "Who knows? If it all comes about, we can make that decision then. For right now we won't be making a change." He paused, "I was serious about those suggestions I made in that letter I wrote to you late last summer. You said you'd read it but you haven't said a word since."

She had said nothing. He had waited and watched as her spirits visibly dropped. Although he had no intent of making an issue of her not responding to his letter, he didn't want to appear weak by dropping his entire 'six month proposal'.

He decided to accept her silence and had added a carefully worded reminder. "I don't want to do anything until at least the end of February, or maybe early spring. We need to see how well we get along between now and then."

Ted recalled that they had then watched the film and afterwards gone to bed. She had cuddled up to him for a few minutes and then announced that she was tired, had some cramps, and really didn't feel like lovemaking.

His emotions had been mixed. He had looked forward to a night of intimacy with this exciting woman. He had felt a sense of relief, however. Supposing, during some of their closest moments, she had chosen to return to the topic of moving in with him? How could he then continue to decline without destroying their love-making? He might not even be able to say "No". It had been a sleepless night for him. Lauren had seemed, however, to be having a blissful, uninterrupted rest.

Ted returned to his present musings and need to face his real life. She had announced her decision to end their romance. What purpose did it serve for him to be even thinking about why he had lost her? Hadn't he even agreed with Lauren at the time that she was doing the right thing?

Maybe he could clear his own mind by putting something down in writing, confirming his acceptance of her need to seek a younger partner. He often felt lacking in his ability to make convincing response on many issues when talking with her. He envied Lauren's ability to put thoughts into words so quickly.

On the other hand, was there still a chance for him? Could she be persuaded to reconsider? Ted shuddered at the thought of her in another man's arms. Why did he love and desire this woman so much and yet deny her request to live with him? Should he reconsider his position, and would this now make any difference?

He thought again about a letter. It could do no harm. He might keep the door open a little without giving ground on the question of their living together. He concluded that events were moving too fast for him. Writing would give him time to sort things through again.

Ted poured himself a final cup of coffee and picked up a legal pad. Letters to other people could wait.

Before Lauren returned from her morning classes, he had opened her front door with his key and placed the envelope on the kitchen counter by the telephone. He saw no reason to take time to pick up flowers.

> *Dear Lauren,*
>
> *I feel the need to say a few things to you in light of your decision to end our relationship. I have thought constantly about it and can't question your logic. I have always tried to accept reality in this awful matter. If I'm here for you, as I've told you I am, I have to accept your decision. No amount of fantasy can take away the meaning of those words spoken last Saturday.*
>
> *You were honest in telling me that you just could not continue as if everything were okay through Valentine's Day and then telling me you were leaving after accepting the money gift I'd planned for you and mentioned in my 'six month' letter. I know you would have been there for me through February had it not been for the reasons you've expressed, so I'm enclosing the cashier's check now and asking that you accept it with my blessing.*
>
> *You will find a new man at some point soon, and I feel justified in making one suggestion based on the tougher sides of our time together as a couple. You are so open and charming with individuals and groups you meet casually, but something seems to change as you deal with people you become close to. I beg of you to reconsider your sometimes hurtful*

choice of words. I felt sad so many times and yet know so absolutely that you didn't intend that to happen. Please don't put your new guy through this ordeal.

I cherish the memories of the time spent as your partner. It began with the surprise lovemaking and grew far beyond that. I've loved our trips, hikes, and times at my lake, and will miss these terribly. However, our situation seems to have demanded a change, and that we must handle together.

I love you, Lauren, and probably will always love you.
~Ted

He received her call at nine that night. Lauren's first words were, "I'm overwhelmed with the check, Ted. You didn't need to do that, you know."

"You're right, of course, but I'm a guy who insists on doing what he promised. Things haven't turned out exactly as I had planned, but there aren't any strings attached. If you ever want to talk about the stock market, let me know. How did your day go?"

"It went along okay. I've ended up with a bunch of essays to review and grade, and a test to prepare for another class this week, so I'll be plenty busy." She paused, "Thanks, again. Goodnight."

The week passed at a snail's pace for Ted. Each morning continued to begin with coffee and his newspaper following nights of interrupted sleep. He mulled over and over his discussion with Lauren about her need to terminate their relationship. His mind usually centered on his responses at the time.

Had he been too hasty? He didn't feel too old for her. Had he given up too easily? He thought through the letter he had written and could find no fault there. He had just acknowledged the need for them to carry through with the break-up, but had left a little room for Lauren to share her feelings. He wondered if she was reconsidering.

Always, though, after short periods of fantasy, Ted accepted that his seventy-eight years was a hurdle he couldn't, with any degree of objectivity, ask her to ignore. He brushed aside his unwillingness to show any enthusiasm when she'd pushed the desirability of them living together.

Early mornings during the ensuing week usually found him busily typing catch-up letters to friends or out of town relatives. If he mentioned Lauren at all, it was to comment on their Cabo San Lucas vacation. A few close friends were informed about her decision. In each, he tried to make light of the change.

"I guess you might say I lost out to a better man."

Ted was certain that most of his friends and relatives would be relieved though wouldn't directly say so. He recalled his letters written two years back to these same people. At that time he alerted them to his excitement over meeting his Polish bombshell. At the same time he had included in most letters an observation that conveyed a degree of concern about the probable longevity of his romantic situation: *I can't figure out what on earth she sees in me!*

He had chuckled at the response of one of his cousins, a woman about his own age. She wrote back: *Well, I can see it clearly! You're good looking, kind, and you're rich.*

Now, as he completed his writing and watched for Lauren's appearance at her kitchen window, he marveled that this lovely, exciting young teacher had found in him what she wanted in a man, a situation lasting as long as it did. Even now, if he saw her working among the few winter flowers in the front yard, or carrying items from her car, there would be a sense of comfort and almost elation.

But then agony replaced the pleasant sensations. Was he now going to see another man fill his place? Ted would find himself choking up, remembering the many times he had lovingly touched or caressed her. Was that all going to end just because he had become two years older? It not only was going to end, it had already! He would slowly recover his composure after reminding himself of that awful truth.

He continued to time his morning activities to be able to watch her departure for work and would be outside with waves and smiles to be exchanged. He knew, though there would be no later call to see if he wanted to visit during the evening or to ask if he had something good planned for dinner.

Twice Lauren called around nine to wish him a "Goodnight" and "Hope you sleep well." She discouraged any prolonged conversation with a now-standard explanation. "I'm busy on the computer getting ready for tomorrow, but you'll be going to bed soon and I wanted to say "Goodnight."

Saturday mornings were almost always sleep-in days for his two teacher neighbors. Often it was almost nine o'clock before any lights indicated some activity. Ted had no letters to get out and had turned his attention to tax-related material for his accountant. He was watching a steady drizzle in the street almost empty of vehicle traffic. The house was completely quiet except for the occasional whirring of the heater fan. He was startled by the phone. It was Lauren.

"Good morning, Ted. I see you're up and working. Your head always seems to be buried in papers. I waved several times but you never looked up."

"I'm sorry about that! I guess I was too engrossed in numbers trying not to miss anything important. I'm glad you called. It's nice to hear your voice! What are you up to today?"

"Same old stuff, but I have a hair appointment at ten-thirty. Mostly, I wanted to tell you that I'll be sleeping with you tonight."

A shocked Ted was momentarily speechless. Why would she suddenly change after jolting him with her decision that their romance was over? But then, wasn't this Lauren's way; seeming to keep him off balance with her mood changes? Whatever. He quickly rallied from her promise.

"Shall we have dinner together?"

"No, I want to have dinner with Ellen. She and I have a lot to talk about. But I'll come over sometime afterwards. I have to go now." She followed with a bright "See you!"

After spending another hour on his tax work, Ted ran two loads of laundry and pushed the vacuum over the carpets in his three most used rooms. He took special care in mopping the kitchen floor. He never again wanted a repeat of the dinner fiasco with her stopping everything and insisting the floor be mopped.

He fixed a light lunch, inserted a Kenny G tape for background music while eating, and then went back to work on his taxes. Ted took a break several times to look out of a back window at his garden area. The grass was growing steadily in spite of the cold rains. He was impatient for the arrival of the early spring sunshine that would allow him to do the needed spading.

He thought about Lauren. It was disquieting to realize that she wouldn't be asking for his help when she prepared her smaller plot for tomatoes, cucumbers and green beans. Ted wondered if the next man in her life would like gardening. Who wouldn't enjoy gardening with her?

But tonight there would be a release from his pent-up yearnings for her. Was she really going to be his again, if only for a short while? The vision of Lauren responding to his caresses was almost overwhelming.

At four-thirty he fixed himself a drink and relaxed with a historic novel that she had loaned him earlier. He had been fitting in time for the book, mostly during the evenings, and wanted to compliment Lauren on her selection.

He was too excited to be really hungry but began fixing his own dinner at six-thirty. A small steak he could grill in a pan plus a baked potato from the microwave and a green salad seemed appropriate. He would carefully sauté the half pound of fresh mushrooms bought yesterday at the nearby grocery.

It was almost eight-thirty when he heard Lauren's whistle and a tap on the front door. "We got to talking and you know how I am once I get started. I didn't forget you! Sorry!" She gave him a big hug and then went directly to the living room couch facing the TV. "Will you get my pillow and a soda? There's a show at nine that you'll like. Then we can go to bed. Are you as excited as I am?"

Ted smiled and did as requested. Without responding, he sat down on the far end of the couch. She placed her feet on his lap after kicking off her slippers. Her smile told him she hadn't forgotten.

"This show lasts only an hour. I just want you to rub my feet for a while. We can stop anytime if you can't wait."

Lauren had always seemed to love their 'mornings after'. He had learned quickly that when she discouraged his suggestion that he jump up and make coffee, she was very serious.

This Sunday morning was no exception. Neither of them seemed to want to hold back their expressions of how rewarding their love-making had been. Ted accepted the blessing and asked no questions.

Lauren did finally express some doubts about the wisdom of her being there with him. He thought she was purposefully being rather unconvincing.

"I don't see how I can be talking seriously with another man while I'm thinking about coming over to see you."

Her tears came as they reminisced about some of their romantic hours together. He thought especially about their Point Lobos trail hikes. Ted was forced to look away from her to avoid tears as he had a brief vision of that lovely body in shorts and sweatshirt moving with such rhythm ahead of him on the trail. As they lay beside each other on this special Sunday, it seemed so cruel and needless to him to have to give this up. Yet, the path to do so was firmly set.

She answered in the affirmative when asked if any of the neighbors was aware of their break up.

"Yes, but only two. We have the right to our own lives while this change is taking place. It's no one's business but ours. I just wanted to sleep with you again."

His response brought a needed laugh from both. "Here we go again! The neighbors will be watching you crossing the street with your pajamas over your arm. We'll get a terrible reputation! But, I'm all for it if you'll promise to handle the neighbors. I'm not going to say a word."

She left at mid-morning with no suggestion that any invitation for dinner or another overnight stay would be accepted. As Lauren started up her walkway, she turned and waved again. The sun was shining.

He took a final half cup of coffee into the backyard and stood studying where to place various rows of vegetable plants and seeds when the weather improved. Maybe some miracle would happen, and he and Lauren would be doing this together again.

Shortly after noon he knocked on her door with a hastily put together letter and a small bunch of carnations.

"I just had to tell you how much I loved last night and this morning. Here's a little letter to go along with the flowers."

She took both, set the flowers on the counter and threw her arms around him.

"Thanks so much, Ted. There's been no one like you!"

He returned to his kitchen. Even with it now mid-day he saw the light go on in Lauren's bedroom. He was sure she would now be reading his letter.

> *Dear Lauren,*
>
> *Just a note to let you know that I'm conscious of the difficulty you find yourself in where our changed relationship, if not our feelings, are concerned. You said you had misgivings about us continuing to be intimate. But you have also wondered aloud if you made a mistake in ending our relationship as you did. I, too, search for answers every day.*
>
> *Making love with me last night was a wonderful thing for you to do. But, no, you didn't make a mistake with your earlier decision. You need to move ahead with your life. Our age difference, and all of the negatives that go with that unchangeable situation, have become too frustrating for you, and I can understand that. The fun of doing things with me, whether it be at my lake, or Carmel, or Cabo, was just no*

longer enough to balance out the increasing problem of my growing older.

From my position, if my health should begin to deteriorate, I don't want you to have to be caught up in that problem.

But I do hope and ask that you find a way to continue your love-making with me until such time as you meet some guy who attracts you enough that you accept more than an invitation to lunch, dinner, a movie, or whatever. Then, I ask that you tell me, and I will have to accept that my intimate times with you are over. It will be painful. I know that you will share that feeling, and that alone may be helpful to us.

It's just that, in the meantime, if we're going to do little things that bring us together, other than just as neighbors, I need to occasionally cuddle up next to you and experience your wonderful lovemaking. I can't be doing things with you and not want you! It's too difficult and too painful, and I won't even try. I know that you understand and hope your heart allows you to do this for me.

There is no going back for us, Lauren, and we both realize and must accept that reality. In so many ways it couldn't have been a nicer time for me, and I'm certain you share my feelings. However, I'll be eighty in two years, and you'll not yet be fifty and still a beautiful young woman. I'll always love you! ~ Ted

EIGHTEEN   Man With A Plan

Ted was elated to have a Wednesday night call from her. "Would you like to have dinner at my place on Thursday? We've been eating at your house most of the time. I've got something in mind that you'll like. I'm not working that afternoon and will have time to prepare it."

His response was that he'd love to, followed by, "What time do you want me there and what can I bring?"

"Come on over about six-thirty. We can have a glass of wine and eat about seven. Would you bring a salad?" This was followed quickly by: "But we can't do much after dinner! I have too much work to do."

His own week had been busy and rewarding. Schools were back in session and Ted had scheduled to give four lectures on Tuesday to individual high school classes at a school forty miles from his home. It had taken less than an hour on Monday to brush up on his planned talk and to make copies of forms he would be using during the presentations.

The day had gone exceptionally well. The health teacher, a Miss Ramos, was in her third year of teaching. Ted had spoken with several of her prior semester's classes and was warmly welcomed.

"I think it's wonderful that you do this. My students just seem to love you. I've never seen them be so attentive."

Ted had thanked her and hung his 'Friends Don't Let Friends Drive Drunk' banner after writing his name and topic on the front blackboard. He had carefully watched the teenagers' faces during the early part of his program and knew he was in for an easy, productive day.

More than half of the students in all four classes had chosen to fill out membership applications. He had collected these with a smile and a "Thank you" at the end of each hour. Each class had given him a rousing cheer, encouraged by Miss Ramos. Three teenagers had handed him personal letters as they were leaving the classroom. He had thanked them, asked if their addresses were on the letters so he could answer, and had carefully folded each letter and stuffed it into his shirt pocket.

Ted had followed his normal routine on Wednesday morning and well into the afternoon, hand-printing fifty-eight I.D. cards and answering the three letters written to him. By two-thirty he had completed the follow-up work and had packaged everything together in a big envelope for the teacher and was at the post office.

Lauren seemed nervous as dinner progressed. She was eating rapidly. It suddenly burst out: "I put a personal ad in the internet the first time we broke up. I had to fill in answers to a lot of questions. I put myself down as above average looking. I looked in the mirror today and think I look awful! Do you think I should have put 'average'?"

Ted ignored the question and asked two of his own.

"Why didn't you tell me you had put in an ad? How many guys have answered it?"

"There must have been a dozen so far. I've deleted a bunch of losers. I have to tell you that I'm meeting with one tomorrow at five-thirty for coffee. He's a teacher. I think he said he's fifty-one. He hasn't any children." Then, barely catching her breath, "There's another man who's driving down from the foothills to meet me at a bar on Sunday afternoon. I can hardly keep their names straight. I called this last guy 'Fred', and he reminded me his name was 'Ed'. I'm surprised that he even wanted to see me after that mistake."

Ted saw no reason to interject any observations about her description of the men responding to her internet ad. He hadn't fully absorbed the reality that she was this far into her search He felt almost numb but tried not to seem surprised or disturbed. He had made a genuine effort to accept a difficult situation and perhaps should have realized Lauren might be making some moves to meet men. But why unload this on him tonight? He had come over for a pleasant dinner, not this revelation! It was as if he'd suddenly become her favorite uncle, completely oblivious to their past.

She resumed eating for a minute or two. Ted sipped on his wine trying to seem casual and not knowing what to say.

"I think you'd be proud of me. I made up a list of questions and sent them back by e-mail to the six men I thought sounded okay. I asked what their favorite and least favorite words were. I asked them to describe 'romantic'. I even asked them about their favorite sayings and colors. Don't you think their answers will be helpful to me?"

Ted gave her a wry smile.

"I'm not sure how, but I'm sure you're right. Is this the way you selected this teacher and your mountain guy, Ed?"

"Yes, I e-mailed my phone number and invited them to call. I needed to hear their voices. You may not think so, but I can tell a lot about people from their demeanor and voices over the phone."

She hesitated again as if asking for his approval. Ted was thinking about her earlier question.

"When I look at you as you are now, all excited and your eyes sparkling, I find you especially beautiful. These men will be pleasantly surprised. You said you're meeting the first one in a coffee shop here in town?"

"Yes, I don't want any of them to have my address yet. Some of them may turn out to be weird. I don't think this teacher is, but I want to be safe. There will be lots of people around the coffee shop at five-thirty."

She stood up and took her dishes from the table. Ted followed suit although he had left part of his dinner uneaten. If she noticed, she didn't comment but continued with her commentary.

"This teacher's name is Bert. His wife died of some illness three years ago. I respect the fact that he hasn't entered into a relationship since then, He's five foot nine, not quite as tall as I'd hoped, but he reads a lot, likes the outdoors and is looking for a long-term partner just like I am."

Ted interrupted. "What do you consider long term? You stuck with that one guy in Arizona for five years, and you and I have made it for two. Do you call these long term?"

"I'm not sure what I mean. We talked about ten years over the phone. What I know I don't want is something that lasts six months. I want some stability and I'm sure not interested in some guy who's just after sex, no matter how good looking he is!"

Lauren had completed rinsing off the dishes and stacked them in the washer rack while she talked. As she was drying her hands, she walked towards the door. Ted reluctantly followed. He thanked her for a nice dinner. She gave him a light kiss while holding the door open. It was still only eight o'clock, but "Goodnights" ended their evening.

He noticed the lights immediately come on in her computer room. They remained on. It was with a feeling of hopelessness that he went off to bed after an hour's reading. Was her heart now beating rapidly in anticipation of a new, younger lover? He finally fell off to sleep.

On Friday, about five-fifteen, Ted observed Lauren about to get into her car. She glanced his way where he was writing at his kitchen table and waved. He hurried outside in time to give her a thumbs-up, then stared after her as she sped down the street on the first leg of her manhunt to replace him. He slowly walked back into his house.

He was finishing dinner when car lights alerted him that she was home. It wasn't yet seven, and the phone rang almost immediately.

"It was awful! This guy was a toad. He wasn't five foot nine. He was hardly five foot seven! He had a silly grin. To myself, I called him Mickey Rooney. I couldn't stand much more than an hour. When he asked me if he could call, I told Bert I didn't believe we were suited for each other."

She continued her description of the meeting with the teacher for several more minutes and then caused Ted's heart to race.

"I'm coming over to sleep with you! I'm going to eat first, though."

He cleaned up the kitchen, put on a favorite tape, and then tried to read a recent copy of Newsweek. His mood was light. He toyed with the idea that Lauren was responding in part to his recent letter and congratulated himself on his decision to write it.

A knock told him she had arrived. Without closing the door she embraced him and followed it with a deep kiss.

"I'm ready for bed! How about you?"

As they undressed, Lauren continued with some additional negative observations about the earlier meeting. Ted listened without apprehension. This guy had turned out to be a toad and no threat to him. He intended to fully enjoy this night with her.

They seemed to share the exciting but now relaxed atmosphere. Ted tried to make sure that their lovemaking was a prolonged and delightful experience for both of them. Lauren was in no rush to turn over and go to sleep. He knew she had something else on her mind.

"I'm not going to tell any of these men that I'm having sex with you. They couldn't possibly understand that I'm still in love with you."

She confided, too, that Ellen and her best friend, Ruth were aghast when she told them she was continuing to have sex with him. She said that both had strongly advised against it as had Ellen's new boyfriend.

"They all said that I needed to concentrate on being appealing to these new men, that sleeping with you would distract me. Maybe we'd better not do this again."

Ted was suddenly in a light and confident mood.

"These people haven't a clue about how you should handle these matters, Lauren! Let's look at it realistically. If you go into these meetings with no 'needs' for a sexual encounter, you can dispassionately appraise the man's more permanent qualities. Look at what a big help I can be to you!"

She gave him a sharp nudge and then joined in with his laughter. "I know you! What a phony argument! All you want to do is justify my sleeping with you. I love you for it, though, but don't know what I'll do in the future."

Lying there beside her now, feeling fully loved, Ted wasn't going to worry about tomorrow. Sleep came easily.

Her Sunday meeting, though again raising his apprehension, was reported as equally fruitless by Lauren. She had called and walked over within an hour after returning home.

"I felt comfortable to meet with Ed in a bar, but I ordered a soda so alcohol wouldn't possibly color my thinking. It seemed to me that he was just looking for a drinking partner and whatever would follow. I'm way past that. I used to think the same way he does now, but no longer have any interest in what goes on between men and women in bars. I want something more now."

She looked intently at Ted across the table.

"You've shown me there is more. I wish all the time that you were younger. I wouldn't be going through this."

Lauren reached over, squeezed his hand and continued.

"I told Ed 'Thanks, but I didn't feel we had the same interests'. He seemed to accept that. He wasn't that good looking either."

She got up to leave. Her hesitant smile and look seemed to be asking for Ted's approval.

"I have a meeting with another man this coming Friday evening at the same place I met the teacher. He's driving up from San Jose. His name is Ron, and he had a great phone voice. He's been divorced for five years and has two children. The daughter lives within fifteen miles of here, and Ron's going to visit her afterwards and stay there overnight."

Ted's answer was toneless. He needed to say something.

"I'm glad you're meeting at the coffee shop. I've read several recent articles, admittedly most involving teenage girls, where e-mail dates turned out to be disasters for them."

He saw little of her during the week. Even with off and on rains, however, he managed to be in a position to wave each morning as Lauren departed for work.

Ted hoped that some of her infrequent calls would be invitations for a visit, but they were brief and seemed mainly for the purpose of wishing him "Goodnight". He cringed when she told him she had enlisted the help of a friend and now included her picture with her internet ad. His response had been, "You're bound to get a flood of guys who want to shack up with you now." He knew he wasn't being fair to Lauren.

Once she was home from teaching, the light in her computer room seemed to him to be always on. How many more men were seeking to replace him in her life? He found little relief from that constant worry. He wasn't anxious for Friday to come. This might be the man.

Again, though, Ted gritted his teeth and was outside to salute her as she left. Lauren gave him an embarrassed smile as if to say, 'Why am I doing this? What can I expect this time? But, please wish me luck.'

She had explained earlier that this man, Ron, was a computer expert working as a consultant for some state function. She said she'd asked him and was assured that he had a fine educational background and a steady work history. This information added to Ted's discomfort.

Two hours elapsed. He caught up on some magazine reading and fixed a drink but delayed preparing any dinner. He was becoming too apprehensive to be hungry. Something could always be put together quickly later. There was no point in rushing through a nervous dinner. He poured another drink. Probably this man and Lauren had talked for a long time and then had eaten a light dinner. Ted didn't see that as a good sign for him, either. The other meetings hadn't progressed that far.

But then her car arrived, and the phone rang within ten minutes.

"Have you eaten yet? I'm starved! Why don't you fix up a big salad? What else do you have?"

"There's some lasagna in the freezer. I'm sure there's enough for both of us. I remember the part I ate was awfully good. My daughter sent it down several weeks ago."

He was thawing the lasagna and was only halfway through making the salad when she arrived.

181

"Get me a glass of wine, please." She said, throwing off her jacket. "I really liked this guy!"

Ted dried his hands and they shared a brief kiss. He winced at her announcement but again decided to accept the role of a favorite uncle as though he were being asked to listen to hints of young love by a sixteen-year old relative. He didn't want to spoil their dinner. Could Lauren not realize, though, that her talking about other men was painful for him? He handed her the glass of wine, continued with the salad and waited.

"I thought that Ron was a real gentleman and a good family man, He was up here to help his daughter get settled into her new house. She has a baby just a year old. He showed me her picture. She's a darling and I can't wait to meet her."

"Why didn't he buy you dinner if he's such a gentleman?" Ted couldn't keep the edge out of his voice.

"Now don't go getting mad! I know he would have, but he had promised his daughter that he'd be there by eight. We had talked so long there wouldn't have been time."

She was now setting the table. Ted carried in the salad and lasagna. Lauren continued as they seated themselves.

"I asked him dozens of questions. I thought it was important to know why he got divorced. Ron said that his wife had gotten to where she didn't seem to want his overtures. He's a very sensitive man and likes to touch and be touched. I may have asked too many questions, I wondered on the way home if he thought I was too demanding of answers."

Ted recalled once calling her 'the interrogator,' a remark that had brought a storm of retaliation. This time he chose to smile and responded briefly.

"Yes, Lauren, I can understand that. You sometimes do it with me. You ask questions and then don't wait for answers."

He tried to steer the dinner conversation to other topics but was only partially successful. She seemed determined to expand on the man's good points. It was apparent that she liked Ron. Ted hesitantly raised a question that had increasingly been bothering him.

"Did you talk about sex?"

"Yes, I did, and I plan to tell each man that I love sex and hope to find a partner who feels the same way. You don't need to worry, though. They will know I want to get well acquainted first. Ron said he's going to call me during the week to see if we can get together for lunch or dinner when he next comes up to help his daughter. He promised it will be soon."

Ted's emotions did flip-flops with her final statement as she reached for her house key.

"Thanks for a great dinner and for being such a good listener! I put in two hours of hard exercise at the fitness center before meeting with Ron, and I'm really exhausted, but I want to sleep with you tomorrow night."

"Tomorrow will be a long but wonderful day for me, Lauren. Let me walk you across the street."

They hesitated at her door. Their kiss held for a long time. It was difficult for him to let go.

"I love you, Lauren. Goodnight."

"Ditto. Goodnight. Hope you sleep well!"

He was a long time getting to sleep. For almost two hours he searched through the six weeks since their Cabo trip trying to sort out what each of her visits since had meant. Again and again he relived the kiss and assurance of love he had just received.

He mentally reviewed each of the several letters he had written to her during the period since Cabo and her jolting "I want to end it" announcement. How was she taking those letters he had so painstakingly penned? Was she reading them as his acceptance of the finality that she was out of his life? Or was Lauren sharing his deeply felt need to somehow hold onto their romance? Had she seriously read his letters at all? Her responses had been almost zero.

Ted knew his age hadn't changed. Was it possible her mind had? It didn't add up. She seemed relentless in her current search for a younger man and yet they continued to make love.

He shivered again when he recalled her revelation of the questions raised around the pool at Cabo by couples her age.

"What on earth kind of a future can you possibly have with that old man?"

Nothing could ever erase the agony he felt in remembering those words. Still, here was that wonderful goodnight kiss just an hour earlier and the unexpected promise of enchantment.

She had sometimes seemed to be embarrassed about being seen in public places as a couple. She would occasionally walk several yards ahead of him on busy sidewalks. Pure strangers seemed to bother her most. He could almost understand that.

With his family members, she mingled fairly easily, although Ted knew that appearances tended to mask his daughter Kathy's lack of acceptance for Lauren.

He thought back to the half-dozen lunches or dinners he had arranged with his older friends and their wives, all out of town. Lauren had seemed to enjoy these. Everyone had been cordial, and the dinners had been light-hearted throughout. Lauren had teased lightly about some of his age-related idiosyncrasies. This had been balanced with her candid expression of admiration of Ted's super-active lifestyle. She had applauded suggestions of repeat dinners and had been welcomed warmly at the few second meetings.

His mind returned to the present. Ted knew how much Lauren loved to travel. If her uneasiness was limited to being seen as his partner when with groups on trips or excursions, could he devise a way of overcoming this reluctance? There had to be a way. He was almost desperate in his desire to keep her.

Finally, Ted hit upon an idea. It would be risky in a way but would accomplish two things he wanted most, to keep an intimate relationship with Lauren for several more years and to assist her in gaining more financial security during that time, giving Lauren a further reason to continue with him.

He couldn't remain in bed past four-thirty the next morning. Once up and coffee made, he was eager to put into writing the ideas he had gathered together before going to sleep. Maybe his plan to add two years to their romance would strike a chord with her. He remembered clearly that she had once suggested that her decision might have been a mistake. Was it possible Lauren would welcome the chance to delay her search for a younger partner if he provided her with a solid reason to do so? The newspaper could wait!

He didn't hurry his work. Each paragraph was thought out and carefully put into print. Ted couldn't believe that he required three pages to finally make his case. He made a few changes before typing the final draft of his letter and then ran an extra copy for himself. It had taken almost two hours.

He then read and reread his typed proposal to Lauren, worried that it might sound too formal. He decided against softening some of the wording. She had insisted on a number of occasions that she 'liked a man with a plan'. He would show her that he was such a man.

With a bouquet of fresh flowers in hand, he was at her door at nine-thirty.

After giving him a kiss and a big hug, and thanking him for the flowers, her eyes fell on the envelope.

"I don't like the looks of that! Do I dare read it?"

Ted grinned. "Come on, now! How often have I given you letters that you disliked after reading them? And, yes, you're welcome."

"I have work to do now. I'll read it later. Thanks, again, for the bouquet. It's lovely."

His spirits dropped though he tried not to show it. He had hoped she'd take time to look at his letter right then. Hopefully, they could spend a few minutes talking about it so he could build some immediate enthusiasm for his plan. Ted was disappointed as she smiled but left the envelope on the counter and began arranging the flowers.

He crossed the street to his own place, a little disturbed by her indicated indifference to his important letter. As he thought more about it, such a response was normal for her. Lauren didn't react well to any sort of pressure. Opening a threatening letter was something she would prefer to do outside the presence of the writer. He felt better.

Ted's spirits further picked up as he mentally tallied this Saturday's work to be done. A full day generally meant a good day for him.

He had watched the lawn grass spurt up from the warmer temperatures coupled with recent rains. This required trimming and would also provide raw material for his winter-depleted compost bin.

He first could leisurely read the early morning paper. After that he needed to do some grocery shopping for the next week. He was sure he had all of the items needed to prepare their dinner tonight. If there was time remaining, he was anxious to get underway on spading part of his garden area. The rains and rising temperature had triggered the emergence and growth of a thick mat of volunteer grass.

As he sat down with the paper, he reminisced back to one of the changes he had made after his wife's death. In an effort to buoy his spirits, he had decided to begin each day by assigning it a 'grade'. A 'four star' day meant it was jammed full of things to do including four activities of interest to him. Ted's spirits picked up even more now as he could easily identify a three star day.

For one, he had already written his letter and had delivered it and flowers to Lauren.

He had purchased some frozen king crab legs. She was bringing asparagus. Their dinner would include bulgur wheat pilaf that he would be preparing. The combination had become a real favorite of theirs.

Lauren would be sleeping over afterwards with no rush to leave his house on Sunday morning. They would be able to cuddle and talk.

There would still be time for coffee and fruit before she made last minute preparations for her drive to San Francisco to meet her older brother for a late lunch. Yes, this Saturday promised to be a strong three-star day for him!

Her single day trip to visit her brother was a recent decision. Lauren had timed it to fit into a two-week stay he was making in that city. She had excitedly told Ted about her brother Stuart's flight out from Wisconsin to apply for an administrative position in a private school.

Ted checked the front lawn and found the grass still covered with dew. He would wait another hour and spend the time getting a few bills paid and some filing done.

He saw Lauren periodically passing her kitchen window; the lights in her computer room remained on. He twice stopped his work for another critical review of his long letter to her. Would she have yet taken time to read it? He hoped he might soon get a call with some questions or comments about the offer he had made. Most of all he wanted her to show an interest in the letter that was so critical in his mind.

Ted's confidence slipped when he reread the part about preferring they not live together during the two years he had projected in his letter. Had he made too much of that worry? His determination to not encourage her to move in was based mainly on his memory of a dozen big arguments that had badly shaken much of the first two years of their being lovers. Was this fair to Lauren?

During the recent autumn, those arguments had almost ceased with few really serious confrontations. She had, at that time almost ceased drinking entirely. Ted had complimented her on that change.

For one thing, he knew that he had, on most occasions, had a drink with her, or they had shared margaritas or wine after her arrival at his house. They both had agreed that there must have been a relationship between her intake of alcohol and the arguments.

With that behind her, why hadn't he encouraged Lauren to move in with him? Why was he still holding back so pointedly in his letter? These questions continued to plague him. Would she see this omission as a silent rejection, a slap in the face? He knew she was one to scrutinize every word. Ted's frown became a smile as he recalled Lauren's reaction when he had sometimes pointed that out.

"After all, I'm an English teacher!"

He quickly returned to his thoughts. If she had made this positive change, why couldn't he respond? Would her feeling of being rejected cause her to turn down the entire proposal?

Ted knew that living with him would not only save her five thousand dollars a year in rent costs, it would keep her close. That was his most cherished dream and now almost an obsession.

Again, though, he decided to let the letter stand as he had handed it to her. He needed an escape! Supposing Lauren became depressed over her work and began using more alcohol? How could he face those angry eyes? At those times her words had cut like knives. It seemed that every oversight or infraction on his part resulted in a mountain of accusations. How could he then ask her to leave? Where would she go? How could he enforce his demand if the confrontations continued and Lauren insisted she had no other place to live?

He went outside and re-inspected the lawn and concluded that it was dry enough to mow. She hadn't called, nor had she come out into her front yard to admire her early-blooming flowers. This was almost a ritual for her.

Ted was half finished with the front lawn when Lauren emerged with a folder of papers. He throttled back the mower engine and walked across the street to her car.

"I've a bunch of copies to make and several short errands to run. Be back in a couple of hours. Don't forget to take the crab legs out of the freezer!"

With a smile and a wave, she was gone. She hadn't even acknowledged his letter. Ted searched his mind again to think through some of the exact words in his almost desperate effort to get her to abandon her move to find a younger man. The letter had read:

> *Dear Lauren,*
>
> *You will be seeing your brother tomorrow, and, from what you've told me, a discussion of our relationship's demise and your ongoing effort to find a younger partner will occupy part of the time you spend with Stuart. I'm glad you'll be doing this. You have told me that he is content to listen and seldom makes rash suggestions. His views might be helpful because this change you are making could be a major turning point in your life. I can't overstate the impact it's having on me.*

If you should review with Stuart the proposed plan I've made for us, it needs to be clear what I'm suggesting. I don't want you to have to say, "I'm not at all sure what Ted means here." I hope you'll have read it thoroughly and will ask me about anything you don't find clear.

First, I would ask that you keep your jobs. Although you have sometimes expressed a different opinion on this point, I feel that your living with me without the responsibilities, demands, and rewards of working would be an absolute disaster.

Our two-year deal would have an escape clause for both of us. You could just walk away by telling me it wasn't working for you and you wanted out. I could get out with a thirty day written notice to you. There would be no place for an argument, nor any reason to be given by either of us.

You would become my part-time employee, a 'Traveling Companion and Housekeeper'. For that service, I would pay you a thousand dollars each month for the two years unless one of us chose to end things. I would go through the needed formal steps for Social Security and tax withholding requirements.

I want the relationship I describe for two main reasons in addition to my self-serving desire to keep you close to me for as long as I can. I have always wanted to see you get ahead financially. It has become very important to me that you look at financial stability as a worthwhile goal, and that you have confidence your life is moving ahead. I respect the fact, as you have reminded me, that you are a 'survivor', but you needn't settle for that.

You have a decent car already, a little money in the bank, and some reduction in your student loan. You've made no secret about your feeling of appreciation for my help. I want to be able to help you continue that momentum.

My second consideration is that you need a reason to give to strangers in response to questions about why you are with me. It had to have been terrible for you to have couples your age you've met (Cabo, for example) ask you directly or by implication, "What on earth kind of a future can you possibly have with that old man?"

You do need to have an answer, and many young women are paid companions for older men. Besides, Lauren, haven't you always told me you'd be willing to help me with my housekeeping? I accept that you 'don't do windows' as you have also reminded me.

At the end of the two-year period, I would expect that you would have added at least twenty thousand dollars to your bank account, and your student loan would be under five thousand. You've made your payments steadily, and I see real progress in getting this burden behind you. It is quite possible that your job will have become permanent and full-time during these next two years. Then your financial future would be fairly well assured.

I know that you will dispute this observation, but I'm telling you that you will be an even more beautiful and desirable woman two years from now than you are today. You will not have lost any ground! Your health habits are excellent, and you will be every bit as appealing to a younger man as you are today.

My preference is that we would not live together but that you maintain your present rental situation or move to an apartment of your own if that should become your decision. It isn't that I wouldn't love to waken each morning with you beside me. I thrill to find you there. You are so extra lovely in the mornings. You're relaxed, rested, and stress-free. Sometimes you are eager, all over again, for more petting and lovemaking. What man, at any age, wouldn't fight to keep that situation alive? I'm at the top of that list of guys!

But, you do have a domineering personality. You insist on having things your way, and you won't let up. I can't handle to be verbally beat on even when your demands are realistic as they are many times. I'm fearful that you wouldn't let up on insisting I change activities not to your exact liking. I'm a little concerned, too, that you'd be pushing me constantly to make big changes in my house. I'd be under stress too much of the time you were there. From my position, it would be best that we live separately during this period. I would give on this point, Lauren, but only with some clear understandings between us.

Too, there is something magic about being able to wave to you each morning as you show up in your kitchen window. I've missed terribly my standing out front and blowing you a kiss as you drive off to work. Never have I ceased to be awfully excited when you tell me you're coming over. There's something truly romantic here! I like that wonderful, yet independent relationship we have developed and would prefer to continue keeping it that way. Your needs as to where you live, as you see them, though, would have a high priority if we work this out and both feel comfortable in our roles.

Would lovemaking be involved? Yes, I couldn't survive without that, but it isn't something that goes into an agreement. If that fell apart, the stress would soon become too great for me. I would cancel out. On your side, if I became impotent, you would have my blessing to walk out. You've made it clear that you would. I believe we feel the same on the importance of intimacy to keep our relationship strong.

So, there I lay my heart out to you! It is a proposal that would be interpreted by some as self-serving. I realize that. But, if you should, now or at some point in your manhunt, want to talk seriously about what I've written, I'm just across the street. I do love you, and I want to do what is best for you without making my life a mess. A man is a fool to not try hard to preserve something that has been, on balance, an exciting and beautiful adventure. ~Your guy, Ted

He had showered and shaved and was measuring the wheat when Lauren arrived home from her errands. Ted watched as she took several trips to unload her trunk of purchases. With her hands full, she gave him a nod and smile when she spied him under the kitchen light.

Forty-five minutes later, she was at his door with a small bundle of asparagus. Ted's pilaf was steamed and ready. He was cutting the long crab legs at the joints to be able to fit them into the steamer rack.

"I don't like the fact you don't want to live with me!"

"Well, I think doing so would be a mistake for both of us. I'm sure you also read where I said it was something we could talk about."

She walked past him and placed the asparagus on the counter.

"Why would you need a thirty day written notice to get out when I could just leave?"

"Because there would be the employment part. It's a normal thing for people to be told several weeks in advance if their job is ending. It would be unfair to you for this not to be part of the agreement."

"It's silly to think that if I told people on a cruise that I was working for you as a traveling companion, they would believe it. Everyone would see right through that!"

"I don't think so. A lot of people with money pay for traveling companions. Besides, it was the best idea I could think of."

He was relieved that Lauren had obviously read his letter rather thoroughly. She hadn't discarded the idea outright. Her adamant statements, though, indicated to him that any further discussion right then would lead to an argument. It was time to move to another subject.

"These crab legs will take about ten minutes to steam. I'll start them. Why don't you take care of the asparagus? If I remember, it requires about the same amount of time.

Ted pulled the steamer pot and rack from a lower cupboard, and then turned to Lauren. "How about a glass of wine?"

"Yes, please."

He pulled her close, kissed her on the forehead, then left to pour the wine. She was putting the final stalks of asparagus in a pot for boiling when he returned. He waited until she was satisfied with the burner heat, then handed Lauren the wine.

"Let's toast your visit tomorrow with Stuart!"

"Yes, to my brother, Stuart. I'm so excited about the chance to see him. I can't believe he might be moving to San Francisco! His whole life has been in Wisconsin."

Their dinner discussion began about her diverse family. Ted had enjoyed listening to her stories about family situations. It had become apparent to him that she admired some of her many siblings, was concerned about others, but loved them all.

Lauren's mother had visited her that prior summer for almost a week. Ted had involved himself to the extent of even preparing dinner at his house one evening. It had been a balmy summer day and they ate in the screened-in patio. He had found her mother, Christina, to be down-to-earth and pleasant to converse with. Lauren had surprised him after her mother's departure.

"I guess I forgot to tell my mother about us before she arrived. Mom was kind of hoping that you and she would make a match. You are almost the same age. Boy, was she surprised when I told her I was sleeping with you! After she got over the shock, she said she thought you were a very nice man."

Stuart's stature among the siblings seemed to be well established. According to Lauren, most of his brothers and sisters respected his judgment on many issues. Ted could tell that she was no exception.

"I phoned his hotel earlier. Stuart was away, but I left word for him to call your number here this evening. He's to tell me where to meet him for lunch tomorrow."

The call came while Ted was washing dinner dishes. He excused himself and went into the living room to read while she visited and made notes.

Ted saw the evening developing as an ideal setting for their love-making. She was visibly excited and yet relaxed at the same time. Lauren asked him to get her favorite afghan and pillow and immediately stretched out on the couch following the completion of her call.

"Stuart said to say 'Hello'." She picked up the TV guide. "Here's the movie I want us to watch. It's only an hour and a half."

He completed the dishwashing, then dried and put away the pans. Soon his caresses of her feet were bringing the responses and murmurs he anticipated. How he desired this woman! Why should he have to let her go? How could the fate of his age have done this to him?

Afterwards, while they were still close together in his bed and relaxing in the afterglow, Ted whispered, "Why does something so wonderful have to end, Lauren?"

In the dim light of their tiny bedside lamp, he could see the tears glistening in her eyes. Immediately, he was sorry he had spoken because her gentle answer was so final.

"Because you're old, Ted, and it must end. I can't stand the thought of losing you either. But it will be worse later, at least for me. That's why I must face it now and find a younger partner."

He had no answer. They held each other in a final tight embrace and then settled onto their separate pillows.

"Goodnight. I love you so much, Lauren."

"Goodnight. Me too."

NINETEEN   Denial

It was five thirty Sunday evening and almost dark when Lauren returned from her visit with Stuart. She called to say she wouldn't be over for dinner, but she would come after to tell him about her day.

His spirits were lifted. The ring of her challenging questions the evening before had been a source of continuing apprehension during the day. Now, without the interruption for dinner, they might have well over an hour to discuss his plan. Hopefully, she wouldn't immediately push the TV power button.

Ted was glad that he had assured Lauren of his continuing love in his long letter. He counted on her having reviewed it several times and that her brother had seen it in a positive way if it was included in their discussion. To Ted, their lovemaking of the night before had been a confirmation of caring. But now, as he prepared and ate his dinner and waited for her, his doubts returned. Why should a few pleasant situations cause Lauren to change her mind? He did see her brother as a possible ally, but wondered now if this was unrealistic.

When Lauren arrived, she quickly spied and opened the box of chocolate candy he had received from his family for his birthday.

"Why haven't you eaten any?"

"It's just that I never think of it. Candy isn't a big thing for me anyway."

"I can't resist the stuff."

She selected one piece and quickly followed it with another. Then she carefully covered the box.

"Get this chocolate away from me!"

Ted enjoyed these little exchanges and marveled at the change in Lauren, in so many ways, since their early days as neighbor-lovers. He recalled the pressure from her to make special trips for individual candy selections she desired. An argument had almost erupted over his stalling until he could combine the five mile drive with other errands in the same area. He remembered one caustic remark she had made:

"Don't I mean enough to you to make a dinky little trip like that?"

Dropping her demands for chocolate seemed to fit the pattern of change. She had needled him on one occasion by saying that she needed to lose a few pounds to make herself more attractive to men after he was gone.

Ted asked her how her trip went. He wanted Lauren to get into the discussion he had been waiting for. She seated herself on the couch without reaching for the remote control.

"We had a good time. Stuart was amazed at how easily I followed his directions to where we dined. But we got to reminiscing, and that wasn't so great."

"What do you mean?"

"Years ago, my family, brothers and sisters one by one, jumped on me for drinking. They said I was thoughtless and abrasive. It was the most awful experience of my life. I couldn't believe it this afternoon when Stuart brought it up. He said he clearly remembered that family meeting and thought it had been beneficial."

Ted could see that she was still smarting from the injustice of that long ago attack. He acknowledged that it must have been painful and waited for her to continue.

"We did talk about your and my relationship. Stuart said he couldn't be of much help as it was a matter of the heart. He said that mom told him you are a thoughtful and articulate person. I think she thinks I am kind of lucky. Stuart agreed that losing you was a fact of life that I will be facing now or later. You know, Ted, you're going to die sooner than me."

Ted watched her closely, and was irritated by her certainty on this. Anything could happen. Anything. And he was still healthy and fully functioning and didn't see his death impending.

"Did you mention my proposal to give us another two years?"

"Yes, he said he could understand how much we loved each other and said that the work-with-pay part was a sort of carrot to encourage me to spend these extra two years with you."

"He's correct Lauren. That's exactly the way I intended it. I felt that you need a number of worthwhile reasons to change your mind. I would want you to enter any arrangement with enthusiasm, not a bunch of doubts."

"I just don't know what to do! If I do stay with you, we're going to get closer and love each other more. Then it will be a lot harder for us when we have to part."

Ted hoped she might be wavering.

"Aren't you forgetting that these next two years could be some of the most wonderful years in both of our lives? Do we have to look ahead as if something awful is inevitable? I realize that I'm looking at it from the selfish viewpoint of an older man, Lauren. I'd cherish each of the next two years with you."

She studied his face but made no response. Instead, she glanced at her watch and stood up.

"We can't forget that I have my class to teach in the morning. And I have a date for an early dinner tomorrow night, a man named Daniel. Will you walk me across the street?"

He sighed and walked with her in silence. She unlocked the door and they embraced in a long hug. His hoped for hour had been twenty minutes of nothing.

Ted plodded through a long uneasy couple of days until Lauren's Tuesday invitation to come over and watch a TV show after dinner. He was very excited to accept, especially when he saw Ellen throw a duffel bag in the car and pull out early in the evening. Perhaps he would get a positive answer to his offer tonight.

After answering the door, she offered Ted a glass of wine and a seat on the couch where they watched the first twenty minutes of the show saying little. At the first advertising break, however, she looked directly at him with a remark that brought an instant frown to his face:

"Ruth said your job offer was only an attempt to pay me for two years of sex. She said I'd be a dummy to accept it."

"Come on now! I do love an intimate relationship with you, but I explained very carefully in my letter why I was bringing up that job idea. I've said before that Ruth is automatically suspicious of men because of her marriage experiences. Why should her opinion count so much?"

"My brother told me the same thing! He said you were hoping to buy sex with me for those two years."

"Why do you tell me this now? On Sunday, you said that Stuart said I was offering you a carrot as an encouragement to stay with me. You indicated you saw nothing wrong with that."

Ted was stunned as she continued to pursue the same line of accusations during advertising breaks and sometimes for several minutes into the show. He listened in disbelief and became ever more uncomfortable. He was sure the pain she was causing him was obvious. Was she never going to quit?

"You didn't tell me this before. What prompted it now? In any case, I'm not sure I feel good at all about your showing my letter to anyone other than your brother!"

"When I first read it, I felt good. Now I feel awful. How could I have been so naïve?"

Ted could stand no more. She was being completely unreasonable. He was mentally exhausted, and stood up abruptly. A nagging thought went through his mind. Maybe she was right. He desired Lauren immensely, but when was it love? He sure as hell couldn't embrace the prospect of living with a woman who would chew on him like this on any issue. Lauren had just confirmed the wisdom of not unconditionally asking her to move in with him. Forget the urge to do that now! But then he glanced at her, that voluptuous young body in her provocative pajamas. How he wanted her! But now he couldn't hide his dismay.

"I don't want to watch any more of this show. Good night."

She didn't offer to get up and see him to the door. He wondered why, if her mind was so full of these questions, she had invited him over to watch a show? Should he cancel their plans to dine out on Friday night? When he had made those plans, she teased him by promising not to make any dates with other men for that night. He'd selected an especially nice restaurant, and didn't want that to be aborted midstream.

Though they had no other conversations during the early part of the next week, she reacted pleasantly to his morning exchanges of smiles and waves when she left for work, and he looked forward to their date.

He spent Thursday afternoon playing cribbage with another friend. For a while, he got his mind off of Lauren. But he immediately phoned her after getting home to confirm that their Friday dinner was still on. Her affirmative response eased his apprehension.

"I'm going to do an hour and a half workout and then will call as soon as I get home and shower."

"Great! Our reservations are for seven-thirty."

Their dinners were put before them in twenty minutes, though they were unhappy with the only available seating which put them very close to the crowded bar. They couldn't talk without shouting. Afterwards, he dropped Lauren off at her house.

"I want to change, and then I'll be right over," Lauren said.

He waited for her for an hour, alternately reading a magazine and peering out the window before she finally came across the street.

"I'm sorry. I got to talking with Ellen. What did you want to talk about that's so important?"

Ted tried not to show his irritation.

"I was really shaken Tuesday night when you told me that both Ruth and your brother said that my job proposal was really a ploy to pay you for sex."

"I told you no such thing!" Lauren said, aghast.

"I'm sorry, but I understood you very clearly. You repeated it twice."

"Then you must have been listening to someone else because I didn't tell you that. They both said it was an age-difference problem that won't go away. I plan to continue to look for a younger partner. I have a date with Daniel tomorrow. It's late and I need to get to bed. Thanks for dinner. Goodnight."

Daniel, Ben, Ed, Fred, whatever their names were, they seemed to have the upper hand with Lauren at this point, and Ted was increasingly concerned that she might not accept his proposed arrangement and might even find that younger partner. Could he stand being treated like an old uncle, feeling forced to feign interest in her actions that threatened to dump him?

Before she had reached her house, he regretted bringing up Tuesday's conversation. Of course, she was tired after a long week of work. But damn it, he was stressed, too! Why couldn't Lauren have added, "But we'll get together soon." He desperately needed assurance that she wasn't closing him out. Not yet.

Over the next few weeks, his visits with Lauren were brief; only for coffee or a drink, but pleasant and casual. She had made no effort to disguise the fact she was preoccupied with her computer e-mail and her hopes for a meaningful relationship with a younger man. If she noticed his emptiness, she ignored it. Ted felt forced to grab any time with her.

One afternoon, she did invite him over to work in her garden alongside her. He showed up with a shovel and rake, and found her waiting in the backyard. Not long after they began working, she insisted on telling him about a promising meeting with a teacher from a town about fifty miles away.

"He was such a tall man that I had to look way up to make eye contact. I think he said he's six foot four. His name is Tom and he teaches math."

Ted tried to show some interest but continued his work with the shovel. "Where'd you meet him?"

"Oh, at a café for an early dinner. I drove to Marysvale to meet him."

"He's a man you met on the internet? Sounds like you moved pretty fast. What happened to the San Jose guy, what was his name, Rob?"

"Ron. He didn't call. He said he would, but it's been almost three weeks without a word. I have to keep looking." She talked as she raked some pulled weeds into a small pile. "Tom has two teenaged boys. He's divorced and his ex-wife has the boys during most weekdays. Tom has them every other weekend. He's trying to be a good father. The oldest boy, I think he's seventeen, came into the restaurant while we were there. He said hello and then ignored me. He wanted to use his father's car." Lauren had looked up and seemed to be gazing into the trees.

"Tom is really quite good looking. He says he wants to keep in shape and works out regularly in a gym. He just towers above everyone else when he stands up."

She seemed to sense his growing discomfort.

"We can start spading now, if you want to. Let's put my garden here again," she said, pointing to the area of the prior summer's garden. It was getting a full three o'clock sun and was covered with volunteer grass about four inches high.

"I don't want any corn this time. It didn't ever look healthy, and the ears were too small. We can buy nicer corn in the stores."

Ted drove his spade into the corner of the grassy plot she had designated, and much to his chagrin, she then continued talking about the tall Marysvale math teacher. After he listened to her express concerns about the distance and the fact that he was a part time dad being obstacles to her relationship with Tom, Ted stopped spading.

"Well, Lauren, those are real drawbacks. But, I think most of the men who answer your ads will be divorced men with kids. You do like young people, though, and those I've seen you with seem to really respond to you. You'll remember that I've always said you'd have made a fantastic mother."

She proceeded to turn a few more shovels of dirt while Ted watched.

"I'm going to wait a few days and then e mail Tom letting him know I'd like to see him again."

They continued their work in silence until the phone rang inside Lauren's house. She went to answer it and he finished the spading, went to the garage for stakes and string to rope off the prepared ground, had raked the spaded area and pounded in the perimeter stakes by the time she returned.

"Sorry. It was Ruth. I had to tell her about Tom. And about this other man I'm seeing on Sunday. He's a hiker. You know how much I like to do that."

"Why yes, Lauren. I do know that."

They sat down at her patio table and she brought him a glass of wine. They chatted for about fifteen minutes before he left with his tools.

Lauren updated him at each of their brief meetings. Her visits to his house were usually terminated by the statement that she had to go home because she was "hoping for some phone calls."

She grew dissatisfied with Tom, who never called when he said he would. She agreed to meet a long-haul truck driver from Nebraska, and in spite of Ted's warnings, defended her decision to meet him. The night of that date, Ted purposefully prepared a late dinner for himself hoping to see her return by the time he went to sleep. She had not.

The next morning, however, Ted had barely been able to scurry to his driveway in time to wave goodbye. She apparently had made it home and slept up until the last minute. There had been no kitchen light and he doubted if Lauren had stopped for any breakfast at all.

She called around six that evening.

"Why don't you have your dinner, and I'll fix up something for myself. Come over after that, and we can visit for an hour." She quickly added, "But then I'll need to get right back to grading papers."

She was just completing cleaning up her dishes when he arrived.

"Why don't you go into the living room and wait for me? I'll bring each of us a glass of wine."

He seated himself and waited. Lauren had an Elton John tape playing and soon arrived with the wine and joined him on the couch.

"Walter was really nice. He's one of the few who said a lot of romantic things. That appealed to me!"

"What did you have for dinner?"

"I had a plate of spaghetti and a salad. I insisted that he order a big steak that was on the menu. He claimed he wasn't that hungry but ate it all. I paid for my own dinner."

Lauren added, "He did have a pot belly, but I don't mind that in a middle-aged man."

Ted finally decided to ask a question that he knew was completely uncalled for.

"Did he ask you to climb into the truck sleeper with him?"

"No, Ted, that was one of the things I liked about him. He was a real gentleman. We sat in the cab and talked for almost three hours." Lauren stood up.

"I need to get to work. Walter is going to send me an e mail or phone me just as soon as he's sure about his next California trip. He thought it would be ten days, but not over two weeks. I think you'd like him. I do."

She walked Ted to the door and embraced him before saying goodnight.

For several weeks, he endured her regular recounting of the details of her nature hike with Bryan, and other less enjoyable experiences with the men she'd met. Her internet ad was obviously getting many responses. There would be more! Yes, Lauren said she had deleted many of them, but Ted's jealousy surged when she told him about any who interested her. It was clear to him that she wasn't wavering in her stated plan to find a younger man to replace him.

Lying in his bed, he found some solace in knowing that she hadn't completely abandoned him during her search. Hadn't she come over, without his asking, to sleep with him on several occasions since announcing that she was ending their relationship? These hours had been comforting and exciting for him. He was sure those occasions had meant something to Lauren.

He knew that Lauren was trying to build a new life for herself that wouldn't include him romantically. He had acknowledged her need for that both verbally and in writing before. She owed him nothing more than what they had already shared. Was it time to accept that? Was it finally time for him to accept the role of neighbor and friend? He shuddered at the prospect but could think of no alternative.

His thoughts turned to the value of writing a farewell letter to her. The newspaper had remained on the front steps while he sipped coffee. It had become daylight and he drew the kitchen curtains. There was no activity on the street, and no lights shown from Lauren's house. It was time to sort out the best words to convey his decision to her.

Forty five minutes later his letter was completed. He saw no rush to deliver it and decided to go ahead with his planned schedule of errands.

He drove to the Sunday farmers' market and then the supermarket. Ted waited until almost ten before gathering up the note and bouquet of her favorite carnations and walking across the street.

"Come on in! It isn't locked," she called out.

He declined her invitation to have a cup of coffee with her, accepted her thanks for the flowers, dropped his letter on the counter, and hurried out the door. He had made no attempt to hand the letter to Lauren. What was the purpose of hanging around? Ted was numb with the thought of the certain consequences of his written decisions, but he had to make them.

His letter read:

> *Dear Lauren,*
>
> *I'm giving up. This is not something I've done often in my life, and I surely don't do it well. It is finally apparent that there is no future for me in your life. You are understandably continuing your search for a new partner, and you will find a suitable one. It's only a matter of time, and that leaves no room for me. I've tried to kid myself into thinking this can change, but it can't.*
>
> *You've told me that you needed space in relation to me. My needs, though, are the opposite. They are for now, not some time in the future, and that situation demands a closeness to you. I can't stand the stress of being near you otherwise.*
>
> *I won't be calling you nor suggesting dinners together. If you want me, or need something, I'm here. You can have all of the space you need. I don't know why I continued to mislead myself into thinking it could be any other way once you told me your initial decision was firm.*
>
> *I'm withdrawing my work offer. A lot of thought and love went into that proposal. Yes, there was a selfish carrot in there. I held the slim hope that you would see two more years with me as being a worthwhile and rewarding part of your life. Understandably, I view a two-year period in our lives in a far different light than a woman of your age would. It also seemed to me to be a reasonable way for me to more*

than double the little money gifts that I've felt so good about giving you.

I am saddened that my motives were so differently interpreted. Perhaps I should have anticipated that as I now look back . I love you Lauren. Good bye. ~Ted

TWENTY   The Car

Ted admired the car as it drove slowly past. It was almost nine and he was at the kitchen sink, cleaning up his few dinner dishes. The driver's head was turned towards Lauren's house. It wasn't a casual glance. Ted could feel the concentration. Although dusk was closing in, he could see a lone male driver.

He half smiled. Lauren must have given this prospect her address. Now the man was examining her neighborhood.

Fifteen minutes later Ted briefly stopped reading to get a glass of water. The same car was passing by again, with the driver's head firmly directed across the street. Lauren's bedroom light was still on. Ted thought of calling to tease her about the drive-by visitor but returned to his book instead.

She had to have read his giving-up letter by now. Would she be relieved? He didn't want to believe that! It seemed to Ted that she just couldn't quite give him up, and he couldn't help entertaining hope even still.

She arrived shortly after noon but instead of going into her house, she came directly to his. They held an embrace for a long time. Finally, Lauren stepped back and looked at his sad expression.

"I may not find anyone," she said.

"You will, Lauren. I can't fill the place of a younger man." Ted thought he saw genuine sadness and compassion in her eyes and finished with a final, undisguised plea: "You can help me in the meantime by being close now and then if you choose to. I can handle the ultimate loss when the time comes."

Lauren left for her house after giving him another deep kiss. She never called although he waited up until almost ten, nor did she call the next morning.

But that afternoon, he was engrossed in some front yard grass trimming when Lauren pulled directly into his driveway, an unusual move for a day when the pressure of her classes was the greatest. She seldom even stopped at her house for her short lunch break.

"Ted, I'm a little uneasy about one of the men I've met. I wanted to tell you two weeks ago but didn't want you to worry. Now, it's sort of gotten out of hand."

"Could it have been a guy driving a new-looking, sporty red car?" Ted asked.

He noticed her head snap back and her eyes open wider. "Yes, why?"

"He drove by slowly twice, a few nights back. There was no doubt the driver's interest was in your place. I almost called you but it was after nine."

Lauren turned off the engine but remained seated.

"I'm not going to get out because you know what a rush I'm in, but I felt I had to tell you."

"Why has it become such a problem? Is this one of your on line guys?" Ted knew that Lauren didn't usually let much rattle her, yet this, for some reason, had.

"Yes, and I've met with him twice. His name's Daniel. He's forty-two. I was really impressed by him at first and flattered because he told me he couldn't take his eyes off me, I was so beautiful." She added, "He's really nice looking and intelligent, too."

Lauren had seemingly forgotten her need to rush away. Ted stood with one hand on the open window of her car and bent down slightly to look intently into her face while she continued,

"He insisted on buying dinner at our first meeting. You know how I don't like that. I told Daniel I wanted to pay for mine, but he brushed me off and said he wouldn't hear of it. He said he has a good job with a travel agency here in town and believes that a man should pay for his date's dinner. I tried to tell him that we were just getting acquainted, but he wouldn't listen.

"I think I made a mistake in having lunch with him on another day, and I even let him show me his nice apartment one afternoon." Seeing his raised eyebrows, she quickly added, "His housekeeper was there. Maybe

I went a little too far, but it meant nothing. You know how impetuous I am sometimes."

Ted couldn't repress a smile. Yes, he well remembered. After all, it was only the second time they met that she had seduced him, in the mostly empty house across the street; that she had helped him to remember that he was a man, a virile man, attractive to women, and had changed his perception of himself and life. Lauren didn't return his smile, seeming intent on presenting her defense. "But you have to understand, Ted, that I'm so discouraged because neither of those other men I liked ever called back." Then, it was her turn to brighten.

"He had roses delivered yesterday, two dozen beautiful red ones. You should see them! This morning he called before I left for classes and insisted we're meant for each other. Daniel wants me to go to Monterey with him next weekend." She finally paused.

"What did you tell him?"

"I was desperate. He seems so sweet and energetic, and he dresses very nicely too. I didn't want to discourage him entirely. I told him that you and I hadn't completely broken up yet and I needed a little time."

Ted stepped back a foot from the car.

"Did you describe me? Did you tell him I was a lot older than you? Does he know where I live?"

"I lied a little and told Daniel you were only fifteen years older than me. I did tell him you were a really great neighbor who lived across the street."

Ted couldn't hide his agitation. Lauren started the engine, slipped the car into reverse, but kept her foot on the brake pedal.

"Maybe I shouldn't have done that. I can't believe he'd bother you, though." The quick flip of her hair indicated dismissal. "I'll talk to you in a couple of days."

Ted moved only enough to be sure the backing car wouldn't hit him. He accompanied his wave with a slight shaking of his head, then watched as her car rounded the corner of their short, almost secluded street before picking up his tools and hanging them in the garage. He vividly recalled the details of her entry into his life. Before she complicated it. How she had added the spice of youth back into his seventy-five year old body, but was now tearing his life apart. He could barely stand the torment.

All thoughts of lunch were gone. He needed to get away from it all for a while at least. Why not drive through the delta agricultural area and along the Sacramento river for an hour or two? He quickly changed out of his gardening clothes.

He drove south along the river levee road, and told himself that there was no way, or reason, for them to get back any significant part of what they had once had. Their age difference was the problem, and he couldn't become younger.

The scenic drive down the winding levee road had become one of his and Lauren's favorites. He recalled having suggested it several times when he felt their relationship needed just such an atmosphere.

The only boats on the water were fishermen trolling for large-mouth bass or anchored in more sheltered stretches of the river, bottom-fishing for catfish. He pulled off the road after thirty minutes and watched the river activity for a while.

Ted ended his down-river drive where he should have known he would, at a popular river front restaurant where he and Lauren had occasionally shared a lunch. He sat in the car for ten minutes wondering why he would torment himself by going in. Why not go to some other place where there were no memories? He finally shrugged that off; he needed to eat somewhere. In his haste to leave his house, he'd overlooked eating anything.

He ordered a beer and asked if he might have a meal at the bar. The bartender seemed to welcome the chance to talk about herself when she wasn't busy with other customers. She had moved up from Southern California.

"I had to get away as far as I could. My boyfriend and I broke up because he started to see someone else. I couldn't stand being anywhere near them. There's not much going on here, but it's really peaceful. Everyone's been nice so far, and there's no pressure in this job. I realize it's going nowhere, but it does pay the rent."

She disappeared and soon returned with his order of a bowl of soup and a small salad. The plate of French bread was especially appealing. From his seat at the end of the bar, Ted watched her handle the drink orders. He continued eating but nodded if the woman made casual observations to him.

He didn't think her face was especially attractive, but concluded that her eyes gave out a warmth that could be appealing. He couldn't help but notice that she had a nice figure. Ted didn't see any reason to share his situation with her. Finally, he did ask her a question.

"Have you met anyone here yet?"

"I've been here about six months. There are lots of nice men who come in as regulars, but most of them are married. I almost went out with a couple of single guys who parked their boats here for a few drinks and dinner but backed out."

"What are your plans now?"

"Oh, I'm not in a hurry to make any."

Ted paid the bill and assured the bartender how pleasant it had been to visit with her. When he arrived home, he was surprised to see that he had missed two calls during his several hour absence. The first was from a high school teacher asking for a return call to set up a date for Ted's next appearance. He played the next call through two times. It was Caroline from Cabo.

TWENTY-ONE   Caroline

Of course he remembered her. It was a little over three months since his and Lauren's winter Cabo San Lucas vacation. He pictured Caroline as maybe ten years younger than Lauren, attractive and soft-spoken. What could she want? Looking at the clock, he decided it was too late to return her call. He would call her the next evening.

When he spoke with Caroline the next evening, she told him that her husband had moved back to San Francisco. "His company had an opening there and he jumped at it. We've separated and I'm going to get a divorce. It just wasn't working out, Ted."

"I'm sorry to hear that, Caroline. But, sometimes I guess there is no point in trying to hold a marriage together, especially if there are no children, and I don't recall you mentioning any. How are you managing?"

"I'm okay. It's meant moving into a small apartment, but it's nice. I've had some luck with my part-time real estate sales job and sold three houses, and I'm now paid for the three days a week at the library where I was doing volunteer work. So I'm getting by fine. It's a big change and I'm rather lonely." She paused before asking, "How are you and Lauren doing?"

Ted hesitated for several seconds. He glanced at the empty spot on the couch where she had kept her pillow for watching television.

"Things have changed here, too. Lauren told me soon after we got back from Cabo that she wanted to find a younger partner. She's met some of the men who answered her Internet ad and has a bunch more who want to meet her. It's been painful for me, and I don't see much of her. I wish I could tell you that things were different. I know that you were concerned for us when we were in Cabo."

"I haven't called Lauren, although I do have her number. I thought I'd call you first. Would you like to spend a few hours at the zoo with me?"

"I sure would. Are you available tomorrow morning?"

"Yes, and I'll treat for lunch there," Caroline said, and the plan was set.

He had hardly replaced the receiver when the phone rang. It was Lauren.

"Would you like to go to a movie with me tomorrow afternoon? It starts at two. We haven't done this for a while, and I think you'll like this one." She paused, waiting for a response. His mind was racing, searching for a reply. "I'll be caught up on my work by noon, and I feel like relaxing and doing something with you."

"Gee, I wish I could, Lauren, but I've agreed to meet Kathy's boys for a game of golf." He was unprepared for how easily he lied to her. Why wasn't he honest with her? After all, she had been the one to first decide to see other people.

He expected an additional argument and was relieved when Lauren accepted his excuse.

The next day, Ted loaded his golf clubs, pull cart and shoes into the back of the Explorer. Lauren looked out from her kitchen window and waved as he pulled away. He spied Caroline waiting near the zoo entrance as he walked up after parking a block away. She hurried to meet him, extending her hand.

"Hello, Ted. It's so good to see you. You look well. I'm glad we're doing this." She then embraced him warmly.

"You look wonderful Caroline. I was almost afraid I wouldn't recognize you. This has turned out to be a perfect morning for a zoo tour. There aren't many visitors this early so we can spend all of the time we want at each exhibit. Let's go in!"

Ted paid the admission fee and then suggested they might like to see some of the larger animals first. Caroline nodded and smiled.

"Yes, you likely know your way around pretty well. Do you mind if we stop for a little while though and watch the flamingos? They seem to be loving this morning sun. I could use some myself." She reached over and engaged her arm in his and drew him a little closer as they watched the stately orange-pink birds stand on one leg.

They leisurely viewed the activities of the Bengal tigers, the lions and the giraffes. Ted outlined the Sacramento Zoo's history as best he could recall from visits and articles he'd read. He felt that Caroline's interest was genuine. He squeezed her hand while they watched the playful though seemingly rough antics of the orangutans. She turned and smiled. "In their own way they show a lot of affection."

Caroline chose to open the conversation about Lauren and his relationship with her.

"You said on the phone that Lauren was seriously searching for a younger man, Ted. Where does that leave you?"

"I hoped for a while that it might be a temporary thing because she continues to express a deep affection for me. Now, I'm convinced that she's bound to find a guy who suits her. We see very little of each other and that may be for the best. Lauren has told me about quite a few of the men she's gone out with. Some are well-established, and she needs a man who's successful. I'm just watching it happen and wish it were over."

Caroline looked at him intently for ten seconds. Ted liked the warmth he saw in her eyes. She touched his arm.

"Maybe I'd see it differently if I were in Lauren's shoes, but I think you're giving her more than she'd ever find in another man. Somehow I feel that she's making a mistake. The men she'll meet may be successful in their work, but are almost certain to be carrying a lot of baggage. Most will be coming off divorces and have children to support or payments to make to their ex-wives. She wouldn't want to share a man with all of his needy relatives. "

Ted laughed quietly, "Yes, it's as if you know her very well. She's very energetic and can be demanding. She has a big desire to travel and would keep any man hopping. Lauren wouldn't accept a lot of excuses as to why a man couldn't do things when they fit her timetable. It's just the way she is. She seems to have a need to dominate."

He hesitated. "But I'm being too critical. She's been awfully good to me. I have no reason to complain."

They walked in silence to the wallaby enclosure before Ted resumed speaking.

"Although I insist on keeping busy, I could usually adjust my schedule to fit Lauren's free time, but then this thing suddenly jumped up about her being embarrassed to be seen in public with me. I can't change my age, Caroline." Ted shrugged and looked at the wallaby without seeing.

Caroline pointed to a tiny head poking out of the marsupial's pouch. "Isn't it wonderful to feel that kind of protection? What a darling baby!"

She turned to Ted. "I'm sorry. I didn't mean to interrupt your thoughts. You look and act so young, and you don't seem to have any of the problems I hear old people talking about. I feel good being with you."

They continued their slow tour past the animal cages and stopped at the hippopotamus tank. The huge animal was swimming underwater the length of the tank and returning. It occasionally emerged just enough to suck in a new supply of air. The dozen young adults with small children seemed mesmerized by the animal's methodical, shadowy movement. Ted stood beside Caroline several feet behind a row of children peering between the heavy bars.

"I used to bring a grandchild here quite often. I remember that there was always a crowd. We would time the hippopotamus' stay underwater to see how long it could hold its breath."

He was pleased to be able to spy two of the three cheetahs in their large fenced compound. One was lying half-hidden among tall clumps of grass. The other was sprawled motionless atop a flat rock apparently enjoying the morning sun. Caroline was openly complimentary.

"You'd make a fine guide, Ted. I wouldn't have had any idea where to look for them."

"Thanks, but that's hardly true. I've even tried hunting but could never spot a deer soon enough. It's just that I especially like these cheetahs and always look for them. They don't pace back and forth like the tigers and the lions do, but seem to be completely content to enjoy their space here."

He glanced at his watch. "If we're going to have lunch, maybe we'd better go now before the lunchroom gets crowded." Ted pointed to a low, white building fifty yards away. "It's warm enough to eat on the patio if you'd like to."

They each ordered a hamburger and fries and picked a small table outside. Caroline asked about his family and listened attentively while he described his early years and the long, barefoot walk to school with his year-older brother. He included a description of the summer encounters with rattlesnakes along the dusty, little-traveled road, and his mothers' frantic pleas to be careful.

Ted was more interested in her recent life changes and asked her about her marriage break up. Her response seemed to reflect only sorrow that it hadn't worked out. "It was his second marriage. I had waited until I was almost thirty to get married because I was busy and really never had anyone who excited me a lot. Randy came along and suddenly I couldn't wait to get married. He seemed perfectly charming."

"Did he change after you married or wasn't he the person you thought he was?"

"I guess I didn't realize how ambitious Randy was and how all-important his work was to him. I admired him for his dedication and still do, but after our honeymoon I seemed to become an afterthought. He would wait until the last minute to tell me he was going to be out of town for several days."

Caroline shook her head. "Many times I would keep a nice dinner ready for him and then he'd come home late and tell me they'd had dinner brought in so the team could continue working. He was full of apologies but would forget to call me the very next time."

Ted watched but said nothing. He could see a tiny tear.

"I know Randy wasn't chasing anyone. He just forgot me in his drive to get ahead. When we had to move to Sacramento he became even more distant. He hated living here. It was almost a relief to me when the opportunity came for him to return to San Francisco. He didn't fight me about my decision not to go with him.

She looked sadly at Ted. "We managed eight years and there were lots of good times in them. He hardly ever calls me now. When he does, it's usually about a technical matter related to our divorce. He says he's been really busy, not dating."

Ted placed his hand gently over hers and then removed it.

"Thanks for telling me about your marriage. That isn't easy. Mine was different because it was a wartime marriage and happened so fast. The war dictated a long separation and a child was involved." He paused. "What shall we do now? I've saved the entire afternoon!"

"Let's go to my place," Caroline said. "I'd love to show you my little apartment, and I have some nice wine and would like to keep talking."

Ted followed her in his car to the address Caroline had penciled out for him in case they became separated on the drive, and parked his car in front of a two story, modern apartment building. She joined him after taking her spot in the covered parking area.

"I'm on the second floor and like it because there's no one above me to disturb me with pounding feet. It gives me a pretty nice view too."

She showed him through the single bedroom apartment. He was impressed with the simplicity of the furnishings and the lack of clutter.

"You'll die when you see my place," he said. "The office is bad enough, but you can barely see the kitchen table for all of the papers stacked around. I work in my kitchen because of the big window. I like to do my own housekeeping and the rest of the house generally looks pretty tidy." They exchanged smiles. "It's not that I'm a slob, but I keep so many irons in the fire that there's no point in putting everything away each evening."

She poured them each a glass of wine and put the remainder of the chenin blanc in an ice bucket. Ted raised his glass.

"Caroline, what would be a good toast? Here we are, a morning at the zoo, our first lunch, your new apartment and a delightful day so far."

She raised her glass.

"Why not just to us? We're both starting afresh. We can't know what's ahead. I've loved our day so far, Ted."

"Yes, wonderful. To us!"

It was almost three-thirty. The bottle of wine was empty. They had explored each others' lives and thoughts for almost two hours. Ted had been careful to steer the conversation away from him and Lauren as much as possible.

Caroline stood. "Come stand by the window with me. I want you to point out the direction to your house. I'd be excited to have you show me the place that's been your home for over forty years."

He walked to the window and put his arm around her waist. She turned to face him. Kisses with her seemed natural. They were gentle, with pauses while they studied each other's faces. Ted could hardly believe what was happening. Their kisses became more passionate and their bodies pressed tightly together.

"Why are we standing here in the front window making a spectacle of ourselves? Come with me!" She grasped his hand and led him into her bedroom. The open shades were quickly drawn.

Lauren's car was in the driveway when Ted arrived home. He was still recovering from the surprise of the tryst. He couldn't shake his feeling of guilt. It was Lauren he wanted. He made up a salad and was seasoning a small steak when the phone rang.

"I saw you drive in a while ago. How could a golf game last so long? I thought we might go somewhere for dinner, but you've likely already eaten."

"No, but I'm about to put a steak in the skillet to go with a salad I've already made up. You're welcome to come over if you'd like to share some of each. I can easily add to the salad."

"Thanks, but I don't feel like red meat. I'll make something up here. Why weren't you home earlier? You left before ten this morning!"

Ted forced a laugh. "Have you ever played with a couple of teenagers in one of their first real golf games? They want to stop and evaluate each shot. We had to let eight groups play through. Talk about impatient people!" Ted thought he'd add a clincher:

"Even the man filling out our foursome asked if he could join a group of three who asked to play through. I tried not to show my embarrassment. The boys were oblivious to all of the static about our slow play. I'm really glad I took them though. Each of the boys made a couple of good shots and just loved it. Did you go to the movie?"

"Yes, Ellen went with me. It was good. Maybe we can see it together later. It's a movie I could see twice." Her voice softened. "I could come over right after dinner, but I wouldn't be able to stay over. I want to get started on my work early."

Ted hesitated, and she added: "We haven't been together much lately."

"I hate to admit this, Lauren, but I'm awfully tired and wouldn't be good company tonight." He hadn't expected her overture, and knew he'd be a disaster in bed. He absolutely could not agree to any intimate visit tonight.

Lauren's voice became brittle. "What the hell's wrong with you? You've never been tired before when I've offered to come over."

"I'm sorry," Ted said. "I just can't explain why I'm so drained. A good night's sleep and I'll feel great. Don't forget me over here across the street. Don't let those other guys take all of your time."

They exchanged simple goodnights and Ted ate his dinner in silence.

During the next two days, Ted gave lectures at two local schools. No evening calls had come from Lauren. Ted couldn't shake his memories of the warm reception he'd received from Caroline. He had a brief fantasy. He could almost see himself as filling her needs as a partner. On Thursday, he called Caroline and set up another dinner date, for Friday. Caroline was quick to accept his suggestion for another meeting. He did not see Lauren, except as she departed for school or a date with one of her potential men.

He was disappointed that Lauren didn't call him, but he didn't want to be the one to call first. It was difficult to suppress a feeling of guilt.

On Thursday, he was awakened by the sound of the newspaper landing on the front porch. Ted could see a cloudless sky through his window. He began to plan his morning while dressing. There was only one letter he wanted to write after completing his paper. Then maybe he'd drive south again but this time on the freeway that also ran through the farming country. It was the same highway he and Lauren had driven on their Carmel weekends. He knew the equipment in the fields would be active. Growers would be anxious to take advantage of the warmer, dry weather to get their land worked up. Ted became enthusiastic about the prospect of the drive. He needed to see people accomplishing something. He felt that his own life was floundering. Ted knew he could make the several hour trip and still be back in time for his afternoon of cribbage with his friend Mike.

He had purposefully kept the kitchen curtains drawn. He was almost completed with his letter when the phone ringing startled him.

It was Lauren wishing him a good morning. He was both surprised and excited by her call. For some reason, she seemed to be in no rush to get off of the line.

"What will you be doing this afternoon? Will you be playing cribbage?"

He acknowledged that this was his plan, and somewhat puzzled, waited for her to say more.

"Could you change it? I want to spend some time with you after my morning classes; my afternoon class has been cancelled."

Ted's mind began to race. Could he be interpreting correctly the words coming over the phone? Or did she just have shopping or a movie in mind and wanted a companion? He wouldn't change his plans for that. Movies were okay, but shopping with her was torture.

But the tone of her voice convinced him.

"Yes, Lauren, I can change the cribbage game if you feel it's important. Count on it being done. I'll give Mike some sort of a reason. He understands that we both have last minute conflicts now and then. What time do you expect to be home?"

"Probably one thirty. Then I'll get a shower and be right over. Her caressing goodbye left no doubt now about her intentions for the afternoon.

Ted immediately pulled open his curtains and received a wave from his neighbor's kitchen window. He went about completing his letter, checked the garden, and was beginning to clean up a few breakfast dishes when he noticed Lauren's car was no longer in the driveway. In his excitement he had failed to watch the time she would be leaving for work.

He decided to change his morning plans. Supposing his vehicle broke down forty miles from home and he couldn't get back in time? He wouldn't take the chance. Ted chided himself on wanting this woman so badly. Why hadn't he just told Lauren that he had other plans and hope she would accept that? After all, he would be with Caroline tomorrow evening.

But he couldn't pass up the chance to be with her. Never! Certainly not with the promise of lovemaking. It was chilling to think that each time with Lauren might be his last.

Ted was still baffled about what had prompted her to be so eagerly lying beside him this Thursday afternoon. She wouldn't have set time aside without a special purpose. But, what was it? Why, after some of the negative things that had happened recently, was this woman here under the light blanket with him? Did it matter? His touches were getting responses. He wanted to keep the feeling going as long as he could. Although he had become uncommonly excited, he forced himself not to hurry. They played and explored and talked about things they loved about each other. Ted felt no sense of any age difference. He was a young man responding to a young woman. Lovemaking was so different in the daytime, He watched Lauren's eyes glowing and now tried to match the intensity of her moves.

"It's going to be awfully difficult for me to give this up. Don't you feel the same way?"

"Yes, Ted, and no man in my life has been like you. So many men are in such a rush to satisfy their own desires. Why don't they choose to see that women have needs too? Why can't you be twenty years younger, Ted?"

"Well, I can't, and that's why you're leaving, Lauren."

Their conversation returned to memories of so many hours and days as their early romance had grown into love. Two hours passed and Lauren sat up and slid out of bed.

"I've got to go grade papers. And check my e-mail messages," she teased. "There may be a dozen men lined up wanting to meet me. I'll never tell them, though, that I've continued to have sex with you right up to the point of meeting them. How could they understand how much we still mean to each other?"

Ted saw the tears come into her eyes. Lauren made no move to hide them. He could think of no response that was appropriate but walked around the bed and gently kissed her. Losing her was inevitable. He felt like a prisoner asking for a final meal.

"If at some point, possibly it will be very soon, you find the right man, I won't welcome the news. You'll need to tell me that our lovemaking is over. Will you give us one final night together? Both of us can hope it will be as wonderfully fulfilling as today. You can't imagine how much that will mean to me. Will you do that, Lauren, for me?"

"Yes, I promise you that, Ted." She brightened. "And will you do something for me? I know that you have that school in Manteca to give your program to tomorrow morning. Will you come home right afterwards and go to a movie with me? It doesn't start until two thirty."

Ted stopped himself from automatically telling Lauren that he'd be happy to join her. He had, after all, scheduled a date with Caroline for the next evening. He was trapped.

"I feel awful about this, Lauren, but I'm meeting with the teacher for dinner. I didn't mention it, but they added an afternoon class. I'll be done before two thirty but there isn't any point in my driving the hour home and going right back down. Do you remember that Miss Ramos I told you about last semester? Well it was only her third year teaching and she admired my approach and she wanted her husband to meet me. I accepted the dinner invitation for six o'clock." He realized he may have been stumbling through his excuse not to meet her the next day and began to worry.

"Why do you even schedule stuff on Fridays! You know it's the only afternoon that I'm able to keep free. You did the same thing with that darned golf game!"

Ted had no answer but watched her walk across the street and into her house, not turning to wave. He worried through the late afternoon and into the evening as he prepared for the next morning's school appearance. He had two concerns. Could he again lie his way through a meeting with Caroline? And, how was he going to handle Caroline if she wanted an intimate evening following dinner? An ageing bull had his limitations.

He called Lauren at nine to thank her for the wonderful afternoon and fell soundly asleep before ten.

He loaded the Explorer and left the house at seven-fifteen. He responded to a wave from Lauren, who had not yet left for work herself. He turned on the music station, changing it only once to pick up the eight o'clock news and stock market numbers during the drive south. The sun was several diameters up from the horizon. Ted normally loved to watch each day develop, but today he couldn't push aside some apprehension. He wasn't comfortable with lying.

He checked in at the school office for his visitor's badge at eight-twenty, and asked for directions to Miss Ramos' room. The office secretary smilingly advised him, "It's Mrs. Williams now."

"Yes, Thank you! I do recall that last fall she told me she was getting married."

Ted welcomed the intensity of a full morning's work. There were only six minutes between classes while he prepared for the next group of thirty students, mostly sophomores, to arrive. Only when the video was playing did he allow himself to think about the evening ahead.

Mrs. Williams insisted she accompany him to get a lunch but said she wouldn't be able to stay and visit because she had errands to run. He knew his programs had come across favorably because she was effusive with compliments. Ted thanked her for lunch.

"I plan to work in the teachers' lounge for a couple of hours, Amy. You can count on all of the follow up materials to be in your mailbox the first of next week. I'll look for a call when the next semester rolls around."

He visited with other teachers while eating. The lounge emptied abruptly shortly before one fifteen. He knew he could fill three hours easily, but he couldn't then drive home and change clothes. As much as he wanted to shower and shave, he couldn't risk doing that. It was almost certain that Ellen or Lauren would be home.

He worked through the afternoon, twice filling a Styrofoam cup with aging coffee. Ted tried to ignore the teachers who passed through for brief stops. At three thirty there was a fifteen-minute flurry as the teachers gathered up jackets from the rack and lunch containers from the refrigerator. He closed his work and watched. At four thirty the janitor entered and asked Ted to go work someplace else.

Ted fitted his car in with traffic heading towards Sacramento. He decided to sit at the bar at Scott's and have a drink while waiting for Caroline to arrive. A drink would probably be beneficial. He was tired and at the same time couldn't shake his nervousness resulting from the story he had fabricated for Lauren.

He chose a seat at the far end of the bar where the curved section allowed a clear view of the restaurant's main entrance. He was about to order a second drink when he saw Caroline enter. He quickly slid off the bar stool and hurried to meet her.

She gave him a quick appraising smile and extended her hand, which he accepted with a compliment to her.

"I've been looking forward to tonight all week long, Ted."

"Let's go sit."

Neither wanted to rush through dinner. He tried to casually change the subject whenever Caroline's part of the conversation turned to Lauren or their relationship.

"Do you see much of Lauren, Ted? She must be awfully busy combining her work and fitting in time for serious meetings with men. I don't envy her."

"Yes, she's in and out a lot and I worry about her concentration on her teaching. I've hardly seen her all week, just a wave now and then. Of course, I've been busy too." He quickly changed the subject. Now he was lying to Caroline and Lauren both!

At almost eight-o'clock, their dinner dishes cleared, Ted poured the last of the wine, set the bottle down and covered Caroline's hand.

"You're a wonderful tonic for me, Caroline. I love your serious but still relaxed approach to life. You're not demanding. I feel very comfortable with you."

Her response was studied: "I was under stress for so many of these last eight years. There's a loneliness now, and my evenings are difficult to fill. I think I'm going to be even more cautious with men. I do feel at ease with you, Ted. You have such a quiet self confidence."

She slowly pulled her hand away.

"Would you like to stop at my place for a while? I'm not tired. One thing I've been having is lots of sleep."

He readily agreed and got the waiter's attention to bring the check. "I still have your address in my billfold, but let me follow you; things look different after dark."

The drive took less than ten minutes. Ted knew he was tired. Worse than that, he was anxious. He and Lauren had just made love the afternoon before. Maybe he should have declined Caroline's invitation to the after dinner visit. He'd do his best if Caroline wanted to complete a romantic evening.

Pretense was no good. Off and on he became aroused. Caroline was patient and encouraging but finally gently told him, "It's alright Ted. Let's don't fight it. There will be another time. I've really enjoyed our evening."

Caroline told Ted she was going to be out of town for a while, but she looked forward to hearing from him again.

He pulled into his driveway late, after eleven, facing an uneasy sleep.

TWENTY TWO   Complications

The phone ringing in the morning startled him. When he picked it up, Lauren's voice on the other end sounded caustic.

"How was your fine dinner last night with that teacher in Manteca?"

"It was great, although it lasted longer than I really wanted. Why do you ask? You sound irritated."

"You lying bastard! Ruth called at nine last night and said she saw you at Scott's Restaurant with a young woman."

Ted was stunned. He had recognized no one at Scott's. Although he had only seen Ruth a few times, he was certain he couldn't have failed to recognize her. He tried to sound composed.

"Look, you can tell Ruth she mistook some other guy for me. I was sixty miles away from Scott's. Incidentally, Amy, that's her name, was a pretty good cook. She fixed a cut up chicken the same way we do sometimes, and served potatoes and gravy with it."

"Why are you lying Ted? Ruth said she walked within ten feet of you but you didn't look up. Ruth said you had your hand over the woman's while she and a friend were walking by. She said it was disgusting to see you drooling over her." Lauren's anger was rising. "How could you possibly do this after all you said on Thursday afternoon?"

"She's nuts! I wasn't near the place. If she saw me, why didn't she stop and say hello? Ruth just saw some other guy who resembled me. You can believe that, Lauren!"

Ted made another quick attempt to bolster his denial:

"Amy's husband's name is Jim. They've only been married four months. He seems to be a sharp guy and is also a teacher, but at an elementary…"

Lauren cut him off. "To hell with the teacher! I'm asking you why you're lying. Have you been seeing this woman all along? Ruth said she's younger than me and quite pretty." There was a brief silence and then almost a choking sound as if she were crying. Ted felt terribly guilty and wished he hadn't lied, but couldn't change his story now.

"I've been honest with you these last few months, Ted. I haven't slept with anyone but you. I feel cheated, you miserable old bastard."

"You'll have to feel any way you want, Lauren, and calling me names isn't helping. I'm through with listening to your accusations. I have some additional work to do and then need to take it to the post office. You can tell Ruth she was mistaken."

He desperately wanted to get off the phone but Lauren speared him with another question.

"Don't try to get out of this! What were you wearing last night?"

Ted needed a few seconds to think. "Why do you ask? Of course I wore the same clothes to the Williams' that I had on at school. I would have liked to have showered and changed, but that wasn't possible."

She was waiting. He remembered seeing several men at Scott's with similar light-tan windbreaker jackets to what he was wearing. He saw an opening. "I was wearing a blue checkered shirt and the tan jacket you gave me a year ago, Lauren. What has that got to do with it?"

"It only proves that you're a liar! Ruth said you had on a light-colored jacket. Why don't you admit you've been seeing this woman."

"The jacket doesn't prove anything, Lauren. I'm sure if you asked Ruth she'd tell you there were several men there in light jackets. They're quite popular, you know."

Ted needed to close the conversation, but he wasn't at all ready to lose Lauren yet. Caroline had been so genuinely nice, but there couldn't be a solid place for him in her life. Lauren's willingness for continued lovemaking always told him she might yet change her mind. Was her present outburst an indication that he was right? He decided to take a long gamble.

"Why don't you call Amy Williams the first of next week. They told me they were going to the mountains this weekend, but they'll both be at work on Monday, I'm sure."

"I know you're lying, Ted. You just think I won't call! You're going to be trapped in this lie. I hate you for it." She hung up the phone.

Ted tried to resume reading but couldn't focus. He poured some coffee and sat in the chair with the paper folded in his lap. He needed to cover every base to avoid being found out. A thought suddenly flashed through his mind. Suppose Lauren should suddenly choose this day to contact Caroline to suggest a casual meeting? He rushed to the phone. She answered after the first ring.

"Good morning, Ted. I only got up fifteen minutes ago, but was standing here by the phone sipping coffee and figuring out what needs to be done today. I'm glad you called. Is there something you need?"

"Yes, in a way, there is, Caroline. I hate to burden you with this, but I had a strange call from Lauren earlier. Here I thought she was well on her way to finding a new partner, but she was all over me this morning about how glad she was that I wasn't interested in another woman. I don't want to get re-involved with her, but also don't want to hurt her feelings or have her get angry. If she should call you, which isn't likely, but if she does, and asks, would you tell her you haven't seen me?"

He felt ashamed as soon as he asked. What kind of things he would stoop to to save his chances with Lauren? He was beginning not to recognize himself.

"Of course I will Ted, if it's that important to you. I don't like to lie, though, and hope she doesn't call me."

Ted thanked her and told her he'd call again soon. Now, he wondered, should he try to reach the Manteca teacher? He had to get to her before Lauren's call. Ted finally decided to gamble that Lauren would wait until Monday. He was certain that as a teacher herself, Lauren wouldn't try to interrupt a class. She would wait until Monday after school. He struggled through the weekend, and made eye contact with Lauren only once when he was outside watering some plants.

On Monday morning at eight-fifteen he called the Manteca-area high school and left a message asking Amy Williams to call him the minute she got a break. While he waited, he read Newsweek and then stared out into his back yard. An hour and a half later, the teacher called.

Ted explained his predicament to her: "I have a real personal favor to ask that may keep me out of trouble. If a woman named Lauren calls and asks if I had dinner with you and your husband last Friday night, would you tell her I did? Please tell her you cut up a chicken, and served it with mashed potatoes."

"Ted, you devil," she said. "What on earth have you gotten yourself into? Here I thought you were busy being a wonderful grandfather."

"Amy, I know it seems strange, and that you have to get back to your class. This woman, Lauren, used to be my girlfriend. I was with another woman Friday night after I left your school, and don't want Lauren to know. She is very jealous, and when a friend of hers said she saw me out with another woman, I denied it and said I dined at your place. I'm out on a limb, Amy. Would you back me up?"

"I can't believe I'd ever be involved in something like this, but I'll do my best. It sounds like a love story gone bad. I need to go now, Ted."

"One more thing, quickly. I told Lauren your husband's name was Jim. What is it?"

"It's Stan. I hear the bell ringing."

"Wait. Wait, please! Tell her I stayed late, until almost nine-thirty. And don't let her keep you on the phone. She'll dig and dig. Tell her you don't want to get involved with other people's personal problems. Thanks Amy."

He was embarrassed about having involved the teacher in his cover up attempt. Amy was a new teacher, filled with ideals and aspirations for her students, had thought of him as a model grandfather and now he just revealed himself as an ordinary man cheating on a woman and desperate for an alibi. As he worked at the household chores throughout the day, Ted chided himself for not taking a more aggressive stance with Lauren when the matter first came up. Why hadn't he said, "You're seeing other men. What's wrong with me doing the same?"

He knew there was a significant difference, though. She wanted to replace him and was open about it. He desired to keep her close but now had been intimate with another woman. Lauren's car was in the driveway when he completed his shower at six. He went about preparing his own dinner and afterwards switched on the TV to watch an hour long National Geographic special. Ted's reading at nine was suddenly interrupted by the phone ringing. Lauren's voice was blunt.

"I talked with Amy Williams in Manteca an hour ago. Why did you say her husband's name was Jim? It was Stan. I had to go through information operator three times and finally got the right Williams."

"Did I make that mistake? Of course his name is Stan. There's another teacher at that school named Jim. I must have gotten mixed up."

"Amy said that you did have dinner with them and that you left after nine-thirty. I don't know what to think, Ted. She sounded like she was telling the truth but seemed anxious to get me off the line. Amy said you were really effective with her students and kept getting back on that subject; I finally thanked her and said goodbye."

"She'd have no reason to go into detail, Lauren. Her interest in having me there for dinner was only because of her appreciation of the positive impact I seemed to have on her students. I don't know what all you told her about our personal lives, but I'm sure she couldn't be interested."

"Ruth still swears it was you and said she couldn't be wrong."

"Well, I don't know what to say. We're all wrong sometimes; I don't blame Ruth. I hope we can spend a little time together before this week is over."

There was a long silence.

"I'll have to think about that, Ted. Ruth said she warned me earlier that continuing to be intimate with you would only detour my effort of seriously looking at other men. Let's don't plan anything. I'm too upset. It may be several weeks." She hung up the phone without waiting for his response.

There were no calls from Lauren as the week progressed. No goodnight calls that he had come to anticipate. He found it difficult to keep busy. He added a needed reorganization of his attic storage area to the regular yard and house chores. Ted knew inwardly what lay ahead. The final chapter of this romance was being written.

She didn't get home before his bedtime on Tuesday or Wednesday night. He wished he didn't have to witness the across-the-street activity at all. He knew he had no right to be jealous of the men she was meeting, but he couldn't suppress a feeling almost of hatred towards them. He tried to appreciate the fact that Lauren had tried to be considerate and meet them somewhere other than at the house.

On Thursday night, Ted decided to call Caroline. If Lauren was keeping herself unavailable, why shouldn't he ask Caroline if they might spend some time together? He put back the receiver. Supposing Lauren should call and suggest she spend the very night he had committed to Caroline? He cringed at the thought of going through that experience again. But, on the other hand, hadn't Caroline said she'd be away this weekend? He picked up the phone and dialed.

"Well, hello Ted. It's so thoughtful of you to call. Everything has kind of gotten tangled up around here. I didn't want to tell you when I last saw you that Randy called me and begged me to meet with him. That's why I told you I'll be away this weekend. I'll be in San Francisco with Randy."

Ted tried to camouflage his dismay.

"I'm surprised, Caroline, but it might be worth your trip. Maybe your husband has come full circle and is willing to rearrange his priorities. Will you be able to spend a little time together next week after you're back?"

"Ted, let's not plan anything. I'm so unsure of my feelings right now. Can I call you sometime next week? You know I've enjoyed our times together. You're a nice person, Ted, but I don't want to complicate my life further now. Do you understand? I'm sorry."

He assured her that he fully understood her dilemma and would await her call. His feeling of deflation was overwhelming. A glance across the street at Lauren's empty driveway only heightened it.

TWENTY-THREE   Reawakening

"Will you come over and sleep with me tonight and stay until nine in the morning? Ellen is going to be away."

What kind of an invitation was this? There was more of a sense of urgency than one hinting of a treat.

"Yes, of course. I have nothing going on tonight or early tomorrow. Might I ask what prompted your call?"

"It's this guy Daniel again. Did you see him drive by last night?" She didn't wait for an answer. "There was a note under my windshield wiper this morning. He wrote that we we're meant for each other, that I needed to understand this and accept it. I'm almost scared!"

"Gosh, that doesn't sound good, Lauren. No, I didn't see the car but I'm not by the window that often. Fill me in."

"He's called at least twice every day this week. Daniel insists he has a great place in mind for dinner and says we can dance all night afterwards, and maybe set a date for a Monterey trip. I quit answering the phone and now he's left three messages since yesterday. He must be calling from work because the calls were spread through the day. What do you think I should do?"

Ted had heard enough. Good memories conflicted with bad ones. "As long as you've told this Daniel as firmly as you can that you're not ready to make a decision about who is to replace me, I don't know what else you can do. If you stall him enough and then decide that he isn't for you, he'll get the idea and back off." He paused, regretting the harshness of his voice. "What time do you want me to come over tonight?"

"I finish school early and will have time to fix a nice dinner for us. Can you be here about six? I've rented a movie. Thanks for helping me out."

Ted walked across the street a few minutes before six. He was relaxed and carrying a chilled bottle of Lauren's favorite wine.

She embraced him warmly.

"You're so thoughtful. You're always there for me." She led the way to the kitchen and opened the oven door. "Look at these chicken thighs bubbling in the creamy mushroom sauce! You can make a salad while I steam up rice. Would you pour each of us a glass of wine?"

Ted laughed. "You haven't changed a bit! Giving orders the minute I walk into the house! But, I can handle it. Where's the corkscrew?"

He felt upbeat as he stooped to reach into the cabinet for the salad bowl.

"Has this guy Daniel called?"

"Yes, there were two calls today. I didn't answer either one. He's such a glib talker and so convincing. I almost wish I hadn't met him because I feel out of control when he's talking."

Ted took the corkscrew, then tapped her lightly on her shoulder with it. "Bring that guy around! I need to take lessons from him."

He poured each a half glass of wine, then raised his glass. "Tonight will be for us. To hell with Daniel."

The night was for them. Halfway through the movie, a romantic comedy that had both of them cheering between intervals of kissing and caressing, Lauren pressed the pause button.

"I can't stand it any longer! Let's watch the rest afterwards. Would you close the drapes in the bedroom?"

Ted wakened first, around six-thirty. Lauren stirred and snuggled her hand into his. He started to sit up in bed.

"Shall I make a pot of coffee?"

She gripped his hand and pulled him back down on the pillow. "Not just yet, Ted. Last night was so special and comforting for me. I need to be here next to you for a while longer." He drew her close.

"Yes, it was almost like our nights together before we decided it was time to go our separate ways. I slept great. How about you?"

"Perfect. I feel so good now."

Their embrace was interrupted by the ringing of the bedside phone. Ted looked at Lauren expectantly. She shook her head.

"You answer it, please."

He sat on the edge of the bed and picked up the phone.

"Good morning, this is Ted."

He heard the man's voice for the first time, pleasant but assertive.

"Is Lauren there? This is Daniel. I need to talk to her."

Ted's hand cupped the mouthpiece. "It's Daniel; he wants to talk with you."

Lauren shook her head vigorously.

"Lauren doesn't wish to take your call, Daniel. Sorry."

The voice became a snarl.

"Listen, you old fuck, I need to talk to Lauren now! It's important! Hand her the phone!"

"I'm sorry, she doesn't want to talk with you. That's final."

"Well, fuck you, Ted. Shove it up your ass." The phone disconnected. Ted leaned over, carefully putting the phone back in its cradle.

"He seemed kind of upset. At least he knows you're firm now about him holding off a little." Ted gave Lauren a weak smile.

"Would you accept the idea of some coffee now? I know where everything is, so don't rush."

At 9:30, Lauren's parting words were: "Thanks, again, Ted, for coming to my rescue. I guess I won't be seeing much of you for a few days. I'm meeting with guys both Saturday and Sunday for lunches, and then have to get ready for next week's classes." She embraced him again. He struggled to understand her.

"Will you understand when I tell you I feel kind of empty and embarrassed?" She asked. "I need to go ahead but suddenly it seems so useless. Do you know what I'm saying?"

"I guess so. But it's your decision all the way. Just don't let this guy Daniel's approach completely distort your thinking. Most guys aren't like that. He does seem a little off-balance."

Ted felt suddenly like Lauren's hero and protector. She'd made love with him. It would be easy now to fill the weekend hours with yard and household chores. His next week contained two days at nearby high schools. That required preparation. He'd fit in a visit with his grandchildren. What more could he ask? He turned to his morning paper after fixing a cup of coffee, and was almost immediately interrupted by the ringing phone. What might Lauren want now?

"Hello, this is Ted." There was no response. He was sure the line was still open and he could faintly hear breathing. Ten more seconds of silence and then the disconnect sound. Ted went back to his paper. Three minutes later the phone rang again. This time, after several seconds, the caller hung up. He stood by the phone for a minute in case the caller might redial. Then, again, Ted attempted to resume his reading.

Twice more in a ten minute period, his phone rang. These times he allowed the four rings to trigger the answering machine. Each time, the disconnect occurred without any communication from the caller. Ted decided not to alert Lauren. It was no big deal for him. Why disturb her? It might not even have been Daniel. He was certain it was, though.

Ted was at his kitchen table Monday night. He had seen Lauren several times over the weekend, usually coming or leaving in her car. It was now almost eight-thirty. His dinner of his homemade vegetable-beef soup, plus a green salad, was over. The few dishes were washed, rinsed, and placed in the dishwasher rack to dry. Ted seldom used the washer.

He was now completing the final notes for his scheduled Wednesday school visit when Lauren's car entered her driveway. She didn't look his way. The phone rang almost immediately after she entered the house.

"It was awful! This note from Daniel was under my windshield wiper when I got to the parking lot after my late classes. I was afraid he was hiding behind one of the cars left in the lot."

"Steady down, Lauren. What did his note say?"

"I'll read it to you: Dear Lauren, it needn't be this difficult. You know we'd get along wonderfully if you'd just give it a chance. Why fight me? We're going to be great for each other. I'll call you soon about dinner."

"That doesn't sound all that bad. I can understand your worry that he might jump out from behind a car and confront you. I'm glad that didn't happen."

Lauren wasn't to be placated.

"I feel threatened. There was a foot-long scratch, a deep one, under the lock on my car door. It was like he was giving me a warning. I just know Daniel did it!"

Ted was trying to think of some reassuring words when she broke in again.

"Can I come over and sleep with you tonight? I'm afraid to be alone. Ellen will be here but she said not to expect her until around midnight. I'd have to leave early. Okay?"

"That's not problem at all, Lauren. I'll keep the curtains open while I finish the stuff I'm doing. Keep your porch light on. No one can stop at your place without me seeing them. Shall I look for you about nine?"

"Perfect." Then a pause. "We won't be making love tonight, Ted. I'm too uptight over what's happening. Is that alright?"

He laughed. "Of course that's alright. I understand. I'll settle for just having you beside me."

At six a.m., Ted was edging out of bed to make a pot of coffee. He didn't want to waken Lauren quite yet.

The ringing phone made him jump. Lauren came awake with a drowsy, "Who's calling you at this hour?"

"Hello?" No answer, he put the phone back in the cradle and sat on the edge of the bed.

"That's strange. My son sometimes calls around seven just before he leaves for work to see how I'm doing, but never this early."

Again the phone rang and no one was on the other end. Lauren now sat upright.

"That has to be Daniel. He must have asked a neighbor what your name was, and then matched it in the phone book. I feel terrible, Ted, that you're drawn into this, but Daniel seems like such a genuinely nice guy most times." She began to dress.

Ted had just turned on the coffee when his phone rang again. He picked up the kitchen wall phone. "Hello? This is Ted. Who is this please?"

He heard a distant but distinct "Fuck You!" just before the phone went dead. He decided not to tell Lauren, but did call out, "It was probably your guy alright. It could have been his way of telling you he knew you were here."

Suddenly by his side, she gripped his bicep and squeezed it just a bit too hard. Ted heard the voice from the phone in his head and tried to decide if he should be afraid.

"What do you think I should do?"

"Beats me! If he gets to be too much of a pest you could get a restraining order. I imagine that involves the courts and might take a lot of your time, though. Why don't you just go about your day and keep alert."

Lauren glanced at the microwave clock and released his arm.

"I'll need to leave in twenty minutes. If you'll slice some melon, I'll make the toast. Would you pour a cup of coffee for me?"

She suddenly put her arms around him. "Thanks so much Ted. Why do you have to be so darned old?"

"Ouch!" He gently disengaged himself, poured the coffee and began slicing the melon.

Ted completed a brief trip to the post office and was back at his dining table with the final coffee from the pot when the sporty red car drove slowly past. The driver barely glanced at the women's empty driveway across the street. Ted knew he was clearly visible under his dining room light and returned the man's stare until the vehicle moved from view.

He half smiled to himself. This Daniel was attractive. He was certainly young. Ted could see why Lauren might have put him near the top of her list of prospects among the internet respondents.

He was still caught up in his thoughts, unconsciously tapping the pencil on the writing pad when the red car appeared again, this time slowing to a crawl. The driver-side window had been lowered. There was no smile, no wave, only what Ted, had he been asked, would have described as an unfriendly challenge.

He wouldn't bother Lauren with the information about the drive-bys. It would worry her even more. Besides, Ted couldn't resist relishing being seen as the competition. Let the guy sweat!

"I think I have some better news."

It was Lauren's first call in several days. Ted hadn't found the silence surprising. He had been away himself for a full day of lectures. Another day he left early in the afternoon for a visit with Kathy's family. Her car wasn't in the driveway either night when he'd gone to bed. Nothing had changed. He was sure she was meeting internet suitors. Ted needed to focus on his own activities.

"That's good. What is it?"

"I went out to do some copying and prep work at the college last night. When I got back to the parking lot late Daniel was standing by my car. He said he needed to talk and I needed to listen. I was apprehensive but the security guard drove up at the same time and began checking cars for parking permits. Daniel was standing by my car door and didn't move when I pulled out my keys. I told him that I needed to put my heavy stuff in the car. I said it loud enough so that the security guard looked up and acted like he was coming over. He was a big guy. Daniel stepped back and I tossed my stuff in and climbed right in myself and closed the door, but rolled down the window.

"'Now we can talk,' I told Daniel. My voice must have reassured the guard that I was okay. He went on checking windshield permits. I'm really good at talking with people, you know, and told Daniel that I thought he was a really attractive man and that maybe there was something in the future for us, but not right yet. I told him that if we ever did go to Monterey together, we'd hike the Point Lobos trail. I told him you and I had done this twice and thought it was great."

Ted gritted his teeth and moved the phone away from his ear and tapped it on his forehead before bringing it back and responding: "You didn't give him too much encouragement, did you?"

"No, I don't think so. Daniel brightened up and said he'd be putting all of the plans together, and hoped it would be soon."

"That doesn't sound like encouragement to you, Lauren?"

"He really seems nice, Ted, but he did get a little pushy again. He said there was no reason for me not to go to dinner with him, and he wanted it to be tomorrow night. He said it was obvious that we are meant for each other, that we enjoy doing the same things. He kept smiling a lot and kept telling me all the things he had planned for us, and that we needed to get started. I kept telling him to be patient."

"I may have talked too much about you, Ted. Daniel kept pushing me for this dinner date tomorrow night. I felt so pressured that I told him you and I were still getting together some, and that these other guys didn't count too much, I know that wasn't fair, Ted, but do you mind?"

"No, I'm still here for you, but did you tell him we've accepted the fact that I'm too old for you as a permanent relationship?"

"No, I didn't. How could I? In fact, I told him I'd promised to have dinner with you tomorrow night, but that he could call me later in the week, though I wouldn't promise anything. What else could I have done, Ted? I needed to get home!"

"I'm not sure, Lauren." What should she have done? CheezNCrackers, just about anything but that! That is, if she really wanted Ted out of her life. She kept pulling him back in, just as he began to accept their altered relationship. What did she want from him, a friend? A protector? A convenient excuse? He felt powerless against her. "Are we having dinner together tomorrow night then? I'm not pressured for time and we could go down to the little Mexican restaurant around the corner. If this Daniel got nosey, he wouldn't find either of us home and wouldn't think about that place."

"Yes, I'll be at your house around six-thirty. I'll run right home afterwards, Ted. I've lots of school work to do. Thanks for understanding."

He hoped she'd find time from her work for a few minutes with him after dinner, but that wasn't to be. He settled for a brief kiss.

TWENTY-FOUR   Daniel

Ted was puzzled. He almost always awakened when his early morning paper landed at his doorstep around four-thirty. Shortly afterwards there would be the sound of an idling car motor revving up and the delivery car proceeding down the street.

He was sure he heard an unusual shuffle of feet near his front door a few minutes after the paper delivery. This was followed by another engine accelerating.

At six-thirty, Ted was up, started coffee, and unlocked the front door to get his newspaper. A torn sheet of paper was Scotch-taped to the door. He carefully removed the message. It was roughly printed in caps.

TED: YOU'RE OUT OF YOUR LEAGUE! WHY DON'T YOU BUTT OUT AND REALIZE YOU'RE JUST A HORNY OLD BILLY GOAT. LAUREN NEEDS A YOUNG MAN. GIVE HER A BREAK. SHE TOLD ME SHE WANTS ME BUT IS STICKING WITH YOU FOR OLD TIMES SAKE. SHE DOESN'T WANT TO HURT YOUR FEELINGS. I SHOULDN'T HAVE TO TELL YOU THIS AGAIN.

Ted studied the note for several minutes, then set it on the counter and carried the paper and cup of coffee to his reading chair. He was still staring at page one of the business section, thinking about the truth of the note: *Lauren needs a young man…*, when the phone rang. This would be about normal for a call from Matthew.

"Good morning, this is Ted." The phone disconnected. Four more times, in intervals of ten minutes, he got up to answer the phone. Every time, until the last, the caller hung up immediately. On the fourth, he heard a growled threat:

"Get out of my way, you old fart, or you'll regret it!"

Even if he was old, even if there was any truth to his scrawled message from earlier this morning, this guy Daniel was bad news. He couldn't deny it any longer.

Lauren's voice over the phone at seven thirty showed no signs of concern, which Ted was thankful for. Her errant suitor had focused his evening hijinks only on him and left her in peace.

"I really enjoyed dinner last night and got a lot done afterwards. I slept great! How about you?"

Ted explained the circumstances of the unsigned note on the door and read it to her. "What do you think I should make of it?"

"I feel awful, Ted. How can he possibly blame you? I felt that Daniel really understood my position when I had that long talk with him in the parking lot."

"I'm a man, Lauren, and can see why he desires you. If the guy is becoming obsessed, there's no telling what he'll decide to do. I guess he somehow sees me standing in his way. I'm not overly worried about myself, but I sure want you to keep your eyes open, and don't get caught alone in the parking lot again. He is obviously not the nice guy you want to think he is. I think he could turn on you anytime. I've read about these stalkers. Saw a movie about one once."

At mid afternoon, Lauren called again.

"Hi Ted. Guess what was just delivered? A dozen and a half long stem yellow roses. They must have cost Daniel a fortune." She hesitated. "I didn't exactly like the note he enclosed. He must have read too much into our conversation in the parking lot. Honestly, I didn't say all of those things. I was only trying to explain why he shouldn't expect me to go to dinner with him that night."

"Do you mind reading it to me? You don't have to, it's really none of my business."

"Well, I want to because I need to stay over with you again tonight. I have his note right here." Ted could hear the rustle of the paper.

"Lauren," she read, "I'm glad you see it my way and like me so much. You don't need any of these other men you're talking with. You sure don't need that sugar daddy who's been doing those nice things for you for a little sex. Tonight will be our night for dinner. Don't let me down. I'll come by about seven. I didn't like it when you locked the car and made me talk through the window. You know you can trust me. Daniel."

Lauren continued, "I told Ellen, and she said she's bailing out if I'm going to be at your house. She's going to call a friend to see if they can have dinner together. Then she plans to come home late. You can see why I need to stay with you."

He didn't hesitate. "Yes, of course you need to be away from the house. I don't know what you told that guy through the car window, but it was obviously too much. I really don't want to discuss it anymore now. Why don't you come over about six or before. We'll fix up something." Ted's voice was firm.

"Thanks Ted, and I'm sorry that Daniel's reading whatever he wants to into what I say. I know now that I should've told him flatly no about any relationship."

He looked through his freezer supplies and selected two trout fillets from the summer catch, thinking how Lauren continues to be a woman who sees things through her own lenses. The green beans he'd purchased at the market would stretch for the two of them. They could bake a large potato in the microwave. He'd need to remember to get another lemon at the store later. The half in the refrigerator would do for the trout tonight.

Ted picked up the two most recent unopened copies of Newsweek and settled himself in his reading chair. The afternoon sun was streaming though the window and left big patches of sunlight on the carpet. He glanced at his watch and said to himself, "it's only three-thirty, but why not? I'll fix an early brandy and soda." He was soon positioned again, with the drink on the low table beside him.

He'd completed reading the magazines, fixed his second drink, and was watching the five o'clock news when Lauren tapped on the window. He hastened to the door.

"I'm glad you're early. We're having trout, green beans, and a potato for dinner. Nothing will take long. Would you like a glass of wine? I've already fixed myself something."

She greeted him with a smile, a brief kiss on his lips, but without an embrace.

"I feel safer being here, but, yes, a glass of wine will help me relax."

Lauren promptly closed the curtains facing his large kitchen window and the smaller ones above the sink.

"If Daniel drives by early, I don't want him to see me here. Do you think I should hide my car somewhere?"

Ted thought for five seconds before responding. "Don't you think that'd be kind of a pain? Where would we put it? Why not just leave it in the driveway? With Ellen's car gone, this Daniel may figure you're out with her. After all, you weren't the one to make a date with him."

"You're right. Let him think what he wants."

Ted carefully poured the wine and handed Lauren her filled glass. No toast was suggested.

"I think it's extremely important that Daniel not see you here. Starting right now I want you to stay in the living room. You can watch TV and we'll set up dinner there. The drapes make it impossible for anyone to see in and you can use the back bathroom."

He drew open the curtains on both of the kitchen windows. Lauren quickly ducked behind a wall.

"What are you doing that for?"

"Well, I've thought about it, and I think it's best if he sees me doing my normal stuff. My hiding behind closed curtains would be a dead giveaway. I'll even clean up the kitchen afterwards. You're the one who needs to be out of sight."

Lauren agreed. They walked together into the living room and switched on the TV, picking a station to watch the end of the early evening news. Ted settled himself beside her, with the residue of the drink in his hand.

"You can peek through the bedroom curtains if you get too curious. It's doubtful that he'll arrive before quarter to seven. Try and relax a little, Lauren."

She gave him a rueful smile and reached over to cover his hand with hers. "I don't know why I get myself into these problems and always seem to come running to you, but thanks."

Twice during the forty-five minutes they watched the news programs, Lauren quietly left for his bedroom. Both times she returned with a shake of her head. At a commercial, Ted picked up his empty glass and stood up.

"I'll start our dinner now. If the red car shows up, I'll let you know."

He had seasoned and floured the trout when he noticed the red car slowly coming to a stop in front of Lauren's house. Ted's glance confirmed that the driver was looking his way. He returned to the trout, trying to appear nonchalant in his movements, although his heart was racing.

"Lauren, the car's there if you want to take a peek. I have the trout ready for the pan but will hold up on that until the green beans have been boiling for five minutes. The potato isn't in the microwave yet, so don't figure on us eating for another fifteen minutes or so."

She peeked into the kitchen. "He is kind of good looking, isn't he? Daniel says he works out regularly and his figure shows it. I'll be in the bedroom watching."

Sounds more like you'll be in the bedroom ogling, Ted muttered, as he checked the beans with a fork, scrubbed the potato, pricked it and set the microwave timer for five minutes. He then observed Daniel intermittently knocking on Lauren's front door, and then stepping back a foot. Ted thought the man's jacket was attractive and went well with the lighter colored pants. He wore an open shirt. Ted mused that most women would find him a most welcome salesman behind a travel agency counter.

When the man started down the walkway, Ted thought he was leaving, but instead Daniel turned sharply and entered the gate to the breezeway, disappearing into the back yard. Lauren's head suddenly appeared again. "Do you think he'll try to break in? Should I call the police?"

"Let's not do that yet. He's likely peering into the back bedroom windows to see if you might be hiding there. So far he hasn't shown any anger. Why don't we wait?"

Ted checked the beans again, removed the pot, drained the water and then placed the pan for the fish on the same burner, turning it to low to preheat the oil.

"Oh, Lauren, here he comes back!" She disappeared back down the hall. Daniel began knocking on the front door again. He alternately looked Ted's way with an intent stare. Ted turned the potato in the microwave. When Ted glanced out the window again before turning his attention to the trout, Daniel had moved to a position several yards to the left of the porch and was trying to see into Lauren's bedroom window. Ted called to Lauren to see where she was.

"I'm going to concentrate on the trout fillets so they don't get overcooked."

Ted heard a muted response coming from his bedroom: "He's heading for his car."

Ted turned the fish and glanced at the stove clock. They wouldn't need but two minutes, just long enough for him to season and butter the beans.

Lauren leaned against the kitchen door frame and peeked out the window. "He's sitting in his car. If you'll hand me the dishes and silverware, I'll set the card table for dinner."

Ted complied with a grin. "Isn't this an exciting way to have dinner, playing like detectives?"

He was carrying the plate with the trout and potato into the living room when they heard a loud metallic slam. Ted ran for the kitchen and Lauren to the bedroom. The man was walking away from Lauren's car. He climbed into his and accelerated down the street. Lauren's voice was no longer muted.

"I think that son of a bitch smashed my car with something! I'm going to look!"

"No, Lauren, please don't. Sure as heck he'll drive around the block and come by again. If he has that kind of a temper, we don't want him to find out you've been here all of the time. Let me go look."

She stood by the door while Ted trotted across the street. He took a quick look at the driver-side door and walked briskly back, first looking quickly up and down the street. "Your vandalism insurance will have to take charge now. It looks to me like Daniel kicked the door hard with the heel of his shoe. It's a big dent."

Ted squeezed her arm gently as he entered the door. "I know it's annoying as hell, but let's enjoy dinner now as best as we can. Dents can always be fixed. We'll decide what to do afterwards."

Lauren shrugged. "I don't feel much like eating, but you fixed such a nice dinner for us." She walked slowly to the table. "And no wine for me please." Ted knew Lauren wasn't one to change opinions easily. He was right. "Daniel seemed like such a nice person. Even when I was sitting in the car in the parking lot, he laughed and agreed with me on so many things. I almost accepted his invitation to dinner. Maybe I should have and this might not have happened."

Lauren apparently couldn't help but notice Ted's silence and deepening frown. She changed quickly. "You're right, Ted. He is strange and I'm better off to do as you suggested. I'm so glad I'm here with you tonight."

"Remember I told you about a movie I watched last month about a stalker? This guy Daniel could have played his role exactly so far. As I remember, it didn't have a pleasant ending." He stuffed a bite in his mouth and chewed slowly before adding, "I hope you'll be awfully careful."

After dinner was finished and the kitchen tidied up, they watched TV. Ted had closed all of the kitchen curtains again and snapped on the porch light. The only light showing inside was the lamp by his reading chair. Ted carefully checked all of the door locks. Daniel's actions concerned him. He tried to match Lauren's apparent concentration on the shows, but found it difficult to do so.

239

By ten, they were in bed. They didn't make love. It wasn't even mentioned. When Ted raised himself up for a goodnight kiss, she responded but quickly settled back, with her bottom nestled into him. Lauren's deep sigh told him this wasn't a night for romance.

He was awakened by a car door closing. A glance at the radio clock told him it was well past midnight. Ted slipped quietly out of bed to see Ellen enter her house. He wakened several times, envied Lauren's evident quiet sleep, and eventually fell asleep again himself. At seven, he arose, made a pot of coffee and then wakened Lauren. He watched as his companion stretched and opened her eyes to smile at him. Why did he have to give up this lovely creature?

"I slept great but I do have to run after one cup of coffee. You know my classes start at eight-thirty this morning."

Ted watched fifteen minutes later when she stopped to view the damage to her car door. He was surprised to see Lauren lift a sheet of paper from under the windshield wiper. The phone rang within three minutes.

"You might be right about this guy, Ted. Let me read you the note. He must have driven back later and left it. It says, 'Lauren, I don't believe you understand. You don't just back out of a dinner date with me. Bad things don't have to happen. You can't deny we're part of each other's lives. I want to meet you in the parking lot for another talk.' He didn't sign it. What should I do, Ted? Tonight is one of my late nights."

"That does pose a problem. I think it's important that you don't walk to your car alone after school. He's sort of given you a warning. I'll come out and escort you if it's necessary, but you can easily ask for the parking lot security guard to go to your car with you. It won't be the first time someone needed their help."

"That's a good idea and I'll do it. I'll call you after I get home. Thanks for dinner last night, Ted, and remember, I haven't forgotten you. I've been so stressed lately. I have to go now. Bye."

Ted was watching a nature show on his PBS station when he heard the car door close. It wasn't yet nine. He got up and glanced across the street. Lauren was unlocking and entering her house. He returned to his chair, relieved to see her home safely. The phone ringing had to be her. He picked up the portable at his side, muted the TV, and answered.

"You were right, Ted. When the security guard left me off at my car, I spotted Daniel's red car parked several spaces down the row. He wasn't in sight. I asked the officer to retain him for at least ten minutes while I got a head start home. He grinned and said, 'Count on me, miss, I'll handle it!' I think he was excited about being able to help a lady in distress. As soon as the officer was standing by Daniel's car, I left. I was still nervous all the way home, but shouldn't have been. I'm going to fix myself some dinner now and work an hour before going to bed. Thanks for your suggestion, Ted, it worked."

Ted wakened from a deep sleep. Who on earth could be calling now? He struggled to find the portable phone he'd carried to the bedroom and glanced at the clock. It was almost eleven. "Hello. This is Ted."

"Oh Ted! I know I woke you, but I just had this awful call from Daniel. He said he couldn't believe I'd been such a bitch to turn the security guard on him. Daniel said he almost got a ticket for parking, even though he was sitting in the car. He said he had to argue with the guard for ten minutes to keep him from issuing the citation. Then Daniel got on last night and kept insisting I tell him where I was having dinner with Ellen. I told him we'd gone to the Red Lobster because they had a good special on crab. He pushed me to tell him all about our dinner and then called me a damned liar. Daniel said he was parked down the street when Ellen pulled into the driveway, and that only one person got out.

I know I shouldn't have, but I admitted that I was at your house. I told Daniel that he had no right to expect me to go to dinner with him because I wasn't ready and hadn't told him I would. I lied a little then," Ted thought he heard her voice change just a bit, was it sheepish? He touched an errant hair on his eyebrow as she continued. "I told Daniel that you were asking me to go back to you, and that I was considering it because in a way we still loved each other." Ted almost choked when she said this. She did still love him.

"That seemed to infuriate Daniel, Ted! He started swearing and damning old guys with money. I finally told him I was going to hang up because you weren't that kind of a person at all."

"Well, thank you for standing up for me."

"Daniel said, in a very quiet voice, 'some people think their money can buy anything. Ted needs to be taught a lesson.' Then he hung up. I'm sitting here shaking."

"I'm sorry he's acting so crazy, Lauren, and putting you through this. It's late and we both need some sleep. Drink a glass of wine if that'll make you drowsy and don't worry about me. I can take care of myself. We'll talk some more about it later. I'm glad you called."

Ted got out of bed and went into his office. There he felt under several items on the bottom shelf of one of the ceiling-high cabinets and pulled out a polished Smith and Wesson .22 caliber revolver. "Stupid crackpot thinks only money could make a woman show an interest in me. Like I'm Warren Buffett or something," He said to himself. "If that son-of-a-bitch gets on my case, he could end up a dead man."

Ted had never loaded or fired the revolver. It had been a gift, after death, from an old neighbor who had been a fishing buddy for ten years. The man hadn't left it via his will, but apparently had asked a close hunting friend to see that Ted got the gun as a token of his appreciation for the many trips to Ted's lake. A box of .22 long rifle shells had come with the gun. Ted had stored the shells separately. He didn't want to risk a tragedy when his curious grandchildren came visiting.

Now he opened the cylinder and loaded six shells. Ted looked the gun over for a safety lock but found none. He was certain that if he pulled the trigger, the gun would fire.

He stood in his pajamas, balancing the gun in his hand. He was now wide awake. He extended the gun in his right hand and aimed at the door knob, but couldn't hold the gun steady. He then held the gun in two hands as he'd seen done in police movies. Ted raised the barrel and visualized Daniel in front of him.

It took a while for his heartbeat to slow, but finally sleep came. He had placed the gun on a folded towel on the headboard. Ted slept fitfully and pulled himself from the bed shortly after six. He carried the loaded gun into the kitchen and placed it atop the refrigerator, started coffee and stepped outside for the paper.

While the coffee was brewing, he retrieved the gun and pointed it towards his front door. He felt a little more comfortable holding the gun and again determined that the heavy revolver required two hands. He felt strangely powerful with all of its weight in his hand, and the handle felt remarkably solid. A small part of him hoped that he'd get to use it. He placed it again on top of the refrigerator, centering it behind a bag of chips.

When Ted returned at five-thirty from the long afternoon of cribbage with his neighbor, he was relaxed and elated. His cards had been good, he felt he'd played well, and had won two dollars and forty-two cents after twelve games. Thoughts of Daniel had seldom entered his mind. A phone message awaited him. He punched the play button and proceeded to fix a drink.

"Ted, it's four-thirty. Daniel just called and I feel a little better. He apologized for his outburst concerning the parking lot security guard. Will you call me when you get home?"

Ted placed the call. Lauren answered after the second ring.

"Hi Ted. Thanks for calling. How did your game go?"

He assured her that he'd had good cards, a pretty good day and won over two dollars, then he changed the subject. "I got your message. Tell me more about this Daniel guy."

"Well, after saying he was sorry for some of the things he said over the phone last time, Daniel said he was sure that you were a nice old man, but that I should understand you are in my history and not my future. We talked about what he did as a young man and why his marriage didn't work out. I feel kind of sorry for Daniel. He said he worked so hard to make the marriage go, but that his wife never seemed to appreciate him. I think I told you earlier that they never had any children."

"Did he press you for a date again?"

"Yes, in a way, and I expected that. Daniel said he's waited long enough. He asked me how I was going to get you out of my hair because us getting back together is unrealistic."

Ted half-heartedly laughed, and said, "He doesn't realize that we managed just fine. It's none of his business to know why we're not partners anymore. What is your next step?"

"I need to stall for time, Ted, while I figure out how to get him out of my life. I told Daniel we were having dinner together again tonight, and that Ellen and I were doing something tomorrow, but that he could call me in a couple of days. I tried to be really pleasant because I didn't want to make him angry."

She paused, and Ted did not speak. He thought she had realized a man like that needed a firm *Go Away*!

"If I do meet with him again, it will be in a place with a lot of people around. Then he likely wouldn't dare show his anger too much if I tell him that I'm not interested in him."

"Wait," Ted said. "Did you just say if you meet with him?" He stood up and walked to the window, pulling back the drape to scan her window for a sign of her. "Are you still interested in him? After he scratched your car and threatened both of us with violence? You've got to be kidding."

"Don't go getting mad. I'm almost sure I'm not. At times on the phone he's a perfect gentleman, just like you are. Then he makes some of these unreasonable statements that are out of character. I don't understand that at all."

"Well, okay Lauren. You and I seem to be regular dinner partners again and I have to admit I like that. Give me half an hour to shower and shave and then come over when you're ready. Between us, we'll figure out something good for dinner. See you later."

When Lauren arrived an hour later, she explained that Ellen had been expressing her concern about Daniel, and that they had talked for longer than she realized.

"She said she had a boyfriend once and he was charming when he wanted to be, but shoved her and even used his fists on her once. He couldn't stand her to be around other men, or people in general. Do you think Daniel would go that far, Ted?"

"He's an unknown quantity, Lauren. You've been around him only a few weeks." Ted paused as he broke apart some cauliflower for steaming. Lauren had seated herself in a kitchen chair.

"Frankly, I think he's totally obsessed with you. He's gone nuts about it. If it isn't me that he sees in this way, it'll be some other man." He gritted his teeth, forgetting to even offer Lauren a glass of wine. "Sure, this Daniel's a good looking and sometimes charming guy, and I know how much you're hurting to find a younger partner, but I'm telling you this man's bad news. Your emotions aren't allowing you to see straight. I'm not blaming you."

He pointed to the refrigerator. "Come and take a look at what's here. This is what I think of your Daniel!"

Lauren stood on her tiptoes and pushed aside the bag of chips. "Oh no, Ted! You don't really think he'd come after you? I didn't even know you had a gun!"

Ted reached up over Lauren's shoulder and pulled the .22 off the fridge. He stood up straighter than usual and pushed out his chest as he held the weapon in one hand and patted it with the other. He looked hard at Lauren's face, but her eyes were on the gun.

"Yes, but I don't tell everyone. It's around, just in case. I didn't buy it, someone gave it to me. It's loaded now, and there's no safety, so I have to be careful."

He slid it back on top of the refrigerator and re-positioned the bag of chips. She remained standing next to the fridge, looking at some point a few feet in front of her. Ted checked the oven temperature and spoke over his shoulder to her. "I'm reheating a piece of pork roast I had left over. We can slice up some oranges to go with the cauliflower and can eat in twenty minutes if you like."

Ted turned and saw Lauren's hesitation before she answered, "I can cut the fruit." He realized he hadn't offered her a drink, and put his arms around her. "Hey," he said right next to her small pearl earring, "I'm glad you're here for dinner. I'm sorry I didn't offer you a glass of wine earlier. Would you slice up two oranges? Try to keep a little out of view, though. There's no gain by antagonizing Daniel if he should drive by. I rather suspect he will." He watched her sip the wine, leaving a pale pink imprint on the rim of the glass. How he had missed washing her lipstick off of his glassware. How happy he will be to wash it tonight.

He was slicing the leftover roast when the red car drove slowly by. Daniel glowered at him, and Ted stared right back. He was momentarily tempted to give him a middle finger, but resisted and looked down to finish slicing. He said nothing to Lauren who had completed slicing the fruit and was seated in the family room watching an audience participation show. He closed both of the kitchen curtains.

Their dinner progressed uneventfully. Ted knew that Lauren's head wouldn't show above the drawn curtains while they ate. He made no mention of the red car. They talked mostly about her teaching. Soon after dinner she excused herself.

"Thanks for dinner, Ted. It was really good! I feel much more relieved now, but I want to get back and talk with Ellen some more. I'm sure Daniel won't bother us."

TWENTY-FIVE   No Going Back

Ted dressed for bed and brushed his teeth. He was toweling off his face when he thought he heard steps out on the small front porch. He stopped what he was doing to listen for a few seconds. *Oh great*, he thought to himself, now *I'm getting paranoid*.

As he hung his towel and turned off the bathroom light, he heard the smashing of glass. This was not his imagination. It sounded like his big kitchen window. Startled, frightened, and energized at the same instant, with his heart pounding, Ted raced for the kitchen as the sounds of breaking glass repeated. He could now make out the outline of a person slashing at the window, clearing out shards of glass with what looked like a two-foot iron bar.

Ted hadn't yet turned off the hall light and it provided a muted light into the kitchen. He knocked off the bag of chips as he grabbed for the gun. He backed up a few feet with the revolver shaking violently in his hand. The person's head and shoulders now appeared as a shadow coming through the low window.

He hadn't felt this overwhelmed with nervousness and excitement since his one-time experience trying to shoot a deer. His older brother had taken Ted deer hunting, assuring him that he'd get a clear shot, but hitting the animal would be up to him. His brother had given him a deer rifle to use. Ted remembered having had an easy shot at fifty yards from a prone position. He'd experienced 'buck fever.' A pounding heart and heaving chest had made aiming impossible. His shot landed five feet in front of the animal, and he never hunted again.

Ted now tried to calm himself as he stood ten feet from the figure emerging through the window. He was surprised at the steadiness of his voice, because he was overwhelmed with fear.

"Stop right now and get the hell out of here!" He shouted at the figure framed in the window.

The figure straightened up. Ted's eyes adjusted to the minimal light. He could see an iron crowbar in the man's hands. The man edged forward and Ted backed up two steps.

"I said stop! Crawl back out that damned window or you're a dead man. I mean it!"

The shadowy figure stepped slowly forward, the bar held at shoulder height. The voice was quiet and measured.

"You wouldn't shoot anybody, you old fuck. I'm going to teach you a lesson. You need to know that Lauren is my girl."

It was Daniel. Ted backed several steps into the hall as he advanced. "If you don't stop, I am going to count to three and shoot. Back off, jerk."

The gun was shaking so violently that Ted put a second hand on the gun and tried to keep it pointed at the intruder's chest. The man's feet shuffled quietly towards Ted.

"Steady old man, and put that gun down. You're not going to hurt anyone. Lauren tells me you're a really nice guy. I only need to talk with you."

Ted thought he saw a strident movement towards him. The iron bar swished at his eye level, a threatening ten feet away.

"Stop, you son-of-a-bitch!" Ted pulled the trigger, not once but three times. The explosions were deafening. Now, the silhouette lunged towards him. Ted pulled the trigger again, and two more red flashes illuminated the semi-darkness.

The man appeared to be flying towards him. In actuality, Daniel was falling. Ted pulled the trigger a last time. He thought this last shot smashed into the man's head. The body slammed onto the slate floor five feet in front of Ted. The iron bar bounced at his feet and then slid down the hallway. The revolver hung limply in his left hand. The light in the hallway exposed the spreading blood.

Ted stared at the body he knew was Daniel. He raised his right hand and gave the corpse his middle finger.

"That's a lesson for you, you dumb bastard. Tell me now whose girlfriend Lauren is."

He shakenly placed the revolver on the kitchen counter and picked up the phone. He took a few deep breaths and dialed 9-1-1. "Hello. This is Ted Butler. I just shot a guy who broke in. I think he's dead, but you might want the police to send an ambulance." He turned his head and looked at the bloody mess that was his stalker. His arms and legs were sprawled out in a spreading puddle of blood. "No. I haven't checked his pulse, and I don't intend to. I couldn't see well but I think I put five bullets in the bastard's chest and one in his head. Your guys can check him out." Ted hoped his voice didn't sound cocky.

He listened while the operator confirmed his address, and responded to her plea to stay on the line by remarking, "I'll be here," and placing the receiver on the counter.

A thick pool of blood three feet across covered the hallway around the motionless figure. Ted stepped back across the feet of the corpse and opened the door to his front yard. A dozen steps down the walkway convinced him that even his close neighbors weren't aware of the shooting. He surmised that the .22 shell explosions that sounded so thunderous to him weren't really that loud.

Ted glanced across to Lauren's house. He saw no activity, no one coming outside. The women were now likely watching TV or playing music and reading. He doubted they were sleeping yet. He returned to the phone, disconnected the 9-1-1 call and dialed Lauren's number. She answered at the fourth ring, but he wasn't sure what to say.

"Sorry to call so late, Lauren." He hesitated. Sirens soon became audible and got closer to the street. "I have to tell you something." The screaming sirens turned down the street.

"What? What is it, Ted. Are you okay? Are you having a heart attack?"

"I think I just killed Daniel."

He heard the thump of the phone as if it hit the floor, and waited with the phone to his ear until Ellen picked it up. "Who is this?"

"Ted. Listen, I just killed a guy. He broke in. The cops are here, I have to go. Look after Lauren."

He was standing in the doorway when the police cars pulled to a halt. Two officers trotted up his driveway with guns drawn. Ted showed them his hands and they put the weapons down. "Are you alright Sir? What's happened here?"

Ted invited them in with a point at the direction of the floor. "He broke in. He came at me with the crow bar." The officers bent over Daniel's body and assessed the situation.

"There's no pulse at all, and he's lost most of his blood. This guy is dead. How long ago did this happen?"

Ted shrugged. "Less than fifteen minutes probably."

"And you shot him?" The officer asked. "9-1-1 said you put six bullets into him? Is that right? Where is the weapon?"

Ted started towards the counter where he had laid the handgun, but the officer commanded him to stop and sit on the kitchen chair while his partner retrieved it with a plastic bag. He reluctantly complied but immediately stood again to face the officer who was questioning him.

"He broke in through that window and I was able to get my gun just in time."

"Where was your weapon?"

"On top of the fridge."

"Loaded?"

"Yes, sir."

"I don't see any cuts on his hands. That's unusual in window break-ins."

Ted pointed under the table at a pair of heavy leather gloves. "Those aren't mine; and neither is that crow bar you can see down the hall."

"Was the guy going to rob you?"

"I don't think so, officer. I have to be honest and tell you there was a woman involved. I think this jerk was planning to get me out of the way."

The officer looked at his partner, then back to Ted. Another police car and an ambulance arrived and filled the immediate street parking. Their flashing lights remained on. Ted watched the attendants pull a stretcher from the ambulance rear door. The single officer in the second car hastened up the driveway and nodded to Ted as he entered the open door.

"You Ted Butler?"

"Yes."

"We have a few questions."

"Of course you do. Can I tape some paper over that open window? I don't want to leave it that way when I go to bed."

"Yes, Mr. Butler, just as soon as crime lab guys arrive for their bit. They'll do a few measurements and take some more pictures. We'll need to take your gun down to the station for some lab work."

"That's okay, just as long as you're sure I'll get it back soon. It was a gift, and I value it a lot."

"That's not our decision, sir. You're an older man, and it looks like a case of self-defense, but a man's dead and there'll be a lot of questions. I'll give you a receipt for it when I leave."

A detective had entered. "Mr. Butler? Sergeant Johnson. I'll take your statement now, but will you come down to headquarters about nine tomorrow morning? I've written down the name of the person you'll need to see here on my card."

An officer walked up with the crowbar in a plastic wrapper.

"You're lucky he didn't get a swipe at you with this tool. We'd have been taking pictures of you."

Ted nodded and managed a grin. He pointed under the table, "Don't forget those gloves; they're important too!"

Ted answered Johnson's questions, trying to leave much of the back-story out of his recounting. But before Johnson left, he insisted that Ted give him Lauren's name, address and phone number. By the time everyone left, thanking him for his cooperation, it was close to midnight.

He stood by the small window over the kitchen sink with the receipt for the gun in his hand, watching the police go. Lauren never peeked her head out all night. Ted brought out his mop and paper towels and cleaned up what the police crew left behind. He struggled but was able to put up newspaper over the window, and reflected on what he'd done. A man was dead at his hands. Lauren would be devastated. She would at least partly blame him. It was self-defense, though. Surely she would accept that if the police did.

Maybe he should have aimed the revolver lower and knocked Daniel down and then dialed 9-1-1. It was barely light, though. Supposing the first three shots had missed the man's legs and Daniel was upon him with the crowbar? Ted became more and more convinced that the police inspector would accept his explanation, but would Lauren?

He jumped when the phone rang.

"What the hell got into you?" Lauren's voice was accusatory. She was almost sobbing. "Daniel was a nice guy, just a little mixed up. We could have worked it out. Now you've gone and killed him? How can you live with yourself! I hope they put you in jail."

Ted took a deep breath. He had somehow known this would be coming.

"He crashed through the window, Lauren. I barely had time to run from the bathroom and grab the gun before he was on me. I didn't know who it was until he threatened to teach me a lesson. He came at me with a big iron crow bar. He was trying to kill me! What would you expect me to do? Come on, be fair."

Lauren's voice modulated somewhat.

"I don't care what was happening, Ted. You didn't have to kill Daniel. Why didn't you shoot him in the legs or feet, anyplace but where it would kill him?"

"Damn it, Lauren, I couldn't see his feet. All I could see was a silhouette. I just aimed at what was coming at me and pulled the trigger. I was scared." Ted paused.

"I'd do the same thing again, so don't tell me what I should have done."

Lauren's voice quieted down. "You just don't kill someone that way."

Ted did not respond and they stayed on the line in silence until finally she spoke quietly.

"Are you okay, Ted? What are you going to do now? Can you sleep? I'd offer to come over but…"

Ted interrupted. "Right now, I'm going to finish taping this window and clean up a bit. I'll try to get to sleep after a little while. You stay where you are and try to sleep. The police will call you."

"Why on earth would they call me? Didn't you tell them it was a robbery attempt? You've never seen Daniel up close, and you said the room was dark."

"Lauren, there was no point in fabricating something. The officer asked if it was likely a robbery attempt and I told him I doubted it. I explained as briefly as I could that I was pretty sure it was a guy trying to get rid of me in a bizarre romantic situation."

Lauren almost screamed. "You didn't involve me?"

"I got drawn into this mess, and I'm going to get out as quickly as I can. The quick way out is to give the police the bare facts, and I'm going to do that tomorrow at nine at the police station. You told me Daniel had a good job with a local travel agency. The police aren't dummies; they wouldn't believe he'd try robbing a house with someone inside."

"What are you going to tell them about me?"

"I'll tell them only that you met this guy and he apparently became obsessed with you and turned into a stalker. I'll have to tell the police that you and I have been neighbors and good friends for quite a while, and that the guy seemed to go nuts and saw me as his competition. I won't say anymore than I have to. Fortunately, I kept the note Daniel taped on my door. I realize it wasn't signed, but the police will have no reason to doubt me."

Ted waited for her annoyed response, but there was only silence on the other end of the line. "What has happened has happened, Lauren. We can't turn back the clock and go in another direction. You know I wish we could. I'll be as brief as I can at the station and you're going to have to play your part carefully. Put your answering machine on so you wont miss the police when they call. And give some thought to what you're going to tell them."

Lauren's response was barely audible. "I'm just sick. How could I have gotten into this awful mess?" She hung up.

Ted felt strangely relieved to be over what he felt would be the worst of it with Lauren. He was confident that the police would absolve him of any crime. After all, it was dark. Ted is an older man; he was defending himself. Daniel was charging towards him with a weapon, the iron bar that was used to smash in the window. Ted would emphasize that even in his fear he shouted several times for the man to stop. His clincher would be that the intruder hissed at him that he was going to teach Ted a lesson.

Ted mixed up a bucket of hot soapy water. When he finished mopping, he carried the blood-colored mixture outside and poured it in the gutter, then hosed out the pail. Lights in Lauren's house were still on.

Several thicknesses of newspaper provided a shield for the exposed window. Ted was soon in the bathroom, again brushing his teeth and preparing for bed. He looked in the mirror before turning off the bathroom light and murmured to himself: "You're not a killer. A guy has a right to protect himself. That son-of-a-bitch had gone mad. There was no other way to stop him."

Ted remembered Lauren telling him that Daniel never had children. That was good. He was sure he had a mother, though, and she will feel terrible. His own mother would, if she were living.

Once asleep, he never wakened until the paper arrived. Ted forced himself from bed quickly. He needed to see what account of Daniel's death, if any, appeared in the metro section. He didn't wait to make coffee, but quickly opened the paper on his kitchen table.

He found no mention of the event, and concluded that the death had occurred too late for the paper's midnight deadline. Lauren would be even more relieved than he was. Ted made coffee and perused the paper, often interrupted by thoughts of the previous night. At seven, he saw activity through his neighbor's window and dialed. Ellen answered.

"I hope you and Lauren got some sleep. That was a wild night, last night, wasn't it?" Without waiting for a response, he asked, "If Lauren is up and available, may I speak with her?"

"Yes, of course, Ted. It was awfully upsetting. Lauren kept blaming you and then herself. I finally convinced her to go to bed around one-ish. Here she is."

"I know it will be a tough work day for you, Lauren. I'm sorry you have to face that."

"I don't know how to feel Ted. Nothing like this has ever happened to me. Is there anything in the paper about it?"

"Not that I've found. Don't watch the local morning news. I'll be leaving for the police station in an hour. They may phone you before I get back. Just let me know what you tell them."

"Ted, our relationship as neighbors has to come across as purely platonic. It's going to be bad as it is, and I have to protect my image as a teacher as best as I can. Do you think the police will talk to the neighbors?"

"I'll back you up on that if it means a lot to you, Lauren. I don't think they'll have any reason to talk with the neighbors. I'll call you if the police interview is different from what I expect."

He hung up and called his children. Kathy first. It was apparent that he had interrupted her preparing the boys for school.

"Kathy, I feel terrible about calling so early, but I want you to hear it from me first. A man broke into my house last night and I shot him."

"Oh my god, daddy. No! Are you okay?"

"I'm fine, Kathy, but I can't talk now. We'll talk more later, okay?" He hung up and dialed Matthew.

Matthew listened for several minutes as Ted got into a bit more depth with his son than he had with his daughter. It was a suitor of Lauren's. He threatened to teach him a lesson. He lunged at him with a crowbar. He had been shot dead.

"Well, dad, all I can say is I'm glad it wasn't you on the receiving end of those bullets. I didn't know you had a gun. What's going on with the police investigation and all?"

"I'm going in at nine this morning to talk with them."

"Call me when you get home and let me know if you need me to come up."

"Thank you, son."

Ted first arranged for a glass company to replace his window during the afternoon, and arrived at the police station a few minutes before nine. He identified himself and handed the card to the desk clerk.

"Mister Butler, Lieutenant Hoskins is this way. Follow me please."

Ted accepted the offer of coffee and tried to appear relaxed. "You must have had a frightening night, Mister Butler," the lieutenant said, reaching his hand across the desk.

Hoskins scanned the papers in front of him and smiled at Ted. "Five bullets entered that guy's chest and one right between his eyes. We need you on the force. Why don't you tell me what happened."

Ted managed a weak smile. "I've never been any good at shooting, especially a handgun. I think I was required to assemble a .45 in the dark as part of my training as a naval officer during the war, but firing the thing accurately wasn't a requirement. I'd never fired this one before last night."

Hoskins' expression told him to continue.

"All I can remember is pointing the gun at the person coming towards me in the half darkness and pulling the trigger a lot of times. I was scared to death and yelling at him to stop."

"My officer's report says you were certain it wasn't a B and E or robbery attempt, but some man who wanted to harm you. Why are you so sure?"

Ted carefully spent several minutes telling the lieutenant how he had learned of this man, known only as Daniel, from his neighbor Lauren Haas. He explained that his neighbor had told him she was concerned about the man's pushiness to enter a relationship with her.

"I live across the street, and saw him drive by slowly a number of times. Lauren even asked if she could stay over at my house three times because she was scared to stay home."

Hoskins nodded, made a few notes and looked directly at Ted. "Was there a romantic relationship between you and this Miss Haas?"

Ted forced an open grin. "Gosh, no! Can't you see my white hair? Thanks for the compliment though. She likes to garden, and we have done quite a lot of that in our respective backyards. I'm sure that's why Lauren feels comfortable with me."

Ted wanted to make sure his point was made. "I can grow better tomatoes, though. My yard has a lot more direct sunlight."

Hoskins pushed the report aside.

"We'll probably call Ms. Haas this morning, Mister Butler. Thanks for your time. Don't go out of town, though, okay?"

TWENTY-SIX   Digging In

Ted called Lauren as soon as he felt she'd be home from her morning classes. He didn't want to be made a liar if she inadvertently revealed an intimate relationship when her turn came with the police.

"I told this Lieutenant Hoskins that my age precluded any intimacy between us and told him that gardening is our mutual interest and that you stayed over at my house three times because of your unease about Daniel's behavior. I didn't show Hoskins the note on my door. That can be done later if I need to."

"Did he say that I'd be called?"

"Only that I was to tell you to expect a call soon for your interview. I think you can be pretty candid as to why Daniel might have misinterpreted my role in your life. He left a trail showing an increasing level of anger. The notes he left you will back that up if you choose to use them. I'd remember though that most of what both of us say to the police may end up in the paper."

"Ted, I'm so numb over this whole awful thing. A man's dead and you're acting like it's part of another good story you're reading. I can't believe it doesn't bother you. You didn't purposefully keep shooting, hoping to kill Daniel, did you?"

"Don't be ridiculous Lauren. As I told Hoskins, I was petrified, it was dark, and this guy was almost on top of me with a weapon. I yelled at Daniel to get back two or three times. What would you have done? I had no place to run. All of the bullets hitting him where they did was just his bad luck."

Lauren murmured, 'I guess you're right. None of us knows how we'll react until it happens. Surely you didn't need to kill him, though." A pause. "I'm glad you called. Talk with you later."

Ted had barely begun the day's work when Lauren called back.

"One o'clock, Ted. I need to be at the police station at one. I'm nervous, Ted! Should I take anything?"

"I'd take the notes Daniel wrote you."

"I'll show them the notes and I'll tell Hoskins about the two parking lot episodes. The security guard will back me up there."

"Yes, Lauren, that's a must. If you want to, offer to show the police the deep scratch and heel dent in your front car door. They'll be looking for proof that Daniel had a violent streak."

"What if they ask why I didn't report the vandalism to the police? The insurance people are going to ask the same question."

"You certainly can be truthful there. You didn't see the damage being done, and couldn't accuse someone of something you couldn't prove. Be equally honest, Lauren, in telling Hoskins that you were still trying to see the best in Daniel."

"I was trying, Ted. Daniel wasn't all that bad." Ted could hear her sobs. He waited while she pulled herself together.

"I wish he wasn't dead. Why didn't you call 9-1-1 and let them handle it? You didn't need to start shooting, did you?"

"Damn it, Lauren. There wasn't time! My phone was in the bedroom. I had to make a choice, run from the bathroom for the phone or go for the gun. When I was grabbing the gun, I could see a man's outline nearly through the window. He was starting to stand up! What would you expect me to do—let the bastard beat me to death with that iron he used on the window?"

"I guess you're right, Ted. It's partly my fault. I should have told the police that I was a little scared and asked them to keep an eye on my house."

Ted interrupted, "Don't blame yourself. Police don't have the time to chase after things unless an actual complaint is filed. You couldn't do that. Besides, everything happened so fast."

"I just know they're going to push me to admit that we were lovers. They won't close the case if they have a hint that you might have wanted to see Daniel dead."

"You might be right, Lauren, but please don't go looking for trouble. Hoskins asked me directly and I pointed to my white hair and said I was flattered. He didn't pursue it. Tell them I'm too old for you. I doubt they'll pursue it with you."

"Ted, you got off easy. I might have to admit that I told Daniel that part of the reason I couldn't go out with him was because of my feelings for you. I'm sure there's a reference to that in one of Daniel's notes."

"Well," Ted tried to think of what he could do with this, "if push comes to shove, acknowledge that we sort of tried to be romantic for a while way back but I turned out to be impotent. The police will accept that you might have said what you did to Daniel to get him off your back. Play up the gardening side and add occasional dinners. You do need to alert Ellen. The police may want to talk with her."

"Oh, now Ellen has to be involved! I hate to lie, Ted. Supposing they interview the neighbors and they mention our trips together. Several know we went to Cabo. I told them about all the things we did."

"In my view that won't happen. The police questions will stop with us, Daniel's work friends, and possibly Ellen. Let's just not open the door to problems. Daniel died because he broke into my house and I defended myself because I thought he was going to kill me. He'd become obsessed with you and came after me. He'd gone nuts! I had to defend myself." Ted was almost shouting.

"I'll do my best. Call you tonight."

Ted called his daughter in the early afternoon before her boys were due back from school to discuss the incident with her. He assured her that he was fine and he'd already completed the police interview and didn't expect a big deal to be made of it. He tried to preclude too many questions by assuring her that his house had been all cleaned up and he was now waiting for the window repair man. Kathy listened without saying much until her father brought Lauren into it.

"It's hard to explain," Ted told her. "A man Lauren met about a month ago became obsessed with her and began to stalk her. He drove by the house a lot of times. She dated him only twice, but the guy went berserk. I'm not too sure about all of it, but Lauren told him she was still my girlfriend just to get him off her back."

"What a bitch! I knew she was trouble Daddy. She dragged you right into her mess. You could have been killed. You should never have been involved with her in the first place."

Ted bristled. "Wait a minute now, Kathy. Get off that kick. I can understand how a daughter might feel when her father hooks up with a much younger woman. Sure, there's been a cost to it, including this unexpected occurrence last night. But I'm telling you that Lauren has given me nearly two years of feeling young again. I'd do that all over again without a minute's hesitation."

"Sorry Daddy. I'm just scared and glad you're safe. I didn't know you kept a gun. I think you should have told me that, because of the kids and all."

"It was a gift and I never keep it accessible or loaded, but I got worried when this man left a note on my front door telling me to get out of Lauren's life. I decided to load it and stick it on top of the fridge. I wasn't even sure how to shoot the damned thing. The police have confiscated it for now."

"Is there anything at all we can do to help? Talk to the police or something?"

"Oh no. Don't make a big deal out of it with the boys or anyone please."

"They'll be really interested at how you fired a gun at a crook. I'll need you to figure out how to discuss it with them."

"I don't look forward to that, Kathy, but I will. Let's plan to get together in about a week. If the boys bring it up, I'll handle it. If they don't let's let it lie for a while."

Ted had no sooner replaced the phone when it rang again. He rubbed his left ear, shook his head and picked up the receiver.

"This is The Sacramento Bee. Are you Ted Butler? We'd like to talk with him, please."

"Yes, this is he."

"We've just read the police report of the shooting at your house last night. I hate to disturb you, Mister Butler, but the report said this man, identified as Daniel Wilson, wasn't attempting a robbery, and there was a woman involved. Did you know the man that you shot, Mister Butler?"

Ted thought quickly. Lauren's interrogation must have been completed and the police released a report to the press.

"All I can say is that this man broke into my house last night right when I was going to bed. It is correct that I own a revolver and was able to grab it as the man was crashing though my kitchen window. I'm sorry someone died, but I had to protect myself."

"Thank you Mister Butler, but we have that information. The report said Lauren Haas was involved somehow? Can you tell us how?"

Ted's mind tried to project what Lauren told the police. He wished he'd insisted she call him promptly after the interview.

"She was involved only in that the man—did you say his name was Wilson?—apparently was a fairly new acquaintance of hers, and had become obsessed and started stalking her. I'm sure you've heard of these situations."

"Why was he after you? What's really going on here?"

Ted's mind whirled again. What had Lauren revealed to the police? Had she expanded beyond their earlier talk?

"There's not a lot I can tell you," Ted replied. "What did Lauren say in the police report? She's been awfully upset, as you can understand, and I've had little chance to speak with her."

Ted waited again.

"It says here that Ms. Haas said you've been friends for several years, and maybe Wilson misunderstood the relationship between the two of you, and that he may have targeted you as an adversary."

"I couldn't have expressed it better. What did you say your name was?"

"I'm Earl Gardiner." The reporter wasn't about to let go. "Tell us something about yourself, Mister Butler. You'll soon be an octogenarian, no?"

"Thank you, but no one is interested in me. I'm just a retired guy who plays golf when I'm up to it, spends a lot of time gardening, does a little fishing during the summers and keeps in touch with his family. There are millions of us. Goodbye, Mister Gardiner." Ted hung up.

TWENTY-SEVEN   Little White Lies

Ted rubbed his ear again, picked up the portable phone, stuffed it into his shirt pocket and stepped out into the early spring afternoon sunshine. He was surprised that there hadn't been more calls. His interest had always spiked when he read of older residents having been confronted with break-ins while they were home. Most were attempted burglaries according to the news articles. He had always mentally applauded when the older guy got the upper hand, usually with a handy gun. Too often, though, and Ted grimaced at the thought, a badly beaten old man ended up in the hospital.

Now he needed to get his mind off of that. His encounter had ended in his favor, one of the lucky ones. For now he'd enjoy the afternoon sun on his back and rethink where all of the garden items would fit. Shortly his soon to be planted tomatoes would be reaching for the sky. His house was paid for, the Explorer was getting old but was fully his and still responded to the turn of the key.

The ringing phone in Ted's pocket jolted him back to reality.

"Ted, what are you up to? I just got back from a couple of days in Reno and here you are making headlines! We can't let you out of our sight. It's a good thing that guy didn't get to you first. I'd have lost my favorite fishing buddy."

Ted was relieved. Five minutes later his conversation with George was over. They'd have another bunch of pleasant trout fishing trips during the coming summer and fall.

Another call came shortly after he had poured himself some brandy and soda.

"Hold on Carl until I find a comfortable chair. It's thoughtful of you to call."

"Ted, old buddy, are you all right? The newspaper article said you were just seconds away from being clobbered. Where in hell did you learn to use a six-shooter? I know we were both in World War Two, but you never talked about guns. You're a fisherman!" and then a pause followed by a jocular, "and if I remember our conversation sitting out in your boat last fall, you've become quite a lover."

Ted joined in with his friend's laughter. "you're right on, Carl, but now matters have temporarily gotten out of hand. I'm not sure where I stand with Lauren. She's kind of standing up for this dead guy."

Their several minutes on the phone allowed Ted to detail the immediate background to Daniel's break-in, the conversation ending with: "Please assure Ida that I'm fine and to count on us getting together before many weeks go by."

It was easier now to concentrate on his news magazine while enjoying the drink. The discussions with two of his closest friends raised his confidence that this Daniel thing was basically behind him.

At four the ringing phone at his elbow startled him. Who could this be?

"Mr. Butler? Earl Gardiner here. How are you doing?"

A hesitant: "Well, okay I guess. Just reading and figuring out what to fix for dinner." Then regaining his composure: "What is the purpose of your call, Gardiner?"

"I'm glad I haven't disturbed your dinner. You'll remember our earlier discussion about this Lauren Hass friend of yours?" Ted made no response.

"Well, a call came to my office this afternoon. It was a man's voice. He wouldn't give his name but said he was a neighbor."

Ted's mind raced. "So what?"

"I don't mean to pry into your personal life but 'so what' is that the guy said it was pretty common talk along the street that you and Lauren Haas were as thick as thieves. He wouldn't answer any of my questions but said he was going to alert the police. It wasn't a very friendly voice, Mr. Butler."

Ted was stunned. He hoped his voice had more conviction than he felt.

"I don't know where anyone dredged up that nonsense. The information I gave you last time still stands."

"Thank you, Mr. Butler. I felt you should know. Our paper won't be printing anything until we get confirmation or the police reports add something. "Good bye, sir.""

A glance out the window now showed Lauren's car in the driveway. Thoughts of dinner were forgotten. Ted paced through the house several times, hands in pockets, staring at the floor. Who could the caller have been? Who would want to see him in trouble with the police. Did it really matter? What mattered now were his and Lauren's answers if that caller to Gardiner did tip off the police.

He grabbed the phone and dialed Lauren, brushing off her greeting. "Have you talked with the police yet?"

"Ted, what's wrong? Your voice is almost frightening. Yes, but only by phone as I had to stay late at school. We talked for several minutes and they said to expect to be asked to come to the station soon. The caller was very courteous and there was no hint of urgency. My classes start later tomorrow so I'll be home all morning if the police call. I'm not as nervous as I was. There were a bunch of calls from my friends, too. I'll take care of them later." Then, "What has happened, Ted, that makes you sound so upset?"

"This Gardiner guy from the paper called a half hour ago. He said he had a call from some unidentified man who claimed he knew that we had a very intimate relationship and that he was going to alert the police." Not waiting for a response, he rushed on. "We need to get together and get our stories right. Can you come over now?"

A gasp at the other end, then: "Damn it! Yes, sure." In the background he heard Lauren call out, "Ellen, I'll be over at Ted's house for an hour. We can work out dinner when I get back." She hung up.

Ted watched her cross the street and held the front door open. There was no greeting, only a brief eye contact, then "I could use a glass of wine," and without asking, "I'll pour one for you, too." He pointed to a kitchen chair.

Their discussion lasted forty-five minutes. It was like an attorney and client meeting. Ted insisted that everything had to carefully be decided and their stories perfectly matching if the expected call to the police had been made.

It was agreed that both would acknowledge the two trips to Cabo San Lucas. Neighbors were aware of those year end Mexican flights. Ellen couldn't deny knowledge if asked.

How could they best handle the key question about intimate relationships, bound to be pursued by the police in their effort to determine if Ted had a reason to kill Daniel.

Each would volunteer the information that a romantic relationship was sort of hoped for at first, but didn't develop. Yes, they had occasionally stayed at each others homes overnight, sleeping in the same bed but with little or no emphasis on sex. Turn the conversation to gardening and friendship.

Ted had to stick with a claim of impotence and Lauren would assert her disappointment and acknowledge her internet search for a younger partner.

If a police interrogator suggested that he had information that Ted had confided to others that his Polish bombshell was great in bed, he would confess that he was bragging to impress his men friends. It would be a weak argument, but Ted insisted he probably could carry it off.

Lauren burst into laughter, reached over and punched him lightly in the ribs.

"You hound dog, I'll bet you did a lot of that." The tension was eased. Ted's stern facial expression relaxed and he smiled. His eyes expressed his feelings.

"Yes, that part has been wonderful and there will never be another Lauren Haas in my life."

Lauren wouldn't agree to his suggestion that maybe she should tell the police that she had a few intimate relationships with prospective suitors during the several months she'd been on the internet. It would back up his claim of impotence and her desire for romance.

She almost exploded.

"Kill that crazy idea! I can just see the headline, 'College professor admits trysts'. I told you before that my job can't stand that kind of publicity. You look out for yourself. You'll get no help from me there, Ted. Remember, it's you who did the shooting. If I were a juror I might even vote to convict you of murder." Neither was now smiling.

Lauren declined a refill of wine, pointing to the still half filled glass. They reached one more agreement as the forty-five minute meeting closed. They would both claim an enduring friendship that possibly was interpreted as a romantic one by friends and apparently triggering Daniel's actions. They would hold fast on this.

At eleven the next morning the anticipated call came from Lt. Hoskins.

"I don't want you to be overly concerned, Mr. Butler, but some additional information has been brought to our attention concerning the break-in at your home. We'll need to meet with you again."

Ted knew his hands were shaking. His response had to be right.

"I'll be glad to come down, but what on earth new information could there be?"

"It involves a phone call that came to our station. Can you be here at nine-thirty in the morning? We're asking Lauren Haas to appear at the same time, though she will be meeting in a separate room with another officer."

Most of the early morning activity seemed to have passed when they arrived. The desk clerk asked their names, then studied the pad in front of her. "Oh yes, Lt. Hoskins asked me to send you right in, Mr. Butler. Lt. Marie Williams will be meeting with you, Ms. Haas. She will be tied up for another five minutes. Will you be seated, please."

Ted said nothing but turned and blew Lauren a kiss as he followed another officer down the hall. It wasn't returned.

The officer tapped lightly on the door, then entered. Lt. Hoskins stood, smiled and extended his hand. He motioned to a small round table set up with two filled glasses of water, napkins, and a half-filled pitcher.

"We'll get right to the point, Mr. Butler. A call came in yesterday. It was a male voice. Unfortunately he surprised us and didn't stay on the line long enough for us to trace the call. The man was very blunt and said we police were missing the boat, that you and Lauren Haas were as thick as thieves, as he put it, and that you had every reason to want Daniel Wilson dead. How would you respond to that, Mr. Butler?"

Hoskins reached into his briefcase and pulled out a small recorder setting it between them. He smiled again. "I'm sure you don't mind if we use this. I'm not good at taking notes and we both want an accurate record of our discussion." Ted could only nod.

"Go ahead, Mr. Butler. What was your relationship with Lauren Haas?"

Ted sat forward in his chair, resting both forearms on the table, first glancing at the instrument before looking at the officer. He realized that he was nervously tapping the fingers of his right hand on the table top.

"Relax, Mr. Butler, that thing isn't going to bite you."

Both laughed. Ted managed to regain his composure. Choice of words was critical.

"Lauren, I mean Ms. Haas, and a teacher friend had moved into a home across the street from me that had been put up for rent. It was summer and I always had a nice garden, especially tomatoes. My wife had suddenly died a year earlier. We'd always shared garden stuff with neighbors, and that's how Lauren, Ms. Haas, and I became acquainted."

"Why don't you refer to her as Lauren if that makes you more comfortable? Go ahead."

It was Ted's turn to smile.

"Yes, thank you. Lauren and I have become good friends. We've spent hundreds of hours in our yards together growing stuff. It's awful that this Daniel Wilson thing had to happen. I never met the man. She had met other guys briefly and sometimes told me about them, but had never mentioned Wilson before this obsession situation developed. Then Lauren asked me several times if she could stay overnight at my house. She had become frightened because of some of the notes he was writing to her."

Ted took a few sips of water, removed his left arm from the table, and waited. What was coming next?

"Thank you, Mr. Butler. Now that we've had this call, we need to clarify the level of romantic relations you had with Ms. Haas."

Ted leaned slightly forward again. This was critical. He knew Hoskins would be studying him.

"Lauren turned out to be thirty years younger than me, as I'm sure your records will show. My wife and I had given up sex several years before and I was keeping extra busy and not thinking much about romance. I'll have to admit that I did begin to think about it with Lauren and wondered how she might respond. One afternoon after we had done a bunch of gardening and were relaxing with a couple of glasses of wine, I did get a little carried away and began teasing her about sex. We ended up in bed. I know she was disappointed. I was embarrassed. Lauren encouraged me several times to try again during the first two or three months. Nothing happened."

Ted looked at the officer and frowned, shaking his head.

"You'll be seventy-five some day, Lt. Hoskins, and you may go through the same experience."

Hoskins didn't smile, but looked puzzled. "But why would this caller say what he did? Did some neighbor dislike you so much that he would call us and try to make trouble for you?"

Again Ted found his fingers tapping on the table. Hoskins eyes were on them. Did he dare give the answer that had popped into his mind? He'd gamble.

"You need to understand Lauren. As you will see, she's a most attractive woman. She's also a big flirt. She told me she likes men's attention, and it shows. She's great socially and within a couple of months, Lauren was on a first name basis with half of the people on our block. One neighbor chidingly told me that all of the single guys and half of the married men on the street likely were dying to get into her pants."

Hoskins eyebrows lifted as if to say "Wow."

"But if Ms Haas was looking for a younger man, didn't that bother you? You don't have to answer this, but did you feel she was responding to some of these men who desired a relationship with her?"

"I don't mind answering that at all, Lt. Hoskins. No, I don't think Lauren gave in to any of them. In fact she told me several months ago when she acknowledged that she had decided it was time to seriously hunt for a partner around her age, that sex would not be involved. Lauren wanted a commitment first. I admired her for that."

Hoskins was now nodding his head slightly and looking thoughtfully at him. For the first time Ted sensed that he was making progress. White lies balanced with some truth can be powerful.

"I know you'll wonder why she stuck with me. We did do quite a lot of nice things together, despite my age, even traveling to Cabo San Lucas twice for a several day winter vacation. I guess Lauren got to feel a sense of stability with me. Her job situation wasn't going too well, and frankly I did pay most of the travel bills. She told me she didn't care what people thought, that she considered me her best friend. You can be sure it made me feel good to have this young companion. It wasn't anyone else's damned business."

Ted hesitated and looked away.

"She's coming down on me awfully hard now about Daniel Wilson. I'm afraid I'm going to lose her trust. She insists I should have found a way to call the police. There wasn't time."

Ted thrust out his chin and sat straight up. Hoskins was staring at him, unblinking.

"As for this jerk who called, maybe it was some guy Lauren had teased and then turned down. Maybe he was getting even and having his fun at my expense. No one knows except him. I didn't go out to kill this Daniel guy. He came at me with that crowbar and I defended myself. Lauren said he was no longer married and had no children. Likely he does have a mother living and she feels awful. I sure feel sorry for her. But I've helped raise a good family, served my time in the war and deserve to live a few years longer. It was him or me."

Ted sat back in his chair, his arms folded, mentally exhausted but hopeful.

Lt. Hoskins glanced at his watch, turned off the recorder and stood. "Thank you, Mr. Butler. If this doesn't take care of our concerns you'll be getting a call from us. Oh, yes, and feel free to travel as you like."

Ted was surprised to find Lauren in the waiting room. Her quick smile eased his worry about her interview. He turned to the desk clerk with a smile. "Thank you for helping set up our appointments."

They left without speaking to each other until clear of the police station.

"How did your meeting with Lt. Williams go? With the clerk saying there would be a wait, I didn't expect to find you finished already."

"I didn't expect that either. She was about my age and asked me to call her Marie. She said she had intended to contact me sooner but got pushed into doing other things. I liked her right off."

Lauren reached over and took his hand as they continued down the almost secluded sidewalk. "I'm awfully glad you insisted on our talk. I did show her the notes Daniel left. Marie said she had to deal with far too many of those types of situations. She appeared a little annoyed that I hadn't called the police but seemed to accept my explanation that I wasn't too concerned at first, then things happened too fast."

"Did she ask about us?"

"Yes, I noticed she had a pad of notes in front of her. I told Marie that you had proven to be a wonderful, dependable and generous friend. She really perked up when I said generous. You know you have been, Ted."

He squeezed her hand but said nothing. "I told her I likely would have married you if you had asked, but this impotence thing got in the way, for you more than for me. Marie seemed to understand when I told her I was sure the reason you didn't ask me was because you feared there was no way I would stay true under those circumstances. I thought I saw a tear starting to form but all she said was 'Men can be so dumb'."

Little more was said until they located the Explorer, paid the parking lot fee and began the fifteen minute drive home. Lauren reopened the conversation.

"Marie said your Lt. Hoskins would be deciding what comes next and that her role was to give him her input. Oh yes, and she told me to tell you she really likes fresh tomatoes, too. How did your meeting go, Ted?"

He was now entering the short stretch of freeway and trying to concentrate on traffic. What should he tell her? More important, what should he emphasize? Sure, she had held his hand on the walk from the station. But Lauren was an emotional woman and very compassionate when she wanted to be. He gritted his teeth. This damned Daniel thing wasn't going to go away even if the police exonerated him. He'd be defending himself forever with her. No, he wouldn't count on recovering a romance he was destined to lose anyway.

"Aren't you going to answer? Did something go awfully wrong in your meeting with Lt. Hoskins?"

Ted took a deep breath, glanced at her quickly, then returned to driving.

"Who knows how it went. Hoskins had a recorder taking down every word. I emphasized a platonic relationship as we agreed to do as best I could. I saw signs of disbelief in his face at times. You can be sure that I made both of us look as good as I could, but I'm not sure of anything. He did say I was free to travel anywhere and that he'd call of there was further need."

His glance at Lauren told him she had more to say. She did, with tears flowing. "Please don't hate me for it, Ted, but I burned all of those letters you wrote to me. I had to. A court subpoena to turn them over would have made liars of both of us."

They were turning into the off ramp. Ted looked at the car clock. "Let's stop and have lunch at that little Mexican place near us," he said. "And I don't want to talk any more about this sorry event."

They didn't. Snatches of conversation about Lauren's teaching fit into a hastily eaten lunch.

Their parting kiss in his driveway was more like one given to a visiting cousin. Lauren stopped halfway across the street, then turned back. Ted waited, puzzled.

"There is something else that you should know. I've been at Bryan's house three evenings this last week. We're not being intimate or anything like that yet, but I feel good just being close to him. I mentioned it in the police interview. Marie said that sounded like a positive step to her."

Ted nodded, momentarily shaken. But why should this come as a surprise? When was an old fool ever going to give up?

Lauren couldn't ignore his crushed expression. She grabbed and held him tightly for a few seconds. Their kiss was one he had cherished so often.

Then, with a cheery "Bye Ted, thanks again for lunch," she quickly crossed the street and disappeared into the house.

The morning paper contained an inside page, single column article. The police had determined that the ageing Ted Butler's killing of Daniel Wilson was regrettable, but was done in self defense. No action by the district attorney would be taken.

TWENTY-EIGHT   Resolution

Calls from friends became fewer over the next two days. Some had never read the brief newspaper article but all expressed their relief with the police decision.

As much as Ted disliked the prospect of long phone conversations, he first called Matthew and carefully answered his son's supportive but pointed questions, deliberately omitting any mention of the impotence discussion in both interviews. Near the end of the call, Matthew asked how Lauren was reacting to the killing and the pressure of the police interviews.

"Women take these events awfully hard, Matt, but she's settled down some now. I'm not sure though, that our relationship will stand this. I'm just waiting and hoping. We've had some great times but I'm worried that Lauren may decide that this mess is too much."

Kathy's call came before he was able to gather his thoughts and call her.

"Hi Daddy. Who on earth were you on the phone with for so long? I must have dialed half-a-dozen times."

Ted Laughed. "Sorry Kathy, and you're right. That's not my style. But I was talking to your brother and you can imagine how many questions he wanted to ask. They hadn't seen any mention about the police decision in their paper. I had to tell him about the whole interview."

Kathy assured her father that her boys were still unaware of the killing, and that she had waited to call until they had left for school.

"I'm so glad you didn't have to get dragged through a long police investigation. Tell me how your police interview went. Weren't you awfully nervous?"

"That's putting it mildly, especially when the Lieutenant turned on his recording machine."

His daughter's questions showed her concern over his welfare. Had she purposefully avoided any questions about Lauren? Ted saw a need for this; he tried a casual comment. "And, oh yes, the police interviewed Lauren in a separate room. She said it went okay."

A blunt: 'What does she have to do with it? It seems to me that she's already got you into enough of a mess. Why did they call her in?"

"The police had to check our relationship out as a motive for my killing this Daniel guy."

"Oh no! How awful! What did you do?"

"To be honest, Lauren and I got together beforehand and agreed what we'd tell the investigators." Ted went on to recount the plan and execution and could tell that Kathy was not happy.

"I imagine you'll feel better when I tell you that this hasn't set well with Lauren and it's more than likely she and I won't be seeing each as much of each other as we have been."

He thought he heard an audible sigh of relief from his daughter on the other end of the phone before they said goodbye.

On Friday afternoon, Ellen pulled into her driveway as Ted was about to leave for the grocery store. She made a sweeping ark with her arm and called out, "Hi Ted, come on over for a minute."

He shut off the engine, walked across the street and sat down on the porch.

"I read the paper and am so glad the police agreed you shot that man in self-defense. I wanted to talk with you before now, but you and I seem to have been gone at the same time. Lauren has been gone herself a lot lately, out with this guy Bryan. They went on a hike somewhere, and she often gets home late."

"Yes," Ted responded, "she mentioned Bryan to me earlier. If I recall, he is the guy with the van and the fancy curtains who was worried about having sex too soon." Both laughed. "Did Lauren tell you about the trail hike?"

"Yes, she said it was a nice hike. He's been divorced, I guess. No kids."

"Umm," Ted grunted.

"She told me nothing is going to happen too soon. There are four other men who she's asked to call. Lauren said it wouldn't be fair just to cut them off. I think she's going a little overboard trying to crowd out the memories of Daniel. How are you handling what's going on, Ted?"

"Not very effectively, I'm afraid. I'm sure you know that we got closer again for a bit after Daniel started to be threatening. I really liked having her around again."

Ted stood to leave. "I'm glad you suggested our visit, Ellen. It's great that you and Lauren are good friends. She needs to be able to talk with someone about the men she meets. You can understand that I'm not a lot of help."

He felt he could see a genuine concern for his feelings in Ellen's expression as she tilted her head and asked if he thought he might start seeing other women anytime soon.

"I honestly don't know, Ellen. Maybe I'm living in a make-believe world of an old man, and try to convince myself that all of this change with Lauren is just a bad dream, one that will go away and leave things like they were. Thanks for your concern. See you later."

He started down the steps.

"Hey, Ted, there's something else."

He hesitated and turned back.

"You're a nice person. One of the most considerate I've ever met. Lauren has gained so much from your time together. She hasn't directly said anything, but I know you've been generous with her." Ted nodded slightly.

"I'm a woman, Ted, and I know what loneliness is. It can't have escaped your attention that I've had men here and hoped something nice would develop, but it hasn't. I envy Lauren."

He nodded again.

"From what Lauren said, she's determined. I'm certain, speaking as a woman, that she's found her man in this Bryan person. She's trying to be cautious, but Lauren's not going to let this man get away, Ted. I'm sure she'll be letting you know about it soon."

He stared at his feet almost afraid to look into Ellen's honest, beseeching eyes. He finally looked up, speaking tonelessly: "I know you're right, Ellen. Lauren's always been straight arrow with me and it won't be any different this time. She likely just wants to make absolutely sure." He smiled at her warmly and stood, then concluded. "Thanks for helping me see more clearly."

Ellen stood and pulled him into her arms. "Ted, you're not old at all. You have so much to offer a woman. There will be someone out there for you, just as I'm hopeful there will be for me."

She released her embrace and led him towards the sidewalk.

Ted tried to scatter his work through the weekend. He wasn't surprised to see Lauren climb into her car at nine on Sunday, clad in bright shorts and a sweatshirt. She'd placed a small ice chest on the rear seat. He'd turned away. He went about his back yard activities during the late morning, enjoying the warm sun. He recalled Ellen's statement on Friday that Lauren had planned another day of hiking with Bryan. Ted was relieved that the man hadn't shown up in the fancy-curtained van. He liked the feeling that Lauren was still showing that consideration for him.

He couldn't throw aside the uneasiness when nine-thirty came that night. He was dressing for bed and her car was still missing. Fifteen minutes later he heard a car across the street. Ted's quick peek confirmed it was Lauren. Was his permanent loss of her as imminent as Ellen had predicted? He slept a little better.

Ted had almost abandoned his routine of seeing Lauren off to work each morning. He noticed that Ellen would occasionally pause in front of the women's kitchen window and wave brightly. Had she told Lauren about their talk? He did miss Lauren rolling down her side window as she left of work, even if it were only for a barely-reassuring "Talk with you later." Now that was gone.

This Friday was different. Ted was out front adjusting the lawn sprinklers when Lauren shoved her book-filled bag onto the front seat and climbed in beside it. She backed into the street, and her car window came down but she seemed hesitant to speed away. Ted walked closer to the car. Her smile was more serene than inviting. She looked so young. It was the face of a happy woman. Ted stood with his hands folded in front of him, looking intently at her, but saying nothing.

"It's Bryan, Ted. I think you'd really like him."

It was her way of being honest and direct. He knew she wanted his approval. He nodded at her through the window to indicate he understood.

"I'm going to move in with him."

Tears were forming in Lauren's eyes. Ted momentarily looked away. The dreaded moment had finally come. He held back his own tears. He had to be the man she had come to love and admire. Hadn't he promised her that when his replacement became a fact that he would be able to handle it like a man?

"I'm happy for you, Lauren. You don't need to feel guilty about finding a younger guy. We both knew it was going to happen."

She dabbed her eyes with a tissue and nodded. A quick glance, smile, and wave acknowledged his blown kiss as she slowly drove away. Ted stood for several minutes staring at the empty street before he said aloud, "and I didn't have to miss the dance." He felt a huge weight had been lifted from his shoulders.

That weekend, Ted watched as Lauren's car followed the van down the street. He then sat in his reading chair and closed his eyes. His part of this story was ended. It was, on balance, a good story for him. He was lonely, yes, but why should his age prevent his finding another companion? He smiled to himself. Maybe she'd have to be a little older than Lauren, but still love mountain trail hikes.

TWENTY-NINE   The Final Chapter

Ted arose early, fully refreshed. He had slept well. An hour into his morning of school follow-up work, he took a break and walked into the back yard, sipping his coffee. Ted examined a small corner strawberry patch he'd been nursing along for two years. The area was flooded with blossoms, but only a few small berries had formed. He glanced at his watch. It was only eight-thirty.

Why not go to the Wednesday farmer's market and see if any of the Watsonville strawberries had arrived? He would enjoy them. He returned to the kitchen, washed the pot and dumped the dregs of the coffee into the sink.

The market was filling with customers when he arrived. Most of the vendors were finishing their displays of late winter vegetables, and of fruit coming out of cold storage. Ted was surprised to find several stalls still displaying apples. He'd assumed that the Sebastopol area apples had sold out several weeks earlier. He wasn't in the market for apples today, but paused at the third stand to examine the fruit. Strawberry sellers, if there were any, would be another dozen stalls down the complex.

"Well, hello—It's good to see you again," said a woman Ted had seen numerous times behind the apple table over the years. He'd casually estimated her to be about fifty. He'd bought apples from her several times to make applesauce for Kathy's boys and for himself, even before his wife's death. The woman always had a quick smile and would thrust several additional apples into his bag after it was weighed.

"It's good to see you too," Ted replied. "I was only coming down for some strawberries and am surprised to see some of last fall's apples still for sale."

"We'd have liked to have sold out sooner, too. Those we have left aren't very crisp anymore, but they'll make good applesauce."

Ted considered the idea for a few seconds.

"Why not? Would you weigh out about five pounds? I've always found that makes a good pot of sauce."

He watched the scale pointer move to five pounds. The woman selected five more nice apples and tossed them into the bag.

"That's five pounds at sixty cents, three dollars even."

"You're very generous," Ted said. "The applesauce will be a real treat for the grandkids and I like it myself."

Ted observed that no one else was close by. "What is your name, by the way. I've seen you many times here, but don't know your name."

"It's Donna. I help some friends in the market when I have time."

"Nice to meet you Donna. I'm Ted Butler. I always thought you were part of this family enterprise. You mean you're not related to any of the guys I've seen working here?"

"No, Ted, these are just friends I've known since high school. They push me to help out because they insist I'm so good with customers. I'm not alone today. Tony just went down the line for a cup of coffee. He's likely met somebody he knows. It doesn't matter. We haven't been that busy."

Ted stood back while Donna helped another two customers. He was now observing her more closely. There was no doubt she was attractive. He estimated her to be almost five feet six, and yes, very nice legs. If it wasn't for numerous fine facial wrinkles, she wouldn't look nearly fifty.

She looked up and smiled after putting the money into the trays on a low table in front of her.

"I'm glad you didn't walk away, Ted. I'm hoping we'll sell out by this time next week. It's slow now but usually gets pretty busy in another half hour."

"If you don't mind telling me, Donna, where do you work as a regular job? You do handle people really well."

"Oh, I'm a bank teller for a small bank. I've been doing that for three years now, but I'm finding there may not be much of a future there."

Ted chuckled, "Here I've been doing business with a banker and never realized it. I'm impressed."

Donna gave him an inviting smile. He was glad he'd worn a cap. He felt younger than his hidden white hair.

"I may not be a banker for much longer. Not many of my friends know it, but I've applied for a position as a flight attendant. My first interview last week seemed to go well and I'm expecting to hear back from them next week."

"That's fantastic Donna. If you like to travel, you might love that line of work. I understand that the pay is quite good after you've been there a while."

Ted again stepped back while two more couples made purchases. He was thinking beyond apples. What could he lose? He'd better act quickly because this Tony was bound to show up pretty soon. He stepped closer when the customers moved along, their purchases held firmly in their hands.

"I don't want to seem forward, Donna, but I have to admit I like you. It's fun talking with you. Would you consider having dinner with me later this week?"

Ted saw no hesitation. "I'd love to do that, Ted. It's not like you're a stranger. What day is best for you?"

"I'm open both Friday and Saturday nights. Do you have a preference?" They agreed upon Friday. Donna declined his offer to pick her up at her apartment. She brightened when Ted suggested Scott's. He offered to make reservations for seven.

"That's perfect! Scott's is only a five minute drive from my place. I'll be driving a small white pick up."

Another potential customer took a position beside Ted and began examining the apples. He backed away, gave Donna a smile and a quick wave, and moved down the line of tables.

Ted was elated to find what he'd come for. The sign above the open rear doors of the bob-tail truck read, Watsonville Strawberries. Two men were taking care of eager customers. He waited his turn and bought a half-crate of beautiful berries for seven dollars. He headed for his truck with the box containing the six baskets balanced on his left forearm and the bag of apples gripped in his right hand. He had a glimpse through the crowd and saw Donna weighing a purchase of apples.

Ted was relaxed on the short drive home. The weight from the memories of the shooting and the loss of Lauren pressed less heavily. He'd thoroughly enjoy his afternoon cribbage with Mike.

It was ten minutes before seven when Ted arrived at Scott's. He quickly glanced at the several dozen parked cars and saw no white pick up. He returned to his car after a survey of restaurant customers revealed no sign of Donna. At almost exactly seven a white pick up arrived and parked in a slot five cars down from his. A single woman stepped from the car and walked briskly towards a small drugstore close to the restaurant. Ted blinked and then relaxed. It was only a coincidence. Not Donna. This woman was dressed in a brief black leather skirt reaching less than halfway to her knees, and wearing high heels. He would be interested later in the face that accompanied this leggy young woman.

Three minutes later the woman exited from the drug store and headed Ted's way.

"Hi Ted. I though it was you, but needed something from the store. I hope you don't mind my ignoring you for that moment."

She held out her hand and then gave him a light kiss on the cheek. Ted was almost speechless as he responded to her extended hand. He tried to be casual. "You look really nice."

Many of the eyes of the diners focused on Donna as the maitre d' led the unlikely couple to their table. Their waiter quickly brought the menus. "May I get you something from the bar?" he asked.

Ted looked questioningly at Donna. "I'm going to have a martini. Gin. What would you like, Donna?"

"That sounds perfect," she said. "But please make mine a double."

They were pretending to study their menus when the drinks arrived. Ted picked up his glass. "I'm so glad you thought this was a good idea, Donna. Is there anything special we might toast?"

"Well, as a matter of fact, I'll be thirty-eight tomorrow."

He couldn't hide his startled expression, and she added, "Some people say I look a little older, but these facial wrinkles run in my family."

"Well," Ted faltered, "Happy Birthday, Donna. To a happy birthday."

Their raised glasses clinked. He quickly changed the subject. They chatted a bit about the airline she interviewed with. Ted reached across the table and briefly touched her hand and asked about her family. She had a brother and sister, both older. Her parents were still living, and living together. Ted chose not to ask her if she had been married.

The waiter walked to their table. "Will you be ready to order soon?" he asked.

Ted responded. "Please give us a few more minutes." He picked up the menu. Donna handed her empty glass to the waiter. "Another one of these please."

The waiter looked towards Ted. "No, thanks," Ted said. "We'll be having wine with dinner."

Donna was looking at Ted with a slight fixed smile when he felt her stockinged foot touch his ankle. He returned a smile and reached over to touch her hand with a whispered "you're nice." Her drink arrived. Ted was pretending to concentrate on the menu items but was almost shaking with the excitement of her foot that was now rubbing on his lower leg.

"I think I'll have the small sirloin. What looks good to you, Donna?" She withdrew her foot from his leg. He could hear the scraping under the table as she slipped into her shoe.

"One of their specialties is the salmon filet. I've had that one before and I'm going with it."

Ted signaled for the waiter and placed their orders. He ordered a glass of the house cabernet. She, a glass of chardonnay, despite her still half-filled martini.

Ted turned their conversation to Donna's banking job, but noticed her conversation was getting disjointed. He saw her slop a few drops from her nearly empty martini glass when she set it down. She responded to his glance by meticulously wiping the glass with her napkin. Their dinners arrived and he began eating. Ted was hungry. He sliced a corner of his steak, tucked thin slices of butter into his baked potato and topped it with sour cream. Donna picked for a bit at her salad and ate a small bite of her salmon.

"This is a really nice dinner, Ted. Thanks."

He felt her foot on his leg again. Ted smiled and raised his eyebrows but said nothing. Donna withdrew her foot and continued pecking at her food. He heard the rustle under the table as she again replaced her shoe. He began to think about driving her home after dinner.

Donna's wine glass was now nearly empty. He could see that she was struggling to cut her food. They had ceased talking. When he noticed that his napkin slid off his lap, he bent down to retrieve the napkin. On impulse, he extended his arm and squeezed Donna's knee. Why not tease her a little?

Her explosion took him off guard. Donna stood up quickly, her thighs knocking against the table. Her half-filled salad plate clattered in broken pieces across the floor. Both wine glasses toppled. Ted barely escaped getting red wine in his lap.

"You old son of a bitch! All you want is sex! All of you men are alike!" she shouted.

The maitre d' and two waiters were hurrying towards their table. Ted could hear himself trying to be helpful.

"Donna, please sit down. You've had a little too much to drink, and I understand, but please keep your voice down. We can leave now if you'd like."

"Don't tell me to shut up, you old bastard, not after you tried to get fresh with me under the table. I came here for a nice dinner and all you want is sex."

Every eye in the dining room was on them. Ted was standing, looking pleadingly into Donnas angry, half-focused eyes. The waiters each had her by an arm. The maitre d' was trying to calm the situation while leading the procession to the door.

"It's all right, lady, but we can't disturb the other patrons. Please come with us."

Ted tried to show some composure.

"Thanks for helping out. Would you get me our check quickly?"

"There will be no charge, sir. We just want this woman out of here. You can understand how this hurts our business."

Donna was screaming as the waiters carefully propelled her to the exit.

"Let go of me you bastards! You can't throw me out. I'm a good customer and I'll never come back to this place again! Ted, tell them to let go of me!"

Ted followed the group. When they reached the base of the steps, the men released Donna's arms. She almost tripped, then ran, half-stumbling, towards her pick up.

Ted felt an impending disaster. He quickened his steps.

"Wait, Donna, please. There's no way you can drive. Let me take you home and we'll come back for your car later."

She didn't respond, but dug her key from her purse and managed to insert it in the lock. Ted grabbed her shoulders.

"No. You can't drive! You'll kill somebody!" He tried to pull her away from the car.

Donna whirled around, loosening his grasp. "Get out of my way, you old fuck!" In a quick sequence of motions, she stomped one heel into his instep and shoved him hard. Ted tried to protect his fall but landed hard on his back. His head thumped solidly against the macadam. He rolled over and was struggling to his feet when Donna backed up, made a quick turn and sped from his sight.

He stared at the spot where her car had turned the corner, then looked at the torn elbow of his jacket. His head hurt but not as badly as his foot. He limped slowly to his car. If he had asked for her address, he could drive by to see if she'd gotten home safely. He could call her, but realized he didn't have her phone number either. Sitting with the engine idling, Ted stared into the nearly full parking lot. A late-arriving couple provided the only activity. He shifted into reverse, backed out, and began the thirty minute drive home.

Ted studied his face in the mirror. What a pathetic old man! If he had a fantasy of acting like a jock this night, his appearance now denied it. He touched a bad scrape on his cheek. The bump on his head wasn't getting larger, but a dull ache remained. His right elbow was already getting black and blue. His jacket looked to be beyond repair.

He thought about the coming Thursday when he was committed to giving five lectures at a Vallejo high school. The scratches and limp should almost be gone by then. Ted assured himself that the man he saw in the mirror wasn't the real Ted who teachers and students bragged up.

He poured a half-glass of wine and turned on the nine o'clock news. There was no mention of a crash involving a woman driver and alcohol. This was some relief.

He could devise a reasonable excuse for not visiting Kathy's family until the limp and scratches were no longer evident. He didn't want to see anyone. He had to repress a grin. What if Ruth had been lurking at Scott's this night as she had been when he was there with Caroline? She would have had her revenge.

Ted managed to spend most of his time in the back yard, away from the house, or working at his kitchen table with the curtains drawn, and most of his battle scars disappeared by Thursday. Friday afternoon was comfortably warm for late April. After getting a good start on the follow-up activity from the Thursday school visit, Ted picked up two flats of impatiens at the nursery and decided to do some work in the front flower garden.

He'd removed the faded patch of winter pansies, worked some fertilizer into the bricked-in area in front of his house, and was busy with the trowel when Ellen's car entered her driveway. Ted turned from his squatting position and waved. Ellen walked across the street, carrying a group of folders. She greeted him warmly.

"I'm delighted to see you filling the front with impatiens again this year. I love your choice of colors, Ted."

He acknowledged her comments and turned to continue his work, but Ellen watched, in no hurry to leave. She spoke again. "I haven't seen much of you lately, Ted. You were away two weekends ago."

"Yes, Ellen, I wanted to get away from everything for a while so I drove to Delano to see my son and his family."

"I can understand that, Ted." She paused. "I was hoping you might come over after you finish planting the impatiens. We could have a glass of wine and visit for a little while."

He relaxed and smiled. "Why, yes, Ellen, I'd enjoy that. There's only another half hour's work here, and then I'd need to clean up and shave. How about an hour from now?"

"I'll look for you then. Don't rush what you're doing, though, Ted. I have a bunch of papers to begin working on until you arrive."

When he arrived at Ellen's house, Ted glanced around the room. A few changes were apparent since the many times that he sat here with Lauren. He noticed some of his favorite novels on the shelves, and a deck of pinochle cards, a Scrabble box, and a cribbage board, none of which he had seen before.

"You've never mentioned liking games," Ted remarked to Ellen as she reentered the room.

"I do enjoy them, but rarely have the time. Lauren, you know, wasn't a big game player. And none of the men I've met want to take the time for games."

Ted didn't respond, and Ellen looked at Ted questioningly.

"Would you like to play some Scrabble while we're enjoying the wine?"

Ted didn't hesitate. He enjoyed her company and found himself laughing out loud, which he hadn't done since the incident with Daniel.

At almost five, he got up to leave. She suggested that they do it again. "It's been fun," she said.

He replied that it had, and added, "I should have known better than to take on an English teacher in Scrabble. I'll promise to do better next time."

"What about next Friday? We could scrape up something for dinner."

"Count me in, Ellen." He reached out to shake her hand.

"Ted, it's been lonesome here, especially since Lauren moved out." She smiled before leaning in and whispering, "Will you bring your toothbrush and pajamas?"

THE END

LaVergne, TN USA
14 August 2010
193273LV00004B/6/P